HERE FOR THE WRONG REASONS

HERE FOR THE WRONG REASONS

A Novel

ANNABEL PAULSEN AND LYDIA WANG

alcove
press

Copyright © 2024 by Annabel Paulsen and Lydia Wang

All rights reserved.

Published in the United States by Alcove Press, an imprint of The Quick Brown Fox & Company LLC.

Alcove Press and its logo are trademarks of The Quick Brown Fox & Company LLC.

Library of Congress Catalog-in-Publication data available upon request.

ISBN (paperback): 978-1-63910-709-4
ISBN (ebook): 978-1-63910-710-0

Cover design by Stephanie Singleton

Printed in the United States.

www.alcovepress.com

Alcove Press
34 West 27th St., 10th Floor
New York, NY 10001

First Edition: May 2024

10 9 8 7 6 5 4 3 2 1

Dedicating this one to each other, obviously.

MEET JOSH ROSEN, YOUR NEXT HOPELESS ROMANTIC!

America watched him fall for Amanda on season twenty-one of *Hopelessly Devoted*, and cried with him when she sent him home after meeting his family. "I just want to be someone's first choice," he said then, his eyes welling up in the back of the Range Rover. Well, now's his chance. As *Hopelessly Devoted*'s first Ashkenazi Jewish Romantic, Josh has thirty-five women dying for the chance to charm this absolute mensch.

Josh, twenty-seven, was born and raised in Long Island, New York, to a line of door salesmen. He plans to take over the family business in the next five years—but not before he finds the hinge to his jamb. His true love is here, he can just feel it, and he's hopelessly devoted to finding her.

Below, catch a sneak peek introduction to just a few of this season's thirty-five contestants:

Krystin
23
Rodeo Queen
Bozeman, MT

Krystin may be young, but she knows she's ready to settle down. After competing in (and winning!) rodeo events for over ten years, Krystin has become one of the most decorated queens in Montana history. Since graduating from Montana State University–Bozeman last year, Krystin has focused on her responsibilities as Rodeo Queen Montana. She's committed to her career and hopes her partner is as happy ringside as he is at the head of the dinner table.

An only child, Krystin wants a relationship just like the one her parents, who are nearing their silver anniversary, have—that storybook romance she's grown up seeing. And with a heart like hers, there's no way she won't find it. "I just think love is what makes life worth living," she tells us. "Even when the world is at its meanest, having someone you love by your side can make everything sweeter."

Fun Facts About Krystin:
Her favorite jellybean flavor is Buttered Popcorn.
She's seen The Chicks live nine times.
She hates shrimp—they look like little sea spiders!

Lily
26
Graduate Student
Austin, TX

She may be named after a flower, but Lily is anything but delicate. Born and raised in Texas, Lily has always been fiercely independent—she moved to Austin to pursue her graduate degree in psychology, and she kicks butt with a personal trainer five days a week. Though she's always valued her education, Lily's looking for someone to share her knowledge with. Her dream guy is curious, adventurous, and unafraid of smart women. She's confident Josh fits the bill!

Fun Facts About Lily:
She's had a *Vogue* subscription since she was nine.
She loves road trips.
She has a tattoo of a butterfly on the back of her neck.

Gabi
24
Italian Princess
New York, NY

Gabi has always known exactly what she wants, and how to get it. She's fearless, confident, and superhot—how else would she have released a chart-topping single at just twelve years old? Now she's working on her debut album, and wants someone to share the spotlight with—just as long as he doesn't steal it!

Fun Facts About Gabi:
She wishes she had written "Fight Song."
Her favorite restaurant is Nobu.
She can't wait to serenade Josh!

McKenzie
25
Scaffolding Heiress
Buffalo, NY

McKenzie is here for the real deal! Since joining her family's scaffolding business as director of social media, she's started taking her career super seriously—but that doesn't mean she doesn't know how to have fun! Sure, she's career-oriented, but McKenzie is also the captain of her recreational bowling team. McKenzie thinks her shared experience with Josh working in construction is more than coincidence—it's fate—and she can't wait to see what they can build together!

Fun Facts About McKenzie:
Her favorite book is *You Are a Badass*.
She hates bananas.
She loves hanging out with her dad, and hopes Josh
    does too!

———————————✖———————————

Sara-without-an-H
22
Intern
New York, NY

Sara-without-an-H is in the house, b*tches! Bubbly and bright, Sara has a lot in common with champagne, but she won't give you a headache, she swears! She's the life of the party, but she's also kind, genuine, and serious about true love. Since moving to New York for an internship with Lilly Pulitzer, she's totally fallen in love with the city life. The only thing NYC *doesn't* have is her dream man—but Sara has a feeling Josh might be exactly what she needs.

Fun Facts About Sara-without-an-H:
She loves turkey burgers.
She loves to sing in the shower.
She can recite the alphabet backward.

Pia
24
Model
Singapore, Republic of Singapore

She might have an inch on Josh, but Pia won't make herself smaller for any man. At 5'11", Pia is a successful model who's turned her biggest insecurity into an asset. Her childhood had a lot in common with the film *Tall Girl*, she tells us, but she'll never let the haters stop her from being herself—one of the most successful models in Southeast Asia. Sure, she's traveled the world, but the one thing she hasn't done is find someone serious to explore it with. She's got a feeling Josh might be that guy.

Fun Facts About Pia:
She hasn't eaten meat in twelve years.
Her favorite place she's ever visited is Monaco.
She wants to adopt a hedgehog and name him Pinkie.

Madison
21
Waitress
Fort Myers, FL

Madison is a white-hot spirit with the blonde hair to match. She loves nothing more than a day on the beach that doesn't end when the sun goes down. But just because she's up for anything doesn't mean she isn't down for commitment. Working as a waitress, waiting for her ideal guy to walk through the door, Madison says she identifies a lot with Sam from *A Cinderella Story*. "She's a hard worker who will do anything for true love," she tells us. Who can't relate to that?

> **Fun Facts About Madison:**
> Her dream car is a Jeep Wrangler.
> She knows how to fly fish.
> She's not a natural blonde—*shh!*

Kaydie
25
Content Creator
Los Angeles, CA

Kaydie has always worked for what she wants, from her Pilates-toned body to her lucrative brand deals. She's a #girlboss, and she needs a man who isn't scared of that. Her ideal guy loves big dogs and warm weather, and is just as excited to hike Mulholland Highway Trail as he is to get cleaned up for cocktails afterward. She loves to travel, and she can't wait to fall in love in some exotic locales during her time on *Hopelessly Devoted*!

Fun Facts About Kaydie:
She is a proud double Leo.
She has over 50k followers on Instagram.
She loves a strong espresso martini.

Sarah-with-an-H:
25
Talent Acquisition Manager
Denver, CO

Sarah is an outgoing lover of life who didn't leave "YOLO" in 2011. Being in talent acquisition means she has to know where to find it! For Sarah, a committed relationship doesn't have to mean settling down—she wants a guy who can keep up with her quick pace and her fiery ambition. But she likes to slow down occasionally, too. "Sometimes the best nights are spent curled up on the couch with a glass of white wine," she says. "And I'd like someone to curl up with."

Fun Facts About Sarah-with-an-H:
She will drink anything with mezcal.
Her favorite movie is *Erin Brockovich*.
She hates country music.

Jen
28
Nurse
Fresno, CA

Since she was a little girl, Jen has known she wants to save lives, and she's dedicated most of her life to learning how. But sometimes the work doesn't leave room for her. "It's time for me to put my own life first," she tells us. She may be one of the oldest women this season, but that's because she's spent her time figuring out what she wants and who she is. Now that she knows, she won't let anyone get in her way. "I'm taking this process extremely seriously," she says, "and I'll have a major problem with anyone who doesn't." Yikes!

Fun Facts About Jen:
She loves pink Starbursts.
She hates when steaks are too rare.
She's been taking tennis lessons for seven years.

Lauren C.
25
Content Creator
Pinevale, NJ

Lauren C. might look like your everyday beauty queen from the suburbs of New Jersey, but she is not what she seems. With big-city style and a small-town, girl-next-door charm, she enjoys a good adventure, but loves nothing more than a girls' night in (with lots of red wine, please!). Her perfect guy will support her professional and personal dreams and understand that sometimes, Lauren C. just needs some time with her close-knit family or her gal pals. Despite having the stunning looks of a movie star and a closet filled with Fashion Nova, she hasn't had much luck with guys—Lauren C. tells us it's difficult to find a man who can keep up with her and fit her very exacting standards. But we have a feeling sparks might fly between this pretty successful social media influencer and our newest Hopeless Romantic!

Fun Facts About Lauren:
She thinks broccoli is disgusting.
She says her dream man does not wear too much
  cologne.
She "never outgrew sleepover parties," and she's excited
  to bring her cutest pajama set to the chateau!

CHAPTER ONE

Krystin isn't thinking about what she's supposed to be thinking about. To be fair, that's usually the case—but what isn't usual is her perch in the left-hand corner of the stretch limousine, precariously balancing on her tailbone so as not to touch her exposed thighs to the vinyl seat. She's sweating—a lot—and it's pooling in inconvenient places, which is raising her already spiking stress hormones, encouraging her glands to produce even more sweat. Her heel taps a syncopated rhythm into the floor; any more force, she thinks, and the stiletto will pierce right through the carpet.

The women around her are chattering nervously, trying to fill up the long space with their expectations for the night.

"I heard they make you stay up, like, all night," says Madison, the twenty-one-year-old waitress from South Florida. "That's why I brought Adderall. I had some left over from college."

"I'm surprised you have any to spare," mutters the brunette sitting next to Krystin. She hadn't caught her name in the introductions.

Krystin wants to laugh, but she also doesn't want to be a bitch, even though no one else heard.

"Do Adderall and champagne mix well?" This comes from Sarah-with-an-H, a twenty-five-year-old talent acquisition manager from Denver.

Madison thinks. "I figure champagne makes me sleepy, and Adderall wakes me up, so like, it'll even out, you know?"

Lily shakes her head, long braids swishing across her shoulders. "That is not how that works, baby girl." She laughs into her own flute.

The conversation devolves into snickers, to which Madison is either oblivious or admirably indifferent. Krystin tries to focus on the jokes, the dialogues splintering out between the women. She tries to rehearse her entrance, the lines she perfected in her bathroom mirror, in the car, on the plane.

She tries to think about anything but what she's thinking about: her best friend since seventh grade, Delia. Well, *ex*-best friend now, but that isn't the point. She's thinking about months ago, when she told Delia that she was doing this whole thing, how Delia choked on her burrito and spewed a wad of spit-logged beef onto the dashboard of her Corolla. Krystin had wiped it up gingerly with a brown paper napkin, dropping it into the to-go bag with the discarded foil wrappers.

"You're *what*?" Delia asked. Then she coughed again. There was evidently still a grain of cilantro-lime rice stuck in her esophagus.

"I'm going to find love." Krystin was resolved. She stared ahead, unblinking, hands steady on the steering wheel despite the car being in park. "I'm leaving here to find love."

"No, you're not." Delia sucked limeade out of a paper straw. "You're going on TV."

"Those two things are not mutually exclusive."

"Huh."

Then they were quiet. They were quiet for most of the burrito's life, and then for the car ride home after its death. They were quiet until they pulled into Delia's driveway and Krystin didn't want to be quiet anymore.

"It's kind of shitty for you to be acting this way."

Delia snorted. "That's rich."

"Frankly, I don't see what it has to do with you, anyway," Krystin said.

"*That's* multimillion!"

Krystin turned from the steering wheel for the first time since ordering their food. "Deels, I want to be happy. I'm not happy. I'm lonely."

"The difference between lonely and alone is up for debate," Delia muttered. "But you certainly won't be alone with one man and thirty-four other women, that's for sure."

"There are no more men to meet in Bozeman. I swear to God, I've run out." Okay, Krystin hadn't dated *every* man in Bozeman. When it came down to it, none of the guys around her made her *feel* anything, other than a twinge of secondhand embarrassment.

If she was being honest with herself, she hadn't tried as hard as she could have—but that had more to do with the maintenance of her Rodeo Queen Montana title than an exhaustion of Tinder.

She took a breath. "Listen, I know you never liked the show."

It was more than that—whenever they watched it together, Delia lamented the idiocy of the show's premise, and spent every commercial break combing the contestants' Twitters for past missteps. Krystin wasn't even sure why Delia kept coming over on Monday nights to watch with her in the first place, that's how mad the whole thing made her. But Krystin had always loved *Hopelessly Devoted*, how there were fireworks on dates, champagne in hot tubs, slow dances in the rain. It was how love was supposed to be: big and grand and luxurious. Even if she wasn't particularly fond of sparkling wine, she loved, well, the romance of it all.

And when they announced that Josh, a runner-up from Amanda's season, would be the next Hopeless Romantic, Krystin genuinely saw herself there. Josh was different from all the guys in Bozeman, and since nothing had ever worked out with them, Krystin thought maybe he was just different enough to work.

Krystin was nearing the end of her royal rodeo reign, and she needed to take a step in a new direction. *Everyone* was getting married—everyone except Delia, but Delia had never wanted the same things as Krystin anyway. The difference between Krystin and Delia was that Delia never needed anything, and Krystin did. She needed what her parents had, what she saw in movies, what they sing about in country songs on the radio. She needed more than a hail Mary. She needed a man.

"I think he might really be—" Krystin started. "I think he might be the one to change things for me."

Delia spun her entire body toward Krystin and said, "You're going to look stupid."

Krystin sat there, quiet again, while Delia climbed out of the car and up the stairs to her porch. She left her limeade sweating in Krystin's cup holder.

She wasn't going to look stupid. She was going to look like herself, and she was going to win over Josh Rosen, and they were going to fall in love and have two houses: one on Long Island and one in Big Sky.

And by the way, today she *really* doesn't look stupid. She looks hot. She knows that because the saleswoman at Dress Barn told her so when she bought this dress.

The limo rounds a corner, and Krystin feels a warm droplet of champagne splatter onto her thigh. The brunette smiles at her apologetically with crimson lips. "My bad."

Krystin smiles back, not wanting the other girl to feel bad, despite her thigh now being sticky in both sweat- and champagne-related ways. "Not your fault," she says, even though it kind of is.

"Okay, ladies!" A producer, a young Black woman named Penny, claps her hands together. "We're pulling up to the chateau now. Let's get some screams for the editing team, all right?"

They scream.

"Let's get a 'JOSH' in unison, huh?"

"JOOOOOOSSSHHHHH!"

The limo pulls onto the property. The women twist against the seats, trying to catch a glimpse of their future soulmate, who is standing at the end of the glistening driveway, cameras in position. Just wait your turn, Krystin wants to say.

"He's soooooooooooo cute," Madison gushes. "I just can't get over his hair. It's *so* curly."

Hilarie cocks her head to the side, her coppery bob sweeping against her shoulder. "He seems shorter in person."

"He's five ten," Madison replies. "That's one entire inch taller than average."

Krystin feels a little sick to her stomach. But then, that always happens when she meets a guy for the first time. Those are called *butterflies*, she reminds herself.

Penny says something into a walkie. It chirps back in response. "Okay, showtime."

Only Krystin and the brunette are left in the limo by the time Penny gives Krystin a two-minute warning.

"Get ready," Penny instructs her, her eyes glittering with the excitement Krystin thought she would only see from the Devotees. She turns to the brunette. "Lauren, you'll be going after her."

Lauren, Krystin repeats silently, as Penny faces her again.

"You have your prop?"

She does. Krystin slides a hobby horse from underneath the seat and holds the stick between her knees. The mane got a little matted during the car ride. She fluffs the synthetic hair, and plucks a stray fake eyelash from its nose.

Lauren gestures at the prop. "Classy."

"I do rodeo," Krystin explains, ignoring the brunette's snark. She smooths out her sash, which proclaims her Rodeo Queen Montana.

"Looks like you more than 'do' it."

"I'm a rodeo champion," she amends. "A queen."

Lauren smirks. "No crown?"

"Ten-gallon hat," she corrects. "Left that at home."

In a few minutes, Krystin thinks, Lauren will probably regret having nothing to distinguish herself from the herd of women that each expect Josh to remember her name. Though, looking at this woman—the left corner of her lips curled up derisively, her eyes wide and brown and framed by a spray of curled lashes—Krystin can't imagine anyone forgetting her.

Penny snaps. "Horse. Go."

Krystin looks at her. "Oh! Yeah. Going." She slides across the seats toward the door. "Going, gone."

The brunette gives her a finger flutter wave. Krystin tips her head before remembering she's not wearing the hat.

Outside the car, the lights are white against the night sky. It feels like the state fair, except it's completely silent aside from the clopping of her rhinestone-cloaked platform heels on the pavement. She sticks the hobby horse between her thighs until it hits the hem of her dress, and begins to half-gallop toward a tuxedoed Josh Rosen. He watches her, amused, as she gives up galloping halfway and just waddles, holding the stick in place.

She approaches him, and the script falls out smoothly. "I wanted to show you that"—she pauses just long enough—"I know how to ride 'em, cowboy."

She stands there for a moment, smiling and waiting. The seconds stretch out, the way they do when she finishes a barrel race and waits for her time. She imagines Delia watching her, shaking her head in disappointment—but no, without Krystin there, she had no reason to watch the show at all. Maybe she is embarrassing herself. Maybe she's going to end this night on a flight back to the Treasure State. But just like her mother always told her, she keeps smiling.

Then Josh laughs.

The chateau is large, and would feel that way too, if not for the hallways and rooms cordoned off like the forbidden wings of a castle. Producers stand with camera operators, their PAs hovering meekly a safe distance away.

By the time Krystin enters the room, the rest of the limo occupants have settled comfortably into the overstuffed L-shaped couch. They all look up at her from their champagne flutes, then at the hobby horse, then back. It reminds Krystin of rushing Alpha Omicron Pi at Montana State. (She got a bid.)

Lauren, the brunette from Krystin's limo, walks (saunters) in after her, flaring her sequined mermaid gown behind her before unfurling herself in an armchair. Krystin tugs at her dress hem.

It takes a while, but eventually the next limo pulls up, and more women stream in. Krystin watches each woman—she really can't help it—how they walk and what they're wearing. Her dress starts to feel shorter by the minute, and the minutes themselves start to feel shorter too.

And now Krystin is making conversation with Sara-without-an-H, the fashion intern to her right. She kind of has to pee (all the champagne), but the succession of women stopped a few minutes ago, which means that Josh could enter at any second, and she doesn't want to be awkwardly standing when he does. She's thought about it, and she wants to be sitting with her ankles crossed to the side like Julie Andrews teaches Anne Hathaway in *The Princess Diaries*.

She crosses her right foot over her left, then left over right. She tries to listen to Sara brag about her semester with Lilly Pulitzer in New York, but she's all fuzzy and can feel her blood rushing in her toes.

"It was just so rewarding, you know? To like, see what goes on *behind the scenes*, like all these people work together to make the *perfect* print. And, I mean, New York. To *die* for."

The alcohol seems to be hitting Sara, because Krystin can see a pink flush begin to color her fair skin.

"Totally," Krystin says, and feels guilty that she doesn't know what she just agreed with. She actually really has to pee.

"Have you ever been to New York?"

Krystin shakes her head. "I've never been much of anywhere, actually. This is my first time in California, too." She hates telling people this. It makes her sound like a bumpkin.

Sara gasps theatrically, French manicure covering her O-shaped mouth. "Oh em *gee*. That is, like, so cute." She places her hand on Krystin's knee and gives it a squeeze. "You know, we're gonna travel, like, all over the world for this. This is totally a new chapter for you."

"Yeah," Krystin says, and actually means it this time. "It is."

Around her, high-pitched cheers spill from glossy lips. When Krystin raises her head, Josh is standing in front of them, holding his own flute and smiling sheepishly.

Josh Rosen, billed as *Hopelessly Devoted*'s first Ashkenazi Hopeless Romantic, is of middling height and stature. But he has those smiley eyes that crinkle in the corners—the kind that make him look like you could tell him any kind of joke and he'd laugh, and really mean it. After his departure from Amanda's season, he started recording and producing a podcast—*When One Door Closes*—about love and relationships. Krystin listened to an episode on the plane ride over; the guest was a past Romantic, administering advice to Josh about the process.

"You know, I'm starting to feel the pressure already," Josh told Danny from season eighteen. "I really want this to work for me. I mean, it almost did last season."

"Ah, yeah," Danny said, commiserating. "It was hard for me too when Casey cut my string."

That's another thing they do—during the elimination ceremony at the end of each week, each Devotee is given a piece of red string to tie around their wrist. When a Romantic sends someone home, they cut the string with these special gold scissors that look like a smaller version of what Krystin used at her first ribbon-cutting ceremony as Rodeo Queen Montana.

"I was sad, you know?" Danny went on. "It took me a while to get over her. But time heals, and any lingering feelings I might have had for her disappeared the second I stepped onto the set as season eighteen's Hopeless Romantic and saw those first few girls, you know what I mean?" He laughed.

"Yeah. I fell for Amanda, I really did." Josh seemed wistful. Krystin remembers the scene exactly—outside the Rosens' Jericho house, the couple shivering in the early spring chill. Amanda didn't even wait until the string-cutting ceremony—she just broke it off right then and there after an excruciatingly awkward dinner with Josh's family. "I wish her and Byron the best, though."

Amanda and Byron broke off their engagement last week.

"Listen," Danny said, sounding like the human embodiment of a clap on the back. "The best advice I can give you is to follow your heart, dude. Like, you'll feel it when it happens. That's how it was with Diana."

"That's my goal, man." Josh sighed. "I just hope the women think I'm cute in person."

Josh is definitely cuter in person—at least, that seems to be the consensus.

He grins, waiting for the squeals to dissipate. "Hi, ladies!"

"HI, JOSH!"

He's already blushing. "I wanted to start off by saying how lucky I feel to be joined by such a phenomenal—and not to mention *gorgeous*—group of women."

"*Awww*," they chorus.

"I'm serious! This is the biggest group of pretty girls I've seen since my bar mitzvah!"

They laugh.

"Words can't describe how excited I am to get to know each and every one of you. I'm sure you all saw how heartbroken I was when Amanda sent me home—"

He's interrupted by a harmony of boos. "No, no, it's all for the best. You know, as I say on my podcast, when one door closes, another opens." He winks. "So with all that said, here's to all of you." He raises his glass toward the women, and they mirror him. "To season twenty-two of *Hopelessly Devoted*!"

They all rush to clink their flutes with his, and Krystin sees a camera swing above them for the aerial shot.

She can hardly see Josh through all the glasses, so many reflections of beautiful women whose makeup, unlike her own, looks professionally done, eyes and lips distorted and magnified like Instagram filters. And then Josh is all she can see, because the glasses disperse and he's looking at her, *only* at her, across the buzzing nucleus of women.

"Krystin." He smiles. "Mind if I grab you first?"

She can feel the Fenty-lined eyes liquefying her, lasers beaming from their doll-like faces. She feels sick to her stomach. "Absolutely."

The women scatter as they adjust to the state of affairs, and Josh moves toward Krystin, elbow extended like an eager prom date's. She accepts it, wrapping her hand around his bicep, which is surprisingly firm.

"Where are we going?" she asks, trying not to look back at the swarm of WASPs flashing their stingers behind her.

"I have a favorite place in the chateau." He smiles sheepishly. "I'm hoping it hasn't lost its magic after last season."

He leads her through the French doors out to the courtyard behind the mansion, down the cobblestone curves looping around the Versailles-inspired garden. The whole property is an America-fied chateau, smaller than its architectural muse; next to the McMansion, the shrunken garden looks like an underdeveloped appendage. Not that Krystin would know—the most she's seen of France is *Emily in Paris*. And besides, the only tenet of Bozeman interior design is a taxidermied stag on the wall.

"So," Josh says as they approach an ivy-covered gazebo, "you're a pageant queen."

"Rodeo," Krystin corrects, trying not to get a heel stuck between the bricks. "Less world peace, more barrel racing."

"My mistake." They stop in front of the gazebo, and he holds his hand out to steady her as she climbs the steps. "We don't have a lot of those where I come from. Actually, I don't think we have any."

Krystin smooths her dress under her butt as she sits. She's still holding the hobby horse, which is starting to feel less funny and more embarrassing the more places she has to carry it. "That's because all the riding y'all do out there is prim and proper. We get down and dirty in the boondocks."

Josh chuckles, which Krystin is beginning to realize he does a lot. She feels the swirling in her stomach start to settle a bit.

"Is that so?" He gestures to the hobby horse, which she's propped up next to her. "Care to demonstrate?"

Krystin feels her cheeks get hot. She picks up the toy horse and strokes the smooth wood. "Well," she drawls, flicking her eyes up to Josh's like she read to do in *Cosmo* when she was fourteen, "a lot of the riding we do is bareback."

Now Josh is blushing, and he seems genuinely flustered.

Delia's face in the car flashes in Krystin's memory, and she tries to ignore the shame nipping at her. Delia is wrong. She is going to *prove* Delia wrong.

But what if she can't? What if she's proving Delia's point right now, insinuating things she doesn't even mean in ways she's never spoken before? She isn't lying, is she? She's just trying to be a bubblier, sexier version of herself, the version she's switched on and off as far back as she can remember—the version that made three guys in high school ask her to senior prom.

She isn't sure how much time has passed, but it feels like eons, and Josh still isn't saying anything. He's just looking at her in this way that she knows she's supposed to want, but it just makes her feel like crawling inside herself. She starts to feel the cameras on her, watching her make a fool of herself.

"I'm sorry," she blurts, and Josh shakes from his horny stupor. "I'm not like this. I don't—"

"Ride bareback?" he supplies, eyebrows raised.

"No—I mean, yes, I do. Like, I know how—" She pauses, looking at Josh, who's smiling at her. She exhales a laugh. "I'm sorry," she says again.

"Don't be." When he says it, she really believes it. "Listen, I don't want you to put on a show for me. I already like you."

She didn't expect that. "Really?"

"Really." He takes her hand in his. "So, Krystin, rodeo queen from the boondocks. What are you really like?"

She tells him—a little bit. How she grew up in a small town in western Montana and rode her first horse when she was three (on her dad's lap), how she started competing in rodeos when she was twelve, how it was the best thing that had ever happened to her because of the community (and college scholarships), how she moved to Bozeman for Montana State and stayed after graduation.

What she doesn't tell him: that she's never had a serious boyfriend, that she hasn't spoken to her best friend since that day in the Corolla, that she doesn't know what she's going to do once she officially outgrows rodeo.

He seems happy with what she provides, though. "That's so cool," he says after she's done explaining barrel racing. "So it's kind of like *Fast & Furious*, but on a horse."

"Yeah, kind of." Krystin laughs, even though she can't imagine a worse analogy. She's still laughing when Lauren, the brunette from the limo, taps her on the shoulder and looks at her, unblinking, red lips spread into a perfectly sultry smile.

"Hey," she purrs, only to Krystin. "Mind if I steal him for a sec?"

CHAPTER TWO

Lauren has never done anything for the right reasons.

And her whole life, nobody's really noticed. Or cared.

At school, she was always nice to everyone, even the horse girls and the greasy-haired kids who ran through the hallways pretending they were in *Avatar*. She told her friends off when they were rude to their hapless teachers. She always tipped at least twenty percent, even when she really didn't have the money, and even that one time she had to wait over an hour for pancakes at the Hillsdale IHOP. She organized fucking *bake sales*. But there was always some kind of reward.

Lauren was young when she learned she was cute and charming enough to be universally liked, but not really loved or remembered—which is still true, which is fine, which is good, actually. "Enough" is great. "Enough" is perfect. When you're pretty and smart and inter-esting *enough*, you get away with the kinds of things that the really beautiful, really talented people don't. Like her sorority sisters from Montclair State, or the stunning, supermodel-tall Southeast Asian girl from the limo (Pia, 24, from Singapore), or even that spray-tanned bottle blonde who teared up during the Hopeless Romantic's toast earlier (Madison, 21, from South Florida).

The girls here are all hot, actually, but they aren't Lauren's type. They can't be, because for the next ten weeks, she's on a quest to win the heart of Josh Rosen, a twenty-seven-year-old door salesman from Long Island. Which is to say that, for a limited stretch of time, Lauren won't be a D-list socialite who quietly hooks up with bicurious models, but rather "hopelessly devoted" to this pretty average, if nice, man best known for getting brutally rejected on national TV.

If Lauren knows anything about herself, it's that she won't win. She won't be able to compete with the Madisons and the Pias and the ensemble of Ashleys squeezed into that cocktail lounge. And frankly, no sponsorship money or follower count could make Lauren want to settle down with Josh, pop out several babies, and turn into a mommy vlogger. What she wants is to make it far *enough*—to the top six, maybe, or top four. Far enough to collect her followers, become a full-time influencer, and maybe travel to a few interesting cities without actually hurting anyone. Her ultimate elimination will be a reasonable and unemotional pit stop on Josh's journey to love, because twenty-five years have taught Lauren that being cute and charming and hot enough doesn't make you capable of stealing—or breaking—anyone's heart.

What she can do, though, is whisk Josh away from the fresh-faced, painfully genuine rodeo queen. So she does.

"Of course," the girl—Krystin?—says, and for just a second, something inscrutable flashes across her face, only to be replaced by a calm, serene smile.

"Hi," Lauren says, leaning toward Josh. He looks like he's making a concerted effort not to check out her cleavage. "Do you remember me?"

Lauren's entrance out of the limo had been perfectly practiced: in front of her mirror, her sister, her best friend back home. "I know you're a man who loves an open door," she'd said, grabbing both of his hands at once. "And I want you to know that my front door is always open. So is my back door. And my side door, actually."

She isn't exactly sure what she'd promised with that last comment, to be honest, but it sounded right. Josh had laughed, and one producer sent her a thumbs-up as soon as she reached the mansion.

"I do." Josh grins. "I don't know if I could forget that dress."

"My friends always told me green was my color. That it brings out my eyes, or whatever," Lauren says.

Her eyes are brown, actually, but Josh isn't even looking at them. He's still trying really, really hard not to look at her C-cups.

Everyone back home told her that this show would be so *hard*, as if straight men weren't the easiest thing in the world.

"So." He puts an arm around her. "Tell me about yourself, Lauren."

"Well, I should tell you up front that I'm a *bit* of a nerd," she jokes.

The women of *Hopelessly Devoted* are always calling themselves nerds, dorks, playacting at growing up unpopular and uncool—the word practically has no meaning anymore. Even Josh looks dubious. "*You're* a nerd. Really?"

"Like, I've only had one boyfriend, ever. He was my first kiss, my first crush, and my first best friend." She sighs, and imagines millions of women sighing alongside her while watching the show's premiere next week. She wonders if one of those women will be Sierra Ashbery, the first person she *actually* fucked. There are a good six to ten women out there who, right this moment, are probably reading Lauren's *Hopelessly Devoted* contestant bio and messaging their group texts about how fake she is.

But her ex-boyfriend isn't fake, exactly. Damian Thomas grew up next door to Lauren and they used to carpool, singing Katy Perry songs and talking shit about their classmates while Lauren's mom weakly told them to be *nicer*. They came out to each other after an eighth-grade dance, and faked a relationship throughout high school and early college.

The entire scheme was mutually beneficial: They already spent all their free time together, and this way, Damian got to buy time before coming out to his hyper-traditional parents. Lauren, on the other hand, got to accrue followers who loved and wanted her hot, wealthy, and extremely fashionable boyfriend. And most crucially, having a "boyfriend" over at another college—not to mention one built like a Marvel superhero—proved a *very* effective way to reject frat guys and explain her lack of attraction to all of Montclair State's most eligible bachelors.

"What happened?" Josh leans in.

Lauren just shakes her head. They "broke up" around junior year of college when Damian was finally ready to come out, just to his parents and frat brothers. She briefly flirted with the idea of coming out too, but ultimately decided against it. By that point, she was actually making a small profit from collaborations and sponsorships on Instagram, and she wasn't sure how her increasingly sizable (and very heterosexual) audience would react to her being a lesbian. The way Lauren sees it, her sexuality is her own private business, something no one besides Damian needed to know.

Well, Damian and the handful of women she's hooked up with on the DL.

Josh is still staring at her, not unkindly, waiting for an answer. Lauren takes a breath. "We decided we were better as friends," she says. "We're still close, actually, but I'm very over him. I deserve someone—I deserve a guy who chooses me. You know?"

Josh nods. "When Amanda dumped me after my hometown visit, I thought, 'Am I ever going to come first?'" he muses. "I've never been the biggest, toughest guy in the room. I've never been like . . ."

"Like Byron," Lauren gently supplies. "Or that fitness instructor who came in third place."

"They're great guys," Josh says, with so much sudden enthusiasm that Lauren assumes this must be somewhere in his contract. "But I've always just been that nice guy from Long Island."

"It's a good thing I like nice guys from Long Island," Lauren lies, and wonders why no one has come to "steal him for a sec" yet.

"And *I* like nerdy girls from—"

"Pinevale, New Jersey," Lauren finishes. "It's a really small town outside of the city." It was actually a midsized suburb, but that sounded decidedly less romantic.

"Nerdy girls from Pinevale, New Jersey. They're some of my favorites," he says, and before she can even digest what's happening, he's giving her a very intentional, meaningful look, and all Lauren can think is, *Oh, fuck.*

But she knows how this show works, and what comes out instead is, "Is it okay if I kiss you?"

He doesn't answer, just presses his mouth to hers, and the truth is, he's not a bad kisser. A little nervous, and his upper lip is sweatier than she'd expected, but she can theoretically see why some straight women might be into this man. Including the very lucky Hopeless Devotee who will win the show; get a massive, free diamond; and date Josh for approximately a year and a half before publishing a cordial, PR-friendly breakup statement on Instagram.

"Hey, girl! Do you mind if I steal a moment with Josh?"

Lauren recognizes the woman from the limo: Gabi, that white girl who clearly spent so much time at the tanning salon that she was left looking half a shade away from a scathing cancellation on Reddit. "He's all yours," Lauren says breezily. Then, as sugar-sweet as possible, she adds, "I'm so glad we got to talk, Josh."

She sashays back into the room and takes a seat next to Sara-without-an-H, a redhead who says she's from Manhattan but actually hails from San Diego. "Well? How did it go with Josh?" she whispers loudly.

"It was great. He's the perfect guy," Lauren says, and for some reason, her eyes flicker over toward Krystin. She's just so annoyingly sweet, the kind of girl about to get eaten alive on this show. But for a small, instantaneous fraction of a second earlier, she'd looked tougher, like someone actually capable of fighting Lauren for time with Josh. *She is* tough, Lauren reminds herself. *She's a rodeo queen, whatever the hell that means.*

Then she thinks, *In one way or another, she's full of shit, too. All these girls are.* A true scholar of the *Hopelessly Devoted* franchise, Lauren knows how this works: Two of these women, at most, are here because they think they'll fall in love with the lead. Maybe a few hope they'll be tapped as the next Hopeless Romantic, with a pool of thirty-five men vying for their hand in marriage. The rest of them are here for . . . well, the screen time. The chance to kick-start an acting career, gain some followers, or promote their shitty line of jewelry.

It's a business opportunity, really. Which is why Lauren didn't put up an argument when her sister and fellow super-fan, Rachel, nominated her for the show. Which is why she's here now.

"It's just so heartbreaking already. See that girl McKenzie, in the red?" Sara says, and Lauren realizes she'd been zoning out for the past minute or two. "She's from Buffalo, and I heard her family owns a scaffolding business. That's gotta make her a front-runner already, and it's like, what *else* does she have in common with Josh, you know?"

"I don't know." Lauren glances over at the bar, wishing she had another drink right now. "You seem to have a lot in common with him too."

"You think?" Sara looks touched.

I feel sorry for both of you. "You're both so expressive. And really here for the right reasons," she says. "If you'll excuse me."

She makes a beeline toward the bar, which serves nothing but too-sweet champagne. Lauren takes a sip from her flute and scans the lounge. There's a game she's been playing with herself since grade school: In a room full of girls or, later, women, she always tries to identify the one hiding the biggest secret. Is it Madison? The other, lesser, blonder Lauren from Cincinnati? That girl with the vocal fry who wouldn't stop talking in the limo about her dreams of becoming an *E!* correspondent?

Eventually, Lauren's thoughts are interrupted by a symphony of murmurs and gasps. Josh is back in the room, and as he walks past each woman, Lauren feels a small knot in her chest (how long has that been there?) expand and loosen at once. "Lauren C.," he says, and she tries to conceal her annoyance at the nickname. Lauren H. needs to go, stat. "Can we go talk somewhere private?"

Lauren blinks, hoping she doesn't look visibly surprised. It's been fifteen minutes since they shared a lackluster kiss and some perfunctory small talk—did she really create that much of an impression? Out of the corner of her eye, she notices Krystin, who's now staring at her heels with an uneasy smile; she can also sense Gabi's wrath, somehow. Lauren forces herself to stay focused on Josh. "Of course," she replies. "Let's go."

Apparently, "private" means no fewer than eight cameramen and producers trailing the couple as Josh leads them down the hallway. "How's your night going?" he asks.

"It's been perfect." Lauren knows that any small talk—especially any made before they get to the gazebo—will likely be left on the cutting room floor. She could comment on how cheap the champagne is; she could ask Josh if he's been a longtime fan of the show too. She could make a joke about her ridiculous, unnecessarily sexual opening line, or compliment Josh's podcast, which she's actually listened to more than once.

Basically, she can say whatever she wants. But there's nothing she wants to say.

At the most, only twenty minutes have passed since Lauren was last out here, but the sky feels darker. A bug lands on Josh's arm, and a wet, completely unromantic sense of humidity washes over Lauren. Despite herself, she shivers.

"Are you cold?" Josh asks.

She shrugs. "Only a little bit."

But he's already pulling off his jacket. "Here, take this."

"Thank you." She sits down and threads her fingers into his. "So, Josh. How's the first night going?"

"It's been terrifying, but incredible. I mean, I may have met my wife tonight," he says. He shoots a look at a producer, like he isn't sure how much he should divulge before the first string-cutting ceremony, and then reaches for a gold ribbon which sits on the bench, surrounded by rose petals.

Lauren knows what it is: the first impression ribbon. Contestants who receive a coveted ribbon each week—on night one, or later during a solo date or group date—are granted immunity at the next string-cutting ceremony. She's so focused on it, she only hears the end of Josh's spiel, which closes with "really, really loved talking to you."

Oh no, she thinks. *He said* really *twice.* "It sounds corny, but I just feel like I've known you for a long time," she replies, her voice smooth as ever.

He visibly relaxes. "Exactly," he says. "I won't lie, I've been nervous tonight. And you're so . . . confident and comfortable with yourself. It really made me feel at home here."

"Well. I don't know if I'm that confident," Lauren says. "I mean, I'm just a girl from Jersey, remember?"

"Maybe this will help you feel a little more confident," he responds. He unlaces their fingers and looks down at the ribbon, like it holds all the answers to life's most dire questions. "At tonight's ceremony, I'll be giving all the women strings to symbolize our connections. Then, each week, I'll snip some of those strings. If you have a ribbon that week, however, your string can't be cut." He frowns. "Of course, if you lose your string in the laundry or something, production can get you a new one. That happened to Chris D., like, three times last season."

Lauren nods, as if she hasn't spent half her life watching this show.

Josh shakes his head. "In any case, Lauren, I'd like to give you this first impression ribbon. Will you accept it?"

"I would love to," she gushes, and Josh ties it around her wrist.

This time, when he kisses her, it feels different. His tongue slips into her mouth and she thinks of the time she and Halley Finch, her ex-hookup from college, fucked in the library and didn't get caught. His arm loops around her waist and she's seven years old, breaking her grandmother's favorite vase and blaming her yappy, beloved poodle. She's fifteen years old, running a seven-minute mile after stealing her sister's Adderall. She's sixteen, tricking her nerdy, acne-prone chem partner into writing their entire lab report by promising him a dance at homecoming—and then hiding from him all night. She's twenty-five, racking up thousands of followers and partnership deals and DMs from exclusive club promoters, finally moving out of her small Newark apartment and into a loft in Chelsea. That's what kissing Josh feels like: getting away with something.

When they get back to the lounge, a few girls eye her wrist with envy; others look outright hurt, or mad. She sits down next to Ashley

F., who immediately blurts out, "You're wearing his jacket already? Should the rest of us be, like, concerned?" She laughs, but doesn't sound amused.

Lauren smiles. She feels buoyant, giddy, as if her Instagram inbox is already full of surface-level compliments and brand partnership opportunities. It might as well be—along with immunity during the next string-cutting ceremony, the first impression ribbon comes with a lot of airtime. "Josh could tell I was cold, that's all. He's such a good guy."

"It's seventy degrees," Ashley responds, her voice light and friendly—but also half an octave higher.

"I have anemia," Lauren lies. "It's mild."

"*I* think it's so sweet he's looking out for us," McKenzie, the Buffalo scaffolding scion, interjects. "I mean, did you even tell him you were cold? It's like he's an empath."

The conversation segues into Josh's best attributes, from his empathy to his sense of humor to his bone structure, but all Lauren can think about is the way her skin feels under his jacket: hot, almost prickly. She blames it on the champagne.

WEEK 1
CONFESSIONALS

Twenty-five women remaining.

Ashley F.
29
Social Media Manager
Tempe, AZ

I really did not expect to be going home on the first night. I think I was taken out of the equation too quickly. [Sniffles.] I just feel like I've been doing this for so long, like when will it be my turn? When will I be enough? [Cries.]

Lily
26
Graduate Student
Austin, TX

Tonight was a real whirlwind. I know it's only the first night, but there are a lot of things I want to talk to him about, like our long-term goals and how he would handle being in an interracial relationship. [Stares ahead.] 'Cause at the end of the day, he is a white dude from Long Island.

Gabi
24
Italian Princess
New York, NY

The girls here aren't sh-t. [Laughs.] I knew going in that there would be no competition, but this is another level. Like, that a literal horse girl? [Whispers.] I think she got her dress from David's Bridal.

McKenzie
25
Scaffolding Heiress
Buffalo, NY

When Josh didn't cut my string, it, like, validated everything. I was not expecting to feel chemistry already. I haven't felt these feelings this quickly, like, ever. But, I mean. [Pause.] With our families, it's kinda meant to be. [Camera zoom in.] I think we could really build something.

Krystin
23
Rodeo Queen
Bozeman, MT

I can't even describe what I felt at the first string-cutting ceremony. [Nervous laughter.] I was so nervous I thought I might drop Jasper here. [Camera pan left to hobby horse.] A lot of really great women went home tonight, so it's definitely scary to think about how that could have been me. But I'm so excited going into next week. [Pause.] Do I think I'm starting to have real feelings for him? [Pause.] Yeah, I do.

Lauren C.
25
Content Creator
Pinevale, NJ

I think Josh and I really connected, so I wouldn't say I was *surprised* I got the first impression ribbon. But the girls here are all so hot and so obsessed with him—which, like, same, obviously! So I know how meaningful it is that I earned this, and really, I don't see it as just an itchy, polyester piece of fabric from Michaels. It's a symbol of our bond. [Pause.] What? Oh, yeah, absolutely. It was amazing. [Lowers voice.] You know the kind of kiss that makes everything else just, like, completely fade away? Yeah. It was like that.

CHAPTER THREE

The chateau is pretty in the morning. Or the afternoon—it's three o'clock by the time Krystin leaves her bunk bed to find food, since she didn't crawl into the XL twin until well past six AM. After the first string-cutting ceremony and the seemingly endless confessional interviews, the women dispersed into their assigned rooms, some neglecting their nighttime routines for the comfort of being horizontal. Not Krystin, though. Her mother taught her to never go to sleep without washing her face before she taught her to ride a bike.

Half the girls are in the common area when Krystin pads in, her bare feet cold on the faux marble tile.

"Hey, girlie," says Sara-without-an-H, twisting around on the couch to face her. She's already in full face, her coffin-shaped nails clinking against the coffee mug in her hands. "How'd you sleep?"

"Amazing," Krystin answers, even though she woke up tangled in her sheets more than once.

She looks around the room. Jen is curled up next to Madison, flipping through Netflix titles. Kaydie stands behind the kitchen island in head-to-toe Outdoor Voices, stuffing celery into a juicer that Krystin suspects she brought from home. Lily's sitting by the window, leafing half-heartedly through an old issue of *Vogue*. Krystin can't help but notice that the brunette from the night before, Lauren C., isn't there.

"How long have you guys been up?"

"Not long," Sara says, taking a sip from what looks like a very milky latte. "Just a couple hours."

Krystin glances at Kaydie, who's making a show of being exhausted from whatever Pilates workout she did from memory. "But our call time isn't until five."

Lily shrugs. "Can't hurt to be prepared," she says without looking up from her magazine. "You never know."

Krystin doesn't know. She feels like the last girl to wake up at the sleepover, still wiping the sleep from her eyes with the corner of her Murdoch's T-shirt. Everyone else is ready for brunch. Actually, everyone else has already eaten.

"Yeah," she says. "Totally." The words stick in her throat. She desperately needs something to drink. "Where's everyone else?" she asks, rounding the corner of the island to fill a cup with water.

"I think some of them are by the pool," Kaydie offers. Up close, Krystin can see the outline of her abs through the color-blocked spandex. She should really ask Kaydie for her Pilates routine.

"Lauren C. definitely is," Jen says, and the girls exchange some looks.

Krystin looks around nervously.

"It's fine," Lily tells her. "The cameras aren't here."

Sara sits up straight on the couch. "Can we just talk about the ribbon? She walked back in all smug. Do we think they kissed?"

"I *know* they kissed," says Kaydie. "I totally saw them."

"No way."

"I mean, is anyone surprised?" Jen lowers her voice. "Do you know what she said to Josh when she got out of the limo?"

"OMG, spill."

"She said, 'I want you to know that my front door is always open.' And *then* she said, 'So is my back door.'"

Madison gasps. Lily laughs.

Jen continues. "And *then* she said something about a side door, which doesn't even make sense."

Krystin wants to leave. She's not part of the conversation, just watching it as if she's back home watching the show with Delia; but still, she feels guilty by proximity.

"Didn't she interrupt your time with Josh?" Sara asks her, eyes wide in doe-like innocence.

"Me?" Krystin asks, but it's obvious who Sara was talking to. "Yeah, I guess she did."

"Well? Aren't you pissed?"

Krystin looks at Kaydie for help, but she just sips her celery juice. Lily's turned back to her magazine. "I mean, not really. I feel good about our time together."

Truth be told, Krystin had been relieved when it ended. It took her five minutes to feel her legs again after Lauren C. had replaced her in the gazebo.

The girls are looking at her, waiting for her to divulge something, anything, but Krystin has nothing.

"I'm gonna go get ready," she says, but no one's listening. They've moved on to Jenna, twenty-eight from Atlanta, who apparently got white-girl-wasted and puked in a potted fiddle-leaf fig the night before. Their giggles fade as Krystin walks back to her room, peeling off her T-shirt before she even closes the door.

The first time Krystin wore fake eyelashes was when she was eight years old. She sat in her bedroom as her mom applied the glue to her eyelids, and then applied the tiny plastic fibers with her Tweezermans. She was competing in her first competition, the junior girls portion of the regional rodeo. She bit down on her Watermelon Lip Smackers when her horse, Ringo, had raced along the fence; her blonde curls bounced against her pearl-button blouse as she gripped the reins.

In the chateau, Krystin steps back from the mirror to assess her work: subtle, but effective. If fake eyelashes could be considered subtle.

She's wearing jeans and a tank top, since all they're doing is receiving date cards. The producers told them "casual-cute." Looking at the remaining twenty-five girls gathered around the living room, Krystin sees how many ways you could interpret those words. She sits next to the remaining Ashley—Ashley O., she thinks—who scoots over to make room for her. The leather pants she's wearing squeak against the leather of the cushions.

Krystin pokes her head around into the various orbits of conversation, but she's not quite close enough to be a part of any of them. She leans back into the couch and looks at the cameramen setting up the shots, the producers alternating between stenographer's notebooks and their phones. Someone in the room is wearing too much Victoria's Secret body spray.

"Hey."

Krystin looks up to see Lauren C. settling onto the arm of the couch beside her, shiny brown hair falling into place all around her. Krystin gestures an offer to make room for her, but Lauren puts up her hand.

"I'm fine here," she says.

Krystin nods, and then shifts away. She's not quite sure what Lauren's deal is yet, and she doesn't want to be associated with someone who might get the villain cut.

But Lauren turns to her like she did in the limo. "Someone in here bathed in chain store body mist," she murmurs, and Krystin muffles a laugh.

"Okay, right? It smells like middle school." Krystin knows, because it's what *she* smelled like in middle school. Janie Tucker, the most popular girl in the seventh-grade class, told Krystin she wore Vanilla Lace, and Krystin had made her mom drive her all the way to the mall after school to get a bottle of her own. "We're not even seeing Josh tonight."

Lauren slips into a glossy smile. "Must be just for us."

"Okay, ladies!" A producer, a white woman in her thirties named Holland, claps three times, like a grade school teacher. "In a couple of minutes, there's gonna be a knock at the door. One of you will answer the door, get the date cards from the tray outside, then read them off. Cool?"

McKenzie raises her hand. Krystin hears Lauren stifle a laugh beside her.

"Excuse me? I'd love to be the one to read the cards," McKenzie says to more than a few eye rolls.

Holland claps again, just once this time. "Amazing! Go for it." She points to the main cameraman, who nods. The red light flicks on.

Like Holland said, knuckles rap at the front door. Around her, the girls fall into exaggerated gasps and whispers.

"I'll get it!" McKenzie stands up and trots to the door, followed by the Steadicam. When she returns, she holds three gold cards, shimmering in the late afternoon sunlight that streams in from the windows. She takes a deep breath, smiling at all of them like a sorority president. Then she reads.

And Krystin hears her name.

"*Krystin.*" McKenzie looks up at her as she says it. "*Let's find out what ten things I hate about you.*"

There's a disparate chorus of "oohs."

"Wonder what that means," McKenzie says, saccharine.

Krystin is suddenly aware of her face, which she's not sure is making any kind of expression. Or, she's sure it's doing *something*, but she doesn't know what. Everyone is looking at her. The red light blinks. She smiles.

"Gosh, I'm so flattered," she says, looking around at the other girls, who all look like they might short circuit. Holland nods at her, gestures to continue. "I knew after the first night we had a connection, and I can't wait to have more time to nurture that." Holland gives her a thumbs-up.

After she's finished, McKenzie reads the next card, a group date with twenty-three women. One name remains.

McKenzie smiles, faux-bashful. "Which leaves me." Her hands flutter up to her heart. "*McKenzie, let's see what we can build together.* Oh my God, that's so cute." She looks up at the couch. "You know, since both our families are in construction."

"Yeah, we know," Lauren whispers, but this time Krystin doesn't laugh. In fact, she isn't really hearing anything due to the blood rushing in her ears. She could barely get through five minutes of alone time with Josh without puking from nerves, how on earth is she going to make it through an entire date?

She counts her breath like she learned to do before competitions. *One, two, three, four, in, one, two, three, four, out.* Is she still smiling? She is now. McKenzie is trying to decipher her date card, the message of which seems pretty fucking obvious, and Krystin nods along in encouragement. She will not freak out. She has gone on dates before. Sure, they weren't very long or intense, and they certainly weren't filmed for the whole of America to see, including her parents and rodeo judges and Delia, but the point is, this isn't her first, well, rodeo. She can *do* this. She likes Josh, remember? She wants this to work. This will work.

"Hey, are you good?" Lauren is looking at her, and actually seems kind of concerned, through the grin plastered on her face.

"Huh?"

Lauren looks pointedly at Krystin's nails, which are digging into her denim-covered knees. "You look like you're about to rip a chunk out of your Levi's."

Krystin releases her legs. "Oh, yeah. Nerves." Lauren's eyebrows raise. "Excited ones, though. Like adrenaline."

Lauren studies her a moment longer. "Totally."

"All right, cut," Holland yells. "That was good. You'll all get your call times and instructions in a bit. Cameras are gonna be around tonight for some B-roll, so just do what you normally do, or not. It doesn't really matter either way."

Krystin's call time is eleven AM. She gets up way earlier, though, after taking NyQuil and falling asleep at eight thirty the night before. When she went to bed, the girls were already shuffling into alliances. No, not alliances, Krystin reminds herself, friendships. The way she thinks about it, the show is as real as you make it, and Krystin is determined to treat it as authentic as her dad's Carhartt work jacket.

She stands at the end of a gravel road in producer-specified gym shoes and leggings. She's braided her hair in two long plaits, which used to make Delia call her Pippi Longstocking, but Holland had coaxed her to "lean into the whole cowgirl thing." She'd started to say there wasn't much to "lean into," but Holland had already moved on to another task.

Krystin spent some time this morning trying to figure out what she and Josh would be doing, but gave up pretty quickly. Whatever it is, she's going to do it. She can't see much from her position on the road, just a long stretch of dust lined with palm trees.

After a few minutes, Holland tells Krystin they're ready to start. The cameras point their lenses toward her.

"Rolling."

Then Josh appears at the end of the stretch and starts walking toward her, so she ignores the wings batting around in her chest and does what they always do: she runs toward him and jumps into his arms.

He catches her, if a bit unsteadily. "Hey, tiger," he says, laughing.

Krystin jumps down, a little out of breath. "Sorry," she says. "I couldn't help myself."

Josh raises his hands in defense. "No problems on my end." He reaches for her hand. "Ready to go?"

She accepts. They walk. Eventually, a red barn appears, the kind too literal to house even cows in Montana. It looks out of place next to the tropical trees.

"So," Josh says as they come to a stop in front of the impeccably painted structure. "Something you should know about me: I love the movie *10 Things I Hate About You*."

"Okay," Krystin replies. "Where is this going?"

"Well, there's something they do that I've always wanted to re-create for myself."

Krystin thinks. "Please don't tell me you're going to make me write you a poem."

Josh laughs. "No, no. But maybe later!"

Then it clicks. "Oh! Oh my gosh, paintball!"

"Paintball."

They're outfitted in vests and pads, and given rifles that look frighteningly identical to the ones hanging in Krystin's grandparents' garage. The course is, as expected, barn-themed; stacks of hay bales populate the ground, triangulated by wooden deer stands—except today, Krystin and Josh are the deer.

"I'm not gonna go easy on you, Romantic or not," Krystin tells Josh, loading her paintball gun.

"I wouldn't expect any less."

And then they're off. Krystin darts behind a haystack, and Josh stumbles away to find his own perch. She exhales steadily, grateful for the adrenaline. Then she flips around, resting the barrel of her rifle on the straw, and waits.

"Jooooosh," she sing-songs, protective goggle-covered eyes glued to the scope. "I should have warned you." She hears him rustle, and moves the gun accordingly. "My dad's big on hunting, and he's taught me a few things."

Josh bursts from behind a haystack and Krystin nails him in the back.

"Ha!" she yells, jumping from her crouch to chase after him.

He turns around, blasting paintballs while running backward, and they splatter the hay around her. He grimaces.

Krystin cackles like a Disney villain. "Wow, you are so gonna lose!"

He's still running, trying to zigzag away from her. "I might have made a mistake choosing this for our first date!"

Right. This is a date. Krystin stops running. "Okay, okay. Go ahead, hit me." She holds her arms up in defeat, letting the paintball gun swing behind her on its strap. "Hit me, baby, one more time!"

Josh pops his head up from behind the stack he dove behind. "What? No way!"

"It's only fair!"

"That's not fair, it's cheating! It is *not* the manly thing to do."

"Oh yeah?" Krystin taunts. "So what's the *manly* thing to do?"

"This."

Josh runs toward her, but he's not holding his paintball gun anymore. Krystin shifts her weight to run away, but he's not chasing her. Instead, he wraps his arms around her waist and kisses her. He really, really kisses her. Krystin is suddenly very aware of her hands, which aren't doing anything, so she runs them through Josh's hair. It *is* curly. It feels funny between her fingers.

"Wow," Josh says, his cheeks flushed when he comes up for air. "You're, like, a really good kisser."

Krystin smiles, even though she wasn't really doing anything. Like most other kisses in her life, she kinda just let him take the lead, projecting whatever he wanted onto her. "Thanks. You too."

"So . . ." He trails off, looking out at the course. "Should we finish the game?"

Krystin takes the paintball gun back in her hands. "You're on."

By the end of the date, they're sweaty and Skittle-colored. It takes Krystin thirty minutes in the shower to scrub all the paint out of her hairline. She feels raw and hot by the time she gets out.

All in all, the first part of the date went well. And Krystin had fun—she barely had time to be nervous between all the running and shooting. Also, she kicked Josh's ass, which she's pretty sure turned him on.

She chooses a long, glittery halter for dinner, and curls her hair into big waves that brush lightly against her open back. Josh blushes again when he sees her. He pulls the chair out for her, and she slides in. The table is already set, red wine in the glasses, plates of pasta in front of them. Krystin's not hungry, though. The producers brought chicken nuggets to her room before she left to prevent any unfortunate chewing on screen.

"Today was really fun," Josh says, swirling his wine around in his glass before taking a sip.

"I had a really great time," Krystin replies. She brushes a piece of hair behind her ear. "I hope I didn't scare you. I tend to get really competitive."

"There's no way that could scare me," he assures her. "I like strong women."

"I'm glad." She smiles. "It's kind of ingrained in me after so many years of rodeo."

"I believe it." Josh pauses. "So, how else has rodeo shaped who you are?"

It's a broad question. "Gosh," Krystin starts, looking out at the empty restaurant. There are other tables, and they're all set, but Krystin and Josh are the only patrons. It makes her think about the cameras, which makes her shift a little in her seat. "I mean, how hasn't it?"

Josh nods. *Go on.*

"Um, okay. Well, I learned a lot about community. The girls who do rodeo are some of the best I've ever known, just the kindest, most talented women, and a lot of them are still my closest friends. And it really connected me to where I'm from—you know, Montana rodeo is a lot about western pride, and I really have a lot of it, I love it. But I guess the biggest thing is that it taught me to go after what I want." She looks at Josh. "That's what brought me here."

Josh whistles. "Wow," he says. "Thank you, Montana rodeo."

"I mean, there are a lot of reasons why I'm here," she amends. "I just mean—"

"No, I understand. Like, genuinely, I thank rodeo. Because I'm really glad you're here." He looks like he means it.

"Me too," Krystin says, and she means it too. "So, what about you? What do you want?"

"Oof, coming in hot, I see. Well, I want a wife, obviously. I want a family. I want what any red-blooded American guy wants, right? A happy home."

"I want that too," Krystin agrees truthfully. "My parents have been married for almost twenty-five years, so it's like, that's all I know. And I want the same for myself."

They talk about their families for a while, and Josh tells Krystin about his younger brother, who is infamously responsible for a lot of the tension at last season's hometown date. Krystin counters with stories of being an only child, and how she feels pressure to be everything for both of her parents, who have given her everything in return. They talk about growing up, how different it was for each of them. When Josh explains the theme of his tenth birthday, Krystin describes the Gallatin County fair and how her mother won first place for best pickled vegetable every year, choosing a different type of vegetable each time.

Toward the end of the dinner, a platter with a single golden ribbon on it is left on the table.

"Krystin," Josh says, taking the ribbon in his hands. "I've had an amazing time with you today. You're smart, and sweet, and you're pretty darn cute."

Krystin doesn't have to remind herself to smile.

"Thank you for sharing so much with me tonight. I'd like to give you this date ribbon, as a symbol of our connection, and so you can be confident your string won't be cut this week. Will you accept it?"

Krystin holds her wrist out for Josh. For the first time since arriving at the chateau, her stomach isn't churning, and she actually thinks she might be happy. "It would be my pleasure."

CHAPTER FOUR

Lauren hasn't missed an episode of *Hopelessly Devoted* since middle school. She remembers falling for the show in eighth grade, eating vegan ice cream with Rachel (and, years later, Damian), and wondering aloud why the Devotees hadn't done any fucking research before humiliating themselves on TV. Everything about the show was predictable, from the manufactured nemeses to the inevitable hometown drama. Everything repeated itself.

And Lauren loved it. She followed every woman on Instagram, lurked every message board, argued with her friends over who had the cutest outfits. She watched her favorite contestants' follower counts skyrocket and thought, *Yeah, I could do that.* While Rachel—and Damian, actually—always joked that they'd love to apply to date the muscular, all-American, vulnerable-but-never-too-vulnerable Romantics, Lauren imagined herself eating catered meals at the chateau, gossiping with and about the other women, and immediately, easily, effortlessly entering an online cult of beautiful people who get paid to shill all-natural wine and face cleansers.

She'd never have to work. Hell, she'd never have to do *anything*. Eventually, she realized she wasn't attracted to men at all, but that didn't change her desire to go on the show, because to Lauren, the show was never really about the men in the first place.

Rachel first nominated her several seasons back when Lauren was about to graduate from college, after a few glasses of rosé and a particularly dramatic episode. Damian had given her a pointed look, one that silently asked *Are you gonna tell her you're super gay?* She had given him a look back (one that silently answered *No*). Months later, the three of them—Lauren, Rachel, and Damian—all assumed that production had passed on her, because they never reached back out. Maybe the casting team found some kind of evidence of Lauren's sexuality, or maybe she just didn't have enough TikTok followers at the time to really stand out. But for some reason, a chipper casting director called her last spring after finding her long-forgotten application in a virtual slush pile. It had been years, but the casting team thought she'd be a *perfect* fit for this season's Hopeless Romantic, he said, and was she still single?

It's weird now, being *on* the show instead of watching it from the couch in her Newark apartment. She still hasn't decided if she'll watch the season back once she gets home. Because the season airs in near real time (every Monday, following the week the episode was shot), the Devotees are all strictly cut off from the outside world while filming. They're prohibited from watching any clips or even reading any commentary while they're still in the running, a rule that Lauren really didn't expect anyone would actually enforce. She thought that maybe she could somehow get on an easy-to-manipulate producer's good side, but not yet. She's only allowed to check her phone every three days, under producer supervision, and post vague Instagram updates with network-approved hashtags. It's hell.

Other than that, though, it's everything she thought it would be.

"I really need to get some sleep," says Lily, the grad student from Texas. It might be the third time she's said this. "Do the one-on-ones always go this late?"

"I'm sure she'll be back soon." Kaydie.

Pia jumps in. "McKenzie, are you excited for yours?"

"So, *so* excited. Lauren, I'm surprised you didn't get one," McKenzie says in a tone that could probably be construed as either genuine or condescending. Lauren *thinks* it might be the latter, but she also thinks that might be giving McKenzie too much credit.

"Wait, me?" Lauren H. responds, a little too quickly.

"No, no, the other Lauren," McKenzie clarifies. "I mean, she got his first impression ribbon."

First of all, Lauren wants to say, I *am not the other Lauren. She's the other Lauren. Hello? Even alphabetically, I come first.* Instead, she says, "Well, I would've loved that, but I'm sure I'll get time with him on the group date. I do feel like we have something, you know?"

"Um, duh. We all do. That's why he didn't cut our strings," says Gabi, the so-called "Italian princess." This girl is clearly gunning for the role of this season's villain, which is a strategy Lauren would respect if she weren't so fucking annoying. She wants to reply that actually, she had an uncuttable ribbon, not a string, but she doesn't know if she'd get a girlboss edit or a bitchy one and she doesn't want to risk it.

Kaydie starts to say something in response, but she's cut short by the sound of heels clacking against the tiled floor. It's Krystin, dressed in a long, sparkly number. Lauren can't tell if she's blushing or just wearing $100 worth of Ulta products—probably both—but she's pretty sure she's the only one actually looking at her face. Everyone else is looking at the date ribbon tied to her wrist.

"Oh my God! Girl, tell us everything," the last remaining Ashley says. She scooches over on the sofa and pats the spot next to her, and Krystin smiles gratefully before taking a seat.

"I . . . truly, I don't even know what to say. It was perfect, and he's such a gentleman, but y'all know that," she says. "It was the most fun I've ever had on a date. I'll tell you this: Josh doesn't know how to play a good game of paintball, but he definitely knows how to make a girl feel special."

The other women all giggle, and Lauren imagines watching the show at home—watching this specific scene, followed by a cut to Krystin's confessional. She'll probably say some shit like, "He also sure knows how to *kiss*." After all, the producers basically begged Lauren to go into vivid detail about Josh's makeout prowess.

"What did you talk about?" Ashley grabs Krystin's arm.

"Well, I got to tell him about growing up in Montana. And rodeo." She looks at the ground and smiles. "We talked about our families, too. I think we really have a lot of the same values."

"That's so sweet," Hilarie gushes. "I hope I get to have a one-on-one soon. I'd love a chance to tell Josh my story."

"I'm just hoping to get some time with him during tomorrow's group date," Kaydie says. "I have a really good feeling about this one."

"I hate to cut this short, but now that Krystin's back, can I go get my five hours of sleep?" Lily interrupts. "Call time's early tomorrow, and I need to run at least two miles when I wake up. My personal trainer will kill me if I don't."

"Fine by me." Krystin stands up and tucks a perfect curl behind her ear. "I'm exhausted from all that physical activity." Even though Lauren's pretty sure she was talking about the paintball, she catches a few of the women exchanging meaningful glances.

As they all head up the spiral staircase, Lauren finds herself walking in step with Krystin. "Physical activity, huh?" she asks.

Krystin blushes. "From playing paintball," she emphasizes, lowering her voice. "We re-created *10 Things I Hate About You*."

Lauren shrugs. "There was a pretty hot makeout during that paintball scene. If I remember correctly."

"We did kiss," Krystin admits. She glances at the other women, who are all several paces ahead. "It was . . . you know. Hot."

The words sound awkward coming out of her mouth, almost forced. She's probably just shy, Lauren reasons, or maybe tired. "I can imagine," Lauren says, not breaking eye contact.

For some reason, Krystin's flush deepens.

About seven hours later, Lauren's in a room with Pepto Bismol–colored walls and a silver, tiled floor. A huge, neon sign insists that *GIRLS SHINE*; Lauren can't tell if it's an order or a statement.

"Where *are* we? Does anyone know?" Pia whispers.

"At least this isn't something outdoorsy," Hilarie responds. "If they try to make us go dirt biking like they did on Nate's season, I might just cut my losses."

Suddenly, the hot pink wall under *GIRLS SHINE* opens to reveal Josh and a dark-haired woman in a jade green dress. Everyone inexplicably starts cheering, and Lauren *thinks* Pia and Hilarie are whispering about how cute Josh looks. But she's staring behind *GIRLS SHINE* at what look like racks and racks of little black dresses, skin-tight skirts, and Y2K-inspired halter tops.

"Hi, ladies. Welcome to the first group date!" Josh looks downright exuberant. "I'd like you to meet a good friend of mine. Melissa Garza is the CEO of ShineGirl—a website that, well, I'm guessing some of you are familiar with."

At that, the girls start squealing. Madison is practically frothing at the mouth, and Pia grabs Lauren's arm.

"At ShineGirl, we believe it shouldn't cost a fortune to look Instagram-ready. Whether you're looking for a dress that will make Josh swoon on your next one-on-one or some cozy loungewear to rock around the chateau, we have, well, *everything!*" Melissa pauses for emphasis, and Lauren won't lie: Now *she's* tempted to cheer. She's been trying to become a ShineGirl affiliate for months. And so has everyone else in the room, given their reactions. "Josh, would you like to tell them a bit more about how today's date will work?"

"Absolutely," he says. "You'll see that behind me is a collection of, um, some of ShineGirl's trendiest looks this season. Melissa and I thought it would be fun to prepare a fashion show."

"You'll have just thirty minutes to create the most 'you' outfit possible. We've got shoes, we've got makeup, we've got accessories," Melissa continues. "Our photographer, Trevor, will snap some pics for ShineGirl's Instagram, and then you'll each have a moment to strut your stuff for Josh, who will pick tonight's lucky date ribbon recipient. Oh, and that winner won't just get some alone time with our Romantic. She'll also get a $5,000 ShineGirl gift card! Are you all ready?"

Everyone shrieks and shouts.

"Go!" Melissa says, and the women make a beeline to the store-room behind Josh and Melissa. It's astonishing to Lauren that, just hours ago, these girls would've mauled each other for time alone with Josh; now, they're pushing past him to beat each other to the perfect miniskirt. The thought gives her an idea, but she knows she needs to wait.

Hilarie's reaching for a pink leather bodycon dress, and Lily is holding two pairs of heeled sandals. Everyone seems to have the same strategy: Hoard as much as you can to block anyone else from creating a runway-worthy look. It's so elementary.

Stalling, Lauren grabs a flimsy black slip dress and some chunky heels, and maneuvers through the room, trying not to physically run into any of the other contestants. Finally, she finds a producer guarding the door. "Twenty-two minutes left," he says automatically.

"Where's Josh?" Lauren asks.

"You'll see him in . . ." The producer looks at his watch. "Yeah, twenty-one minutes and thirty-three seconds."

"No, no, I need to talk to Josh. It's important. On-camera is totally fine."

The producer—Lauren thinks his name might be Tim, or Tom, something like that—sighs. "Wait here."

Moments later, Tim returns with Josh (and a cameraperson) in tow. "Lauren! Hey!" he says, his eyes lighting up.

"Josh," she says, before taking a deep, dramatic breath. Her voice lowers. "I don't know if I can do this."

"Hey, hey. Let's go talk," Josh says, nodding at the camera. He puts his arm on the small of Lauren's back and leads her back into the Pepto-pink waiting room. The other women are, for the most part, too wrapped up in playing dress-up to even notice Josh, but Lauren briefly makes eye contact with Gabi, who narrows her eyes.

"It's just that, like, you've seen those girls, right?" Lauren tucks a strand of hair behind her ear. "Their bodies are *insane*, you know? They all have perfect, toned arms and Kendall Jenner legs and—" She cuts herself off before she accidentally mentions any of their asses. For some reason, an image of Rodeo Queen Krystin riding her fake little horse flashes through her mind, and she swallows, her throat suddenly dry. "It's just hard not to feel insecure on a group date like this one."

Josh nods. "Honestly, I'm just so glad you're opening up to me about this. This is the kind of thing I want to know about you."

"I know I'm hot. Like, I know that on paper, my friends always say I have weirdly perky boobs and princess hair." Lauren sniffles. "But seeing how confident these girls are is just getting to me, you know? Kaydie has an actual *modeling agent*. How can I compete with that?"

"By being Lauren C.," Josh responds, with so much stoic sincerity that she almost wants to laugh. "You know, when I first saw you, I thought, 'That girl's drop-dead beautiful, and she's got confidence.'"

"And now?" She gives him a shaky smile.

He reaches for her hand. "Now, you're letting me see the real you. And I have a feeling you're about to wow me on that runway."

Lauren lets out a small, forced laugh. "There probably aren't any good dresses left. I'll have to get creative."

"I'm excited to see what you come up with." Josh stands, squeezes her hand, and gestures back toward the treasure trove of clothing. "You've got this."

"Ten minutes," Tom-or-Tim says. He gives Lauren a stern look, which, honestly, is pretty rude—she's making great TV right now.

"Thanks so much, Jim," Josh replies, clapping him on the back.

Jim. Well, Lauren was pretty close. "Thank you, for real," she echoes.

"Nine minutes and twenty-eight seconds. Hurry up," Jim says, and Lauren gives Josh her best grateful, girl-next-door smile before returning to the now-depleted ShineGirl showroom. No one is left, and no *clothing* is left on any of the rotating racks, either, aside from a lace-trimmed, cow print nightie, a cropped graphic tee, and a few sad, tie-dyed halter tops.

"Shit," Lauren mutters. She looks down at the dress and heels she snagged fifteen minutes ago. She *could* wear that and hope for the best. Or . . .

Lauren drops the outfit on a nearby neon orange armchair and follows the din of chatter and laughter toward the fitting rooms. Many of the doors are locked shut, but evidently, more than a few women have already moved on to hair and makeup. The smart ones, of course, left their dressing rooms locked, but Lauren easily slips into an abandoned stall full of someone else's reject items.

"Five minutes," another producer announces. Someone shrieks from the next fitting room over, and Lauren hears another door slam open and shut. Heart pounding, she tears through the pile of dresses and rompers with the kind of intense, fast-paced focus and fervor she usually reserves for scrolling through Newark Tinder. Finally, she lands on a metallic, emerald-colored bandeau bikini top, and within seconds, she's stripping down naked. The cups are a size too small; the cheap polyester fabric scratches Lauren's skin as she tries to fix a pretty unfortunate underboob situation. But with a little strategic reassembling, she looks Jersey Boardwalk-ready.

"Three minutes, ladies."

Lauren shimmies into the matching bikini bottom and reaches for a baby blue flannel robe. She takes a deep breath, steps into the nearest pair of size seven heels, and heads back to meet the rest of the women back in the waiting room.

Pia, who looks stunning in a deep red maxi dress, fixes her dark eyes on Lauren's get-up. "Well, you look cozy."

"I'm really out of my comfort zone here," Lauren says under her breath. "But anything for Josh, right?"

"Right," Lily interjects, sidling up to them both. She pulls at Lauren's bathrobe sleeve. "Wait, I could've sworn I grabbed this one."

"Five . . . four . . . three . . ." Jim walks out of the showroom, trailed by two straggling contestants. "Two . . . one. Okay, everyone, it's go time. Follow me."

He leads the women into a massive elevator with mirrored walls that make Lauren feel like she's in a funhouse. A few of the Devotees are eyeing her outfit, but for the most part, the women are chattering about Sarah-with-an-H and Jenna, whose satin, plunge-neck dresses are nearly identical. Jenna is glowering, and Sarah looks like she's one pointed comment away from a panic attack.

"I should've just said 'fuck it' and worn glorified pajamas like Lauren C.," Jenna snaps. "At least *she'll* stand out."

"Trust me, modeling is about way more than what you wear," Kaydie pipes up. "It's how you wear it. How much *fun* you have in it. There's a reason Revolve pays me—"

"More than your friend Arielle. We know," Lauren mutters to herself, but even though about twenty people are packed into the elevator, no one catches her comment; no one else even reacts when Kaydie finishes her sentence by bringing up her modeling frenemy for the billionth time. For a moment, Lauren feels completely, disarmingly alone.

The elevator opens into a green room, and the girls spill out onto the pastel velvet couches. Jim murmurs something into a headset and then clears his throat. "Got that. Kaydie, you're up first," Jim says. "Pia's next. Follow me."

"I hope I'm not last," Hilarie says. Her shiny pink top is, for lack of a better word, *shedding*, and she keeps nervously brushing rogue sequins off of her black leather pants. "Or do you think it would be good to go last? Maybe, right?"

"Maybe." All Lauren can think about is the tight fabric under her robe. She's slightly concerned about an accidental nip slip, but hasn't decided yet if that might actually help her chances at winning that gift card. Josh, like many men, seems very susceptible to the damsel-in-distress thing.

Hilarie looks like she's about to reply, but she's interrupted by another directive from Jim. "I'm going to need you all to line up, okay?" he says. "Hilarie, Jenna, Sarah K., you're on deck." Because of course the two girls in the matching dresses have to go back-to-back.

"Wish me luck." Hilarie sucks in a breath, taps Lauren's sleeve, and jumps out of her seat.

Lauren's name is the last one called, just after Gabi's. "Here goes," she whispers to herself—really, to the cameras. And then, she strides onstage to the beat of the music, a clubby remix of what sounds like an Alessia Cara rip-off. By the time she's made it to the end of the stage, she shakes off the robe; after deliberating for a split second, she tosses it into the audience. Her eyes lock on Josh's, and he mouths something she can't decipher. She blows him a kiss and struts back to the green room, dizzy with the confidence that she's just twenty minutes away from a win.

The second Lauren walks through the door, the room goes silent—except for Madison, who lets out a gasp. "Did you . . ."

"I was really nervous, but wanted to challenge myself. For Josh, of course." Lauren plops down on the couch. "You know what they say: fake it 'til you make it."

"Sure," Gabi says, crossing her arms and giving her a full-body scan.

She's probably drafting out her next scathing confessional, but Lauren couldn't give less of a shit. Especially when Penny, the fresh-faced producer who looks like she could be on *Hopelessly Devoted* herself, bursts through the door. "Hi, girls. If you'll follow me, it's time for a *very* special announcement."

After another quick jaunt in the elevator, they're back in the showroom. Josh and Melissa walk in moments later.

"You ladies really wowed me today," Josh says. "I mean, I had no idea there were so many ways to accessorize a dusty pink cocktail dress! But Jenna and Sarah K., you both really made that outfit your own."

Jenna tries to hide her scowl, and Lauren wonders if it was Melissa who fed Josh this line or a drama-hungry producer. Either way, there's no world in which a twenty-seven-year-old man dressed in khakis would have thoughts on someone's ability to "accessorize a dusty pink cocktail dress."

"As Josh said before, with each date comes a date ribbon! Now, he's going to give one lucky Devotee a date ribbon—and some extra one-on-one time before tonight's cocktail party," Melissa adds. "*And a $5,000 ShineGirl gift card!* Josh, I'll let you take it from here."

"Thanks, Melissa." His eyes jump from woman to woman, and they linger on Lauren for a beat too long—which reminds her she's still in a skimpy bikini and heels. "Pia, you clearly know your way around a runway. And Kaydie, I was so impressed that you managed a wardrobe change halfway through! You all brought your damn best to this group date, but one person really stood out."

Lauren has to remind herself to breathe.

"Lauren C.," Josh says. "I know today wasn't easy for you. But you really put yourself out there, and if there's one thing I want in a partner, it's someone who can let herself be vulnerable, even when it's scary. Will you accept this group date ribbon?"

"Of course I will," Lauren says, unable to stop smiling. "Excuse me, Jenna."

She's pretty sure Gabi is muttering something under her breath to Madison—and Jenna, of course, is still fuming—but she doesn't care.

"Thank you," she whispers to Josh. Then, because she can't help it, she turns to Melissa. "I have to tell you that, as a woman who's also built her own brand from the ground up, I think you've done something so amazing with ShineGirl. I'm *so* excited to keep wearing your stuff."

"Well, you'll probably want this, then," Melissa says, handing her the gift card. "And ladies, I mean it: You *all* sparkled today. I wish I could give out twenty-three gift cards—and unlimited time with this special guy right here—but unfortunately, I can't. I would, however, love for you all to keep the outfits you're wearing right now."

The reactions to this are varied. Pia, Hilarie, and Lily look excited, but Jenna looks like she'd rather send herself back to Atlanta than ever match Sarah-with-an-H again.

"I hope the rest of your journey with Josh is magical," Melissa gushes. "And remember: Never let *anyone* dull your shine."

WEEK 2
CONFESSIONALS

Sixteen women remaining.

Krystin
23
Rodeo Queen
Bozeman, MT

I was really happy to receive the date ribbon after my time with Josh.
I definitely think we got closer . . . [Blushes, giggles.] [Cut to shot of
Krystin kissing Josh during paintball date.] Yes, he's a good kisser.
[Hides face in hands.]

Pia
24
Model
Singapore, Republic of Singapore

I was definitely bummed to be on a group date instead of a one-on-one with J—that's what I call him—but I'm confident I'll get that time with him soon. [Pause.] I mean. [Pause.] I *was* a little surprised when I didn't win that group date ribbon. Just, like—*considering.* Because I'm a real model. [Blinks.]

Lily
26
Graduate Student
Austin, TX

Being an academic, I take the honor code really seriously, you know? And cheating is a big accusation. [Pause.] But I swear I had that robe first.

Lauren C.
25
Content Creator
Pinevale, NJ

My whole life, I've struggled with confidence. Like, I was always the girl who made it to Homecoming Court, but I was never prom queen, you know? So for me, it was really empowering to open up about my insecurities and try to just be myself out there. Getting the group date ribbon was, like, exactly the kind of validation I needed. [Smiles.] And God, I can't *wait* to spend this gift card. I just wish I could get a cute outfit for my next date with Josh!

CHAPTER FIVE

Even growing up in Montana, waking up at dawn to brush Ringo and take him for a spin around the ring before school, or spending a few summers at the FFA camp with friends who milked cows and fed pigs—even then, Krystin never anticipated standing in front of a pen filled with mud, and being expected to wrestle in it.

Yet here she is, wearing bike shorts and a sports bra, surrounded by thirteen other women wearing variations of the same thing, staring at how they'll be spending the next five hours. She looks around the room, some repurposed warehouse-cum-CrossFit gym, walls painted the shade of gray someone imagines when they think "gray." Krystin blinks. This is probably what Delia had in mind when she said Krystin was going to look stupid.

She can't help but feel this couldn't possibly have been Josh's call. Sweet, fun Josh, who based their last date on a classic scene from a '90s rom-com. But maybe that hadn't been Josh's idea either.

"The rules are simple," says Michael, season fourteen's Hopeless Romantic. He's their guest host for today's group date, still in the show's orbit despite breaking up with his fiancée on *After the Final String*. "We're gonna pair you guys up, you'll get in the pen, and you'll wrestle it out. Safely, of course."

"On Amanda's season, it was really important for us guys to let out some of that pent-up aggression," Josh says. "And I know, as a feminist myself, that it's just as crucial for women to express those feelings."

"There's no time cut-off, but you'll have to pin the other woman for five seconds in order to win the fight. Then the winners will wrestle each other, until eventually there's one Mud Queen standing." Michael holds up a rhinestone crown. "Now, you might be wondering what's at stake here."

Krystin isn't. She's seen enough seasons of this show to know what's coming.

"Well, the lucky lady who wins the title of Mud Queen will get some extra one-on-one time with my buddy Josh tonight."

The women gasp as if they hadn't also anticipated this "twist," then size up their competition. Lily looks smug, arms crossed over the hard-won abs she maintains with the personal trainer she never shuts up about (and maybe seems to have a thing for). Gabi, though Krystin's pretty sure she's got an aversion to sweating, is definitely not afraid of some hair-pulling. Krystin has to train a little for rodeo, but there's no question she's more comfortable on a horse than on her own two legs.

Michael runs through a list of rules that Krystin's sure go largely unnoticed by the girls. Besides, it's not like any of them are in real danger, surrounded by three cameras and a field medic on site. Wait—are they going to need a medic?

Pia and Jen are up first. Krystin watches as they enter the ring, Pia stepping delicately into the mud like she's testing a hot tub's temperature. When they're both inside, they just kind of stand there for a minute, looking at each other and wavering like Wii avatars.

"Come on, guys," yells Holland. "You have to actually touch each other."

Pia looks down at her golf skirt, a pristine cream—until Jen lunges toward her and collides with Pia's tan torso, knocking Pia onto her ass in the mud. It takes a second for Pia to recover and mourn her soiled outfit, but then she's back on her feet, and remembers the six-inch advantage she has over Jen. Her long arms wrap around Jen's compact frame and she uses her weight to force Jen into the mud, where she stays for the five count.

Michael rings a bell. "Nice job, ladies! Pia, great form."

Krystin glances at Josh, who looks a little scared.

The girls climb out of the pen, dripping brown in their path.

"Okay, next are Madison and Lauren H."

Lauren H. emerges victorious, as do Lily and Kaydie in their respective matches. Lauren C. hops into the ring with Gabi, who's wearing head-to-toe leopard print, and they last for longer than the other women. Gabi's strategy is mostly slapping, which seems to annoy Lauren, because she stops playing defense and starts actually wrestling. Krystin can't look away, her eyes pulled as if by a magnet by Lauren's lithe, catlike movements. She whips her head up, mud sliding off her dark hair, slicking her poreless skin. It's kind of like the rodeo, Krystin thinks, the spectacle of it all—which means she knows how to win.

Lauren pins Gabi pretty quickly after she starts trying, and Gabi sulks out, wringing wet dirt out of her extensions. "This is so unfair," Krystin hears her mutter, which Krystin can't help but think is extremely unattractive. If she loses, she tells herself, she'll be graceful and dignified. As graceful and dignified as she can be while wrestling other grown women in mud.

And then it's her turn, and she faces Ashley O. The mud is warmer than she expected. Is that the heat generated by an hour's worth of women pinning each other? She inhales, *one, two, three, four*. She's riding Ringo. She's Rodeo Queen Montana. She's on top of Ashley O., rolling around in the dirt.

Ashley grunts under Krystin's weight and wedges her foot under Krystin's stomach. They rock sideways, but Krystin doesn't let go. Krystin brings her knee up to Ashley's sternum, stabilizing her enough to grab her wrists and hold her down.

"One, two, three, four, five!" Michael rings the bell. "Krystin wins."

She stands up, holding her hand out to Ashley, who just looks at it before reluctantly accepting. As they leave the ring, Krystin glances at Josh, and winks. He directs a golf clap toward her, and she laughs.

After a couple more showdowns, they're paired up for Round 2, which goes by quicker than the first. Now that she's warmed up, Krystin easily beats Kaydie in their match, and then watches as the victors emerge. It's kind of fun to watch everyone get all *Lord of the Flies*, survival of the literal fittest. Lauren C. absolutely decimates Lauren H., with the kind of unbridled energy that Krystin thinks has to be premeditated. The girls are barely paying attention to Josh at this point, so utterly obsessed with the competition, and Krystin feels a little bad for him. Then again, he already watched her defeat him on the paintball course, and he seemed to like that.

Eventually they hit Round 3; only a handful of matches left. The competition has activated the less . . . diplomatic part of Krystin's brain, and she wants to win. *Badly*. She feels pretty confident too, having spent the last two hours watching the girls use their best moves and studying their strategies. She's already thinking about how she'll place her rhinestone crown right next to her rodeo sash.

"Krystin," Michael says, and she steps forward, not even caring about the mud that's dried in rivulets down her cheeks. "You'll be going against Lauren C."

Lauren grins and flips her hair behind her shoulder. "Easy," she says.

"Ooooh," Michael whistles, nudging Josh. "We've got some fire."

"All right, all right," Josh says. "Play nice, you two."

Krystin steps into the ring. "Oh, I'm not playing at all," she says, looking directly at Lauren, whose grin has evolved into a smirk. It ignites a burning sensation in Krystin's gut.

"Mm," Lauren replies, a razored edge to her silky voice. "Watch out, cupcake. I've been doing cardio kickboxing for eight years."

"Well, I can tie down a calf in seven seconds. And they're a lot quicker than you."

"Ho, ho!" Michael laughs. "Josh, you've certainly got some fiery women this season. I hope you can take it."

"Trust me," Josh says. "They're just as sweet as they are fiery."

But Krystin isn't feeling very sweet. She's feeling like she wants to win.

The bell rings.

Krystin and Lauren both leap forward with equal strength, going right for the shoulders, but neither falters. They step forward, then back, and Krystin's reminded of the time her dad took her to the father-daughter dance on Valentine's Day when she was seven. Then she remembers the time her dad taught her how to escape a captor—God forbid she ever got attacked when she went away to college—and does a variation on the move to destabilize Lauren and get her on the ground. Mud splatters on Lauren's face, and she squints in surprise.

"You okay, *cupcake?*" Krystin asks, her knee planted firmly on Lauren's pelvis.

Michael starts counting. "One, two—"

"I will be," Lauren mutters.

Then she pulls Krystin down with her, using the momentum to roll until she's practically straddling Krystin, her dark hair hanging in damp vines around her. She's so close that Krystin can smell her rose-scented face cream. They lie there for a moment, just breathing. Lauren is nearly covering Krystin's body with her own, her stomach pressing into Krystin's, her thighs pinning Krystin's in place. She feels warm, warmer than the mud, warm like the sun is hitting her, like she's in direct light. For a split second, she thinks she wants to hold Lauren there.

But then she hears the sports-like commentary from Michael, and she hears Josh chuckle, and she remembers. Krystin thinks she sees something flash across Lauren's face, but it's gone before she can decipher what it is.

"One—"

Krystin pushes up to flip Lauren over again, and they roll some more. Krystin has so much mud on her face that she can barely see, but she locates Lauren's wrist in the flurry of movement and wraps her fingers around it. Now she only has to—

"Ow!"

Krystin sits up, still pinning Lauren, knees on either side of her tiny torso. "What?"

Josh rushes to the side of the ring. "Lauren, are you okay?"

"I think—" Lauren starts, then gives a little gasp. "I think I'm injured."

"What?" Krystin repeats. "How?"

Lauren doesn't answer. She wriggles under Krystin's weight, and Krystin swings her leg around to release her. Lauren sits up, rubbing her arm.

"Where does it hurt?" Josh asks, leaning against the rubber ropes.

"Kind of everywhere," Lauren answers, only to him.

Krystin starts to feel like she's intruding on something. She just sits there, legs crossed, watching Josh watch Lauren whimper. "But I—"

"Let's get the medic over here?" Josh waves to one of the producers, then helps an almost comically shaky Lauren stand. Krystin's surprised no one's handed her a space blanket.

A person in scrubs meets them on the other side of the ropes and ushers Lauren to a corner of the room where a gurney stacked with medical supplies waits. Lauren looks back at Josh, and—is that a tear in her eye? Is she kidding?

Around her, the other girls stare in awe. Krystin's kind of impressed by the performance, except she's also fucking pissed.

"Josh," she calls, trudging through the mud to the edge of the ring.

He holds a finger up to Lauren on the gurney to gesture *one minute*, and Lauren nods solemnly. Then he rips his concerned gaze away and walks to Krystin. "Hey," he says.

"Hi." Krystin is suddenly very aware of her skin. It starts to feel itchy under all the mud, drying and caking behind her knees and in the crooks of her elbows. "I didn't hurt her, I swear. Or I didn't mean to, but seriously—" She lowers her voice. "I really don't know how she could have gotten hurt."

"Hey, hey, it's okay." Josh softens, and his eyes crinkle at the edges in a way that makes Krystin feel safe. "Accidents happen. That's why we have medical professionals on set."

Krystin shifts. "No, but—" *There was no accident! I didn't do anything!* She knows how to lose, and to lose with honor, but she didn't even lose. She didn't even get the chance.

Josh's eyes start to look less like comfort and more like pity. There's nothing she can say now; anything more and she'll start to look like a whiny baby. Things aren't always fair. Krystin learned that back when Toni Milburn told a barrel racing judge that Krystin moved a marker before a competition—a total, absolute lie which got her disqualified. She takes a breath, and steadies.

"I'm sorry. I really hope she's okay."

69

Josh puts his hand on top of hers, where she grips the rope. "Nothing to be sorry about." Then he steps back and turns to the rest of the room. "All right, I think that's enough wrestling for today. You guys really showed up!"

The women exchange looks, some of which are pointed toward Krystin. Krystin looks down at her feet. Or the mud.

"But what about Mud Queen?" Lily asks. She'd made it Round 3 too, but hadn't yet won her match.

Josh looks at Holland, who nods. "I know I promised some extra time to the Mud Queen, but since we've had to cut this short, we're not gonna have the chance to crown her today."

The women groan, and now Krystin's getting full death daggers.

"But," Josh says over the objections, "as much as I loved seeing you get dirty, I'd love to see how you all clean up later tonight."

They cheer.

"You're *all* invited to the Victor's Cocktail Hour, all right?"

Krystin's heart settles a little in her chest, not so much for the chance to see Josh but for the women having less to be mad at her for. She looks over at Lauren in the corner. Some PA is fanning her with a folded up *People*.

The producers start to lead them out of the wrestling room, all of them leaving muddy footprints in their wake.

"Thank God," Krystin hears Jen say from a few feet behind her. "I would have hated to have the whole date ruined just because *some* people don't know how to leave the competition in bumblefuck."

Krystin thinks about spinning around and showing Jen how girls from bumblefuck deal with twats from Fresno, but keeps walking without so much as a glance behind her.

The evening portion of the date is held in a fancy hotel lobby—the kind of hotel you see in those shows on TV about an undercover CIA agent or a torrid affair, that plays nondescript untz-untz music and has a giant fish tank in the middle of the room.

There is a fish tank, but there isn't any music. "They edit it in, in post," Lily tells her, which is kind of depressing because it means that they all have to sit in a big room listening to each other talk about the same guy.

"Wasn't this just so generous of him?" Madison asks the group, as they wait for Josh to join them. Lauren isn't there yet. Krystin wonders if she broke a bone out of pure determination.

"I think it was the *least* he could do," Jen says, and Krystin just keeps smiling.

Josh walks in, and they all commence with the giggle-greeting.

"What are we all talking about in here?" he asks with a grin.

Kaydie answers. "You, obviously!"

Josh fans the air in mock humility. "Me?"

The women laugh. Krystin tries to match their enthusiasm, but she's still preoccupied with the events of that day. She really doesn't want Josh to think she's some raving lunatic with anger management issues, even though when she thinks about it, she *is* angry, because what the fuck? Lauren C. is not only evidently untrustworthy and manipulative, but she's a cheater, and if there's one thing Krystin hates, it's cheaters.

While she's stewing, they break off into little sections.

Krystin turns to Sara-without-an-H next to her. "Where'd Josh go?"

Sara raises a tawny eyebrow. "Um, Lily literally just pulled him. Weren't you watching?"

"I guess I spaced out."

Sara shrugs, then turns back to her conversation. Krystin wishes she were drinking a whiskey neat, but all they ever serve is champagne, which Krystin doesn't even like. She hates bubbly drinks. She doesn't even like soda, and she hates Pop Rocks.

But she drinks it anyway, because there's nothing else to do. She knows she should go join a conversation so she doesn't seem like a loner, but she can't seem to focus on anything because she keeps seeing Lauren C.'s dumb face under her. It was just such a cheap move. She thought Lauren was smarter than that.

She wanders over to the fish tank, a large rectangle right smack in the center of the room, filled with tiny sharks and tinier fish. She watches them chase each other around through the glass, going in circles because there's nowhere else to go. She pictures Lauren again, squirming under her weight, and her cheeks get a little hot. She's just, like, so *annoyed*.

And then Lauren's body appears through the water, wavy and distorted, and Krystin thinks she's imagined it, until the other women stop chattering and turn toward her too. Krystin steps out from behind the fish tank to see for herself.

Lauren walks daintily down the little steps in her skinny little heels that she would never be able to balance in if she were actually injured, and—Krystin can't believe she's seeing it, but yes, there's an ACE bandage wrapped around her elbow, which is snuggled into a sling. Krystin almost drops her flute.

Lauren crosses the room to the love seats and tables the women have congregated around. "Hey, guys," she says, her voice like a ribbon unfurling.

"Oh my God, Lauren!" Madison says, jumping up to give Lauren a hug that Lauren seems not to actually want. "Are you okay, girly?"

"Yeah," Pia adds, pointing to the sling. "That looks serious."

"I'm okay," Lauren responds as soon as she shakes Madison off. "It's really not as bad as it looks."

I'm sure it isn't, Krystin thinks.

"I barely even need this," Lauren continues, gesturing to the sling. "It's really just to be completely safe."

"Totally." Hilarie nods. "Here—" She pats the cushion next to her. "Come sit."

Is everyone buying this? If they aren't, they're playing like they do. Krystin decides to play along. The more she sulks, the pettier she'll look.

"Lauren!" she says, running over to join the group. Lauren's taken the seat next to Hilarie, so Krystin towers above her. "I'm so glad you were still able to make it tonight."

Lauren smiles sweetly. "Same, even if I was a little late." She laughs like she just made a joke. "But seriously," she says, looking up at Krystin. "No hard feelings."

"For sure."

Lauren holds her gaze for a moment, then breaks away. "Where's Josh?"

"I think he's with Lily," Madison says.

Pia shakes her head. "No, I think Gabi interrupted them. See, Lily's over there." She points to a table where Lily sits with Sarah-with-an-H.

"Hm. Well, I'm gonna go find him," Lauren says, standing up even though she just sat down. "I just wanna make sure he knows I'm okay."

Krystin's pretty sure he already knows, or else this cocktail party wouldn't be happening, but whatever. She watches as Lauren excuses herself, and can't fight the nagging feeling that Lauren did all of this to her, on purpose. And then, as if proving Krystin right, Lauren tosses one more glance at her before she flips her ninety-percent cocoa hair behind her shoulders and walks away, swinging her hips purposefully in her silky dress.

CHAPTER SIX

As far as Lauren can tell, Josh seems to have three states of being: flattered, excited, and distressed. Occasionally, he looks amused or slightly turned on—during that mud wrestling date, he was a bit of both—but Lauren would probably classify those moods as slight variations on "excited," anyway.

Right now, he looks extremely distressed. His brows furrow and he sucks in a breath as he rests a large, warm hand on her thigh. "You have no idea how happy I am to see you."

"Really, I'm fine." Lauren covers his hand with her own, but can't bring herself to weave their fingers together. "I just have low iron, so I have to be careful. It's the anemia." Did she tell Josh about being anemic, or just the other women? She can't remember. *Get it together*, she tells herself. *It hasn't even been three weeks. You can't let some cowgirl from the middle of nowhere totally unravel you.*

"I'm just glad you made it back here," he says. "We were all really worried."

"We?" Lauren echoes. Krystin wasn't actually worried she hurt her, was she? Something flips in Lauren's stomach, and if she didn't know herself any better, she'd think it was guilt.

Well, fine. Maybe she does feel just a *tiny* bit guilty, only because throwing Krystin under the bus wasn't a part of her master plan. It was a survival instinct: She was rolling around in the mud with a pretty blonde, their legs locked together, and all the emergency alert systems in her brain told her to *shut it down, shut it down.*

"Okay, okay, you got me," Josh says, sounding sheepish, and Lauren remembers where she is. "*I* was worried. Between this and the fashion show date, you've had a rough go of it."

"I've been pushed out of my comfort zone, that's for sure. But it's all worth it." Lauren moves a quarter of an inch closer to him. She can smell his woodsy, husky cologne. It's way too strong, and makes her feel even more light-headed than all those thoughts about Krystin and mud wrestling. She soldiers on, though. "Whenever I see you, everything else, like, disappears."

Instead of answering, Josh just gives her this puppy dog look and kisses her, soft and sweet and quick. Lauren uses her sling as an excuse not to lean in any closer.

"What happened out there, anyway?" he asks. "It was like, one second you two were going at it and having fun, and the next . . ."

"Oh, you know. It was an accident," Lauren says. She feels pained at the idea of rehashing everything. "It wasn't, like, her fault."

"Krystin's fault," Josh clarifies.

"Right. I mean, she couldn't have known about my iron deficiency. And I think Krystin just got really into the competition component, which isn't a bad thing," Lauren adds. "I don't know her that well, of course, but she's clearly an athlete. And she's one of those people who's just so . . . *focused.* She's kind of a fighter, right?"

Josh doesn't answer right away. His lips quirk into a small, thoughtful smile, and Lauren wonders if he's remembering their paintball one-on-one from last week. She wonders how easily Krystin beat him—because obviously Krystin beat him, even though Lauren knows nothing about how paintball works or how you win. She wonders if he just let her kick his ass or made her work for it, if they kissed during or after their match, if Krystin's hazel eyes go molten and dark and determined every time she really, really wants to win . . .

Before she can stop it, Lauren has a flash memory of Krystin's body under hers: her tanned skin streaked with mud, her hands clawing at Lauren's arms. Their thighs slotting together and Krystin's soft but strong grip on her wrist. The way her whole fucking body seemed to react to Krystin's warm breath, her too-close mouth. She might have used the word *focused* to describe Krystin, but for a moment in the ring, it was Lauren who couldn't hear or feel anything besides her opponent's unsteady, fevered breathing.

Suddenly, Lauren's whole body feels hot, and Josh's hand is way, way too high up on her thigh. She gently squeezes and moves it.

"Let's not talk about the other women here," he says, and even though Josh has no way of knowing what Lauren was thinking, her heart rate ratchets up. "I want to know about *you*. Tell me something about your family."

It's a sharp conversational pivot, but a welcome one. "Well, my dad works in sales. My mom's a real estate agent. We're all really close," Lauren says. "And then my sister, she goes to my alma mater. She's, like, one of my best friends."

Growing up, Lauren and Rachel *were* close. There was this game they used to play: They'd round up every chair in the house, except their dad's heavy armchair, and bring them outside, all while chanting the words "Garden Wedding Special" over and over again. Rachel would fill every seat with a doll or stuffed animal, and Lauren would sneak into their parents' bedroom and steal her mom's makeup—Rachel tried to do this once, but she got caught—and they'd switch off, with one as the bride and the other as the maid of honor. The bride had to wear all white, the maid of honor had to do her makeup and take photos, and after that, the game was over. Despite the name and all the setup, there was never an actual wedding. It was all about the preparation. (And their mom inevitably lecturing them for moving so much furniture to the backyard, or getting lipstick on their white dresses.)

One time in sixth grade, Lauren had some friends over. Damian, of course, and this girl Alisha, who lived down a couple blocks over and had the prettiest, silkiest, longest black hair. Rachel, who was still just six or seven years old, walked in on the three of them watching some paranormal teen show on the CW. "Laur, Laur, I have an idea," she said, her face all lit up. "Let's do Garden Wedding Special. We can do it for real this time! Damian can be the groom. Alisha can be a bridesmaid!"

Before Damian or Alisha could say anything, Lauren rolled her eyes. "Rach, I'm way too old for Garden Wedding Special. Go away."

Rachel looked confused, probably because they'd played the game just a few weeks before. She walked up to Lauren and lowered her voice to what she clearly *thought* was a whisper. "Are you scared to kiss Damian?"

"No," Lauren snapped. She could hear Alisha giggling. "It's just a stupid game for kids, and I'm almost a teenager. Leave me alone."

Later, Damian left for dinner, and Alisha spent the night. She borrowed a pink pajama set and tied her thick hair back into two loose braids, and they crawled into side-by-side sleeping bags on Lauren's bedroom floor. "That wedding thing sounded so dumb, but you should've done it, just to kiss Damian," Alisha said. "I mean, *I* would have. He's so cute."

77

Lauren's chest seized, and she suddenly worried she might throw up. She felt ridiculously, uncontrollably jealous—which was weird, because she'd never seen Damian that way. But Alisha was snoring steadily within minutes, and Lauren stayed up for another hour, thinking of Damian and Alisha cuddling up on bus rides to field trips and holding hands at the end-of-year dance and hanging out without her. She stared at Alisha's sleeping body, her chest rising and falling with each snore, and imagined the way her feisty, cocky smile might turn soft and serious in the seconds before someone kissed her—in the seconds before *Damian* kissed her. The thought made something fall in Lauren's stomach, and she suddenly wanted to cry. Maybe she did like Damian, after all.

You just don't want to be left out, she told herself, and the conclusion was convincing enough that she was finally able to fall asleep.

The next day, she found Rachel reading a chapter book in her room. "We can play Garden Wedding Special now," Lauren said. "You can even use my new strawberry lip gloss. I only said it was stupid because you were embarrassing me in front of my friends."

"It's fine," Rachel said. "You were right. That game's for babies."

Lauren isn't about to tell Josh Rosen about Garden Wedding Special, and she isn't about to tell him that, dramatic as it sounds, she thinks her relationship with Rachel was never the same after that. That some sort of chasm opened up between them as teenagers and then adults, and even though they borrowed each other's shoes and commented on each other's Instagram posts, they never actually talked about anything substantial, or knew anything about each other's lives. Even their weekly *Hopelessly Devoted* watch parties came to a temporary, then permanent halt once Rachel left for college.

Alisha, on the other hand, stayed friends with Lauren for another three months, until Lauren kissed a boy Alisha liked at Sammy Giordano's birthday pool party. Shortly after, for hopefully unrelated reasons, Alisha's family moved to Atlanta. Lauren never saw her again.

"You have a brother, right?" Lauren asks Josh. "What's that relationship like? Did you have any traditions or anything, like, growing up?"

Josh smiles and shakes his head. "We used to get in so much trouble together. Jeremiah was always pranking our parents—moving things around the house, putting sugar in the salt shaker, stuff like that. His signature move was hiding under the couch and reaching out to grab someone's leg whenever they sat down."

"Let me guess. You were always the well-intentioned bystander who got roped in?"

Lauren gives him a look, and he laughs. "The worst was this one time, he dared me to jump out at my mom from behind the kitchen door. It was Passover, and she was bringing all this food out, and—well. We thought she'd drop it, and it would be funny."

"You're literally evil." Lauren elbows him with her good arm. On some level, she knows that they're flirting, even though this is possibly the least sexy conversation she's ever had in her life. But if Lauren learned anything from her sorority sisters, it's that flirting with men is as easy as getting them to tell a long-winded story, then somehow touching and insulting them in tandem. The formula never fails.

"It gets worse." Josh winces. "My *grandfather* walked out instead, and we scared him so much that he had to go sit down for a while. Thankfully, he took it in stride, but I was grounded for weeks. Anyway, I learned my lesson."

"So you won't be jumping out at any of us, will you?" she asks. "Because I can really only sustain one injury at a time."

"For real. I'm glad you're okay," he responds, his voice low.

Lauren's still deciding what to say next when she gets a pungent, sudden whiff of Daisy by Marc Jacobs. "Mind if I cut in?" asks Ashley.

"All yours." Lauren smiles sweetly, then smooths a wrinkle in her rose gold dress. "Thanks again, Josh. Seriously."

Josh's earnest, beaming face is the last thing she sees before turning and walking back to the lounge.

Because no one was crowned the Mud Queen, no one gets the group date ribbon, either. It doesn't go over well.

"We really bonded today," Lily laments as she takes her contacts out. Although the contestants are divided with three or four to a room, they all have to share one bathroom, which only has three sinks, two stalls, and four showers. It isn't ideal for a group of sixteen twenty-something women, each with her own Sephora haul and personalized skincare routine. "I told him about my parents' divorce, which is something I never share with guys. And we, um, kissed for the first time."

Hilarie, all while actively brushing her teeth, whips her head toward Lily. A speck of Colgate MaxFresh lands on the mirror. "You kissed? How was it?"

Lily chews her bottom lip, then erupts into giggles. "It was perfect. The whole night was perfect. Or at least it would've been, if there'd been a group date ribbon."

"You're not going home, girl. If he kisses you, you're safe," Kaydie adds. "I'm going to bed. Today was long as fuck." She gives Lauren a weird look, tosses a cleansing wipe into the trash can, and walks out.

Lily and Hilarie follow her soon after, and for the first time in weeks, Lauren is completely alone—no cameras, no contestants, no producers, no Josh.

At that moment, of course, Krystin walks in. She's in sweats and an old T-shirt, her hair piled up into a messy bun, but she's still wearing a full face of mascara, lip gloss, and blush. She smiles tightly at Lauren and then pulls out a purple makeup bag.

"Hey," Lauren says. Even to her own ears, her voice sounds bored, but she feels the need to fill the silence.

"Hi." Either Krystin doesn't want to look Lauren in the eye, or she's just really, really laser-focused on washing her face. Before Lauren can reply, she adds, "Glad to see your arm's feeling better."

Lauren glances down. She'd taken off the sling to pull her hair back into a ponytail. "Like I said, it was mostly a precaution," she says. "I'm not upset or anything."

Krystin's face contorts in frustration, and she starts scrubbing at her cheeks just a little more vigorously. "Good. I'm glad."

What Lauren should really do is nod and move on, if not leave the bathroom altogether. But she isn't done with her nighttime routine yet, and she doesn't know what to do with this nagging sense that Krystin's icing her out. Obviously, Lauren isn't *sad* about it or anything, but it's like a hangnail or a split end—an annoying inconvenience that she'd really rather just rip off and then forget about forever.

"Look, it was an accident. No one's mad at you," Lauren reiterates. "I mean, I'm not mad at you. Josh isn't mad at you. Everything's fine."

"You're sure about that?" Krystin stops what she's doing and turns to face Lauren. Her skin is now almost makeup-free, but there's a small mascara smudge on her left cheek. "Because I'm pretty sure everyone thinks I'm some kind of vindictive, hyper-aggressive monster who ruined the group date and caused someone personal injury. And who knows how they'll edit this on-screen. It could hurt my rodeo career."

For the second time tonight, Lauren feels a pang of guilt. After all, if the roles had been reversed, she'd be *pissed* if someone messed with her image and burgeoning influencing career. In fact, she'd probably find a way to fight back, but Krystin seems too noble to pull any kind of revenge stunt—which only makes Lauren feel worse. Still, she can't bring herself to apologize.

"Josh doesn't think you ruined anything," Lauren tries. "That's what matters, right?" She's not sure if she's trying to convince Krystin it's okay, or herself.

"I don't know what you're trying to do here, but this isn't a game to me," Krystin says. She sounds haughty, but looks exhausted. "This could be my future husband."

"This isn't a game to me, either," Lauren lies, keeping her eyes level with Krystin's. It's both easy and impossible to stare this girl down, because as much as she hates to admit it to herself, Krystin's pretty. And genuine, too, in a way that keeps catching Lauren off guard. For a second, neither moves, and it's like they're back in the mud pit: Lauren can feel almost every nerve in her body. She isn't sure if Krystin's about to burst into tears or curse her out.

There's still a mascara smear on her cheek. A fucked-up, almost imperceptibly small part of Lauren wonders whether Krystin's eyes would flicker shut if she leaned in and smudged it away. *Shut it down, shut it down.*

"Right," Krystin says finally, tearing her gaze from Lauren's. "Just . . . stay away from me, and don't interfere with *my* relationship, okay?"

She leaves the bathroom before Lauren can think of a response.

WEEK 3
CONFESSIONALS

Eleven women remaining.

Krystin
23
Rodeo Queen
Bozeman, MT

Yeah, the group date was . . . challenging. I definitely never want to be seen as a violent person. [Cut to replay of Krystin wrestling Lauren C.] I feel really bad. I mean, I don't really see how I could have hurt Lauren C. [Cut to shot of Lauren C. wearing a sling.] I wouldn't accuse her of *lying* . . . [Shakes head.] I don't want to say anything bad about her, but she does rub me the wrong way.

Jen
27
Nurse
Fresno, CA

Listen, I wouldn't say Krystin hurt Lauren on *purpose*, but I think all that competition really *affected* her, you know? I would be worried she might get like that with Josh, like, I don't think he wants a wife that might, like, *snap*. [Snaps fingers.] It's a little scary.

Lily
26
Graduate Student
Austin, TX

Yeah, I was pissed when the date was cut short. I could have really used that alone time with Josh that the Mud Queen was supposed to get. But instead of having a whole night, I just got a little bit. Plus, there wasn't even a group date ribbon, which means all of us were at risk for going home at the string-cutting ceremony. It's not fair that the rest of us got punished for something between two of the women—and honestly? I'm disappointed Josh didn't see that.

Lauren C.
25
Content Creator
Pinevale, NJ

Do I think Krystin hurt me on purpose? Oh my God, *absolutely* not! Honestly, I don't think she'd even slap a mosquito if it were biting her. But she grew up competing, you know? And I think that, like, *conditioning* can mess with your head sometimes. Kinda like how football players have brain damage.

CHAPTER SEVEN

Krystin is running out of ways to occupy herself between filming. She didn't bring that much to do because, really, she figured she wouldn't be bored, what with all the dramatics. But with the near real-time airing schedule, they can only shoot one episode a week, so there's a lot of downtime. Tomorrow the remaining Devotees are almost certainly going on another group date, though they're withholding the activity for prime on-camera reactions. At least that'll be something to do.

She's lying prostrate on a pool chair as the Palm Springs sun bores its UV into her back. She thought she'd have more friends by now. She thought she'd have *any*. She'd thought about texting Delia during the week's allotted Instagram-posting time, but couldn't bring herself to type out anything even mildly insinuating that Delia had been right. Lauren C. could have been her friend, or friend-adjacent, but any possibility of that had been left behind in the mud pen. What do they do with all of that mud, anyway? Do they drain it, or scoop it up with a massive shovel, or recycle it for the next match, or—

"Hey!"

Krystin pulls her head up from the chair and waits for the sun-blur to clear from her vision. Kaydie's standing in front of her, holding two cups of green juice and a folded-up *Women's Health* under her arm. She extends one drink to Krystin.

"Thanks," Krystin says, mildly surprised, but no less appreciative. "What's this for?"

Kaydie unfolds on the chair beside hers, pushing her hair back with her tiny sunglasses. "Nothing, really. I made too much green juice and figured I'd share."

Krystin sits up, and tries not to look too disappointed. "Oh."

"Also," Kaydie says, turning her highlighted head to hers, "I think we should be friends. You know, since we're both gonna be here for a while."

"You think so?"

Kaydie nods. "Oh, yeah. We're both front-runner material. I feel it." She takes a sip from the glass, careful to avoid any green residue around her mouth.

Krystin isn't sure how to feel. Is Kaydie proposing an alliance? Or does she actually want to be Krystin's friend, which she was literally just thinking she needs? She decides to hope for the best.

Krystin drinks her juice, and the lemony kale tastes genuinely refreshing. She guesses Kaydie's had a lot of time to perfect her recipe. Or maybe she got it from Instagram. "So does this mean you're not mad at me for taking you down in the ring?"

Kaydie laughs, a light, chiming thing. "Please. I knew coming in that the physical dates would not be my forte. I prefer my exercise to take the form of yogalates in a heated room."

Krystin smiles. "I think you held your own."

"Well, I'm glad I got out when I did. Otherwise I might be the one with my arm in a sling."

Krystin reddens. She puts the glass down on the side table a little too hard.

"I'm kidding. Look, Lauren C.'s full of shit. She told Josh her hair is naturally wavy when I see her using her Dyson AirWrap every single morning."

Krystin laughs half-heartedly. "I just don't want everyone to think I'm this, like, competitive freak. Or a petty bitch."

"Oh." Kaydie sips her drink. "They do."

Krystin sits up so violently the chair teeters a little. "What?"

"I mean, they don't think you're gonna leave used tampons in their suitcases like Shauna from season twelve, but yeah, you're not a huge hit in the chateau right now."

"No one's even said anything."

"That's because they don't want to end up in an ACE bandage."

"But it was the date! It was, like, a challenge."

"Yeah, on *Hopelessly Devoted*, not *Survivor*." Kaydie swings her tanned legs around to face her. "Listen, who cares what they think? Lauren C. thinks I'm a bimbo with fifty thousand followers. But you know what? I worked hard to build my business, which I own, and frankly I make a lot of cash doing it. She's just jealous that she doesn't also have a Revolve deal."

Krystin's not exactly sure how Kaydie's successful influencing career fits into the conversation at hand, but she lets it go. "Yeah," she sighs. "You're right."

Kaydie nods, then leans back in the pool chair and tips her sunglasses onto her nose.

Krystin does the same, but inside she feels squirmy. She hates the idea that the other women don't like her, and especially that it's not for a good reason. If her reputation is ruined because Lauren C. decided to fake damsel, she'll be pissed. And she doesn't even know how the editors are cutting it together. What if they make her look insane? Krystin combs her memory for what she said in her confessional. She didn't sound too cocky, did she?

Krystin finishes her juice. She wonders what Lauren's doing right now. Actually, why isn't she at the pool? That's where she usually is, and probably why she always smells kind of like coconut tanning oil.

The French doors facing the pool open and Gabi walks out, silky animal print billowing out behind her. She's trailed by Madison, the camera crew, and one of the producers. They don't even look in Krystin's direction.

"I'm SO excited for this week's dates," Madison gushes, stepping gingerly into the pool, as if it isn't heated to seventy-eight degrees.

"What are you most excited about, Madison?" Jim prompts, standing off to the side of the cameraman.

"I just can't wait to see what Josh chooses next," Madison continues, looking back at Jim for approval. He shakes his head and points to Gabi. Madison directs her attention there. "I mean, he's been so creative."

"Totally," Gabi agrees. "This whole experience has been so magical. And I can't wait for my one-on-one." Then Gabi looks at Krystin. "Krys, doesn't it kind of suck that yours is already done? I mean, if I were you, I would have wanted mine to come later, after we'd already gotten more serious."

Kaydie looks up at Krystin from her *Women's Health* in expectation. Krystin feels her face get hot from the inside, distinct from the sun hitting her cheeks.

"Actually, no," Krystin responds from her seat in the chair. "I'm really happy with how everything's gone so far. It shows he's interested in me and excited to see where things go."

Gabi smiles and clearly doesn't mean it. She looks like the girls who are bad at losing gracefully to Krystin in competitions. Then she continues, trying another angle. "I would just be worried. I mean, personally. I wouldn't want my spark to burn out too quickly, you know? There's still six weeks left."

Gabi's mouth is twisted in some imitation of concern. She unties the zebra-printed sarong from her waist and drops it daintily on the poolside. *The only thing you should worry about is your self-tanner polluting the pool water,* Krystin thinks.

She wants to defend herself, but she also doesn't want to add fuel to the apparently spreading Krystin's-a-crazy-bitch fire. "Like I said, I'm confident in our connection," Krystin says. She should leave it at that, but she can't help herself. "The only reason I'd be worried at this point is if we hadn't . . . tested our physical attraction."

Gabi's mouth drops into a line. She hasn't kissed Josh yet, and everyone knows it.

Krystin stands from her chair. "I'm gonna go make a sandwich," she says, and then she does.

Krystin doesn't listen to podcasts. She kind of missed that wave, along with furry loafers and matcha. And there isn't a lot of time to listen to them anyway, except for in the car, which is when she listens to 102.4 *The Bear.* She likes the radio, how it feels somehow more special to hear her favorite song when it comes on, instead of playing it herself. She tried to listen to *Serial* once when she was driving to Missoula for a bachelorette party, but her thoughts kept wandering off about how her friends kept getting married to the guys Krystin thought were just something to do at frat parties, and then she had to rewind, before eventually turning the podcast off altogether.

So when she listened to Josh's podcast *When One Door Closes* on the plane to the chateau, she was committed to paying attention. Every detail was important, every pause, every laugh, every lead-up to a door-themed punch line. She stared at the seat back in front of her and traced the edges of the tray table; she looked out the window at the cloud cover, terrifying in their bigness, in their deceptive denseness.

What she learned: that each episode of the podcast revolves around the love life of its guest, their relationship highs and lows, and why they're single—or, usually, why they're not. At least, that's how they start out. After about twenty minutes of relationship talk, Josh and his *Hopelessly Devoted*-sourced guest pivot inevitably to the show and what goes on behind the cameras.

It was interesting to hear then, before she was on the show herself—but now, sitting at a round table in a sound booth, it feels uncanny.

Josh looks at home in his swivel chair, one big padded headphone covering his ear, and one nestled behind. "So, usually on this podcast, I'll have on one guest, and we'll talk about their love life, and we'll learn a bit about each other. This time is a little different"—he smiles—"because the love life involves me. Say hi, ladies."

Everyone leans into their mic. "Hiiii, Jooooooosh!" A few giggle at the novelty, but some look comfortable with the recording equipment. Gabi strokes hers like the nose of a horse. Kaydie rests her wrist on the microphone stand like she would the arm of a couch.

"I'm gonna ask some questions, but I really want this to be a natural conversation. Almost forget the mic is even there, you know? Except you do have to speak into it. Sometimes I forget and then I have to go in and re-record, and it's a whole mess." Josh laughs.

Usually, they're telling Krystin to forget the cameras are there, but now she has to forget about a microphone on top of the cameras, which are also set up in the corners of the studio. Krystin is suddenly very aware of the several versions of herself that are being recorded. Except, wait, they're not *versions*. They're just her.

"Anyway, this should just be a good time. How are you ladies doing today?"

McKenzie leans in immediately. "I think I speak for a lot of us when I say that we're always happy to be with you."

Josh laughs. "Don't make me blush."

"I'm just happy to be in a studio again," says Gabi, twirling a piece of curled hair around her finger. "As much as I love the chateau, it's been so hard to be away from my recording booth."

Krystin looks at Kaydie, who bites her lip. Gabi's father had paid for her song "Rich Like Me" to be produced when she was twelve. After it went viral on YouTube, he built her a home studio so that she could keep making music, which means he must really love her, because Krystin's heard Gabi sing in the shower. Actually, Lauren had been there too, but Krystin is still too annoyed to share any knowing glances with her right now.

"Right," Josh says. "Gabi, you've got some experience in front of a microphone."

"You could say that," Gabi responds, feigning humility. "I mean, I'm no Rachel Platten. But yeah, music is my passion."

Lauren H. leans in. "I actually remember when your music video blew up. I was in seventh grade."

"Oh my God, same," says Sara-without-an-H. "We all watched it on our walk to school."

Everyone is talking around the real uniting quality of Gabi's song and corresponding music video, which is that they all made fun of it, because it was really, hysterically bad. Even in Montana. A handheld camcorder framed twelve-year-old Gabi, lounging poolside in a fuchsia Juicy Couture tracksuit, fanning herself with plumes of feathers; when she smiled, you could see a small dark cavity next to her incisors, where she'd lost a baby tooth.

But Gabi seems to be enjoying the attention anyway. She turns to Josh. "What about you, J? Did you ever listen to 'RLM'?"

Josh runs his hand through his curls. "Hey, I'll be honest. It was a carpool staple that year."

Gabi meets his eyes across the table and drops her voice real low. "I think that sounds like a sign."

Now Krystin can't help but look at Lauren, who is looking right back at her with a wicked gleam in her eyes, her lips quirking up in a smirk. Krystin looks away.

"Let's get down to business," Josh segues, and Gabi looks more than a little miffed that the spotlight has flicked away from her. "I know why you guys are on the show, and that's to form a connection with me—at least, I hope that's why." Josh pauses, then smiles. "But what *brought* you here? We all walked through a new door to get to this place, here with each other. What, or who, was in your hallway?"

When she'd listened to episodes, Krystin had assumed Josh read these kinds of lines from a script, but it appears they just come to him on the fly. To be honest, Krystin is a little impressed by his seemingly infinite arsenal of cheesy lines.

Madison raises her hand. "For me, it was my ex-boyfriend Steve. We were homecoming royalty, king and queen junior *and* senior year." She pauses for a reaction, which doesn't come. "Anyway, we were high school sweethearts, and I thought—I thought he was the one. But . . ." She trails off, looking at something that isn't there. "Then we went to college. He was unfaithful."

"I'm so sorry, Madison," Josh says gravely. "That's really hard."

"It was." She nods, and her balayage flares out. "It left me with a lot of trust issues, you know? But I think it was actually good in the long run. It taught me a lot."

"Sometimes we have to close the door on a relationship, even if it's hard, in order to open the next door ahead," Josh says. "Thank you for sharing, Madison. Who wants to go next?"

Lily talks about how her last boyfriend dumped her when she beat him in an arm wrestling match. "My strength emasculated him. Which, like, screw you. I can bench ninety pounds *and* I'm sexy as hell."

"Damn straight!" Pia yells. Then she elaborates on her struggle as a tall woman to find men who aren't intimidated by her height.

The more they talk, the faster Krystin's heart beats. It jumps over itself and into the base of her throat, which makes her feel like she's choking. She wipes her palms on her jeans, but they just get sweaty again. What is she going to say when it's her turn? That the last guy she kissed was Logan Bullock at the last Sigma Nu party before she graduated two years ago? That she can't even remember the last devastating crush she had on a guy? That the two times she'd had sex were weird, uncomfortable, and generally unfun, which made her feel guilty during and embarrassed after? That she couldn't even talk about any of this without feeling like a total prude?

Kaydie clears her throat next to Krystin. "I'll go. I was actually with my last boyfriend when my influencing career started taking off. I was getting a lot of followers from my lifestyle blog, and then a bunch of companies just started reaching out, and all of a sudden I was just swimming in brand deals. And it was actually really hard, because even though I was getting exactly what I'd always wanted, I was losing something too—Brad." She takes a dramatic breath, then continues. "He couldn't deal with my success, and it ended our relationship. But I'm glad, because I don't want a man who can't handle being with a girlboss."

"That's so effed up," says Sara. "Your man should support your dreams."

Kaydie nods. "But Josh, like you said, I closed the door on that relationship. I closed the door on Brad."

"And I'm really glad you did," Josh says. "Because it brought you here."

"Thank you so much for saying that. It really means a lot."

"Actually, it makes me wonder . . ." Josh swivels in his chair. "Lauren C., you're also a content creator. Have you ever experienced anything like this?"

Lauren's eyes widen at the question. "Honestly? I wish I hadn't. But yes, unfortunately, it's not uncommon among our community."

Josh gestures for her to continue. Krystin knows she would have even without his prompting.

"With my ex, I wouldn't say that was *why* we broke up, but my career was definitely an aspect of it." She looks up at the ceiling, considering. With her head tilted up, Krystin can see her lash line, the dark feathers flowering out from her eyelids. "We had a lot in common, but it was almost too much. Kind of like how magnets repel each other? We're best friends now, actually. It just didn't work out romantically."

"Wow," Josh says. "That's really impressive, that you're still close."

Gabi cocks her head to the side. "Yeah, how *do* you manage that?"

Lauren shrugs. "I think when someone's really important to you, they stay that way. I mean, we were together through high school *and* college."

The revelation mildly shocks Krystin. She can't imagine Lauren staying with anyone for that long, let alone anyone staying with *her*. And she would be impressed if she didn't think Lauren was lying out of her StairMastered ass. But everyone else is nodding along, even Kaydie—which means she was either lying yesterday at the pool about distrusting Lauren or is lying now. How did Krystin get to be surrounded by liars? What happened to just being yourself?

"But I'm sure this experience isn't unique to content creators," Lauren says now. "Men get jealous of successful women all the time. Krystin," she says, and turns to face her, a saccharine smile on her ever-glossy lips. "What about you? I'm sure guys get intimidated by all those blue ribbons."

Krystin feels hot all over, and now she's not sure if it's from anxiety or anger. She decides to play it off.

"Yeah." She exhales a laugh. "I once beat my boyfriend's steer-roping time and he was a real sore loser."

Lauren rests her chin in her manicured hands. "When was that?"

Krystin swallows. "Eighth grade."

Everyone laughs, thinking it was a well-timed joke. Everyone except Lauren, who's still looking at Krystin like she can see right through her. "But like, be serious. When was your last boyfriend?"

Krystin wishes she really had broken Lauren's arm in the ring. She doesn't know how to explain that her last boyfriend really was Brady Tucker in ninth grade, or that she only went along with it because all her friends said he thought she was pretty and just liked her *sooo much*, and her parents said they looked sweet together. Or that when they kissed for the first time, her first time, she could feel the seconds tick by and she didn't know what to do with her hands, and after a few minutes she asked if he wanted to stop and play a card game. And even though he obliged, he went and told everyone that she was weird, and broke up with her the next day.

But they were young, *she* was young, and that was around the time she'd started to get serious about competing, really considering it as a career path. And after that, she didn't have time to even think about dating, or to feel guilty about not wanting to.

Krystin smiles, even though her lips feel tight, which means it's not going to seem natural on the camera. She wipes her hands on her jeans again, and then she imagines she's riding Ringo, rhinestone-bedazzled hat on her hairsprayed curls, and faces her judges.

"Actually, I've never had a serious boyfriend before," she says. She keeps going, even through the overdramatic gasps. "Rodeo queens contractually aren't allowed to be in a public relationship—it can literally cost you your crown. And competing has really been my whole life."

Even Josh looks taken aback. "I had no idea," he says. "So you've never been allowed to date? That's like having the world's strictest parents."

Krystin shakes her head. She feels a little calmer now that she's said it. "You can't even be seen holding hands."

"I could never do that," Sara announces. "That's actually insane."

"Me neither," Madison agrees.

"Okay, but you said *in public*." Lily puts her hands on the table. "What about in private?"

Sara slaps her hand over her mouth. "OMG, like in secret? That's so hot."

"What? No," Krystin says. She tries not to sound too defensive. "I mean, I was always focused on training anyway. It would have been a distraction."

Lauren isn't even talking anymore, just watching the whole thing devolve.

Josh points a finger into the air. "So, wait a minute. If you're here, does that mean you're forfeiting your title?"

Krystin pauses, then nods slowly. It's technically true, even though her tenure was coming to an end soon anyway.

"Wow."

Krystin considers her words. This is her chance to prove how serious she is about this process—to Josh, to Delia, to everyone. "This is important to me. I did sacrifice a lot to be here, but it's because I'm committed to finding love."

She feels a warmth around her hand, and then realizes Kaydie's squeezing hers for support. Krystin looks up at her and smiles, and then her eyes flicker to Lauren, who's staring blankly at Kaydie's hand on hers. Krystin squeezes Kaydie back and pulls her hand away.

"Well, that was really illuminating," Josh says, rubbing his hands together like a fly. "From the bottom of my heart, thank you all so much for digging deep with me. I really feel like we crossed a threshold today."

CHAPTER EIGHT

Tonight's cocktail party really shouldn't feel that different from the past three cocktail parties leading up to the past three string-cutting ceremonies: Once again, everyone's wearing heels and false lashes, and once again, producers and cameramen are circling the women like gnats as they wait patiently for a turn with Josh. But this time, there's an anxious, frenzied energy in the lounge, and half the contestants are already rosy-cheeked and glassy-eyed from champagne. Maybe everyone's still on edge after reliving their biggest relationships and heartbreaks.

Or maybe, like Lauren, they're just all too aware that three more women are going home tonight.

Lauren isn't nervous, though—well, not really. So far, the season is unfolding exactly as she expected: She knows she's making enough of an impression to survive another few weeks, collect another few thousand followers. But Josh hasn't even chosen her for a coveted solo date yet, meaning she's clearly not in the front-runner ranks with McKenzie, Kaydie, Krystin, and Lily. At the rate things are progressing, he'll cut her string right before hometown visits.

Everything she wants—everything she's planned—is materializing perfectly. So why does Lauren feel just as unsettled as the rest of the contestants look?

"Talking about Steve was really difficult," Madison says. Her eyes look slightly puffier than usual, and Lauren wonders if she's been crying, losing sleep, or both. "I had no idea it would bring back so many emotions."

Gabi immediately pounces. "Are you saying you miss him? Because if you're not here for Josh, there's the door."

Lauren takes a sip from her flute. If she never hears the word "door" again, it might be too soon.

"Oh, not at all. It's just painful to remember, especially since Josh is really the first guy I've been vulnerable with since then. In fact," Madison says, stepping up, "I'm going to go tell him all of that right now."

Gabi glares at Madison's retreating body. "I need more champagne," she announces. "Anyone else want a refill?"

"I'll come with," says Lauren H. She's been glued to Gabi's hip since the podcast date, probably hoping to get some kind of attention from Josh and the rest of the women. After all, as insufferable as Gabi is, Lauren has to admit she makes a strong impression.

Lauren sloshes the liquid in her glass a little. She doesn't exactly want to follow Gabi and Lauren H. anywhere, but she's tempted to grab another drink, if only to have something to do. She stands up and starts to make her way over to the bar, but she's intercepted by Penny. "How's it going?" she whispers conspiratorially. She's flanked by two men with cameras. "I'd love to pull you aside and hear your thoughts ahead of the string-cutting ceremony."

She nods. "Sure."

They pop into a small side room. "So. Do you feel good about your chances tonight?" Penny asks.

Lauren takes a seat and folds her hands into her lap. "I really opened up to Josh on yesterday's group date, and I definitely think our connection's stronger than ever. I just hope he feels the same way."

"Is there anyone you think *should* go home tonight?" Penny leans in.

They ask this every time, and Lauren's answer is always the same. "Not at all," she says. "I think everyone was really vulnerable on yesterday's group date, and I think Josh has some really difficult decisions to make."

"What about Gabi?" Penny crosses her arms. "I don't know that she's a huge fan of yours."

"Oh, Gabi's definitely a presence at the chateau," Lauren says. "But really, I'm just trying to focus on my relationship with Josh."

"Would you say you're, you know, not here to make friends?" Penny phrases the question like an in-joke, but Lauren can tell she's hoping for a good sound bite.

"The other women are all wonderful," Lauren says diplomatically. "But at the end of the day, we're all here for the same reason: to find love."

"What about Krystin?"

"Sorry?" She remembers Krystin's strong, firm arms pinning her down and holding her in place; that little smudge of mascara on her perfectly smooth cheek. *Just stay away from me.*

"Is everything okay between the two of you?"

"What, did she say something?" Lauren blurts out before she can stop herself. *Fuck.*

"A lot of the women are still talking about your incident from last week," Penny says, blatantly dodging the question.

"Everything's fine between me and Krystin," Lauren says, hoping they won't intercut her quote with some snippet of Krystin shit-talking her. "We're both adults, and again, we're both here to find love. That's what matters, right?"

For a moment, Penny just stares at Lauren, willing her to elaborate. She doesn't.

"That was really great," she says, although her tone implies she feels otherwise. "Thank you, Lauren."

"Any time." She gives her a pleasant smile. "I'm going to head back out there. Talk soon?"

The energy is even more tense when Lauren gets back to the lounge. Lily is laying into Gabi, probably because Lauren H.—Gabi's only real ally at this point—is nowhere to be seen. "What you said to Kaydie *was* uncalled for, so don't play dumb. You're always provoking anyone who gets a group date ribbon," Lily says, tossing back her braids. "It's transparent, and frankly, it's tacky."

Lauren automatically glances at Krystin. Krystin immediately looks away.

"All I said was that it's really interesting she hasn't had a one-on-one yet. That's basically a compliment." Gabi rolls her eyes. "You're acting like I accused her of buying followers."

"Everyone needs to calm down!" Sara-without-an-H interjects, somehow louder than both Lily and Gabi. Her lip quivers, and Lauren wonders if any of the producers keep Ativan on hand. "There's way too much toxicity in this house."

"You haven't had a one-on-one yet, either!" Kaydie snaps, completely ignoring Sara's outburst. "You keep trying to undermine everyone who has a real connection with Josh. You did the same thing to Krystin." She points a finger at Krystin, who looks like she wishes she'd melt into the plush sofa.

"I don't think—" Krystin starts.

"Josh likes me because I'm real and genuine, and I tell it like it is," Gabi interrupts. "If you can't handle one little question, maybe this isn't the environment for you, babe."

At that, Lauren heads over to the bar cart, pours herself a generous glass of champagne, and wonders if she should go get her five minutes with Josh out of the way. As soon as she puts the bottle down, though, another perfectly French-manicured hand reaches for it.

"Gabi isn't a bitch, you know." It's Lauren H. "She's just trying to . . . weed out the weakest people. The ones who aren't really here for the right reasons."

"Hmm," Lauren says. She doesn't exactly want to participate in this conversation, but she doesn't want to go back to the lounge, either. Maybe she *should* go make out with Josh.

"Like, you're really here to get married at the end of this. I can tell. It's so obvious that Kaydie just wants Instagram followers," the Other Lauren adds. Lauren follows her line of vision back to the other women. She doesn't disagree about Kaydie, but it's hysterical that the Other Lauren thinks Gabi, of "Rich Like Me" notoriety, isn't here for fame, either. "And then there's Krystin, who's just . . ."

Lauren takes a sip of champagne. "Just what?"

The Other Lauren lowers her voice, even though there are still cameras within earshot. "I was just telling Josh that, like, she can't be real, right? She's never had a relationship, and now she's ready to risk her entire rodeo princess thing for some random guy we just met? Something isn't adding up."

Lauren looks back over at the women. Krystin's flute is still completely full—she hasn't seen her take a sip of champagne all night. "Josh isn't just some random guy," Lauren says, mindful of the mic clipped to her dress, even though, well, he kind of is. Actually, nothing the Other Lauren has said feels like a stretch, but her vigilante act still bothers Lauren for reasons she can't really pinpoint. "He's special. That's why we're all here, right?"

"Of course," the Other Lauren says. "But come on. You've seen her, right? Is she really ready to get married?"

Lauren narrows her eyes. She knows she's not one to talk, but the Other Lauren herself has *wrong reasons* written all over her perfectly made-up face. After all, she's spent more time discussing future Tik-Toks she'll make with Gabi than her interest in Josh. "Are *you* ready to get married?"

"Yeah. Obviously." She looks down at her champagne as she says it, though, swirling the sparkly liquid in her flute.

"Right." There's something equally comforting *and* depressing, Lauren thinks, about being surrounded by people who are just as fake as she is. She thinks of Krystin again—genuine, naïve, secretly strong enough to pin her down—and then something clicks into place. "Wait. Did you say you told Josh all of this, about her not being ready?" Lauren asks. "Like, just now?"

"I know. I didn't want to be that girl, either," the Other Lauren says. "But I feel like at this point, it's our responsibility to tell Josh if we see any red flags."

"Red flags," Lauren repeats.

"If one of the girls here hasn't committed to anyone in her entire life, I just think that's a red flag," she says. "That's all I told him, and you of all people should be *thanking* me, seeing as she almost broke both your arms."

On that note, the Other Lauren turns and marches back toward Gabi with purpose. Penny approaches Lauren, but Lauren speaks before she can ask for another quick interview. "Is Josh still in the sitting room?"

"Yes," Penny says. She looks defeated. "I think he's with Hilarie now? But you should definitely grab him. Don't be afraid to interrupt. It's important to be bold."

"Right. I'll do that," Lauren says, starting to feel almost sorry for her. She's clearly working overtime to catalyze some kind of rivalry since, honestly, Gabi's days are numbered, and after that, who's left to stir shit up? Lily and Sara?

From the sound of it, Josh and Hilarie are recapping their entire one-on-one in the sitting room. "I can't believe they got Hayden McGranger to perform a private show for us," Hilarie gushes. "I don't know about you, but 'Jesus, Jameson, and Blue Jeans' was on my Spotify Wrapped a few years ago."

"Hey," Lauren says, resting a hand on her shoulder. "Do you mind if I steal him for a minute?"

Hilarie looks at Josh, her face suddenly sullen. "Yeah, sure," she says. "But Josh, don't forget: 'Passenger Seat of My Pick-Up' is our song, right?"

He hums a few notes, and it's enough to make Hilarie smile again. "I'll see you back out there, Hilarie."

"Hi." Lauren sits down and rests a hand on Josh's thigh. "Did you miss me?"

"Not anymore." He grins. "You really impressed me on that group date, you know. Have you ever thought about going into podcasting?"

"It wasn't a big deal," she says, taken aback by his earnestness. "All I did was open up about my ex."

"Well, it wasn't just that," Josh counters. "You listened, and riffed off the other guests, and asked all the right questions. You're a natural out there."

"That's nice of you to say." Lauren lets herself wonder whether she could actually make a lucrative podcast after her *Hopelessly Devoted* stint. It's not a bad idea, but it would definitely require a lot more work than the Q&A vlogs she'd been envisioning. "It was a really illuminating group date, by the way. I mean, trust and vulnerability are so important in a relationship. If someone can't even talk about their relationship history, how can you trust anything they say?"

Unfortunately, Josh doesn't take the bait. "You mentioned you were still friends with your ex-boyfriend," he says, then clears his throat. "There aren't, er, any lingering feelings there, are there?"

"No. He's totally over me, I'm totally over him." Lauren decides to try again. She's not sure how much time she'll get with Josh before a contestant "steals him for a sec," and she might have to hit him over the head with this one. "Listen, Josh. The last thing I want to do is start any kind of drama, but I know Lauren H. said something to you, and I just don't know if she's trustworthy."

Josh frowns, and Lauren can practically hear the dramatic music that will be superimposed over this moment. "What do you mean?"

"Well, she didn't even open up on the podcast date. She said nothing," Lauren says. "And now she's going around and making some pretty huge assumptions about women who *were* vulnerable with you today. And if I've learned anything from reading a lot of Taylor Swift interviews, it's that you can never trust women who backstab other women."

"I hear you," Josh says. "She did say something to me, but . . . you know, can I be real with you for a minute?"

"We're Josh and Lauren," she says smoothly. "We're always real with each other."

"It's just fucking hard sometimes." He shakes his head, and for half a second, Lauren worries he might start crying. "It's so damn hard trying to figure out who you can trust. I have Lauren H. saying one thing, and then . . ."

"Look," Lauren says, trying to buy a few seconds of time. No part of her wants to be the season's snitch; time and time again, she's watched contestants get sent home (and, even worse, mocked on Twitter) for whining about other Devotees instead of focusing on their own bond with the lead. But she has one card left to play. "I didn't want to say anything, but she called you 'some random guy we just met.'"

Josh blinks. "She did?"

"You can ask her yourself. I don't want to be the one who tells you who you can't trust." She puts her other arm around his shoulders. "But I think you know who you *can*."

He looks into her eyes. "Yeah?"

It would be so painfully easy to become a front-runner right now, to secure her spot for another week and beyond. All Lauren would have to do is implore Josh to trust *her*, and then kiss him until he spews some bullshit about how he's falling for her already. Instead, Lauren says, "You can trust those of us who actually opened up to you yesterday, right? You can trust the women who told you the truth about their romantic history, even if it was terrifying, or even if it gave everyone else room to speculate and judge them. Especially the people who really put themselves out there."

"That's . . . wow." Josh lets out a whoosh of breath. "You're absolutely right."

Lauren nods sagely.

"Again. I think *you* should be hosting a podcast." He chuckles.

"I'll think about it. But in the meantime, if you ever need a co-host . . ."

Instead of answering, Josh kisses her. And when they're interrupted just a minute later, it isn't by another Devotee—it's Holland.

"Ceremony in ten," she says. "Josh, come with me."

Lauren is in the front of two rows, sandwiched between Pia and Madison, but she can *feel* Lauren H. right behind her, emanating smugness like a signature perfume. Krystin, meanwhile, looks petrified. And alone. *Not my problem*, Lauren thinks. *She won't even look at me.*

"Wow. What a week, right?" Josh says. "You know, these ceremonies get a little harder each time. It's still surreal to me that I'm standing in front of eleven beautiful, strong women. It's even more surreal that among them is my future wife. Am I the luckiest man in the world, or what?"

There are a few compulsory, inebriated giggles. But Pia and Madison, anyway, both look nervous out of their minds.

"I have to do what I've done every week, though." Josh takes a deep breath and reaches for the pair of golden scissors in front of him. "I need to follow my heart in order to find my person. And I hope all of you know how special, wonderful, and gorgeous I think you are. McKenzie?"

"Excuse me," McKenzie whispers to a disgruntled Gabi. She walks up to Josh, who takes both of her hands in his. He pointedly glances at the string tied around her wrist, then back up to her face.

"McKenzie, I'd really love to continue our journey together," he says. "And if you'd like that too, you can take a seat with Kaydie and Hilarie over there."

"Of course," McKenzie says earnestly. She sits down next to Kaydie and Hilarie, both donning their golden immunity ribbons. Hilarie, of course, received her ribbon on her solo date; Kaydie, on the other hand, nabbed the group date ribbon after "opening a pretty heavy door to her past" during the podcasting date.

"Madison."

She steps forward.

"I know you haven't always felt appreciated—but tonight, I appreciated your vulnerability and honesty. And I'd really love for you to stay another week."

The next two women are also invited to stay: Lily, Sara.

"Lauren C."

Lauren takes a breath and approaches Josh, her heart pounding. They kissed—that has to mean she's safe for another week, right? Then again, she did break the cardinal rule of tattling on another contestant . . .

"I can see a future with you," he says, and Lauren exhales. "And I'd love for you to stick around."

"I'd like that," Lauren says. She can't help it: As she walks across the room, she shoots a look back at the Other Lauren and Krystin, standing side by side.

Josh heaves a sigh. "This is hard," he says, almost like he's talking to himself. "Really hard. Lauren H."

The Other Lauren saunters confidently toward Josh, leaving Pia, Gabi, and Krystin behind. Lauren's Glossier-coated lips go dry, her heart sinks to her stomach, and a thought hits her, one that's more a fact than a feeling: This isn't just about wanting the Other Lauren out. She wants Krystin to stay.

"Lauren H. Did you . . ." He clears his throat. "Did you say I'm 'just some random guy you just met'?" He makes little air quotes, and a few of the women gasp.

The Other Lauren opens her mouth, then closes it. She looks directly at Lauren, then back at Josh. "No. Of course not," she says, but she's inexplicably blinking like there's a dust mite caught in her eye. "I mean, yeah, I did, but I didn't mean it like—"

"So did you say it, or not?" Josh asks. He's never sounded this authoritative before, and clearly, the rest of the women find it hot: Lily is pretending to fan herself, and McKenzie's smiling like a proud girlfriend.

"There was context," the Other Lauren says weakly, and Lauren tries to keep her face appropriately solemn.

"Trust is the most important thing to me here, and I don't know that we have that," Josh says. "I'm sorry, Lauren, but I'm going to have to cut your string."

The Other Lauren reluctantly reaches out an arm. "I just hope you find what you're looking for, I guess," she says as he snips the string off her wrist. "I hope you make the right choices." It would sound pretty menacing and cold, if not for the fact that she's clearly staving off tears. Josh half-heartedly tries to hug her, but she shrugs him off and walks away.

The room is silent. Sara, seated next to Lauren, is almost vibrating; Pia, Gabi, and Krystin, still in elimination purgatory, are gazing at Josh, waiting for his next move. Only one of them will get to stay.

"Krystin," he finally calls, and until now, Lauren didn't realize how fast her heart was beating. She walks past Pia, her stilettos clicking against the tiled floor.

"As difficult as it was, you were real with me today, Krystin." He squeezes her hand. "I have to trust my instincts, and my instincts are telling me that we have something special. That we could create something special, down the line. And I think you're ready for that."

Lauren swallows down a laugh. She had no idea he'd lay it on this thick.

"I'd like you to stay another week, Krystin," he says. "What do you think?"

She gives him a winning smile. "I think that sounds perfect."

"Gabi and Pia," Josh says. "I'm sorry, but I'm going to have to ask you to step forward so I can say goodbye . . . and cut your strings."

All things considered, Pia's exit is a graceful one. She gently thanks Josh for the opportunity as she hugs him goodbye, then walks over to the rest of the girls. "DM me if you're ever in LA, okay?" she tells Lauren. "And good luck with all of"—she gestures around broadly—"this."

"Thanks. And I will," Lauren says. She can't really imagine hanging with any of these women outside of the *Hopelessly Devoted* incubator, but Pia was genuinely kind of cool, someone she might have actually elected to follow on Instagram. It's a bummer she got cut, Lauren thinks, but she'll probably be a shoo-in for the show's free-for-all reunion spin-off, *Summer Lovin'*.

Gabi, on the other hand, doesn't take the high road. "Whatever," she grumbles as Josh cuts her string. "As if I'd ever want to move to Long *fucking* Island." She gives the rest of the women a withering look before exiting. Unfortunately, based on Lauren's comprehensive understanding of how this show works, she'll probably get invited to *Summer Lovin'* too.

"Well," Josh says, staring off after her. "That was an emotional night." He coughs, turns back to the contestants, and tries to smile, but it doesn't quite meet the corners of his eyes. "I have a good feeling about tomorrow, though. And you know what they say when one door closes, right?"

It took Lauren a week or two to get the hang of sleeping in the chateau. It's not that she can't cohabitate with other girls—she lived in a sorority house throughout college, and she stayed at countless Airbnbs while studying abroad in Europe—but the small, tightly packed, wallpapered bedrooms are even worse than the hostel she braved in Copenhagen. Thanks to her silk sleep mask and earplugs, though, she's been able to sleep well enough.

Not tonight.

With Pia gone, Lauren's alone in the room with Hilarie, who's snoring steadily in the bunk bed five feet away. Eventually, unable to take it any longer, she slides out from under the linen sheets, grabs her empty black Hydro Flask, and slips outside. She's surprised to see another woman sitting on the floor at the end of the hall, in a matching flannel pajama set, leaning against the wall with an earbud in, connected to an ancient-looking iPod that may or may not be contraband. Krystin.

Before she even realizes what she's doing, Lauren walks over to her. "Hey."

Krystin hesitates before taking out her headphones. "Hi."

Lauren holds up her water bottle. "Just refilling this."

Krystin just nods. "I thought I was going home tonight," she finally says.

"Oh." It's all Lauren can think to say back. "Well, that didn't happen."

"Yeah." They're quiet for a second, and Lauren's about to say something when Krystin speaks again. "I know you somehow . . . got him to eliminate Lauren H. You ratted her out, didn't you?"

"You don't know that." Lauren sits down on the ground, too, across from her. The hallway is narrow enough that Lauren has to pull her thighs to her chest so that their slippers don't touch.

"Yeah, I do."

"What makes you think that?" Lauren challenges.

Krystin gives her an incredulous look. "She was so busy glaring back at you, she almost tripped on her way out the door."

Lauren doesn't answer. Instead, she pulls at a loose thread near the sleeve of her pink satin pajama top. She's so close to Krystin—closer than they've ever been without camera surveillance—and it would be terrifyingly easy to touch her. Brush her hand, maybe, or adjust her seating position and graze Krystin's leg with her own.

She shouldn't be thinking these kinds of things about another contestant. Hell, she shouldn't be thinking these things about an absolute textbook straight girl, whether or not she's a fellow Devotee. But then she remembers the Krystin she saw on the podcasting date: her complete lack of experience with men, her hand in Kaydie's.

Suddenly scared that Krystin can read her thoughts on her face, Lauren pulls her legs in even closer.

"So you really care about Josh," Krystin continues. "If you wanted to warn him that she called him—what was it? Some guy—"

"Of course I care about Josh," Lauren interrupts, but it doesn't sound very convincing, even to herself, so she adds, "He's, like, our boyfriend."

Krystin bites her lip. She looks like she's trying to hold back a laugh, or maybe a sigh. "Lauren H. was trying to get me eliminated, wasn't she?"

"You don't know that," Lauren says again.

"Yeah, I do." This time, Krystin doesn't wait for Lauren to argue back. "She and Gabi were standing by the bar cart and talking about it for, like, twenty minutes."

"Well, she and Gabi can have fun talking about it some more at Palm Springs International Airport."

"Seriously," Krystin says, adjusting her whole body a bit as she turns to look Lauren in the eye. "Why are you suddenly trying to help me? What do you want?"

Why *is* she trying to help Krystin? And the biggest question, really: Why is she still sitting in the hallway with Krystin, having this conversation at two in the morning? The former is only slightly easier to answer. "You seemed so upset after the whole mud wrestling thing. I guess I . . ." She feels helpless. "I just wanted to show that I, like, care or whatever. About you staying here."

Krystin chews the corner of her lip. "That's a really weird way to show you care about someone."

Lauren holds eye contact. "Did it work, though?"

Krystin's silent again, but her gaze is steady. It's not completely unlike the way Krystin stared at her during mud wrestling; the way she looked at her later that night, in the bathroom. This time, though, her expression is more quizzical, like she's trying to figure Lauren out—but it's equally intense, and Lauren feels a jolt somewhere in her chest.

After what feels like minutes, Krystin gives her a quick flash of a smile, then stands up. "I'm exhausted," she says. "I'll see you in the morning."

WEEK 4
CONFESSIONALS

Eight women remaining.

Lauren H.
27
Real Estate Agent
Cincinnati, OH

I never meant for my words to be twisted like that. [Sniffles.] I was literally just pointing out that, like, some women here haven't even had serious *boyfriends* before. Like, how are they ready for marriage, and I'm not? I'm twenty-freaking-seven—I'm running out of time! [Turns away from camera, cries.]

Lauren C.
25
Content Creator
Pinevale, NJ

I think Josh—I mean, I think *everyone* knows that the last thing I ever want to do is start any drama. And as much as I want every strong woman here to find happiness, sometimes you just have to stand up for the person you're *really* there for. And *me* . . . well, I'm here for Josh.

Gabi
24
Italian Princess
New York, NY

This is so majorly f--ked up. It's like, I shouldn't even have to say I'm better than all those other girls, it's that obvious. And Josh wears *khakis*. All this for a guy I could have met at f--king 1 Oak?

Kaydie
25
Content Creator
Los Angeles, CA

Josh's actions this week really proved that he's nothing like the insecure boy-men I meet in LA. The fact that he sees a future with me, knowing everything he does about my brand? I really trust him.

Krystin
23
Rodeo Queen
Bozeman, MT

I'm so grateful that Josh still believes in us after I was vulnerable with him this week. To be completely honest, I did feel animosity from some of the women. I was hopeful that I wouldn't be judged for my experiences, but if rodeo has taught me anything, it's that you can't let the stares of other people slow you down.

CHAPTER NINE

Krystin was supposed to leave the country for the first time with Delia. They had a plan, post-college graduation: to go to Europe and see all the things pictured in their Italian textbooks, to practice saying *ciao* and *grazie*, and then sit in dark pubs and talk to boys who thought their American accents were endearing. But then Krystin won the title of Rodeo Queen Montana, and couldn't leave the state.

They were disappointed, obviously. But Krystin was excited, and Delia was proud of her, which made up for any guilt Krystin felt for canceling their trip because Delia's approval was a precious resource and Krystin felt lucky for feeling its glow. Any time Krystin found herself thinking about tossing coins into Trevi Fountain, she remembered Delia's grin when Krystin rode Ringo around the ring, waving the Montana state flag. And Delia never said a word about it, just showed up at Krystin's events and told everyone she was her best friend.

And she was—up until she wasn't anymore. Actually, Krystin doesn't know what they are. Because friendship, at least the kind she had with Delia, doesn't just *end*. Not after thirteen years. Krystin still doesn't understand why Delia was so mad in the first place. She genuinely thought Delia would be happy for her; or, if not happy, then accepting of the situation. But it really wasn't about happiness at all. It was about Delia's respect, and Krystin had lost it, and she's afraid she'll never feel that glow of admiration ever again.

"Mind if I sit?"

Krystin looks away from the clouds she's been staring at through the plane window. Lauren stands in the aisle, a furry neck pillow cradling her head. Her hair is tucked into a silk sleep mask with *Shh . . .* embroidered across it. She should look silly, but she doesn't. She looks . . .

Krystin shakes her head and gestures for her to sit. "Didn't like your seatmate?" Krystin asks as Lauren slides her carry-on under the seat.

Lauren makes a sour face. "Some old guy that kept asking me probing questions like, why is a pretty girl like you traveling alone? And I was like, I am literally traveling with nine other women and a production crew." Then she sticks a water bottle, a pack of gum, a magazine, a book, and a gratitude journal in the seat-back pocket.

Lauren catches Krystin watching and explains. "Water because airplane air is incredibly dehydrating, gum for when my ears pop, a gossip rag for entertainment, a bestseller for when I get bored of celebrities, and a journal for personal growth."

"Wow," Krystin replies, surprised that Lauren spares even a minute trying to grow personally. "You're really prepared."

"Aren't you?" Then Lauren looks at Krystin's empty seat back. "Oh. Are you just a plane sleeper?"

"I don't really know," Krystin says. "The longest flight I've ever been on was from Bozeman to Denver, and that was only an hour and fifteen minutes."

"Wait, really?" Lauren looks like Krystin just told her she shoots and eats bunnies. "So, you've never been out of the country?"

Krystin shakes her head.

"Not even Mexico?"

"Nope."

"Huh. You're really living up to your reputation."

"What reputation?"

Lauren's expression says it's obvious. "Naïve horse girl."

Krystin rolls her eyes. "Great." She looks back out the window. She can see mountains below, and the shadows painted like water-color onto them by the clouds. "I was supposed to go to Europe with my best friend a couple of years ago, but then stuff came up, and we had to cancel."

"So? You can still do that."

"I don't know if I can." Krystin turns back to Lauren. "I don't even know if we're still friends."

Lauren twists the cap of her water bottle until it snaps. "Why?" she asks, already drinking.

Krystin tries to think of how to phrase it without offending Lauren, who is ultimately someone Delia would hate. In fact, she's everything Delia hates about *Hopelessly Devoted*. "She didn't want me to come on the show. She doesn't . . . like it."

It doesn't work. Lauren already looks suspicious, which is just one step away from her being annoyed. "Why?" This time the word is razored.

"You know, the usual reasons," Krystin hedges. "It's fake, anti-feminist, blah blah blah."

"So your friend thinks the show is anti-feminist, but doesn't think you not being able to have a boyfriend while being a rodeo queen or whatever is?"

"Huh? What are you even talking about?"

Lauren sighs, and speaks more slowly. "You said you can't have a boyfriend, right?"

"I was not allowed to have a boyfriend while holding the state title, yes."

"So your best friend was totally cool with that, even though it seems like a fucked-up old-timey rule that some might call anti-feminist."

Krystin is starting to glean her point. "Okay, sure, I see what you mean. But it was never about that. Rodeo's about our connection to the west, and the importance of agriculture, and, like, being a role model—" She stops herself before she gets too corny. "It's a whole culture."

"Based on not having a boyfriend so you can seem attractive and available."

Krystin bristles. "Why do you care?"

Lauren shrugs. "It just sounds like your *best friend*'s a hypocrite."

Krystin is starting to regret letting Lauren take the seat next to her. "Yeah, well, you don't know her."

"Honestly," Lauren says, slipping her magazine out of the pocket and onto her lap, "it sounds like she just doesn't want you to have a boyfriend at all."

A muted *ding* from the speakers. "Ladies and gentlemen, the captain has turned on the fasten seat belt sign."

Krystin hears Sara give an excited yelp in front of her. Then Sara pops her head above the seat and looks back at them.

"Isn't this so exciting? I can't believe we're going to Buenos Aires!"

"Totally!" Lauren says, an octave higher than her normal voice. Krystin just nods.

Sara beams at them until a flight attendant tells her to sit down and fasten her seat belt.

Krystin looks outside as they enter a patch of clouds. Next to her, Lauren flips through her magazine, her face partially obscured by the fuzzy pillow that brushes against the skin of her cheeks. She looks warm. Krystin wonders what it would feel like to curl into her. The plane jostles slightly, and Krystin feels herself pushed into her seat.

Lauren reaches into the seat pocket and retrieves her gum, and Krystin watches as she pops a square out with her acrylics and places it gently on her tongue.

Krystin did, in fact, wish she had prepared for the flight like Lauren. She could only sleep in thirty-minute increments, and the time she really *was* sleeping, Lauren shook her awake for their connecting flight. Krystin's first instinct when she felt Lauren's hand had been to lean into it, but Lauren had pulled away.

By the time they land in Argentina, Krystin feels like a balloon is about to burst behind her eyes. Lauren, though, just pushes her sleep mask up into her hair and blinks.

"You look like hell," she tells Krystin, who ignores her.

Holland and Jim wrangle the women off the plane. Josh, who had been siphoned off from his Devotees in his first-class seat, is nowhere to be seen.

"He's getting a separate ride to the hotel," Holland says as they walk through the airport. "You'll all see him tomorrow for the date cards."

Sara pouts. "I can't believe we were so close to him for, like, sixteen hours and couldn't even talk to him. I would do literally anything to see him right now."

Lily turns to her. "You want him to see you like this?"

Sara shrugs. "It would be good practice for when we're waking up next to each other."

Kaydie laughs. Lily rolls her eyes.

When they arrive at the hotel, Holland and Jim stop in the middle of the lobby and motion for the women to gather around them.

"Okay, ladies, we have your room assignments," Jim says. "You're all gonna share a room with one person—"

"And *don't* come to me saying you need a single because of some middle school sleepover trauma," Holland interrupts, holding up a finger. "I will *not* believe you."

Jim waits for her to be finished. "As I was saying, you'll all have one roommate, which is an upgrade from the bunks, right? Right. Okay, so the rooms are: McKenzie and Lily, Kaydie and Madison, Hilarie and Sara M., and last but not least, Krystin and Lauren C."

"It's just Lauren now, Jim," Lauren says. "There's only one."

"Congratulations."

"Thank you."

Holland gives them their room keys and itinerary packets for the week. "Meet on the private pool deck at seven PM so we can get the shot of all of you shouting 'Buenos Aires,' all right?"

They all nod in agreement and then head to the elevators.

Lauren walks next to Krystin, rolling her AWAY suitcase smoothly across the tile. "It's like one *long* sleepover," she says, stretching out the word *long* in her mouth.

They board the elevator, which spits them out on the top floor.

"See you guys soon!" Madison yells down the hall, skipping to keep up with Kaydie, who looks like she's one excited exclamation away from pushing Madison into the wall.

"Just the two of us now," Lauren sing-songs. Then she slides the keycard into the door, which unlocks with a click.

Krystin pushes into the room. "Just so we're clear, I don't all of a sudden trust you again just because you did the right thing, like, one time."

"Come on." Lauren sets her bag down on a chair. "Don't tell me you'd rather share a room with any of them."

Krystin thinks of Kaydie, who once told Krystin that Madison's shrieks made her want to be deaf. "No," she admits.

"Then we're on the same page."

They only have a few hours before their call time on the pool deck, so they pass the time unpacking their makeup bags and hanging their cocktail dresses in the closet. When she's finished, Krystin sits down on her bed, which is way nicer than the mattresses back at the chateau, even though it's still a twin. She wishes she could just sleep now, even though it's only 6:17 and—shit, it's already 6:17 and she hasn't even started styling her hair.

Lauren's sitting on the floor in front of the windows, hunched over a magnifying mirror. "Are you good?" she asks, her tweezers poised in the air. "You look—"

"Like hell," Krystin finishes. "I know."

"I was going to say 'out of it,' but sure."

"I'm just so tired," Krystin says as she plugs her curling iron into the bathroom outlet. "Is it normal to be this tired?"

"You're asking me if it's normal to be tired after not sleeping during seventeen hours of travel?"

Krystin sighs, wrapping a chunk of hair around the hot iron. She doesn't know why she's expecting Lauren to say something comforting. They're barely even friends.

"I'm just not used to all of this," Krystin says. "That's all."

It's quiet, and Krystin starts to think they really aren't friends at all, until Lauren walks into the bathroom and places two Advil on the counter in front of her, followed by a plastic water bottle from the mini fridge.

"Here," Lauren says. "This will make us *both* feel better."

She says it like a dig, but the normal edge—the condescending one usually reserved for, well, everyone—is missing. Krystin turns away from the mirror, observing Lauren like one might a new species. Her typical glare has softened, her bottom lip pulled ever so slightly behind her teeth. Before Krystin can respond, she flips her already-perfect hair behind her shoulders and walks out of the bathroom.

"In any case, you'd better get used to it," Lauren calls from the other room. "It's week five. It's only going up."

Krystin wades through the rest of the evening in a hazy stupor. She can barely focus during filming, just keeps yelling "Buenos Aires" into the hot air while the women around her beam into the sunset.

"¡Arriba!" Kaydie yells, shimmying her hips.

McKenzie rests her elbows on the balcony edge and smiles at the city. "This is it," she says. "This is it."

Madison is told she has the week's first date, and she better go get ready because they leave in an hour. Krystin dips out the second they cut the cameras, leaving the rest of the women to splash each other in the pool and guess what the dates will be that week. She feels Lauren watching her as she passes the producers without a glance, but doesn't look back.

When she reaches the room, she goes straight to the bathroom and locks the door behind her. Then she strips off her too-tight dress and leaves it in a sad tangle on the floor.

It might be the nicest shower she's ever stepped in, or it might just be that she's never wanted a shower so badly. She rakes shampoo across her scalp until her hair feels squeaky under her fingers; she rubs shower gel into her skin, and spends several minutes washing her face. Every time she looks at her hands, more mascara has flaked onto her fingertips.

She stays even after she's clean. The water glitters as it hits the shower tiles. No matter how much she turns the dial, she can't get the water hot enough. Eventually she just sits down, resting her toes on the curve of the tub. The water rains down onto her, pushing her hair in front of her face; she lets it hang there like a curtain in front of her eyes.

Then she cries. It's probably the jet lag, because she's so, so tired, and she doesn't even know why she's sad. But then she thinks of the time she and Delia went to get their passport photos taken before their trip was canceled, and remembers. She thinks about Delia eight years ago in Krystin's bedroom, on a hot summer night, somehow hotter than this, than Buenos Aires. And she remembers. Remembering feels like swimming through molasses.

Why is it so hard for her to be happy? She's in Buenos Aires with a guy she really likes, and who likes her back. For some reason, that thought only makes her cry harder. The steam fills up the bathroom until breathing feels thick and hot. Her back feels raw from where the water's been hitting her skin.

She waits for her breathing to steady, then reaches back to turn the shower off. She wraps a towel around her body and wipes a hand across the foggy mirror, which reveals a more-than-flushed Krystin staring back at her with puffy eyes.

"Fuck," she whispers, then puts on her moisturizer.

When she emerges from the bathroom, Lauren looks up at her from her bed. "Finally. I have to pee."

"Sorry," Krystin says, hoping she sounds normal. "I thought you were still at the pool."

"It's fine," she says, turning the TV off. "I've been watching Argentine telenovelas."

Krystin busies herself with rifling through her suitcase for a T-shirt. "Well, it's all yours now."

She hears Lauren bounce off the bed and close the bathroom door. Krystin changes into her Murdoch's shirt and Montana State sweats and then dries her hair with the towel. By the time Lauren's done, Krystin's managed to maintain a neutral face while combing out her waves. She's confident Lauren hasn't noticed anything different until she sniffles and has to blow her nose.

"Allergies," Krystin lies.

"Bullshit. You haven't had allergies this entire time."

Lauren looks at Krystin, who tries to hide behind her hair. "Hey," Lauren says, softer now. "Are you okay?"

Which makes Krystin start crying again.

Lauren looks confused, and kind of uncomfortable. "Is this because of when I called you a horse girl?"

"What?" Krystin says through tears. "No."

"Well . . ." Lauren pauses. Krystin doesn't expect her to finish, but finally she just asks, "What's wrong?"

"Delia," she blurts out, too exhausted to care.

"Who?"

"My best friend."

"Oh. You never told me her name."

Krystin reaches for another tissue. "I didn't? Well, there it is."

Lauren hasn't moved from her position on her bed. "If you're sad because she doesn't want to be your friend anymore, then fuck her."

"She's my best friend," Krystin chokes. "Don't you have a best friend?"

"Well, yes," Lauren replies. "But we're, like, different."

"Bully for you."

"That's not what I mean," Lauren says, and Krystin can hear that she's actually trying. "I don't know. We like a lot of the same things."

"I think she's ashamed of me," Krystin says suddenly.

"Did she tell you that?"

"No," Krystin says. "But she didn't have to." She decides to just tell Lauren the whole car story, because it's too much work to talk around it. She doesn't tell her the other stuff, the stuff that started to peel back in the shower before she frantically smoothed it back up again.

"What a bitch," Lauren says when she's done.

"She's not," Krystin insists. "She wants the best for me." She meets Lauren's eyes from her bed. "What if I really fucked up coming here? What if I made a horrible, awful mistake? And I can't even go back to rodeo—"

"Krystin," Lauren interrupts. "You—"

"She's not proud of me anymore," Krystin spits. "I ruined it."

Lauren looks at Krystin, her eyes dark with determination, a stern stitch in her brow. "You don't exist just for someone else to be proud of you. Who gives a fuck if some cunty hick doesn't approve of your choices? You can't live your life constantly afraid of disappointing people. And, like . . ."

She trails off, directing her gaze to the ground. Krystin's a little afraid of what she's going to say, because it looks like Lauren's steeling herself for something.

"I know *my word* doesn't, like, count for much, but . . ." Her eyes flick up to Krystin's and there's something in them that feels like fire. "I think you have a lot to be proud of. And if you need someone else to see it for you, I do."

Krystin feels like Lauren's hands are wrapped around her lungs, squeezing the air out bit by bit. She doesn't know what to say, so she just says, "Thanks."

Lauren straightens a little. "Yeah, well."

Krystin pulls her legs up to sit cross-legged on the bed. "She's not a cunt, you know. We've been friends since sixth grade."

"She sounds like a cunt."

"Okay."

They sit in silence for a while. Krystin blows her nose again.

"Hey," Lauren says, and Krystin turns to look back at her. "You're a rodeo queen."

"Are we just listing facts now?"

"You're a rodeo *queen*," she repeats. "That sounds like something to be proud of."

"Mm."

Lauren turns off the light without Krystin asking. Then she flicks on the TV to more telenovelas, and mutes the sound.

Krystin folds the duvet back and crawls underneath the blankets.

"You can turn the volume up," she says, and the words sound slurred to her own ears. "I don't mind."

"It's fine," Lauren says softly, and Krystin can barely hear her over the sound of her own steady breathing. "I can't understand it anyway."

CHAPTER TEN

Lauren slept like shit last night. Again.

"Mimosa?" A production assistant hands her a flute as soon as she steps foot on the pool deck.

"Sure. Thanks," she says, scanning the group. Kaydie and Lily are chatting with their legs dangling in the infinity pool, and Sara's slathering herself with sunscreen. Hilarie's in the hot tub, paging through a thriller that was recently adapted for Netflix. The group's gotten small enough that Lauren can immediately sense every absence: there's no Madison, no McKenzie.

And no Krystin. Krystin was still in bed when Lauren left this morning, curled into the fetal position with her hair fanned around her face like a halo. She thought about waking her up, but even gently tapping her shoulder felt illicit, somehow, so she just clomped around the hotel room loudly and waited for her to startle awake. She never did.

"Morning," Lauren says, taking a seat next to Sara. "No date card yet?"

"Not yet," Sara chirps. "But it's gotta be you, right? You haven't had a one-on-one yet."

Lauren shrugs. "Anyone's guess, really." She glances toward the sliding door. "Any idea how Madison's date went?"

"You didn't hear?" Sara looks genuinely sympathetic. "He sent her home instead of giving her the date ribbon. I guess we've really reached the part of Josh's journey where it's, like, he knows who he wants." On that ominous note, Sara drops the lotion back into her oversized Kate Spade tote, then shifts back into perky mode. "Anyway, whoever gets today's one-on-one is so lucky. I can't believe we're in Buenos Aires! This is, like, the most romantic city I've ever been to, and I grew up summering in Mykonos."

The sliding door opens with a smooth whoosh, and Lauren's oddly disappointed to see it's McKenzie, a mimosa in one hand and a date card in the other. "Hey, ladies," she says. "Everyone sleep all right?"

"That was the comfiest bed I've ever slept in," Hilarie half moans, stepping out of the hot tub and walking to a lounge chair. When Lauren meets her eye, she gives her a sheepish, semi-defensive look. "Hey. *I* didn't grow up vacationing in the Mediterranean."

"Wait, who's missing?" McKenzie slides off her sunglasses and squints at the women. "There are only six of us here."

"Madison got axed last night," Kaydie supplies. She sounds distinctly less sad about this turn of events than Sara did. "Poor thing. Lauren, where's your roomie?"

Right on cue, Krystin opens the door behind McKenzie. "I'm sorry," she says. "I hope you all weren't waiting for me." She looks achingly pretty: Her makeup's a little more stripped down than usual and her hair's pulled back into a perfect ponytail. Lauren never would have guessed she'd been asleep just twenty minutes ago.

"Don't worry about it," McKenzie says, even though she literally just got to the deck too. "Anyway, guess what, girls? I have a date card! Who's excited?"

While she speaks, Krystin glances between the hot tub and the empty lounge chair between Lauren and Hilarie. She decides on the lounge chair.

"You turned down the mimosa, huh?" Lauren asks. It's possibly the most stupid attempt at a conversation starter ever, but whatever. "It's actually not bad."

Krystin pauses. "I'm not a huge Prosecco girl, actually."

"Really." Lauren frowns. "How have you survived here the past five weeks?"

"Lauren!" McKenzie interrupts loudly. "¿Me concedes éste baile?"

Everyone's eyes are on Lauren, and for the first time, it's actively difficult to muster the kind of undignified enthusiasm expected of her.

McKenzie, however, interprets this as a poor understanding of the Spanish language. "It means, 'May I have this dance?'" she explains.

"Oh! Thank you," Lauren says, then flips her hair. "I took a few dance classes in college, so this will be *so* fun."

"Well? Go get ready, girl!" Sara says, patting her thigh.

Lauren raises her eyebrow at Krystin and stands up.

Once again, Krystin looks away.

The date is on the third floor of a large, industrial building. Once they've made it up the staircase, Jim waits for the two cameramen to go first, then reaches into his backpack for a bottle of water. "Here," he says gruffly. "You'll need this."

"Thank you." Lauren's pretty sure she knows what to expect— after all, "May I have this dance?" doesn't leave much room for interpretation—but still, she's a little bummed. She was hoping for a bike tour of Buenos Aires, or maybe a scenic picnic with authentic local food, but this venue looks almost identical to that barre place she used to frequent back in Woodland Park during her college years.

She follows the cameras into a midsized room with hardwood floors, pale yellow walls, and a few framed prints. Josh lights up and gives her a "come here" gesture, and Lauren reminds herself to focus on her date instead of the middle-aged, hyper-accessorized white woman inexplicably standing next to him.

"Hi!" Lauren walks over to give him a hug, and he pulls her off the ground for a little spin. "How's it going?"

"Me? I'm great," Josh replies. "I'm in a beautiful city with an amazing girl. What more could a guy want?"

"You look pretty good yourself," Lauren says. She can't help but glance back at the woman. "And who's this?"

"Dawn is a renowned tango instructor here in Buenos Aires," Josh explains. "She's going to show us some moves, and later tonight, we'll put our newfound skills to good use."

"You're a lucky girl," Dawn says in an American accent, before literally *winking* at Lauren. "Josh here will be taking you to dinner at the Puente de la Mujer, and then out to a milonga, an event for locals and tourists alike to bond over the art of tango. Trust me, you haven't been to Argentina until you've been to one of these."

"Awesome," Lauren says. "I'm ready to do this."

Dawn beams. "Josh will lead, of course. I'm going to need you to put your arm around Lauren's back, just like this . . . exactly, right under her shoulder blade. And, Lauren, your hand around his neck . . . *Perfecto.*"

Lauren's spent the past several weeks touching Josh: kissing him, wrapping her leg around his, carefully stroking his modest biceps. But now, Josh is really touching *her*, and his large, proprietary hand on her back somehow feels more invasive than his tongue down her throat. When Dawn encourages them to move chest to chest ("Like an inverted 'V,' *muy bueno*"), Lauren feels completely dwarfed. Small.

Plus, even with Dawn guiding their each and every step, he keeps fumbling. When one of his pristine white Air Force 1s comes in contact with Lauren's toe, he leans down. "I'm sorry I'm so bad at this," Josh whispers. He gives her an aw-shucks, self-deprecating grin.

"I'm having fun," Lauren promises, but she can't bring herself to look him in the eye as she says it. "Don't apologize." Josh pulls her closer, and she can feel his heartbeat through his blue button-down.

The back of his neck is very, very sweaty. Or maybe it's just her hand.

"Tango is all about two things," Dawn yells over the up-tempo music. "Chemistry and confidence."

"Well, I think we've got the first one covered," Josh says, his eyes not leaving Lauren's.

"I think so too," Dawn yells back. "Your physical chemistry is palpable. *Caliente*, even."

He steps on her foot again.

"It's okay," Lauren murmurs, because Josh is actually starting to look a little mortified. "Just hold onto me, all right?"

And then she's leading, while Dawn shouts out random facts about the history of the dance and a few pointers. "Posture is *key*," she yells. "Following is about *trust*. Leading is about *confidence*."

"Well?" Lauren's hand slides down Josh's back. "Do you trust me?"

Her tone is teasing, light. She knows trust as something that's earned—after all, Damian is the only person who has hers. But when

Josh says, "You know what? I do," it's straightforward, simple. She wishes she hadn't said anything at all.

It's fine, Lauren, you're not actually winning this, she tells herself. *He's spent a handful of hours with you, tops. He didn't even give you a one-on-one date until five whole weeks in.*

It tempers the guilt, somewhat.

Then he steps on her foot again, and they both laugh. The moment is gone.

It's just after sunset when a producer drops Lauren off for the nighttime portion of her date. She had under two hours to shower, shave, moisturize, put on a full face of makeup, decide on a magenta ShineGirl mini dress, and recurl her hair into perfect waves, but clearly, all the hustle paid off: Josh is looking at her like she's a fucking Hadid.

"There's my favorite dance partner," he says, wrapping her into a warm hug.

She kisses him, then pulls away to look around. "So where are we, exactly?"

"Near Puente de la Mujer," Josh explains. Before Lauren can ask for more information, he starts spitting out facts probably fed to him by a producer: It's a rotating footbridge, it was built in the late 1990s by the Spanish architect Santiago Calatrava, and the design is said to resemble a couple dancing the tango, isn't that perfect?

"Very appropriate," Lauren agrees.

"So." Josh claps his hands together. "Ready for some sustenance before we go show off our moves?"

Lauren follows him to a candlelit table set for two. "This is so beautiful," she says, and it's not a lie. There's a man strumming a guitar several feet away, lanterns and rose petals littering the ground, and cameramen blocking any tourists from entering the bridge's vicinity. For the first time today, Lauren actually feels like a VIP. "I've never had a guy do anything like this for me, you know." Or anyone, really.

"And *I've* never danced the tango with a pretty girl, then taken her to dinner," Josh says. He pulls out her chair and helps her shrug off her black jacket. "We're in this together."

"You're not a huge dancer, huh?" Lauren asks.

"'Not a huge dancer' is an understatement. Back in middle school, I learned that I have zero coordination on the dance floor." He shakes his head and chuckles. "You should see the videos from my bar mitzvah. Even the party motivators couldn't save me from the humiliation."

"Party motivators?"

"Yeah. We had these . . . bar mitzvah dancers." Josh looks sheepish. "Parents hire them to get the party started, drum up some excitement. I swear, I thought I was the coolest guy around dancing with these ladies, but the photos . . . oh, man."

"Well, you heard what Dawn said earlier," Lauren replies. "Dancing *is* all about confidence."

"And chemistry," he adds, reaching an arm across the table.

Lauren grabs his hand right back, and like the flip of a light switch, the entire scene feels less beautiful: the cheap lanterns, the golden champagne flutes, and even the bridge itself seem manufactured, as fake as everything else on *Hopelessly Devoted*. She gazes across the water at the moonlit city. "Definitely."

"A toast." Josh lifts his glass of champagne with his other hand. "To having just a little more game than I did in seventh grade."

"Just a little," Lauren teases, and it's so *easy* that she can almost forget all the artifice.

"Something I've noticed about you," Josh says. "You're great at picking up new skills. Dance, modeling, even podcasting—I mean, I don't know how you do it."

"Not everything comes easily to me, if that's what you're saying." Lauren takes a sip of champagne.

"Of course not," he quickly clarifies.

"I've had challenges," she says. "I know I put on a good front, but I've always had to, like, *work* for things. And it sometimes feels like no matter how hard I work, it still isn't good enough."

She's briefly worried she shouldn't have hinted toward faking anything, but Josh just nods solemnly. "That must be really hard."

"Like, in college." Lauren looks at the ground. "I didn't get into my dream sorority, and my two freshman roommates both did. I think that's the first time I really felt like I wasn't enough."

Josh's voice goes soft. "Do you feel that way a lot?"

Lauren pauses to consider his question. If she's being honest with herself, she doesn't feel less than—like, ever—because she actively, skillfully avoids putting herself in any kind of situation that could potentially make her feel that way. She doesn't work a job, aside from influencing and the freelance marketing work she does from her apartment. She's never had a romantic relationship, aside from her fake one with Damian (and, well, whatever kind of relationship she has right now with Josh). And since she first realized she was gay in eighth grade, she'd started keeping her friendships with girls casual, light. She'd hang out with them in group settings, planning mall trips in high school and pregames in college, but she avoided deep conversations at all costs. Even with the girls she's hooked up with—Halley Finch from her sorority, for example, or Sierra Ashbery back in high school—the more *drawn* she felt, the more she kept her defenses up.

And *fine*, it's a little sad, when Lauren thinks about it like that. But it's also smart. It's foolproof.

"I mean, working as a content creator," Josh says, prompting Lauren out of her own head. "That's gotta be constant competition, right?"

"Oh, yeah," Lauren says, grateful their conversation's moving toward an easier topic. "There's always a girl out there who's prettier or hotter or has more money. It's hard."

Josh shakes his head. "It's so sad to think about powerful women getting pitted against each other like that."

Is it? Because we're currently filming a reality show based on that exact premise, Lauren thinks, but she has a feeling that if she pointed that out, production would chastise her for breaking the fourth wall. "It's pretty competitive," Lauren agrees.

"I can't imagine," Josh continues. "I mean, my dad has an ongoing rivalry with this door guy from Syosset, and I know he takes it really hard when he sees Ralph's van in our neighborhood. But at least he doesn't know how to use Instagram."

"It's been nice to be off social media a bit while filming," Lauren lies. "And just focus on our relationship."

"I know that must be difficult. It's your career," he says. "But I'm really happy you're here, and I'm so happy you feel that way about . . . us."

"Of course I do." Lauren tucks a stray piece of hair behind her ears. She can see this conversation's finish line, and she knows what she needs to do: follow the one-on-one date script, one she's watched contestants follow year after year, season after season. "This is all so surreal. I think I always knew we'd have a connection, but I never expected to fall so fast."

"Lauren." Josh puts down his flute. "I know we haven't even made it to the milonga yet, but I told myself I'd follow my heart throughout this journey, and I just . . ." He shuffles through his jacket pocket and procures a shiny gold ribbon. "I need to ask if you'll accept this date ribbon. I don't want to wait."

"I'd love to," Lauren murmurs, but to her shock, he doesn't reach over; he *stands up.* She has no choice, really, but to stand up, too.

He walks her toward the guitarist and pulls her in. Before wrapping the ribbon around her wrist, he kisses her with purpose. "You're enough," he whispers, his breath hot against her cheek. "You're more than enough."

There's nothing to say to that, so she just kisses him again. It feels cheap and saccharine, like a glass of producer-provided champagne.

The lights are out when Lauren slips into her hotel room, gracelessly removes her heels, and drops her purse on the desk. Krystin must be asleep already, which isn't a surprise—the clock by her bed reads past midnight. Lauren beelines to the bathroom, beyond eager to shower for the third time that day. Eager to be alone for a second, honestly.

As she slathers coconut-scented shampoo into her hair, she remembers the way Josh kissed her at the bridge. She remembers the way he "didn't want to wait" to give her a ribbon, the way he *needed her to know* how *enough* she was, and her heart starts to pound in an anxious, unfamiliar way. No matter what Dawn or even Josh said, there was no chemistry, no sexual tension, no desperation at all. But there *was* a sense of certainty, at least on his end. An earnestness.

Lauren knows she won't break Josh's heart. They hardly even know each other, and besides, she doesn't think she's capable of breaking anyone's heart. But as hot water cloaks her body, she has the nauseating, terrifying, sudden-as-hell feeling that maybe she's in over her head here, because Pia's gone. Gabi, all the Ashleys, and the Other Lauren are all gone. Tomorrow night, Josh will cut two more women loose, but the date ribbon around Lauren's wrist is a too-tight reminder that she won't be one of them.

She remembers the way Josh looked at her at the loud, crowded milonga, the way his eyes never left hers as they danced, and an unwelcome thought pops into her head: *What if you actually win this thing?*

Lauren showers until her body feels swollen red, brushes her teeth until her gums hurt. If it comes down to it, she doesn't want to have to self-eliminate—with a lead as beloved and nice as Josh, she just knows she'd get eaten alive online, labeled a heartless bitch who hurt a good guy's feelings. And if she's being honest with herself . . . she doesn't want to hurt Josh's feelings. Sure, she came on this show for purely selfish reasons, and yeah, this man would probably give her the ick even if she were into guys. But that doesn't mean she wants to hurt and humiliate him on national TV.

This is ridiculous. *You won't win,* she tells herself. Spits. *You have two weeks until hometowns, and three weeks until overnight dates. There's plenty of time for him to cut your string. McKenzie or Krystin will win, probably, and you'll make it far enough for an* Us Weekly *feature, a bottomless well of brand partnership opportunities, and a lucrative, performative friendship with Josh. A lucrative, performative friendship with the rest of the Devotees, too, including your roommate over there.*

She spits again.

Even after showering, brushing her teeth, flossing, doing her multistep skincare routine, letting her hair dry, and crawling into bed as carefully and quietly as possible, she's wide awake, too tense to move. The air in the hotel room feels sticky-hot and charged.

And then Krystin flicks the bedside lamp on, and Lauren almost jumps.

"Jesus, you scared me," she says. "I thought you were asleep."

"I was. I just need to pee," Krystin responds, but after spending a few nights in a hotel room together, Lauren knows how she sounds when she's just woken up: raspy, slow, and sleep-laced. Right now, meanwhile, her voice is crystal clear, if quiet. She heads to the bathroom, and Lauren takes the opportunity to sit up, smooth her hair, and pull off her pink satin sleep mask.

"Trouble sleeping?" she asks the second Krystin returns.

"Not really."

"Okay." Lauren gives her an up-and-down scan, and tries not to smirk when Krystin blushes and looks away.

"How was your date with Josh?" Instead of getting under the covers, Krystin just sits down on her bed, legs crossed. She doesn't move to turn the light off, either.

"Oh, you know." Lauren sits up a little straighter. "A hippie from California taught us how to tango, and then we went to this nightclub where we did it in front of, like, half a dozen cameras. So we really had the authentic Buenos Aires experience."

Krystin cracks a smile. "Well, it sounds fun."

"I guess I'm glad I got that time with Josh. He's cool," Lauren says, because it's what she's supposed to say; it's a sentence she's heard a million times. But Krystin's smile dissipates, and Lauren remembers how flushed and happy she looked after *her* one-on-one with him, weeks ago. Lauren's positive that all the other contestants are playing the same game—maybe each to a different extent—but Krystin? She might really be here for this guy. For the *right reasons*.

"You don't talk about him a lot," Krystin says. "As much as some of the others, I mean. But you must have a strong connection, right?" She zeroes in on Lauren's ribbon.

"Yeah, I guess. We get along." Lauren's caught between feeling guilty and defensive. "But the conversations just start to get repetitive, you know? And kind of creepy. We're just sitting in a circle, making the same observations again and again. It starts to feel like we're in the Cult of Josh or something."

She's worried she might have gone too far, but Krystin lets out a laugh—a real one—and Lauren's stomach and heart both settle at once, like she just reached the end of a roller-coaster or downed a can of ginger ale. "It's pretty depressing, actually. Especially at the cocktail parties," Krystin agrees. There's a pause. "The one-on-one time with him is always nice, though. Right?"

Lauren meets her eyes, trying to figure out what she's angling toward here. "I thought we just agreed all the Josh talk is redundant," she says, but it comes out with a harsh edge, and Krystin looks away. She sighs. "Listen. I'm not . . ."

Not what, exactly? Not a threat? Not interested in Josh like that? Luckily, she doesn't have to finish the thought, because Krystin pipes up again. "I'm jealous you learned how to tango," she says softly. "I feel like we came all the way out here, and I've hardly even gotten to leave the hotel."

They both know she isn't really jealous of the tango lessons. She's jealous of Lauren's supposed *connection* and *time* with Josh, which is, like, laughable, really. But she looks at Krystin, and she doesn't look like a renowned rodeo champion or a reality show star; she just looks uneasy and sweet and ridiculously cute in her old Montana State sweatpants and form-fitting gray tank. Her top's just cropped enough to reveal a small sliver of skin, and the sight makes Lauren way too aware of her own fingers, her own heartbeat.

She can't believe she's spent so much time quietly pitying Josh when, really, he's the luckiest fucking person in the world.

"Come here," Lauren says, climbing out of bed. "I mean it. Stand up."

Krystin frowns, confused. "What?"

Lauren gives her an appraising look. "You wish you learned how to tango, so I'm going to show you everything I know. Which, really, is not very much. Production probably shelled out two hundred bucks for this, max."

Krystin visibly softens, but she still doesn't stand up. "It's the middle of the night."

"Yeah, and neither of us are tired." Lauren rolls her eyes, but then Krystin does stand up—slowly, hesitantly—and Lauren feels herself smile. "I'll lead. You have to start with an upside-down V, like this."

Lauren wraps an arm around the small of Krystin's back. She doesn't know if it's okay to pull her any closer, but Krystin easily lets herself fall into place, reaching around Lauren's neck. "Like this?"

"Yeah," Lauren says, more than a little distracted by the feeling of Krystin's breath against her neck. "So then just follow me, okay?"

Leading Krystin doesn't feel like dancing with Josh. For one thing, there's no New Agey blonde yelling at her about posture and chemistry and the art of dance, and for another, she realizes she isn't faking anything at all: She actually feels confident, sure of each step. Even when she and Krystin bump into each other and even though there's no music, what they're doing doesn't feel clumsy or awkward. It's . . . kind of fun. Almost intimate. For the first time since stepping out of the limo—actually, for the first time in years—she doesn't feel like she's hiding something. It's like there was a thin layer of film separating Lauren from the rest of the world, one that's somehow dissolving underneath Krystin's touch.

"I feel like you're holding back on all the pro tips," Krystin says. "Is this really all it is?"

"Well, your posture is perfect," Lauren says, stepping forward, then forward again. "No surprise there."

"What about my rhythm?"

"Also perfect," Lauren says again. "You're a natural."

"I guess I have a good teacher," she says quietly.

There's something shy and nervous in her voice that Lauren doesn't recognize, and it stuns her silent. She wants to do something, wants to tell Krystin not to worry about her relationship with Josh, wants to say something stupid and snarky and watch a slow smile spread across her face. But even though Lauren usually knows the perfect thing to say to get what she wants, she doesn't know what to say this time—maybe because what she wants feels too convoluted and impossible and unfamiliar.

So she doesn't say anything, and she realizes that they've stopped dancing altogether. But her arm's still holding Krystin close, and their chests are still flush against each other. And then Krystin tilts her head just slightly, takes a shaky, nervous breath, and kisses her. And Lauren doesn't even have to think about it, doesn't try to process what's happening, doesn't stand there in shock—she just kisses her back.

It isn't like kissing Josh. It isn't like any kiss Lauren has ever had, actually.

It's chaste—*sweet*, like everything about Krystin—but still real and full and deep. Kissing Krystin feels like sinking into freshly washed sheets after a long, arduous day of . . . well, sweating and primping and drinking and fawning over a man she doesn't want. Eventually, Lauren's lips find her collarbone, her earlobe. She kisses Krystin's neck, just under her clavicle. She feels her suck in a breath, then feels herself smile against her skin.

A small part of her wonders if this is a huge mistake or even some kind of trap, but every time she thinks Krystin's about to push her away, she just pulls her closer. And then they're making out—*really* making out—and then Krystin's pulling her backward, until Lauren's practically straddling her on the hotel bed, and then—

And then, Krystin's eyes snap open.

"I, um." Krystin glances around the room before her gaze lands somewhere behind Lauren. "I really need to go to bed."

Lauren wants to ask what the *fuck* just happened. Even more than that, she wants to ask if Krystin's all right. It's actually borderline overwhelming, how much she wants to just talk to this person and hold her close, maybe make her laugh. Make sure she's okay, or something. It's a foreign feeling.

Instead, she just says, "Sure, whatever," heads back to her own bed, and takes nearly two hours to fall asleep.

WEEK 5.5
CONFESSIONALS

Seven women remaining.

Lauren C.
25
Content Creator
Pinevale, NJ

I've always said that when you're alone with someone, you can be who you really are, you know? They just, like, see the real you. So it felt so special that I finally got that one-on-one with Josh, and it was, like . . . just us. And production, obviously, but mostly just us. [Pause.] These emotions I'm feeling, they're . . . real.

Madison
21
Waitress
Fort Myers, FL

[Sniffles.] I've been true to myself throughout this whole journey, and if Josh realized that's n—not who he wa—wanted . . . I just hope he finds what he's lo—looking for. [Pause.] My makeup's probably a mess right now, huh? [Sniffles.] I just hope he finds what he's looking for. Did I say that already? God, I need a nap.

McKenzie
25
Scaffolding Heiress
Buffalo, NY

Being here with Josh, and falling in love—I feel like the luckiest girl in the whole world. But at the same time, it's scary, you know? It's just getting real. [Nervous laugh.] I know I already had a one-on-one date, but every time we get a date card, I just start, like, *manifesting* that they'll call my name again. Maybe next week, right?

Krystin
23
Rodeo Queen
Bozeman, MT

Buenos Aires definitely heightened a lot of feelings—I think everyone's feeling the pressure. But I'm really looking forward to seeing what's next for all of us. This is my first time out of the country, and it's been exhausting. [Pauses.] Not in a bad way! I couldn't be more excited to explore it all with Josh!

CHAPTER ELEVEN

Krystin feels like she's been fighting off a panic attack the entire night. It's like the minute before she tears into the ring, the sloweddown sixty seconds of girding Ringo before they run, her heart like lead in her chest, rattling against her lungs. No matter how deeply she inhales, she can't get enough air. She's mildly nauseous.

And Lauren's asleep in the bed next to her.

Fuck. What was she thinking? She can't say she blacked out. She can't even say it's a blur, because it isn't—she remembers everything. She can still feel it.

She tries to do her breathing exercises, but it doesn't work. Her body is operating without her. Is this why people use paper bags? She pulls the covers over her head to try to simulate the experience, but that makes her feel like she's suffocating.

She can't help it—she looks at Lauren. She's facing Krystin, her fists curled up in the duvet. Her hair tangles behind her, a few strands stuck to her lips, which are slightly parted. Krystin wants to brush her hair away. She wants to drag her thumb along Lauren's bottom lip. She wants to do it all again.

Her face feels hot, then her neck, then her entire body. She squints her eyes shut and focuses on the black. Josh smiles at her. Josh, the whole reason she's here. Josh, the man she wants to marry. The man *Lauren* wants to marry.

Doesn't she?

Krystin peels the duvet back. This doesn't have to mean anything. It didn't mean anything the *last* time . . . but the last time, it hadn't been Lauren.

She plants her feet on the carpeted floor. Her group date doesn't start for another two hours, but that doesn't mean she can't get there early. She thinks about showering, but worries it might wake Lauren, so she just changes into the outfit she'd laid out for herself as quietly as possible and then treads out the door.

The day happens around Krystin. She participates in a *Hopelessly Devoted*–themed beach volleyball tournament that Josh watches from a lifeguard chair. Lily and Kaydie take their team captain titles way too seriously, and Krystin wonders how *she* was ever painted as the "competitive" one. Especially after Josh gives Kaydie the date ribbon for "really standing out" and "leading her team to victory." Lily looked like she might use her personally trained biceps for evil.

They head right into the cocktail party after that. Krystin keeps to herself, ignoring Lauren's relentless stare. Instead she talks to Sara, which basically guarantees Lauren's distance, since Lauren once told her she'd never willingly talk to someone who wore that much Lilly Pulitzer. She has a vaguely "intimate" conversation with Josh in which she shares that she misses home, and he thanks her for "opening up." After what seems like an eternity, they line up for the string-cutting ceremony and she watches blearily as Josh cuts Hilarie's string.

She takes a moment before letting him walk her out, and says in one dignified breath, "I don't think you ever really saw me in the passenger seat of your pickup."

After they wrap, Krystin hangs around with Kaydie until she's certain Lauren will be deep in REM. She falls asleep counting the minutes until she has to wake up again.

The hotel lobby is relatively empty, given that it's 6:32 AM. A front desk agent watches as Krystin drags her suitcase through the silent space and chooses a couch to sit on. She's early again, this time on purpose, and she intends to use her time productively.

She pulls out her headphones and the old iPod she convinced Holland to let her have, scrolling through her music library until she sees the episodes of Josh's podcast she'd downloaded to listen to on the way to the chateau. She needs to remember why she's here. She selects a random episode and tries not to feel weird about listening to her quasi-boyfriend's disembodied voice. It's kind of like training, right? Like practice.

Holland rolls into the lobby an hour later. She looks suspicious.

"What are you doing here?" she asks as she parks her luggage next to the couch.

Krystin pulls an earbud out of her ear. "This is where we're supposed to meet, isn't it?"

"Yeah, in—" Holland looks at her phone. "Another hour. You're all usually late, which is one of the reasons I have a Xanax prescription."

"Then you should be thanking me. Maybe I should ask what *you're* doing here."

Holland smirks. "I'm a producer. I have to do things that *you* can't know about."

Krystin shrugs. "I couldn't sleep. Travel anxiety."

"Well if you're a puker, do me a favor and don't eat, all right?" Holland taps at her phone. "I do *not* need a repeat of last season. You remember Monica?"

Krystin nods. A four foot eleven strawberry blonde who went home after a bad group date involving a Guinness World Record.

"It was bumpy on the way to Aspen. Passed me in the aisle on the way to the toilets." She looks up at Krystin. "Did *not* make it there on time."

"Noted."

Holland goes back to tapping, a fervent determination in her eyes. Krystin wonders what it might feel like to be on the receiving end of one of those emails. Not good, she thinks.

She's about to put her earbud back in when Holland looks up at her again.

"You know," she says, resting her phone in her lap, "it's normal to be nervous at this point, once it starts feeling really serious. It happens every season."

Krystin pauses. "Yeah."

"If there's anything you wanna talk about . . ."

"No," Krystin replies, a little too quickly. Holland raises her eyebrows slightly. "It's just travel," she repeats.

Eventually, Jim steps off the elevator, trailed by a few PAs. He tosses Krystin a questioning glance, which Holland bats away.

Krystin watches them settle into a table a few feet away and slide out their laptops. Holland and Jim dip their heads together, probably to discuss next week's dates, and how they'll meddle from outside them. Krystin presses play on another podcast episode. And another. And another—

"Hey, baby."

Krystin rips her ear buds out and whips her head up. "What?"

Kaydie stands above her in an Exercise Dress, sipping an ever-present green juice. "Jesus, you're squirrely this morning."

"Sorry." Krystin releases the breath she's been holding. "Long morning. And night."

Kaydie pouts. "Yeah, poor Hilarie, right?"

Krystin scoffs. "You're full of shit."

Kaydie smiles. "Yeah, I am." She sighs, tossing herself onto the couch next to Krystin. "This week has been great for me. I crushed volleyball, got a date ribbon, and I've slept so well since Madison was dumped. No shrieking, no singing Journey in the shower, no asking me if I want to trade clothes for our dates. I've never been happier."

Kaydie leans serenely into the cushions. Krystin thinks about Kaydie's Instagram bio, which self-proclaims *empath*.

Kaydie turns to Krystin. "But what about you? You've had a pretty good week."

Lauren's lips on her neck, the smell of her shampoo . . .

"Huh?"

"The cocktail party last night," Kaydie supplies. "Your conversation with Josh? Come on, don't play coy."

"Oh, yeah." Krystin shakes Lauren out of her head. "Josh is great. You know."

Kaydie waits.

Krystin swallows. "We talked about traveling. I've never really been anywhere before, it feels kind of weird."

"You must have had a lot to say," Kaydie says, blithe. "Since you talked for so long."

Krystin pauses. Was that a dig? She doesn't know if she considers Kaydie a friend, necessarily, but she doesn't want to think of her as an enemy either.

She decides to play dumb. "Did we? I guess I always feel outside of time when I'm with Josh."

Kaydie smiles stiffly. "Next time I'll give you a watch."

"Hi, girlies!" Sara bounces across the lobby, so chipper that Krystin feels Kaydie bristle beside her. "Ready for our next adventure?"

"Totally," Kaydie gushes, and Krystin feels something like guilt gnaw at her stomach.

Sara settles into the couch across from them. "It's gonna be so cold in Patagonia. Do you think there'll be a hot tub?"

"God, Sara, do you really need another reason to wear a bikini?" Lily walks up behind her and sits on her suitcase.

Sara sits up so fast she almost knocks her copy of Rupi Kaur to the floor. "Okay, what's up everyone's ass this week? First Hilarie rips my head off for singing in the shower, and now you're coming for my throat over *bikinis*, which by the way, I've worn *two* one-pieces." She holds up two fingers.

Lily cocks her head to the side. "Well, what were you singing in the shower?"

Krystin interjects before Sara can dig her grave deeper. "We were all sad to see Hilarie go."

"But now you can sing as loudly as you want," Lily laughs.

Kaydie turns to Krystin. "What about you? Where's your roomie?"

"I'm right here," Lauren says, and she is, flipping her blown-out hair over her shoulder. "You guys talking about me?"

Krystin forces her gaze to her lap, where she plays with a stray thread on her sweats. Lauren either doesn't take the hint or doesn't care, because she squeezes between Kaydie and Krystin on the couch, ignoring the open seat next to Sara. Krystin feels a buzz jolt through her thigh where it touches Lauren's and inches away.

"We *were* talking about hot tubs in Patagonia," Sara answers.

Krystin can feel Lauren looking at her, but she won't meet Lauren's eyes. All it takes is focus and determination, both of which she has.

She avoids Lauren for the rest of the conversation, and then avoids her in the car, and on the airplane, and all the way to the next hotel.

Krystin spends most of the day alone. They're in single rooms now (thank God), and she's been rotating between sleeping, eating, and looking out the window at the snowy peaks. She keeps steaming out her dresses even though they don't have any wrinkles. She could see what the other girls are up to, but she can't be around Lauren without feeling like she's somewhere between horny and throwing up. She figures the best she can do is a detox: She just has to wait it out, and eventually Lauren will be out of her system. It's like how skin regenerates so that every seven years you have completely new cells covering your body. Or like flushing out toxins. Or going on a juice cleanse.

Sometimes she gets caught up in herself and realizes she hasn't thought about Lauren in a few minutes, but then that means she remembers what she's trying not to think about. She just needs to get through this week so she can focus on bringing Josh home next week.

It's a good plan, solid and simple—until they get their date cards.

They're sitting in a mock living room, on a few love seats facing a fire, when it's announced that Kaydie and Lily have this week's one-on-ones, today and tomorrow morning.

Krystin feels herself sink deeper into the fuzzy cushions when she hears her name called after Lauren's on the group date card. She knew it was coming, but she was really hoping to get by on the avoidance tactic.

Sara immediately bombards Lily with questions about the date and what she's going to wear, which tests Lily's ability to maintain her composure in front of the cameras. Kaydie just smiles smugly into her mug of hot cocoa.

The hotel's decoration almost looks like Montana's log cabin aesthetic, which does more to displace Krystin than comfort her, because two of the walls are windows facing the Andes. She can't help it—she feels homesick. And the more she thinks about home, the more she thinks that she never should have come on this godforsaken show in the first place.

When they arrive at the group date, Krystin nearly bursts. Josh stands in the rocky landscape, squinting in the sun as they spill out of the car and fawn over what stands behind them: six gorgeous horses standing in a line, equipped with saddles and reins, ripping at patches of grass below them.

Krystin can't help it—she gasps. Then her hands fly to her mouth in embarrassment.

"Holy crap," Sara says, staring at the horses with eyes like saucers. "We aren't gonna . . ."

"Ride them?" Josh supplies with his ever-present smile. "You bet."

Sara nods stiffly.

"They're so pretty," McKenzie says, and Krystin wonders if she ever breaks character.

"You okay, Lauren?" Josh asks. They all turn to look at her, even Krystin.

Lauren manages a nod, but she looks like she's biting back acid reflux. "Absolutely," she answers. "I've just . . . never done this before."

"Well, that's a-okay," Josh says, and then gestures behind him at an appropriately rugged man who has appeared behind the horses. "We've got Diego here to guide us on this trail ride, and obviously—"

He turns to Krystin. "We have Krystin here for some additional expertise."

Now they all look at Krystin. She blushes. Josh continues talking about the date, and then steps aside to allow one of the guides to explain some safety rules for riding. But McKenzie's gaze lingers on Krystin a little longer, and when Krystin turns to meet her, she's pretty sure she can see a glare of envy in her eyes. Maybe she can break character, after all.

The minute she swings her leg around onto the saddle, Krystin feels her stomach start to settle. She trots the horse around a little, getting to know his movements, then circles back to join the rest of the group. Josh looks outrageously out of place, his curly hair sprouting out from under his hat. Sara and McKenzie seem steady, if a bit rigid. Lauren, however, has knotted her fingers into her horse's mane, and has a manic flash in her dark eyes. Krystin feels the stone in her stomach reappear as she fights the urge to take her hand

They set off calmly. It's beautiful—azure, unbothered skies, the air crisp as it nips at their cheeks. The trail takes the group through the mountains, curving around rocky bluffs and looking out onto miles of grassland. Krystin's horse moves steadily under her, his legs melting into her hips. As she feels her mind sync with her horse's movements, Krystin realizes she hasn't felt this much herself in weeks.

She can't say the same for the other Devotees. McKenzie flinches every time her horse kicks a pebble, and Lauren's holding her reins way too tight, which Krystin can tell is starting to grate on the horse. Sara actually seems like she's doing okay, but that's because she's been humming the same Hayden McGranger song for the past twenty minutes.

Krystin tugs on her reins, letting McKenzie and Sara pass her. She glances back at Lauren a few feet away. "Hey," she calls softly. "You have to loosen up your grip. He's getting a little antsy."

It's the first time Krystin's allowed herself to look into Lauren's eyes, and it hurts.

"I think I can handle it," Lauren says. "Thanks."

Krystin waits back as Lauren passes her, wishing she hadn't said anything at all.

They keep climbing steadily, and Krystin isn't even listening to the guide talk about the land. To be fair, she can't really hear him from the back of the pack, but still. Sara and McKenzie are trailing Josh, neither able to get their horses up next to his. Krystin could—and she should be using this time to talk to Josh—but she doesn't. It feels too good to be riding again, and she doesn't want to share it just yet.

Eventually, the trail plateaus, and Josh turns back to face them. "This is supposed to be the most beautiful view in all of Patagonia," he announces, and Krystin wonders why everything they do always has to be *the most*.

But it is. They round a corner, and a massive field expands in front of them, waving with wildflowers. Sara shrieks in delight.

"Wow," Krystin says.

"It's really something," says Josh. "Really something."

Krystin looks to find Lauren to see her expression, to watch her take in something so stunning, but Lauren's not looking at all. Instead, she's wrestling with the reins as her horse huffs and shakes his head underneath her.

And then she takes off, galloping into the field.

Well, the horse does. With Lauren on it.

Krystin doesn't even think, just takes off after her. She clicks her teeth and kicks her heels into the hide until she's as fast as the wind, and her hair whips out behind her. She leans forward, going faster and faster until she's gaining on Lauren, who, bless her heart, is holding on for dear life.

"Hold on, Lauren!" she yells as she kicks again, and her horse bolts under her.

"Obviously!"

And then she's beside Lauren, looking at her as the trees blur past them.

"Okay," Krystin shouts. "I need you to grab one rein in each hand, and pull really hard!"

Lauren technically follows her instructions, but she's yanking so chaotically that it's ineffective.

"One long pull, with all your strength, and don't let go until he stops," Krystin instructs. "On the count of three. One, two, three," and then she shouts "*Whoa*" as Lauren pulls, really pulls, until her horse gives up and stops under her.

Krystin keeps going, then loops around back to where Lauren sits, pale and sweaty on the horse's back. Krystin dismounts, then helps Lauren down off her own horse. Lauren stumbles back into Krystin, and Krystin steadies her. She's shaking slightly under Krystin's hands, and Krystin stifles the urge to pull Lauren completely into her arms.

She releases Lauren, and steps away. "Are you okay?"

Lauren swallows. "I was getting used to asking you that question."

Well, at least her humor's intact. "It's the adrenaline," Krystin answers, even though Lauren didn't ask. "You'll feel fine in a bit. You have to get your land legs back."

Lauren nods.

"It's honestly a miracle you didn't fall off," Krystin says, reaching for Lauren's horse. He's still agitated, kicking up the grass with his hoof.

"I told you I could handle it," Lauren mumbles.

Krystin laughs. "Okay, yeah. Sure."

Lauren eyes her horse warily. "I'm not getting on that thing again."

Krystin frowns. "He's not a thing. He's a majestic being."

"I'm not getting on that majestic being again," Lauren deadpans.

"Fine," Krystin says. "Then you will just have to get on this one."

Lauren shakes her head. Then she crosses her arms for good measure, like a four-year-old at bedtime. "I'm walking."

"Lauren." Krystin sighs. "You may not realize, but your horse was very fast. It took me a while to reach you after you bolted off, and now we're really far from the others, wherever they are, and we—" Krystin pauses, and looks at Lauren, who is—because when is she not?—smirking. "Look, just get on, all right?"

"Fine."

"Fine."

Krystin guides Lauren to her horse. "Jump up, and I'll give you a little lift."

She does, and Krystin lifts Lauren from the hips. Her hands linger there, on the soft flesh separated only by a thin layer of stretch denim, before helping the other woman swing her leg over.

She hands Lauren the reins to her horse. "Hold onto these," she instructs. At a noise of protest, she explains, "You won't have to do anything, just hold them. I promise." Then she hops on herself, settling her hips into the curve behind Lauren.

Lauren feels warm against her. Her posture is rigid, almost reluctant. Her hair is motionless against her back, and Krystin fights the urge to brush it to the side, to kiss the place behind her ear. She wraps her arms around Lauren, and Lauren flinches slightly.

"I'm just getting the reins," Krystin explains. Lauren is silent.

Krystin holds the leather ropes outward and guides the horse forward, leading the other horse behind them. Lauren starts at the sudden movement.

"I've got you," Krystin says, and maybe it's despite herself, but Lauren softens a bit, melting into Krystin just a little.

They ride in silence, listening to the wind rustle the flowers. Krystin isn't sure how far they are from the group, but figures they must be somewhere over the hill that rises in front of them.

"Why did you come after me?" Lauren asks suddenly. "Like, why didn't you just let the guide or whatever come get me? Or let me fall?"

Krystin thinks. "I don't know. I didn't really think about it. Instinct, I guess."

"How very heroic."

"Well, look around." Krystin gestures at the expanse of field, empty except for the two of them and the horses walking with them. "It's a good thing I did, because that guide sure as hell didn't."

"Or maybe you just wanted to play white knight."

Lauren turns around to look at her, and Krystin expects to see her features drawn into icy lines—but they're not. Lauren's eyes are wide under softened brows; her lips are parted slightly, and she runs her tongue lightly across her bottom lip. Krystin recognizes Lauren's expression as the same as the other night's, and all at once realizes the futility in her plan.

They're so close, and the cameras are nowhere to be seen. And Lauren's nose is rosy from the chill, and Krystin wants to kiss the very tip of it, and then make her way down.

Krystin breathes. "I guess I didn't want to see you get hurt."

"Thanks," Lauren replies, without looking away.

Krystin thinks she should probably say something else, but she sees Diego trotting over the hill at a clip. Josh bumbles after him, and the other women behind him.

"Are you two all right?" Diego calls.

Krystin can't see Lauren's face, just hears her say, "Just fine."

They keep walking until they reach Diego. Josh catches up to them soon, and fumbles with his reins until he gets his horse to stop.

"Thank God you're both okay!" Josh says, and he looks genuinely relieved. "Well, I knew Krystin would be fine. But Lauren! You're in one piece."

Lauren smiles, and Krystin can tell it's forced. "Yep, all thanks to my savior here."

Josh turns to Krystin. "Hey, are you gunning for my job?"

Krystin pushes out a laugh more like a bark. "Ha! No, just doing my due diligence. Earning my crown and all." She hands the reins to Diego, then dismounts. "She's all yours."

The rest of the group date goes relatively smoothly. Lauren spends the rest of the trail ride on Diego's horse, grudgingly holding onto the guide as they descend the mountainside. Josh trails them to the best of his ability, and McKenzie and Sara are plainly irritated by the attention Lauren's garnered from her bucking bronco experience. Krystin tries to return to the serenity she felt before the date went left, but the tranquility has been irreparably disrupted. It's like she was a crystal clear lake, and some asshole steered a motorboat through her no-wake zone. She's all buzzy.

A few hours later, they're showered and changed and on their way to the evening portion of the date, which is getting weirder the fewer women there are on them. Josh waits for them outside a small brewery that looks more like a yellow farmhouse. He waves as they wait in line to hug him, each woman desperately wishing there wasn't another woman waiting behind her.

Krystin tries not to look at Lauren, but it's hard when there are only five of them. She's wearing high-waisted jeans and a plunging red top that has to be a bodysuit, considering how tightly it's clinging to her torso, and lipstick to match. Krystin wonders how easy it would be to smudge.

The inside of the brewery is dim and sparsely populated, its wooden walls lined with beer bottles and coasters from various locales. It's warm, a welcome relief from the plummeting mountain temperatures outside, and smells like salt and firewood. Josh leads them to a table near the center of the room and tells them that they're going to do a beer tasting.

"I wanted to get the local experience," he says, scooting his chair into the table. The camera crew hovers a few feet away. "When in Patagonia, right?"

"Right!" Sara responds, even though she's told Krystin she thinks beer tastes like puppy pee.

Krystin, on the other hand, is grateful for the break from bubbly. It's starting to taste acidic, the carbonation burning the back of her throat, and not in the good way.

McKenzie settles in next to Josh, flipping her hair purposefully over her bare shoulder. "What a great date," she says to him, ignoring the other women. "I can't imagine today getting any more perfect."

"Just you wait," Josh says with a wink. "I've got something really special in store for all of us."

The girls *ooh*. Krystin can't imagine what more could be in store for them, and hopes it doesn't involve a hot tub.

McKenzie doesn't wait. "Josh, mind if I steal you?"

He doesn't. They stand from the seats they literally just sat in and walk through an open doorway to another part of the bar. As soon as they're out of sight, Holland approaches them.

"Sara, can we borrow you for an interview?" she asks, though she's not really asking. Then they leave the room for the dwindling afternoon light, followed by a Steadicam.

Krystin scans the room. A few parka-wrapped skiers huddle around a table recounting their day on the slopes. She eyes the doorway that Josh and McKenzie walked through, but she knows that they won't come back until someone makes them.

She looks at Lauren from across the table. Lauren looks studiously at the woodgrain of the table.

Krystin sighs. "So . . . how are you doing after your little mishap earlier?"

"Swell," Lauren responds silkily. "I actually feel great. I've really caught up on my sleep. I know some of the other girls have had a hard time catching those Zs."

Krystin ignores the dig. She chooses her words carefully. "I think this process can get a little overwhelming. Maybe they just need some time to decompress."

Lauren's eyes are steely. "I actually think it's pretty easy when you know what you want. Really, I'm *energized* by it."

"Well, I think it doesn't come as naturally to everyone. I would give them the benefit of the doubt."

Lauren shrugs. "If you can't take the heat . . ."

She leans back in her chair with what Krystin's mother calls that devil-may-care flair, usually when talking about 1980s movie-star heartthrobs. Well, the devil may care, but Krystin won't.

"I'm gonna . . . go freshen up," Krystin says, and scoots her chair away from the table.

The restroom is just two stalls and a sink, with an unlit candle labeled "Fireside" on the counter. Krystin places her hands on the edge and leans forward, examining herself in the mirror. Her makeup is impeccable, her hair falling in perfect beachy waves. She washes her hands, dries them, but doesn't leave. Instead, she closes her eyes and inhales the "Fireside"-scented air.

"Are you performing some kind of ritual?"

Krystin startles, flicking her eyes open. Lauren stands behind her, reflected in the mirror. Krystin turns around to face her.

"I figured you didn't want to talk to me," she says.

Lauren raises her eyebrows. "That defense might work if you hadn't snuck out of our room before sunrise yesterday. Kind of made it seem like it was you who didn't want to talk."

Krystin grimaces. "Okay . . . that's fair." She searches Lauren's face for any sign of uncertainty, but Lauren is resolute, almost daring. "I guess I assumed the . . . kissing . . . was a mistake, given where we are." She gestures around them.

Lauren crosses her arms. "I don't do anything I don't want to do."

Krystin can't say the same. Except she did want to kiss Lauren. And she wants to do it again.

"So what are you doing in here?" Lauren asks. "Because it seems like you're trying to put some distance between us."

Well, it's clearly not working.

As if to prove her point, Lauren takes a step forward, leaning into Krystin. "Are you worried what could happen," she whispers, "if we get too close?"

Krystin can feel Lauren's words on her lips. She can feel them between her legs.

Lauren lifts a finger, drags it up Krystin's arm to her neck, raising the hair as she goes.

Krystin swallows. "I'm gonna go get a drink," she says, and leaves the room.

When she gets back to the table, whiskey in hand, Sara's returned from her interview. Her cheeks are ruddy from the chill.

"There you are!" Sara says, rubbing her hands together. "I thought you'd gone to get Josh."

"Oh," Krystin says, realizing that she could have done that. Lauren is back to ignoring her. "No . . . I got whiskey instead." She lifts her glass.

Sara eyes the brown liquid. "Are we allowed to do that?"

She doesn't know. "No one stopped me." She hovers awkwardly above her chair. Suddenly, the prospect of sitting down with Lauren and Sara feels more than unbearable. "Um," she starts, shrugging her cardigan off and draping it across the chairback, "I actually am. Going to get Josh, I mean."

"Okay," Sara says, and seems disappointed that she didn't get to him first. Lauren just stares at her stonily.

"So." Krystin raises her glass half-heartedly. "Cheers." Then she sets off in the direction of Josh and McKenzie.

The adjoining room is cozier, embroidered pillows littering the floor and stacked against the window benches. McKenzie and Josh are snuggled into one. Krystin sees a hand high up on a thigh and considers turning around, but they've already seen her. McKenzie sits up abruptly, her smile immediately falling.

Josh doesn't lose his cheer. His hand does drop from McKenzie's leg, though. "Krystin!"

Krystin swirls her glass lightly. "Mind if I interrupt?"

"Not in the slightest," Josh says, though she's sure McKenzie disagrees.

As soon as Krystin replaces McKenzie on the window seat, she realizes she doesn't have a thing to say. She clocks the cameraman in the corner, Jim standing next to him.

"You were a superstar today," Josh starts. "Seriously, I looked around and you were gone like that." He snaps. "Diego didn't even have a chance."

Krystin wishes they could stop talking about it. "Instincts, I guess."

"Great ones. You really saved the day. You're the only reason Lauren's all right."

Krystin drinks instead of answering. "I hope I didn't show you up," she says after swallowing.

"Don't worry about that," he says, and his eyes look heavy and dark. "I think it's really hot."

And then his lips are on hers, wet and sloppy, and all Krystin can think about is how scratchy his facial hair feels against her chin. His hands grip her waist. Did he hold her this tight when they kissed before? Maybe he's turned on from McKenzie, Krystin thinks, but wait, why is she thinking about McKenzie? Don't think about McKenzie. Think about Josh. His cologne. His tongue in her mouth. His fingers scraping against her denim-covered hips.

Shouldn't someone be coming to interrupt them? Where's Sara? Where's Holland? And then she remembers the camera, and she opens her eyes and sees the red light blink back at her. Oh God, did it see her open her eyes? She doesn't want to be like that one Bruno Mars song. Her heart is beating really fast, and she doesn't know what to do with her hands. She tries to take a breath, but Josh just sucks in her air.

She pulls away, panting slightly. "Maybe we should . . . stop."

Josh blushes, then nods, and Krystin realizes he thinks she said that because she's turned on. She tries to play off like he's right.

"Just a preview of Honeymoons week," she smiles, and hopes she doesn't look too twitchy.

Josh squeezes her knee. "I can't wait."

In another world, she'd be flying on that reassurance. She should be elated that he wants to keep her until then, and that he's telling her as much. But she just feels like she asked him to play cards. She feels like she wants to be kissing someone else instead.

"So." Krystin twirls a finger through her hair. "What was that big surprise you had planned for us?"

"Ah! Yes." He points to Jim, who signals that it's all ready to go.

Krystin looks between them, and then follows Josh back out into the main room, where a mic stand and a screen have been set up in front of the bar, in direct line with the table the other women sit around. Sara waves excitedly, while Lauren zeroes in on Krystin's lips. Krystin fights the urge to cover them with her hands. *You're not doing anything wrong,* she reminds herself, but she's never been less sure that's true.

Several glasses of beer sit on a platter in the middle of the table, but it seems that the intention of tasting has been forgone in the desire to be drunk.

Josh gestures for Krystin to sit down, and then grabs the mic. "Ladies and gents," he says, loudly, "I have here in my company four gorgeous women, who are crazy enough to want *me*."

The bartender whoops.

"Well, they're all gonna grace us with a song or two—"

"*What?*" Lauren shouts. Sara shrieks in delight. McKenzie smiles uneasily.

"But first," Josh holds up a finger. "This little kid from Long Island can't believe his luck tonight. So I'm gonna sing a little number from another small-town East Coaster." He points to the bartender, who nods. And then Krystin recognizes the keyboard melody from Bruce Springsteen's "I'm on Fire."

He's not good. The song is entirely too low for him, and he also doesn't quite know the words so he keeps tripping over them as he reads them on the screen. Even McKenzie stifles a laugh when he tries to hit the high *oooh ooohs*. But Josh doesn't care, and Krystin thinks it might be the most endearing thing about him. He growls his best Bruce impression, all brooding and mysterious, two things he couldn't be further from.

Josh detaches the mic from the stand and dances over to them. He pulls McKenzie from her seat and twirls her around until she stumbles dizzily back to the table; even Lauren is tapping her block-heeled boot along with the beat. When he finishes, he bows dramatically to a roaring applause. One of the skiers howls in support.

"Thank you, thank you," he says, and starts to ask who's next, but Sara pops up like a Whac-A-Mole and grabs the microphone out of his hands.

Sara, true to herself, sings Katy Perry's "Roar," and gets everyone to clap along with her. Krystin's glad Kaydie isn't there to claw her eyes out, but then she looks at Lauren, who seems ready to take up Kaydie's mantle.

She decides to try again. "Not a fan?" she asks Lauren, leaning across the table.

Josh is busy watching Sara, and McKenzie is busy trying to make him pay attention to her instead.

"It's not my favorite Katy era," Lauren responds, taking a swig of her beer.

"Yeah?" Krystin says. "What's that?"

"'I Kissed a Girl.'"

Krystin can't tell if she's joking. Lauren's looking at her straight-faced, and the rest of the room starts to warp around her. Krystin looks down at her drink, but it's empty.

"I'm gonna get another one."

When Krystin returns with her second whiskey, Sara's finished her rendition and has taken Krystin's seat, forcing Krystin to take the open chair next to Lauren. She waits for Lauren to make a comment about it, but she doesn't. She just watches McKenzie take the stage and start singing Kelly Clarkson.

Krystin's body feels like it's static TV. Every time she wants to look at Lauren, she tenses a muscle in her body.

But then Lauren looks at *her*. "Aren't you glad Gabi went home before this date?"

Krystin meets her eyes, but it doesn't do anything to assuage the buzziness. "Yeah, she would've had a field day with this."

"Maybe we should sing 'Rich Like Me' in her honor."

Krystin laughs.

McKenzie places the mic back in the stand, and Josh high-fives her.

"Krystin?" He points to her. "You ready, girl?"

Krystin stands, more confidently than she'd expected. Maybe it's the whiskey, but the anxious hum is evolving into more of a glow. She walks to the stand and types her song choice into the screen. It might be a little on the nose, but fuck it.

"Kenz, you're gonna be a tough act to follow," she says, and then hears the signature sliding guitar.

Krystin can tell everyone is shocked, and Sara a little dismayed, when she starts actually singing, and she realizes she never told anyone that she's been a regular at the local bar's karaoke night since well before she could legally drink. She's comfortable in front of a crowd. She loves it.

She belts as the song swells to the chorus. "*Hopelessly devoted to youuuu,*" she wails, squinting her eyes shut. When she opens them, they find Lauren, who looks unraveled. Just one tug, and her whole tapestry would fall apart. Krystin breaks her gaze and takes a sip of her drink before the next verse.

Josh looks thoroughly enthralled. He keeps pointing at Krystin and yelling, "That's our show! That's our show!"

When she hits the second chorus, her eyes flick back over to Lauren, and stay there. Her hands sweat around the microphone, and she adjusts her grip. She knows she should look at Josh, but she can't. Not when Lauren is looking at her like she invented the song, the whole bar, all of Patagonia. And mid-lyric, she feels it: what she sees in movies, and what they sing about in country songs on the radio. She feels it all over her body, a simultaneous sensation of goose bumps and flames, that undeniable, ballooning feeling of want.

She's lucky she ruined her tape of *Grease* from hundreds of viewings, or else she'd have forgotten the words.

And then the song is over. She sustains the last high note, holding her drink high in the air.

Josh jumps up, clapping enthusiastically. "That! Was! Amazing!" He pulls her in for a hug, and she looks at Lauren over his shoulder. McKenzie shifts in her chair when Krystin passes her, probably peeved that all she got was a high-five.

"So," Lauren says when Krystin takes her seat next to her. "Another secret you've been keeping. Surprise, surprise."

Krystin opens her mouth to ask what other secret she's talking about. Lauren raises an eyebrow. *Come on, you know.*

"Well," Krystin says, drawing circles on the table with her glass. "I guess I'm not as predictable as you thought."

Lauren shakes her head, but she's smiling. "And the hits just keep on coming."

CHAPTER TWELVE

Everyone's shuttled back to the hotel in a too-tight, too-sterile van with dark leather seats—well, everyone except Josh, who's always deliberately pushed into his own taxi, limo, or first-class airplane seat. The point, Lauren knows, is to remove him from any part of the *journey* that isn't romantic and magical and perfect. He's not supposed to see the women like this: Sara, with a rosy cheek pressed against the glass of the window. McKenzie, currently squished next to Lauren, humming under her vodka-scented breath. And Krystin, several rows back, out of Lauren's line of vision.

Sara startles awake when the car pulls up in front of the hotel. "All right. Everyone out," Jim says. "Remember, call time's not until three tomorrow. We have Lily's one-on-one date, and then we're shooting some more B-roll."

Lauren climbs out of the shuttle as gracefully as possible, then pauses to sift around in her purse for her room key. Krystin gently bumps her shoulder on her way out, then all but jumps back. "Sorry," she murmurs.

"It's fine." Lauren's eye catches on Krystin's wrist, adorned with a glittering date ribbon. After karaoke, Josh had thanked her for "always putting herself out there" and "going out of her comfort zone" and "doing scary, brave things for the sake of finding true love." McKenzie had visibly tensed, and Lauren tried, for the fortieth time, not to think about how Krystin really *put herself out there* in their Buenos Aires hotel room.

"I can't believe hometowns are next week." Lauren's been so focused on Krystin, now scurrying into the hotel elevator alone, that she didn't even notice McKenzie—who's sidled up next to her, for some reason. "And Krystin's going," she continues. "Maybe Kaydie, if she got a date ribbon. I haven't seen her since her one-on-one earlier."

Hometowns. Lauren didn't expect to make it that far; chances are she'll get her string cut tomorrow. She just nods politely at McKenzie, then buzzes the elevator, letting the events of the day play through her head like the world's most confusing slideshow. For someone so good at *going out of her comfort zone* and *doing brave things*, Krystin seemed pretty damn determined to book it to her hotel room without so much as saying goodbye. Then again, she *did* save Lauren from a homicidal horse earlier, and for a split second in that dimly lit bar, she could've sworn Krystin was singing directly to her. "Not as predictable as you thought" might have been pretty accurate after all.

Then, at once, two things happen: The elevator dings, and McKenzie blurts out, "I really, really like him, you know."

At that, Lauren turns to look at her. She's clearly buzzed: Her face is flushed and glistening with sweat, and her dark hair's slightly frizzy. For a moment, McKenzie doesn't look like the ideal *Hopelessly Devoted* contestant or an airbrushed influencer, but a regular person. A drunk girl in a shitty bar bathroom, maybe, or someone Lauren could've crossed paths with back in college. She's about to respond that yeah, they *all* really like Josh, but she can't bring herself to play along.

They step into the elevator, and McKenzie jabs the button for the sixth floor. Someone really should've cut this girl off after her third vodka soda. "Look," Lauren says. "I'm telling you this because I *know* you really like him. You should probably stop talking. Play it cool, okay?"

"I just . . ." McKenzie trails off. She looks like she wants to continue, but instead, she takes Lauren's advice and stares straight ahead until the door dings and opens.

Lauren swipes her keycard into her room and flicks the light switch on. She changes into a black tank top and red pajama shorts, then heads into the small, attached bathroom to wash her face. She's in the middle of moisturizing when someone knocks.

Her gut tells her it's McKenzie, drunk and sloppy and still looking for moral support. Her brain, armed with an encyclopedic knowledge of *Hopelessly Devoted* plot twists, tells her it's Josh, trailed by cameramen and an exhausted producer, ready to either send her home early or kiss her good night and seal her fate as a front-runner.

But it's Krystin—notably alone, and still wearing her checkered two-piece set from the group date. Lauren swallows, suddenly unsure what to do with her hands.

"Are you sleepwalking or something?" she asks. Still, she lets her in, closing the door behind her.

"No."

Lauren squints. "Still drunk?"

"Not really."

"You're sure about that?" After all, Krystin's eyes keep jumping nervously from the drapes to the floor to the rose gold dress hanging in her open closet.

"Positive." As if to prove it, she finally looks at Lauren and attempts a nervous smile. It's . . . cute. Everything about her is cute, actually, and Lauren's torn between kicking her out right this second and kissing the smooth spot underneath her jawline again.

She *wants* to kiss Krystin again. Badly. She wants to watch her give up control, completely, trace a gentle line from her throat to her waist to her hips until she involuntarily whispers her name. She wants to make her forget about the producers and the cameras and Josh and the entire *Hopelessly Devoted* operation, just for one night. She's spent the past forty-eight hours trying to look at Krystin and think of anything other than the soft noise she made when Lauren's lips brushed her neck.

Anything other than the way she then jumped back and snapped her eyes open, horrified, like she'd just woken up from a nightmare.

"So. Nice concert earlier," Lauren says, because now Krystin's walking over to her *bed* and sitting down, and it's conjuring up images of . . .

No, she reminds herself. *Focus.*

"Oh. That." Krystin giggles uncomfortably. "You know, it's funny this show is named after a song from *Grease*, because it was always one of my favorite movies as a kid, and now—"

"Krystin," Lauren interrupts. "Are you sure you're not drunk? Do you want, like, water or something?"

"I'm not," she says again, and this time Lauren believes it. She sounds lucid, just . . . "I'm just nervous, okay? Are you happy now?"

"You're completely fine riding a rabid horse, casually saving my life, and doing karaoke in front of tons of cameras," Lauren says flatly. "But *now* you're nervous."

"You're really going to make me spell it out?" Krystin sounds pained. "Do I have to?"

"I mean, you don't." Lauren crosses her arms. She's a little annoyed, but mostly confused. "But *you* came to *my* room. And the other night? *You* kissed *me*." *And then ignored me*, she wants to add. But she doesn't.

Krystin chews at her lower lip. "I can't figure out why I did that," she finally says.

"Maybe because you . . . wanted to?" The suggestion pops out before Lauren can stop it.

Krystin opens her mouth to speak again, then closes it. Lauren's kissed enough straight girls (and "straight" girls) that she should be able to read Krystin's expression, should practically hear the gears turning in her mind. But Krystin doesn't seem like the kind of person who drinks a few glasses of champagne and decides to have a 2008 Katy Perry moment. In fact, Lauren can hardly imagine Krystin even kissing a *guy*—even her future husband and America's heartthrob, Josh Rosen—as impulsively, fervently, and suddenly as she kissed her the other night.

Which is why it's so weird that somewhere, deep down, Lauren isn't exactly surprised it happened.

"I did."

The raw honesty in her voice makes Lauren's breath catch. "Krystin," she says, taking a seat next to her on the bed. "I know I was teasing you at the bar earlier, but it's fine with me if you want to just, like, move on. It doesn't need to happen again."

"I know. You're right." She looks down at her hands. Lauren's tempted to reach out and hold them. "But what if that's . . . not what I want?"

There are too many variables at play—Lauren's faux heterosexuality, Krystin's clear emotional crisis, the fact that Josh Rosen is somewhere *down the hall* and they'll both probably kiss him tomorrow, the fact that Krystin kissed her two nights ago, the fact that

Krystin kissed her at all, the fact that she might want to do it again. It's enough to make her dizzy.

Krystin looks up at her. "What do *you* even want?"

For the first time since she joined the cast of *Hopelessly Devoted*—actually, for the first time in years—Lauren doesn't even think about hiding or doctoring the truth. "I mean, I don't know how or why it happened, but it's like I said before. I . . . care about you."

Krystin smiles a little. "Well, this sounds promising."

"Let me finish, okay?" Her heart is hammering, and her hand finds Krystin's. "I think you're courageous, and I think you're a good fucking person, and I think you're, like, beautiful. I've thought you were hot since you stepped out of the limo on that stupid little horse. And even if you don't realize it, I think you're someone who knows how to go for what she wants, and I want—I want you to do that. If you want to leave here engaged to Josh, I want you to do that. If you want to go home and keep your championship title, I want you to do that."

Krystin's silent. Lauren takes a deep breath, then continues.

"You asked what I want, and, like, if you really don't know, I'll tell you." Lauren licks her lips. They're very, very dry, all of a sudden. "I want to kiss you again. But I want you to think about what you want, Krystin, because it's fine if you don't know, but if you *do* . . . and if you just don't know if you're, like, *allowed* to want it, or if you *want* to want it . . ."

She's getting dangerously close to babbling, so she stops. For a moment, there's a silence, and Lauren finally turns to look at her. She expects to see panic in Krystin's eyes, but instead, she just looks *soft*, maybe a little contemplative. And then, just like last time, Krystin drops her hand, grabs her face, and kisses her.

It's real this time—less of a question, and more of an answer—and there's nothing Lauren can do but rake her fingers in Krystin's hair and pull her closer, closer, closer; kiss her the way she's wanted to for a week or maybe a month; inhale her shampoo and swallow a gasp when Krystin tentatively slides a hand up her tank top.

"I do," Krystin sighs, her voice practically a breath. "Want it."

It takes almost no effort at all to push Krystin onto the bed—in fact, maybe Krystin's the one pulling her down, but in any case, their legs lock together, Krystin's skirt slides all the way up, and Lauren distantly wonders how the hell she spent so much time around this person without touching her lips, kissing her jawline, holding her in place with her hips and thighs and hands.

Lauren's fucked women before: a few of her college friends who wanted to experiment, a couple of microinfluencers and Tinder girls, even one D-list actress who never texted back. She wouldn't say it was life-altering every time, but it was usually fun—fun enough, anyway, that she always left with the smug, satisfied feeling of *Yeah, I don't think I could do this with a guy.*

But whatever's transpiring with Krystin right now is something more than *good*, more than *fun*. Nothing's even happened yet, really, but she's already turned on out of her mind. And she can't even bring herself to feel embarrassed about it, because the girl in front of her—lips swollen and parted just slightly, shiny-smooth hair framing her face, hot breaths tickling Lauren's cheek—isn't someone out of her Rolodex of wine-drunk fantasies. She's flushed, so real and so wrecked and so fucking *pretty* that, with every gasp and anticipatory look, Lauren can feel her own heartbeat pulse between her thighs.

"Remember our mud wrestling group date?" she whispers, leaning down again to kiss the warm, soft spot behind Krystin's ear. "You hated me."

"I didn't . . . hate you. You cheated." Krystin practically sighs out the words as Lauren kisses down her neck. Then, in one surprisingly fluid motion, she reaches out with both arms, pulls Lauren in, and helps her shimmy out of her tank top. Her fingers delicately trace the skin on Lauren's back, eliciting a lone shiver.

"No, you hated me," Lauren repeats, pushing her back down onto the bed. She unclasps Krystin's front-close bra with ease, and continues kissing her neck, her collarbones, her chest. She carefully positions herself between Krystin's legs, well aware that the moment her lacy underwear brushes Krystin's thigh, she'll be able to tell how fucking wet she is already.

"You know what I think?" Krystin asks, her voice achingly slow but certain, like she's a few seconds from solving a Rubik's cube. "I think you just liked me under you."

"Hmm," Lauren murmurs. Her lips make it to one of Krystin's nipples, and suddenly, Krystin is a lot less cocky. Her body rocks against Lauren's, and she lets out another deep, audible breath. "Well, what about you? What do *you* like?"

"I, um . . ." Krystin trails off, biting her bottom lip. She pulls Lauren's face up to hers, kisses up her jaw.

"You can tell me. Whatever it is," she says softly, savoring how it feels to be this close. "I want to know."

"It's not . . . that," Krystin says.

Even in the dim, Lauren can see the blush crawling up Krystin's cheeks. She waits, not wanting to interrupt Krystin's thoughts and puncture this already delicate moment.

Krystin exhales. "It's that I don't know . . . what I like." She brushes her forehead against Lauren's. "I haven't done this a lot. With anyone."

"Have you had an orgasm before?" Lauren asks softly. She kisses her ear, then the spot right under it, and feels her breath hike.

"Just on my own." She runs a hand through Lauren's hair, and Lauren shivers at the mental image of Krystin touching herself, making herself come.

"Okay." Lauren's hand gently brushes down Krystin's body, and she takes stock of each reaction, even the smallest ones: The way Krystin's breath hitches when she passes her chest, the goose bumps on her upper thigh. "Do you want . . . do you want to find *out* what you like? Like, together?"

Krystin's quiet, and Lauren tilts her head up to gauge her reaction. She looks *fond*—that's the word for it. Relieved, almost. She runs a hand through Lauren's hair, and Lauren's heart seizes. "That sounds really good," she says.

Lauren kisses up her body again, and then reaches for her hand and gives it a gentle squeeze. As soon as their lips meet, Lauren slides a leg between Krystin's thighs, revels in the way she undulates. She isn't sure how much time passes as they kiss, but by the time she starts to move back downward, she sounds thicker, raspier. "Is this okay?"

"Yeah," Krystin murmurs. Her voice is thicker now, too. "It— yeah. Please."

Lauren lands a small kiss near Krystin's hipbone. "There's something *I'd* like to do. I mean, if you want . . ."

At that, Krystin slips out of her black thong and gives Lauren a meaningful look. "I do," she says, her voice so small but plaintive that Lauren's heart squeezes again like she's in some kind of cheesy soap opera or something. She doesn't even try to stop from moaning as she kisses up Krystin's perfect thigh again; she feels herself fucking *smile* as Krystin sucks in a gasp and a sexy-as-fuck little *oh*.

"It's okay if you don't come, you know," Lauren says, her lips moving closer to Krystin's vulva. "I just want you to feel good, okay?"

At that, Krystin's strong thighs lock her in place. She gasps as Lauren circles her clit with her tongue slowly, then faster, as rhythmic as a heartbeat. "You look so *pretty* like this," she says. "You look perfect, you *feel* so perfect, you taste . . ."

Each word is quieter than the last, until Lauren isn't sure if she's speaking or thinking, until Lauren isn't sure of anything, really, because the only thing that matters is . . . well. Krystin whines, pushing against her in a silent plea for more, and finally seeing Krystin like this—*feeling* Krystin let go like this—turns Lauren's whole body into a live wire. A litany of "oh, God" and "yes" and even a solitary, strangled "oh, fuck" spills from Krystin's pretty lips; she squeezes her thighs tight around Lauren's head when she comes, cries out her name in a desperate sob.

It's the sexiest thing Lauren's ever heard.

But it's also possible that, up until now, the sexiest thing she'd ever heard was, "You just won a $5,000 ShineGirl gift card."

For a moment, after she climbs back up to Krystin's side, everything in the room feels still. Then Krystin breaks the silence. "Well," she says, slightly breathless. "I liked . . . that."

Lauren can't help but grin. And sure, it's *somewhat* out of pride, but she also just feels *happy*. It's a good thing Krystin didn't explicitly ask what *she* liked, because she's worried she would've said something like stupid—something like, *I like you. I like sexy, fearless, freakishly competitive, and unabashedly kind horse girls. Apparently.*

A tiny part of her wants to say it right now, actually.

But she knows she can't, and besides, maybe that's not what this is. She must just be in some kind of jet-lagged, sex-fueled haze, because Lauren's *never* liked anyone like that—the way her friends always like their boyfriends, the way McKenzie likes Josh. The way *Krystin* likes Josh . . . probably.

This will probably never happen again, Lauren tells herself. But even as she does, Krystin plants a small, open-mouthed kiss under her ear, and Lauren thinks it again. *I like you.*

She isn't sure when she falls asleep, only that they keep kissing and touching and discovering new ways to hold each other—Krystin's head tucked under her chin; Krystin's smooth, strong arms pulling her close; Krystin turning around and then reaching a hand back to thread their fingers together—until, finally, she finds herself waking up in the morning. She expects Krystin to be long gone, or at least in the shower, but she's blinking awake, too. And instead of looking visibly panicked, she's almost *calm*. Or maybe she's just tired.

In any case, she's not running away. And she's still completely naked. For the first time, Lauren realizes she must've taken off her date ribbon before showing up to her room.

"Hey," Krystin says softly.

"Hi." Lauren's positive that she's never wanted to touch someone so badly, but she's half afraid that the second she does, Krystin will evaporate into thin air or something. She reaches out and tucks a blonde curl behind Krystin's ear; it feels like a compromise. "Are you freaking out right now?"

Krystin doesn't answer right away, but she absently starts to trace lines across Lauren's collarbone. "A little," she finally says. "Are you?"

"Not really," Lauren says, and Krystin squeezes her eyes shut. She briefly wonders if she somehow said the wrong thing, then decides that's not the part to focus on. "Do you . . . feel okay about last night?"

"I feel okay." Krystin's voice is small, and what she says next sounds like a realization as much as a confession. "I feel . . . really nice, actually. And a little freaked out."

Me too, Lauren thinks, but she remembers what she told McKenzie last night. At the end of the day, *Hopelessly Devoted* isn't that different from the real world: If you show all your cards, you lose. You get hurt; you scare people away. As it is, this *thing* with Krystin feels fragile and fresh—not to mention completely temporary. She's bringing Josh to her hometown next week, after all.

So Lauren doesn't tell her that she wants to kiss her again. She doesn't tell her that she's thought about kissing her for weeks, that she doesn't want her to leave this bed, that she *likes* her or whatever. She just says, "Have I mentioned you're really fucking pretty?"

"Um." Krystin blushes. "Last night. Once or twice."

Lauren rolls over until she's on top of Krystin—slowly, giving her the space and time to tell her to fuck off. But she doesn't. Krystin just sighs and twines their legs together, runs her hands down Lauren's back, over her ass, from the back of her neck to her elbow. No one's ever touched Lauren like this before: like every inch of her body is a small discovery.

"I guess we should get up," Krystin finally says.

"He's going to be on his one-on-one with Lily all day," Lauren replies. She lands a kiss on Krystin's shoulder. "It's okay."

"I just really need to brush my teeth." Krystin sits up, and Lauren watches something like panic flash across her face. "And McKenzie and Kaydie and everyone are, like, down the hall. They'll see me in the dress I wore last night, and—"

"Hey, hey. Breathe." Lauren sits up too, and sifts around the bedsheets for her tank top. "If you're really freaked out, I can lend you a top or something. Then if someone sees you leave, you can say you came here this morning to borrow an outfit."

Krystin just looks at her.

"What?"

"That's just . . . smart thinking." She stands up and makes her way to Lauren's suitcase. "I can't believe you just came up with that right now."

"I wasn't, like, plotting something. *You* came *here*," Lauren says, suddenly defensive.

"I didn't say you were." Krystin gives her a tentative smile. "I just think you're smart. And alarmingly good under pressure."

Lauren waits for her to continue.

"That's it," Krystin says. "I'm complimenting you."

"Oh." And then, because Lauren can't fight her impulses when it comes to fashion and beautiful women, she adds, "You should try on the knit lilac one. You look good in purple."

"Yeah?" Krystin pulls it out of the suitcase. Lauren could swear she's blushing.

"Definitely." Lauren watches as she pulls on the ribbed top, and realizes that it was a self-serving idea, really. The thought of Krystin walking around the hotel grounds in Lauren's cropped little shirt, unbeknownst to Josh or any of the producers, is more than just a slight turn-on.

"Well?" Krystin fixes her hair with one hand, and reaches for a nearby pair of nondescript sweats.

"You look like you got a perfect nine hours," Lauren says.

"Okay." Krystin takes a breath. "I'm going to head out, then."

"Okay."

But she doesn't. She lingers near the foot of the bed, her eyes scanning Lauren's body with something like tenderness. "I'm going," she says again, this time shaking her head like she's trying to snap herself out of a trance.

"Sure." Lauren yawns. "I'll see you in a few hours."

She pauses by the door, then whips her head to face Lauren again. "You know," she says, "you're really pretty, too."

Lauren can't help it. She fucking smiles.

It takes her hours to get ready after Krystin leaves. Part of it is that there's nothing to do while she waits for filming to start: She's pretty sure there's a hot tub somewhere, but after last night, she's ecstatic to take a long shower and do a face mask while a low-budget nature show plays on the small hotel room TV. She doesn't make it to the lobby until twenty minutes before call time, and by the time she does—dressed in skinny jeans, a cami top, and a cropped sweater—McKenzie, Krystin, and Kaydie look like they've been there for a while. Kaydie and Krystin are seated on a sofa in front of the fireplace, and McKenzie's on a velvet armchair.

When Lauren walks in, though, McKenzie jumps up from her seat and runs over. There's a manic, restless look in her eyes as she digs her perfectly manicured fingernails into Lauren's arms. "*Where* have you been?"

"I got a long night of sleep." Lauren has to force herself to look at McKenzie—with Krystin curled up on the couch directly behind her, it feels next to impossible. "Feeling reinvigorated, really. What's wrong?"

"Sara left," Kaydie says, swiveling her head around. "Hours ago. I was the only one who even got to say goodbye to her, since the *rest* of you were all sleeping in."

"What do you mean, she *left?*" Lauren releases herself from McKenzie's clutches and heads to sit on the sofa, right next to Krystin. It's a bad idea: She can smell her shampoo, and it reminds her of how Krystin's hair slipped through her fingers last night. It might be her imagination, but she thinks she hears Krystin inhale when Lauren's thigh accidentally touches hers. "Did she self-eliminate?"

"Josh stopped by her hotel room before his one-on-one with Lily," Kaydie says. She sounds bored, like she's already gone over this a few too many times. "Like, super early. He told her she was, quote unquote, 'an amazing woman, but he has to follow his heart.'" She makes air quotes with her fingers as she says that last part, not so subtly showing off her shiny date ribbon.

There are questions Lauren wants to ask, but then she glances at the small camera crew in the corner of the lobby. "Wow," she says. "I mean, poor Sara. And that must have been hard for Josh too. But I really do feel so lucky."

It's not a lie: She *is* lucky. If Josh had knocked on her door to end their journey first thing in the morning, he would've found another naked contestant in her bed.

"That's what I said." McKenzie returns to her chair, and sits down with a dramatic plop. "I can't believe we didn't even get to say goodbye to her and now she's gone. This is, like, getting real, guys."

"Don't worry," Lauren says. "Knowing Sara, she'll DM all of us as soon as she gets home."

"I'm just so nervous." McKenzie's eyes dart from woman to woman. "The fact that Sara was here last night and now—"

The elevator dings, and McKenzie abruptly quiets. Lauren watches as a few production assistants wheel out a sleek suitcase and two matching carry-ons. Lily's luggage.

Bravo for production, Lauren thinks as McKenzie lets out an audible gasp. *This must be a perfect shot.*

Lily pushes through the front door, followed by Jim and another cameraperson. Her dark eyes are watery, and her wrist is bare.

"Hey." This time Kaydie's the one to jump up. "Are you okay?"

"He cut my string. Right after we went kayaking together, no less." Lily chokes out a dry, humorless laugh. "He just said our con- nection isn't as far along as his others, and with hometowns coming up, he's—he just has to make hard decisions."

"It's a bloodbath. He cut Sara this morning, too," Kaydie says. Her voice sounds sympathetic, but Lauren can see a sharp, competi- tive glint in her eye, like she really only heard the bit about how strong Josh's other connections are.

"He's not . . . He's just not the one for me. It's fine." Lily's voice is scratchy. "And I will *absolutely* be okay."

"Come here." Kaydie wraps Lily into a tight hug. "You *will be*. I promise."

Krystin slowly rises, too, and hugs Lily as soon as Kaydie's done. The whole thing reminds Lauren of the receiving line at her great-grandmother's funeral ten years ago. As she awkwardly waits her turn to bid Lily farewell, her mind starts to jump ahead. Sara left this morning. Lily's leaving now too. There's supposed to be a string-cutting ceremony tomorrow, but . . .

"There are just four of us left," McKenzie says softly. It's for Lauren's ears only: Krystin and Kaydie are still watching Lily as she gives a shaky smile and walks back outside, and the camera crew is focused on her retreating body, now trailed by the PAs with luggage in tow. "Do you know what that means?"

Lauren doesn't answer, because she does. It means she made it further than Lily, further than Sara, further than she expected—further than she wanted. It means she doesn't even have a day in Patagonia to process the events of last night, or figure out what she's doing next. It means she's in this thing for real. And Krystin is too.

"There are just *four of us left*," McKenzie repeats, her voice somehow even quieter. "We're all going to hometowns."

WEEK 6 CONFESSIONALS

Four women remaining.

McKenzie
25
Scaffolding Heiress
Buffalo, NY

It's been a long time since I brought a guy home, but with Josh, it just feels right. I couldn't be more excited to show him all the sights of Buffalo! Obviously, he's going to have *so* much to discuss with my dad, who also works in construction. And I just can't wait for him to meet Mikayla and Reagan—those are my best friends—and maybe even visit my high school. Upstate New York, here we come!

Kaydie
25
Content Creator
Los Angeles, CA

Our one-on-one was just unbelievable. I still can't believe we actually got to ride in a hot air balloon! It just cemented how excited I am to bring Josh home to my family, but I hope he knows I won't go easy on him when we're hiking Mount Baldy. And neither will my goldendoodle, Cody.

Krystin
23
Rodeo Queen
Bozeman, MT

It felt amazing to be on horseback again. I mean, after I told Josh about putting my rodeo career on pause for him . . . [Pause. Smiles.] Yeah, part of me does think he chose that date for me.

Lauren C.
25
Content Creator
Pinevale, NJ

I mean, hey. The things we do for love, right? [Cut to footage of Lauren nearly falling off a horse.] This journey hasn't been an easy one, but when it feels so right with someone, you'll kind of do anything. You know?

CHAPTER THIRTEEN

The chateau feels different when Krystin walks through the French doors, wheeling her suitcase behind her. Somehow, it seems emptier with fewer women left to populate it, like how a new apartment looks smaller without any furniture. There aren't even any cameras—because they're not filming there this week. Instead, they'll all be heading back home in waves, with Josh visiting them. Krystin can't help but imagine it like a map in *Indiana Jones*, a cartoon airplane flying from destination to destination. (The real Ark of the Covenant? Their hearts.)

McKenzie flew directly to Buffalo, with Josh in tow. She seemed pretty happy to be his first stop on his tour of the US, despite Kaydie's rather specific quips about earlier dates being easily forgotten.

Krystin isn't even thinking about home. In fact, she can't comprehend Josh in Bozeman. Every time she tries to imagine him walking down Main Street, it's just a cardboard cutout version of him hopping along the sidewalk. And she's gonna have to think about it seriously soon, because she's supposed to tell Jim and Holland what she wants to do with Josh when they get there.

And who will he meet? Aside from her parents, who will just be happy she's bringing any man home, Krystin has nothing to show for a personal life in Bozeman. She can't introduce him to Delia, for more reasons than one. She's already losing touch with her sorority sisters, mostly because Delia always hated them. Honestly, Delia hates most people. She probably hates Krystin now, too.

Krystin rounds the corner to the residential corridor. Jim told them they could take any bunk they wanted, in any room, since it'll only be three women in the house at a time, so Krystin chooses the one she'd been assigned when she first got to the chateau, out of habit. She slips the suitcase under the bottom bunk and leans into the top, resting her head on her hands.

She breathes. *One, two, three, four.*

She hears the clatter of heels in the hallway, and then feels slender fingers walk across her back and into the curve of her hips. And then they press gently into her skin, and pull her close.

Lauren breathes into her neck, matching her rhythm. *One, two, three, four.*

"Did you close the door?" Krystin asks, without moving.

"There's no one on this floor." Lauren's lips graze Krystin's ear. "I checked."

Krystin knows she should feel paranoid, be extra careful, but she can't bring herself to care. She wants to feel Lauren, everywhere.

Lauren curves her pelvis into Krystin's hips and holds her there.

"Kaydie's gonna be here soon," Krystin tries, but Lauren slides her fingers under Krystin's shirt.

"Kaydie's giving Penny a list of things she wants to do with Josh in LA," Lauren whispers. "Trust me, it's gonna take a while."

Then she kisses Krystin's neck gently, carefully, and brushes her hair aside. Krystin sighs, twists under Lauren's grasp, and kisses her lightly on the lips, exhaling into her mouth. Lauren rakes her nails along Krystin's spine, and Krystin kisses her harder.

Kaydie's laugh echoes down the hall, and Krystin leaps back.

Lauren looks mildly startled by the severity of her movement. "Easy, tiger. She didn't see anything."

"I know, I'm just—" Krystin rolls down her tank top, which had ridden up to under her bra. "We have to be careful."

Lauren shrugs. "If you say so." She unzips her suitcase.

Krystin hears Kaydie's suitcase approach, and then she appears in the doorway.

"Hey, girlies!" She's grinning, which, for Kaydie, means she looks like she's plotting something. Her eyes dart deliberately from Krystin to Lauren. "Still bunking together?"

Krystin looks at Lauren unpacking across from her. "Yeah," she says, trying to think of a reason two adult women would share a room when given the option for privacy and space. "I get . . . lonely." Kaydie blinks. She continues. "It makes me feel like I'm back in my sorority."

Kaydie looks like she has something to say about a twenty-three-year-old woman unable to spend a night alone in a house full of security, but she just nods. "Suit yourself." Then she rolls away. Krystin closes the door behind her.

"So," Lauren says, leaning back on her bunk. "How long were you in a sorority for?"

"All four years."

"And you're telling me you went four years sleeping in a house with however many women without kissing any of them?"

Krystin sits down and pulls her legs in. "That's not that crazy."

Lauren snorts. "You couldn't go two nights sleeping next to me without making a move."

Krystin thinks. It's not that she never thought about it. She was always closer with girls growing up. All the girls in Alpha Omicron Pi were pretty, and sweet, and she did like them a lot. But she thought it was normal to want to kiss your girlfriends—because, if you wouldn't want to date them, why are you even friends with them at all?

But maybe she just confused attraction for that intense closeness that blooms between women. No one ever told her those feelings were different.

"And after that," Lauren goes on, "it wasn't long before we—"

Krystin interrupts her. "Okay, yeah, I know what we did." Heat crawls up to her face at the memory.

Lauren smirks. "I'm just saying. I'm kind of impressed you never planted one on a sister."

"Wait," Krystin says, unfolding her legs. "Did *you*?"

"Obviously."

It takes Krystin longer than it should to understand. "Are you . . . ?"

"Don't tell me I seemed out of practice in Patagonia."

A memory flashes: Krystin looking down at Lauren, whose tongue slipped expertly in and out of Krystin's tastefully waxed—

"Not at all."

"You're cute."

Krystin looks out the window. The Palm Springs sun is high and bright, bouncing energetically off the pool water below. "Should we, like, do something?" she asks.

"Like what?"

"I don't know . . . What did we do before we left for Argentina?"

Lauren thinks. "We talked shit."

Krystin narrows her eyes.

"And tanned?"

The object of the show is even more stark in its removal—without Josh around, without dates to plan outfits and cocktail parties to primp for, they have nothing to do. It's kind of depressing.

"I just don't know what to do with myself," Krystin laments as she and Kaydie sit on the pool's edge. After years of obeying a color-coded schedule, Krystin is starting to get antsy with the empty hours, like a toddler during preschool-sanctioned naptime. "I feel like my brain is starting to melt out of my ears."

"Hello, this is a dream," Kaydie tells her. "It's like we're in a time vacuum. We have zero responsibilities and an entire mansion to ourselves. Literally, how are you finding a negative?"

Krystin shrugs. "I'm just not used to it, I guess."

What she really isn't used to is spending this much time by herself. Even when she's training, she has Ringo there, and usually Delia to cheer her on from the other side of the fence. The past month and a half, she hasn't had much time to think about anything but the show; and for most of that time, she was surrounded by other women—lots of them.

"So what's up with you and Lauren?"

Krystin's leg twitches, sending a stream of water into the air. "What do you mean, what's up with us?"

Kaydie leans back. The sunlight glints off her sunglasses. "You're, like, joined at the hip since Argentina. Are you besties now?"

"I mean, we had to spend time together, you know?" Krystin drags a finger along the water's surface. "Since we were assigned the same room."

"Right."

The heat feels weighty, and it leans on Krystin's eyelids until they fall closed. She unfurls until her back meets the pavement. The chateau is as quiet as she's ever known it, without pods of women chatting in the cabana and playing chicken in the pool. Krystin half-expects Sara to burst through doors humming Top 40, or for McKenzie to offer her some eggs she just scrambled.

But McKenzie's not there—she's in Buffalo with Josh. *They're probably having the time of their lives together*, Krystin thinks. *Discussing the merits of cedar versus oak.* Josh and McKenzie's father are likely getting along famously. Krystin doesn't have the slightest idea what her own father could have in common with Josh, besides an appreciation of hard work and blondes. She supposes she'll find out soon enough.

"So, you guys are close?"

Krystin sits back up. "What?"

"You and Lauren."

"Have you been thinking about this the whole time?"

"Well, are you?"

Krystin hesitates. "I don't know." It's the truth—she doesn't know half of what's going on between them. "I guess, kind of."

"Do you think she has a shot?" Kaydie asks. "With Josh?"

Her sunglasses are perched on the bridge of her nose, and Krystin can see the curve of her eyes behind them. Her brow arches slightly, something like a challenge hardening the ore of her irises. A few weeks ago, Krystin might have thought the emotional wall she sensed Kaydie building between them was evidence of Kaydie's burgeoning crush, each brick an effort to distance herself from heartbreak. But now, after sharing velvet couch cushions and plane rows and hotel rooms with an ever-dwindling group of women who would clearly sacrifice anything to win the perfect life dangling in front of them like a carrot, Krystin suspects Kaydie is merely sussing out her competition.

"Yeah," Krystin says finally, because she does, even if Lauren doesn't want a shot at all.

"Hm," Kaydie mumbles, and then jumps into the pool.

A few hours and several SPF reapplications later, Penny pulls Krystin aside for a "quick chat." She leads her to the confessional room, and Krystin sits in the fold-up director's chair, which she's always felt to be a strange choice for the Devotee seating, considering they're not the ones directing anything.

Penny settles onto a stool opposite her and nods to the cameraman to start rolling.

"So," she begins, looking back at Krystin. "How are you feeling heading into Hometowns? Are you nervous?"

Krystin responds to the camera lens, like they taught her to do during the first week. "I'm really excited to bring Josh home to Montana. I can't wait to show him all the things that make me who I am."

"Are you nervous?" Penny asks again.

Duh.

"I think it's always nerve-racking to bring someone home for the first time," Krystin says carefully. "But it's a super important step in any relationship, and I'm ready to take it with Josh."

"Have you ever brought a guy home before?"

Hadn't they already been through this? Krystin sighs, rephrasing the question in her answer like they always instructed her to do. "I've never brought a man home to meet my family."

"So how do you know what it's like?"

"I'm assuming."

"How do you think your lack of experience will affect your Hometown date?"

Krystin feels blood starting to pool in her cheeks, and takes a measured breath. She's just doing her job, she reminds herself. "Josh will be the first guy I've ever brought home to meet my family, which is how they'll know just how special he is. And how serious I am about this entire process," she adds, for good measure.

Penny nods. "How do you think things are going with the other women?"

Krystin gives a variation of this answer every time. "Every woman here is amazing, and I think Josh would be lucky to marry any of them. But I can only speak to my experience, and I'm confident in our connection."

Penny looks bored before she even finishes speaking. "What about Lauren C.? You had an altercation with her earlier in the season. Is it uncomfortable being around her?"

Yes, but not for the reasons you think. "I wouldn't say Lauren and I had an altercation," Krystin says, but she can already imagine the slo-mo footage of the mud wrestling debacle spliced with her interview. "Lauren and I are definitely very different people, but I don't have a problem with her."

"She seems to get a lot of attention from Josh. Do you think that's fair?"

"I think the fact that we're all still here shows that Josh is interested in each of us."

"But do you think it's fair that she gets more attention from him by making out with him?"

Wait, what? "Haven't we *all* kissed Josh?"

"Some women have been more forthright than others."

"Some women," Krystin repeats. "You mean Lauren."

Penny shrugs. Then she points to the camera, and Krystin realizes she'd been talking to Penny instead of the lens.

Her skin is starting to feel sticky under the layers of sunscreen. She desperately wants to shower, but she knows Penny won't let her leave until she gets a sound bite.

"I try my best not to think about Josh with any of the other women," Krystin says. "But it's really hard. Especially when we're all living in the same house together. But if there's one thing rodeo taught me, it's that you can't compare yourself to other women." Krystin pauses, and hopes what she's about to say doesn't sound too canned. "Unless you're comparing barrel racing times."

Penny doesn't look happy, but she doesn't look mad either. At least no one can tell her she didn't lean into the cowgirl thing.

When Krystin exits the room, she sees Lauren leaning against the kitchen sink, washing strawberries under the faucet. She looks up when Krystin pads across the tiled floor.

"You give 'em anything juicy in there?" Lauren flicks her head toward the confessional room.

Krystin watches Lauren bite into a berry and discard the stem. Then she imagines Josh tasting the sugar on her lips. "No."

Lauren holds out the carton to Krystin. "Want any?"

"I'm good."

"You sure?"

"Yeah." Krystin plucks a piece of stray hair from her bikini top. "I'm gonna take a shower."

Lauren leans across the kitchen island and lowers her voice. "Want company?"

She does. She wants to be warm with Lauren, to feel streams of water flood them until they're both undersea. She wants to forget what air feels like.

"I'm really gross," Krystin says instead. "I'll see you later."

By the time Lauren returns to their room, Krystin is showered and lying in her bunk, wearing a full sweatsuit. She hears Lauren close the door behind her, but doesn't look up.

Lauren crosses the room, her footsteps stopping in front of her bed. Her voice is soft when she speaks. "Krystin?"

"Yeah?"

"What, like . . . happened today?"

Krystin sits up in the bunk. She tries to think of an answer that doesn't sound too evasive, but she takes too long.

Lauren tries again. "You've been so . . . distant all day, and—" She takes a breath. She looks uncomfortable, eyes darting to different parts of the floor and avoiding Krystin entirely. It sends a pang through Krystin's chest. "I don't know. I just thought, after South America—"

"Do you like Josh?" Krystin blurts out.

Lauren falters. "What?"

"When you kiss him, do you like it?"

Lauren looks mildly horrified. "Why are you asking me this?"

"I'm trying to understand something," Krystin says, because she is. "I like Josh, a lot. He's sweet, he's charming, and he tells bad jokes, and I think he'd be a really good husband, and a good father—"

Now Lauren looks mildly pissed. "And he'll take care of you and build you a house with fifteen different kinds of doors and you'll live happily ever after. I get it."

"No, you don't." Krystin rubs her eyes. "I like Josh, but I like—I like *kissing* you." She lets it hang in the air before saying it again. "I like kissing *you*."

Lauren sinks down to the floor, resting her back against the bunk. "I like kissing you, too."

"What you said about your sorority sisters. You liked kissing them?"

"Do you want an itemized list of everyone I've liked kissing?"

"Lauren, please." Krystin meets her eyes, and a dare flickers in them. "Do you like kissing Josh?"

"Krystin," Lauren says, and it sounds like a sigh. "I don't like kissing boys. I never have."

Somewhere buried, Krystin knew the answer as Lauren said it. But even though she expected the words, they still feel something like relief.

Krystin picks at a loose thread in the blanket. "I . . . don't think I have either."

Lauren's eyes are round and dark. "Really?"

"Really."

They sit there for a moment as the words dissolve in the still air. The room feels like the minutes before a thunderstorm in the dead of summer, sticky and heavy and crackling with anticipation. And then the anticipation is replaced by action, because Lauren crawls across the floor and onto Krystin's bunk, and they're no longer *talking* about kissing.

Lauren's lips taste like minty toothpaste, and then they just taste like Lauren. Krystin leans into her, smells her hair, and drags her lips along her jawline. Lauren wraps her hands around Krystin's waist and guides her onto her back, and Krystin kicks the covers over them.

"So," Lauren says between kisses, "you like kissing me?"

Krystin's way past the point of blushing, but she feels the blood rush to her cheeks anyway. "Don't make fun of me," she says, only half meaning it.

Lauren looks down at her through a curtain of dark hair. "I'm not," she says softly, and then smiles, like she can't help it. She looks so pretty Krystin thinks she might explode, and confetti and glitter might fire out of her.

Krystin doesn't know if this is what happiness feels like, but she also doesn't want to spend much time thinking about it. She just wants to feel Lauren's skin on hers, to sink into her universe.

Lauren flicks her fingers inside the waistband of Krystin's sweats, and Krystin strips them off entirely. Lauren smirks and looks as if she might have something to say about Krystin's enthusiasm. But then she just sighs and trails her fingertips featherlight along the velvet of Krystin's inner thighs.

Krystin's breath hitches, as if Lauren can conduct the oxygen moving through her body. Lauren traces a line up, up, until her finger slides easily into Krystin's slit, and Krystin shudders into her.

"You looked so pretty today," Lauren says, dipping her fingers slowly into Krystin.

Krystin tries to think of something clever to say, but words are hazy, and she can't grasp any of them. "I was so sweaty," she manages. "I smelled like—" She gasps as Lauren curls her fingers inside her, cupping Krystin against her hand. "Like Banana Boat and deodorant."

Lauren laughs, breathy, against Krystin's chest. "Don't make me say some cheesy shit," she says, "about you looking beautiful without knowing it." Then she pulls her fingers from Krystin and slides them into her mouth.

"Okay," Krystin says, looking up at Lauren through blurry vision. "You've proven your point."

Lauren kicks her legs around Krystin, settling onto her hips. "What point is that?"

"That you've done this before."

Lauren's lips spread into a grin. "I'm not done."

When Lauren presses her lips against Krystin, it feels like agony and respite at once. Lauren grips Krystin's thighs, holding them down while she sinks her tongue into her. Krystin knots her hands into Lauren's hair, and Lauren moans against her.

"You feel—so good," Krystin stutters, because she can't manage anything else. She's melting into the bed, into the dark of the room, tethered only to Lauren's lips. She feels the heat coil through her, around Lauren. Krystin whimpers, stifling a groan. She's still afraid of someone hearing, as if Kaydie could hear anything over the sound of her workout video. But then Lauren slips her tongue inside Krystin, and she no longer cares about anything.

"I—" Krystin starts, but she doesn't even know what she was going to say. She holds Lauren's head between her legs, curving her hips up, and comes into Lauren's mouth.

Krystin covers her face in her hands, feeling the warm skin of her cheeks as the rush dissolves. Lauren kisses the inside of Krystin's thigh while she catches her breath. Krystin hooks her hands under Lauren's arms and pulls her up, despite protests.

"Excuse me," Lauren says when she settles next to Krystin. "I was just in the middle of a conversation."

Krystin giggles. "I heard a strong closing argument."

"I was driving it home. Really, I was emphasizi—"

But Krystin interrupts her again, this time with her lips. She's gentle and slow, following a path from the soft curve of Lauren's neck, to her nipples, to the fleshy part of her abdomen. She follows it to the crease of Lauren's thigh, and further down.

Lauren's breath hitches. "You don't have to do this," she whispers. "You haven't—"

"I know," Krystin says, because she does. "I want to."

"Okay," Lauren breathes. "It's fine if I don't—"

Krystin lifts her head. "Shh! Let me try."

Lauren's quiet after that. Kind of.

Krystin kisses her, then slips her tongue into the soft folds. Lauren relaxes into her, and Krystin applies more pressure, circling Lauren's clit. She follows Lauren's sounds, adjusting and responding like she's learning a new language. When Lauren whines, Krystin clutches Lauren's thighs closer to her, desperate to hear it again.

"Oh my God," Lauren gasps, and Krystin thinks the same.

Oh my God.

Krystin opens her eyes, lifting her gaze to Lauren's perfect face, and realizes she's never seen her look so . . . open. Unafraid, unguarded. She wants to protect this woman who's never needed anyone. She wants to hold onto her forever.

When Lauren comes, Krystin feels as if a ray of sunlight is beaming from her chest. Lauren's breaths are shallow, then slow and deep. Krystin crawls up to her, nestling her head into Lauren's neck.

"That was a surprise," Lauren says. "A good one."

Krystin feels as giddy as she did the first time she won first place. "Really?" she says. "It was okay?"

Lauren leans into her, and kisses the top of her head. "It was perfect."

CHAPTER FOURTEEN

"Have you ever been to LA?"

Krystin's voice cuts through the dark of the room, and Lauren automatically turns—as if she's turning to face Krystin, even though she's *not*, even though she's still on the top bunk and Krystin's on the bottom. They haven't actually fallen asleep in the same bed since Patagonia, but it's starting to feel like every night they spend more and more time in a post-sex cocoon until Krystin squeezes her hand and rolls over or Lauren yawns, climbs back to her bunk, and tries not to feel her absence.

And then, sometimes, Krystin starts talking again. About Montana, or about Ringo, or even her parents or Delia. Lauren likes it best when she's almost too tired to respond, when the steady but excited cadence of Krystin's voice is the last thing she hears before falling asleep. When she's exhausted, it's easy to forget how temporary all of this is. How Josh can, and will, cut her string and send her packing, probably any day now.

"No," Lauren says. "Just Disneyland when I was, like, six."

"I'd like to go, I think." Krystin pauses. "Just to visit. It would be fun, right?"

Kaydie left for Los Angeles this morning, which means McKenzie's been buzzing around the chateau all day, gushing to anyone who will listen about how she went skydiving with Josh in Buffalo. Lauren was appropriately polite at first—in a weird way, McKenzie's starting to grow on her, maybe because she generally minds her own business and never takes too long or leaves a hairy mess in the shower—but eventually, her ramblings got so repetitive that Lauren started to wish Josh would pop up out of nowhere to make them go to a cocktail party or therapy-themed group date.

She *must* be exhausted from dealing with McKenzie all day. It's the only reason that now, from the safety of the top bunk, Lauren lets herself imagine going back to California with Krystin: massaging sunscreen into her tanned back, taking stupid photos of her at the Santa Monica Pier, making her come in airy hotel rooms.

"Maybe," Lauren says, after realizing Krystin's been waiting for her response. The fantasy pops and falls to the ground like a pierced balloon, because really, she's never traveling anywhere with Krystin again—unless, of course, they somehow both make it another week to overnight dates. When Krystin thinks of visiting LA, she's probably imagining a cozy Airbnb with Josh, dressed in cargo shorts and looking up the best local sports bars on Yelp.

"Does your family ever go on vacations?" Krystin asks.

"We used to." Lauren rolls over again, until she's facing the wall. She wishes she could come face-to-face with Krystin, but in a way, it's almost easier to talk to her like this. It's definitely easier to quietly think about *traveling out of state with Krystin* when they're separated by an entire tier of the bed—when Lauren can think about whatever she wants, really, and not worry about Krystin or anyone else trying to read it on her face. "When my sister and I were younger."

"What was it like?" Krystin asks softly. "Growing up with a sister?"

"When we were kids?" Lauren asks. "Or when we were, like, in high school?"

"Both." Lauren hears Krystin turn in her bed, too. She wonders which way she's facing now.

"We're not that close anymore." Lauren just stares at the wall. "To be honest, I'm not close with a lot of people. Some college friends, kind of. Damian, I guess. But not Rachel, or my parents."

She waits for Krystin to ask her why, or even snort and make a joke. Something like, *Yeah, huge surprise there,* or *Are you saying you're closed off? Didn't you tell Josh your doors were always open?* But obviously, those are things *Lauren* would say, and Krystin, in classic Krystin fashion, just says, "That sounds lonely."

"I mean, I'm not always great at talking to people," Lauren admits.

"I don't think that's true," Krystin says softly.

"Yeah. Well." Lauren shrugs, even though Krystin can't see her. "I'm sure my sister's watching me on TV. And I guess she's going to meet Josh at Hometowns."

"Right," Krystin says, after just a slightly too-long pause. There's something hard to decipher in her tone, but then she lets out a breath of a laugh, and it's gone. "I don't know anyone who's watching me on the show. I'm sure my parents are watching, but it's not like they know anything about it."

"Rachel does. And Damian," Lauren adds. "It's the only thing she and I ever really did together in high school. We all watched *Hopelessly Devoted* every Monday night."

She can practically hear Krystin smile. "Your sister's a Devoted Fan?"

"She nominated me, actually. Several years ago." She squints, trying to think. "I guess that would've been . . . Danny's season?

Anyway, the producers clearly thought Josh and I would be a better match. So here I am."

"So your sister—I mean, Rachel. She doesn't know that you're less into leads like Danny and Josh, and more into leads like Amanda from season twenty-one?" Krystin's tone is light, teasing, but there's a real question there.

"Amanda and I wouldn't have worked out. I think I'm more into the blonde cowgirl type," Lauren replies. She can't see Krystin's reaction, of course, but she wishes she could. She can picture it: Krystin's cheeks flushing pink, her lips curving into an embarrassed, private smile. "But to answer your question, no. She doesn't."

They're both quiet for a few moments. Lauren's about to speak again—maybe to explain that she's not ashamed of being a lesbian or anything, but that her sexuality just feels so big, so real, so personal. It's the most glaring, obvious thing that makes her different from the other women in every environment she's inhabited: her suburban high school, her sorority, her mutuals on Instagram, the *Hopelessly Devoted* cast.

But then Krystin beats her to the punch. "People would like you," she says. "If you did want to get close to them."

Lauren doesn't know what to say to that. Frankly, it's a little terrifying that she's apparently that transparent. "How about you?" she asks, opting for a subject change. "Did anyone nominate you?"

"Uh, no." Krystin's silent for a beat. "I nominated myself."

"Why?"

She lets Krystin take her time to answer. "I guess . . . I was pretty lonely too."

Her voice sounds so vulnerable that Lauren lets herself *imagine*, yet again. Taking Krystin back to New Jersey, or even New York City, and introducing her to Damian. Going back to Montana, meeting

Krystin's family and horse—doing all of the things that Josh will get to do in a matter of days. Something in her aches. "So you were a fan of the show, too?"

"I am," Krystin says. "I mean, I wasn't watching every single Monday night like you and your sister . . ."

Lauren smiles. "Rachel's always super obsessed with the lead," she says. "She especially loves the promos, when they show a shirtless guy rubbing soap all over his abs while he squints and moans like he's constipated."

"That's not what they look like," Krystin tries weakly, but Lauren can tell she's stifling a laugh. "You're ruining it."

"Sorry," Lauren says. "It's true. Even Damian agrees that the gratuitous shower scenes are overkill."

"Wait." She thinks she hears Krystin sit up. "Damian, your ex-boyfriend, likes *Hopelessly Devoted*?"

"He likes the guys they cast."

"He . . ." Krystin's voice trails off. "Oh. Really?"

"Yeah." Lauren laughs. "What, you thought I really dated a guy for years while I was hooking up with girls? I might be a bitch, but I'm not, like, a cheater."

Krystin's response is so instantaneous, it's almost alarming. "Well, you admitted to cheating at mud wrestling—"

"I wouldn't cheat on a person who actually had feelings for me," Lauren says, because maybe she's *technically* cheating on Josh with Krystin, but he doesn't count: He likes a shoddily edited Wikipedia version of her, if anything. Besides, aren't they *all* kind of in an open relationship right now? Krystin starts to say something, and Lauren, nervous that she's already brought this conversation somewhere way too vulnerable, cuts her off. "How tired are you?"

"Um . . . not really tired," Krystin says, confused. "Anymore."

"Cool. I have an idea." Lauren dangles her seal-smooth legs over the bed. "Let's go for a swim."

Technically, they aren't breaking any rules.

It's not like there are rules about how much the Devotees have to sleep, or how late they're allowed to wander around the chateau, or even when they're allowed to use the pool. To be fair, there's probably an implicit rule that they're not supposed to go night-swimming with other contestants while the Romantic's away on a hometown visit, but there's also an implicit rule that the contestants shouldn't have sex with each other, and Lauren's now broken that one, like, seven times in as many days.

"What if there's a security camera?" Krystin asks softly. Still, she places her towel on a nearby pool chair. "And what if they catch us, like . . ."

"We're just swimming," Lauren says before dropping her bathrobe and revealing a black string bikini. "In a G-rated way. Get your mind out of the gutter, babe."

The nickname just slips out, but Krystin doesn't even seem to notice. She's staring at Lauren's body like she's never seen a woman in a swimsuit. "You usually wear that pink set," she says. Maybe it's Lauren's imagination, but her voice sounds a little strangled.

Lauren grins and ties her hair back into a ponytail. "I didn't realize you were taking inventory of my bathing suits."

"I just feel like I'd remember this one."

"Yeah, well." She takes a step closer to Krystin. "It's too skimpy for network TV."

"And here I thought we were also having a G-rated night," Krystin says, a smile slow-dancing across her face.

Lauren runs a hand down the curve of Krystin's body, then turns to step into the pool.

For all the time she's spent *by* the pool, Lauren hasn't actually gone swimming yet. The water feels warm against her skin, and then there's Krystin, quietly following her in. It's dark, but she can see Krystin's eyes go from anticipatory to glimmering, teasing. "Race you to the end of the pool?" she asks. "Or are you too scared to get your hair wet?"

"Not at all." Lauren smirks. "I'll even play fair this time."

Krystin counts down from five, and then they're off. As she swims, Lauren realizes that somewhere along the way—between their flight to Buenos Aires and their impromptu tango lesson and the nights she's spent relishing, memorizing the way Krystin looks when she's turned on—this girl has actually become her friend.

"Okay." Krystin's head pops up from underwater just as Lauren's feet touch the pool wall. "I can't tell who won."

Lauren adjusts her bra; this bikini really was not made for swimming laps. "Rematch?"

"You're on."

This time, Krystin's the clear winner, but it's okay. Because her moonlit face looks so *triumphant*, happy and at peace in a way that suits her nicely, and then she's wrapping her arms around Lauren's waist and kissing her, urgently. When Lauren slips a thigh between her legs, she whines, pulling her impossibly closer.

"Wow," Lauren says softly, moving her lips to the spot right underneath Krystin's earlobe. "Winning really turns you on."

"Winning," Krystin agrees, "and this." One of her arms snakes further down Lauren's back, and the other traces the thin fabric of her bikini top. It takes her little to no effort to move the bra to the side, and then, in a haze, Lauren unties it altogether and tosses it somewhere near her bathrobe. The feeling of Krystin's soft, certain hands on her bare skin—especially paired with her soft, certain lips on Lauren's—is fucking lethal.

And, really, just *good*. Krystin's lips make their way down to Lauren's chest, and as they start to find new ways to fold their hips and thighs together, Lauren takes the opportunity to squeeze Krystin's perfect, firm ass, then pick her up. Krystin's legs automatically wrap tightly around Lauren's waist and she rocks her body against her torso, like she's desperate for contact. Like she's riding her underwater.

"Here." Lauren gently lifts her to the edge of the pool. She leaves an open-mouthed kiss on the crease of her bikini bottom and feels Krystin's thighs twitch. "Wanna take this off?"

She doesn't even hesitate. As she slides off the fabric, Lauren takes a moment to just look at Krystin: this strong, huge-hearted, occasionally obtuse, but irresistibly hot rodeo queen completely splayed out in front of her. Her whole body is glistening wet. Her lips are parted, and her heavy eyes are set on Lauren.

Lauren doesn't say anything as she kisses up Krystin's thighs again, spreads her legs with her hands as she traces her clit with her tongue. "You win," she murmurs eventually, and Krystin breathlessly giggles. She's positive *she's* making obscene noises too, especially when Krystin tosses her head back and sighs out Lauren's name like it doesn't even matter if she won, if she lost, if a sleepless producer walks out right this second and sees her come against another girl's lips, like nothing matters except this.

And when Krystin gasps out that she's *so close*, that *it feels so good*, that *Lauren, I'm gonna—*

Nothing else *does* matter. Definitely not a fucking TV show.

Krystin starts breathing again in relieved, bone-tired heaves, and then she smiles, bright against the dark California sky.

And then Lauren pulls her back into the warm water.

The shower they take afterward, on the other hand, *is* completely innocent. Well, it's almost innocent. Lauren lands a few kisses on Krystin's chest, and she *does* accidentally groan when Krystin massages shampoo into her scalp, and at one point, after Krystin's thoroughly cleaned her body with bar soap, she slips three fingers into her like it's the most natural thing in the world, and fine. Like their dip into the pool, it isn't G-rated at all.

But they don't fuck when they climb into Krystin's bunk. Instead, Krystin curls her naked body into Lauren's like she's a Tetris block fitting into the perfect place. Their legs tangle together, and Krystin's breath is hot and gentle against Lauren's neck. She's positive Krystin's nodding off, but then she hears her speak.

"You said you don't get close to lots of people." Her lips tickle the sensitive spot right above Lauren's sternum. "But we're . . ."

She doesn't finish her thought. "We're what?" Lauren asks quietly. She hates how vulnerable she sounds. She hates that every atom of her being is suddenly on high alert, waiting for Krystin to elaborate.

"I just feel like I know you."

Lauren can't tell if it's what Krystin initially planned to say, but either way, it's a jarring thing to hear—and anyway, she's not sure if it's true. Sure, Krystin knows how she likes to be touched; Krystin knows that she doesn't like men, that Damian is also gay and her best friend in the world, that she's not always a good person but she'll put her ass on the line to help someone who matters. Krystin knows she can be a liar. Krystin knows she's cold and strategic. Krystin knows she can't even manage a healthy relationship with her sister that stretches beyond *Hopelessly Devoted*'s two-hour airtime window.

Krystin doesn't know Lauren, necessarily, but she knows all of *that*. And somehow, none of it stops her from tilting her head upward to kiss Lauren one more time, gently, and nestling her head back near the curve of her right boob. She falls asleep there before Lauren can think to move back to her own bunk.

WEEK 6.5 CONFESSIONALS

Four women remaining.

McKenzie
25
Scaffolding Heiress
Buffalo, NY

Seeing Josh with all the people who matter most to me just, like, affirmed *everything* I already knew I felt about him. Even my parents pointed out that I hadn't looked this happy since our family's business hit 10,000 followers on Instagram. [Pause.] Of course, I'm worried about his other hometown visits, but I've got to just try to focus on our connection.

Kaydie
25
Content Creator
Los Angeles, CA

God, being back in LA was incredible! Seeing my friends, getting to introduce them to my new guy. [Cut to footage of Kaydie and three friends in West Hollywood.] I mean, they've always been the toughest critics. But I think Josh really passed all the tests.

Josh
27
Hopeless Romantic
Jericho, NY

Seeing the sights of LA with Kaydie was amazing. It's going to be hard to beat the hometown visits I've had so far, but I'm so excited to fly out to Montana next week and meet Krystin's folks—and her horse too. Who knows, maybe I'll even get to watch some barrel racing!

CHAPTER FIFTEEN

The first thing Krystin notices when she returns to Montana is the smell. The air is sweet and light, fresh and woody, and like sunshine. It's completely untainted, nearly untouched by man. There's nothing else like it.

She fills her body with it. When she exhales, it feels as if she's breathing out the past seven weeks. But then, of course, she'd be letting go of Lauren, who's sticking to the back of her skull like toffee to the roof of her mouth. She would do well to remember that she's not home for good. In fact, the only reason she's home at all is to introduce Josh to her family, who have never met a single man she's ever dated, because, well, she's never really dated anyone before.

It's early enough in the fall that some green is lingering, persisting among the washes of orange and yellow. The trees rustle in the breeze, which knocks a few leaves off the branches.

Krystin watches as they swirl to the ground. She's waiting for Josh in the middle of the street that production has blocked off. In past seasons she's watched, the Hopeless Romantic just kind of

215

appears. Now she knows that a big black car will deliver him to her at the end of the block and then drive away.

She rocks back on her heels. It actually is a little chilly, just standing around. She wraps her arms around herself, tucks her nose into her turtleneck, and pauses, because it smells like Lauren's perfume. She hasn't washed it since she last wore it at the chateau. She panics for a moment, wondering if Josh will be suspicious if she smells like another Devotee. She almost hopes he'll notice and then make her leave, because the decision would be made for her.

She shakes her head, willing the thought to tumble out of her ears. She hears a car approaching, then sees it.

"The eagle has landed," says a PA from behind her. Penny glares at him, and he withdraws.

Then Penny turns to Krystin. "Remember your one-on-one a few weeks ago?"

Krystin does. She nods.

"It was really great when you ran into his arms," Penny says enthusiastically. "You know, like jumped?"

Krystin nods again.

"You should totally do that again."

Krystin knows it's not a suggestion. Penny looks like her old sorority president, and young enough that she could be. Krystin's a little scared of Penny—and, knowing Penny, that's purposeful.

And then, because Krystin isn't paying attention, Josh *does* appear, without a car in sight.

"Rolling."

So Krystin does what she's told and runs to Josh, lightly enough that she won't look too bouncy on camera. The distance feels longer than it did the first time in Palm Springs, even though it's only half a block. Josh wraps his arms around her waist and twirls her around. She wonders if it looks anything like it does in *Beauty and the Beast*.

When they kiss, it feels longer too. Josh brushes his fingers through Krystin's hair, and she sees Lauren on the back of her eyelids. She pulls away.

"I'm so excited you're here," she says. They start walking down the street, cameras following.

Josh reaches for her hand. "Me too. I even stopped shaving so I'd fit in with the rugged look."

Krystin laughs. "I think it'll take more than a five o'clock shadow for you to fit in here."

"Fine," Josh says, eyes narrowing, coy. "We'll make a bet. If I pass for a local, even just *once*—" He holds up one finger to emphasize. "I get to watch you barrel race."

"Why? I do that all the time," Krystin says, slipping her free hand into her pocket for the tiny clip she'd slipped in there earlier. She fiddles with it, squeezing and releasing as she speaks. "You can even watch my best times on YouTube."

"I want to see you do it in person. I want to see everything about you." He says it like it's the easiest thing in the world.

A month ago, an admission like that would have pleased Krystin. It would have settled peacefully in her stomach like a rock sinking to the bottom of a crystalline lake. Now all she feels is the acid, threatening to climb up her throat.

She swallows it back. "So what do I get if I win?"

Josh gazes at her, heavy-lidded. "You'll just have to win to find out."

The day passes relatively smoothly. Krystin leads Josh through the center of town, the storefronts of which were mostly constructed in the mid-1800s, and look like the set of an old western film but less convincing. The twentieth century tried to usher western architecture into the modern era, which led to a lot of wood paneling and minimalist paint jobs.

There are a few places in Montana that boast historical main streets, all unpainted wooden sidewalks and saloon doors. Incidentally, most of these destinations are famous for being ghost towns, but that's not the point. Krystin kind of wishes the modern era had never reached Montana at all. She'd rather see the history, ghosts and all, than the desperate attempts to keep up with the rest of the country.

Josh actually doesn't look too out of place. Krystin still suspects he'll never look like a local, but he has a quality that makes him seem comfortable anywhere. It's part of what Krystin likes about him, really—that he's a stabilizing presence, an anchor. Which is all Krystin's ever wanted.

They go into a couple of shops: a general store, a western supply depot, an antiques market. Josh places a wide-brimmed hat on his head and bows to Krystin. Krystin slides on a pair of old cowboy boots, the leather cracking in the toes.

She starts to feel like herself again, surrounded by all the things she's seen for twenty-three years, before these past eight weeks of mud wrestling and wining and dining. Sure, between rodeo and her sorority, she's seen her share of eyelash extensions and sequined dresses, but it feels like all she's done in the *Hopelessly Devoted* world. If she really started to think about it, she might wonder if she'd started to lose herself in all the glamour. She's gotten wrapped up in it, in more ways than one.

After they finish up in town, Krystin leads Josh through a nature path, until they reach a small clearing. Jim and Holland have done exactly as Krystin asked: a wicker basket boasts bread and cheese and jam, sitting atop a flannel blanket. And, most importantly, there isn't a bottle of champagne in sight. Instead, a bottle of whiskey is nestled beside a baguette. Krystin smiles.

"All this, for me?" Josh fans himself. "Gosh, you sure know how to make a fella feel special."

Krystin chuckles. "All right, we're in Montana, not *Oklahoma!*"

As they sit, Josh wraps his arm around Krystin, pulling her into him. Krystin lets him kiss her again, then breaks away.

"Should we, um, eat?"

If it bothers him that she stopped kissing, he doesn't show it. "Let's dig in."

Krystin hasn't brought a man home. Ever. Not even for Senior Prom, because she didn't go—there was a rodeo competition a county over (she won). Her parents used to ask about it, but Krystin never gave them anything to hold onto. When she was twelve, she made up a boy in her class just to have something to tell them. She named him Will, because she always liked that name after she saw *Pirates of the Caribbean*, and said they had English class together.

Her mother was ecstatic. "Your first crush!"

Krystin was doing algebra homework at the kitchen counter. "Yeah, I guess."

Her mother looked up from the sink, where she was washing dishes. "Well, tell me about him."

Krystin thought. "He's really nice. He has a friendly smile." She paused. Her mother was smiling to herself, looking down at the sudsy pot in the sink. "And he makes me laugh."

She kept up the ruse for a couple of weeks, answering questions when he came up at dinner and fabricating details on the fly when she needed to. It was the only time Krystin ever lied to her parents. Eventually, it stopped feeling like a lie at all.

Josh feels like the closest Krystin's ever gotten to Will. She wonders if they'll mention him, even though there's no reason they would. She never told them he was fake, and she can't imagine what she would say to defend herself. The whole thing was so involved.

She looks at Josh now, standing at the end of the path leading up to their house. He's holding a bouquet for her mother, and a bottle of single malt for her father, and he doesn't look nervous in the slightest.

There have been moments before this one where this whole experience has felt real—their first paintball date, Buenos Aires, karaoke—but it's never felt as real as it does right now, as she stares at the house she grew up in and Josh squeezes her hand. The top of her nose feels tingly in the way it does before she cries.

They take a few steps forward, and newly fallen leaves crunch under her boots. The light is dimming, the sun already below the jagged line of the mountains. She takes a long breath when they reach the front door.

Josh squeezes her hand again, then looks at her. "Don't worry, it's gonna be great."

Krystin nods. She squeezes her eyes shut, but Lauren winks at her there.

Josh raises a fist, raps his knuckles against the wooden door. Then he opens it.

It's bright inside, where a cameraman is already waiting for them. The lens pans over them as they walk down the corridor that opens into the living room.

"Knock, knock!" Josh announces, and Krystin trails him as if this is his house rather than hers.

And then her family is there, sitting on the brown leather couches, and they see Krystin and stand up, but Krystin can't look at them—she can only look at Delia, who's standing timidly to the side of the couch, holding a glass of sauvignon blanc.

Delia's mouth quirks up at the corner. Her coppery bangs fall into her face, and she pushes them out of the way. Krystin just keeps smiling.

"Sweetheart," her mom coos, pulling her in for a hug. Then she's hugging her father. And then she's hugging Delia, because she's not sure what else she's supposed to do.

Once all the handshaking is done, they settle onto the couch. Her mom tells Josh to call her Peg. Glasses of wine appear in front of them, and Krystin drinks.

Krystin's dad clears his throat. "Well, isn't all this something."

Her mom grins. She's expertly applied eyeliner for the occasion, as well as donned her lucky belt buckle. "Isn't it? You must feel like you're waking from a daydream." She leans forward. "Or are y'all still in it?"

Josh squeezes Krystin's knee. "I know I am. I just feel like the luckiest guy."

Delia grips the stem of her wine glass. "I'm sure you do."

"I mean, I do have to commend you on raising such a great girl. Woman," he corrects. "A great woman."

Peg smiles graciously. "Thank you. She is pretty special."

Krystin knows she should say something, but she doesn't have a thing to say. And she doesn't for the life of her understand what Delia is doing there, and who invited her, because it certainly wasn't Krystin.

Delia, for her part, doesn't seem like she particularly wants to be there. She sits awkwardly on the couch that she's spent countless nights curled into, near the edge as if she's going to have to run at any moment. She hasn't looked at Josh once.

He's talking about their first date, how Krystin kicked his ass at paintball.

"That sounds like my Krystin," her dad says. "Never let a man win a damn thing in her life. Or a woman, for that matter."

Josh smiles at Krystin. "So I've heard." He nudges Krystin's shoulder. "When do I get to see the trophy room?"

Krystin looks down at her drink and wills it to turn darker. "It's not a room . . ."

"Oh, she's always like this." Peg stands up and motions for Josh to follow her. "Come with me, I'll show you."

Josh looks at Krystin for permission, which she grants, and they leave the room. One camera follows them, another settling into the corner of the room. Penny stands beside him. Krystin can feel Penny looking at her, practically willing her to say something.

Her dad speaks instead. "So, Krys." He's looking past her at something on the wall, or in the yard. He pulls his gaze back to his daughter. "Tell me the truth. You're happy?"

Krystin responds immediately. "Yeah. Yeah, definitely." She leans back into the couch. The space next to her is still warm. "He's all I've ever wanted." She glances at Delia, who's eyeing the camera warily.

"He sure is something," her dad says again. "I'll say we, uh . . . we didn't expect you to be gone this long."

Krystin shifts. "You're saying you didn't expect this process to work."

"No, no, I didn't say that," but it's clear he did. "It's just been a change, is all. We're used to seeing you more often. The way things were."

"I mean, sure," Krystin nods. "But things change. People change."

"You're saying that you've changed," Delia says.

Her dad must sense the sharp edge in Delia's voice, because he tries to redirect the conversation. "I think you're the same old Krystin we've always loved. And we always will."

"Thanks, Dad," Krystin says, but she's looking at Delia.

Voices echo through the hall, and Josh and Peg return arm-in-arm. She's telling him some story about Krystin when she was a child; when Josh throws his head back in laughter, Peg looks at Krystin and gives a thumbs-up.

As soon as Josh sits back down next to Krystin, her father stands.

"Let's go take a walk, son," he says, and Josh squeezes Krystin's shoulder before following him out of the room.

"Well," Krystin says, turning to her mother. "What do you think?"

"Oh, Krystin." Peg sighs, and she has the same smile on her face as she did when Krystin told her about Will. "He's just a lovely man. I'm so happy for you."

"Really?" Krystin isn't sure if what she's feeling is relief. "You really like him?"

"I really do, hon." Peg looks at Delia, then back at Krystin. "And how has everything else been? Do you like the other girls?"

Krystin takes another sip of wine. "Mhm."

"Have you made any friends?"

She thinks of Lauren, in Patagonia, in the chateau bunk bed. Then she thinks of Kaydie, and decides she won't be lying if she says yes. "Absolutely. Some of the best in my life."

Delia chokes on her drink. "Sorry," she says. "Wrong pipe."

"Well," Peg says, "I'm gonna give you girls some time to talk. I'm sure you have a lot to gab about."

She leaves, and Krystin hears the front door close. Penny and the cameraman stay firmly planted in the corner of the room. Delia tilts her head toward them.

"Do they have to be here?" she asks.

"Yes, Delia, it's a TV show."

"Fine."

223

Why are you even here? Krystin wants to ask. "I didn't realize you were coming tonight," she says instead.

"Some producer reached out to your parents about any friends or family they thought should be here. So they called me."

Krystin hadn't told them about the fight. She hadn't really gotten the chance. "Honestly, I'm kind of surprised you showed up."

"You can just say it," Delia says. "I don't mind." She looks directly at the camera. "I don't like this show."

Penny rubs her temples.

"Deels," Krystin pleads. "Come on."

"Twenty-three years, and *this* is the guy? This is the guy you want to marry?"

Krystin swallows. She remembers when they announced Josh as this season's Hopeless Romantic, and how he seemed, by all accounts, like a genuinely good guy. He had been kind and genuine with Amanda, supportive of her choices and leaving obligingly when she asked, despite how embarrassed he must have been. If she can't love Josh—who is flawed and more than a little corny, but has never done anything truly wrong—she would have to give up. And she doesn't know what that looks like.

"Yes," Krystin says. Then she adds, petulant: "And I really don't understand why it's so hard for you to believe me."

"Krystin," Delia says, in nearly a whisper. "You've never even had a serious boyfriend."

"He knows that. Everyone knows. I told them."

Delia scoots forward. A little wine sloshes out of her glass. "It's not about what *he* knows. It's about *you*, and what *you* know."

Krystin's heart rate is trying to beat its own record. "Why are you being so cryptic?" Krystin tries to level her voice, but she can't help it, she sounds a bit shrill even to her own ears. "Do you know something I don't?"

"I know you're not ready to get married."

They let the accusation hang in the air for a moment. Krystin can already see Penny's gears turning, hearing this after all that drama after the podcast date.

"What do you know, Delia?" she says finally. "You've never had a serious boyfriend either."

Delia tucks her hair behind her ear. "Well, I'm different."

"How? How are you different?" Everything from the past two months starts flooding back to Krystin. She's back on the plane to Buenos Aires, Lauren needling into her past while settling into the seat next to her. She's in the hotel bed, eyes puffy and achy from crying, a telenovela muted on the television. *You don't exist just for someone else to be proud of you.* Lauren told Krystin that she had a lot to be proud of. Lauren told Krystin *she* was proud of her.

Why the fuck is Delia in her house? What was she telling Krystin's parents before Krystin walked in on Josh's arm? Why should she trust anything Delia has to say, anyway?

Krystin can feel it happening. Her chest feels hot, and something bubbles up that could, in any other circumstance, be mistaken as laughter. "You love to tell me how to live my life, and you don't even know how to live yours."

Delia looks like she did when they were in grade school and Jaden Bader hit her with a volleyball in PE: stunned, pissed, and mildly hurt.

Fuck. She should not have said that. And especially not in front of the cameras. Even Penny looks a little mortified. This night, one of the most important of her life, is quickly morphing into a different kind of TV show. She has to fix this.

She takes a breath. "All I'm saying is, I wish you would just support me in this journey. I believe that this process works, and I'm really trying."

225

Delia's lips have settled into a stony line. She looks at Krystin when she speaks. "Maybe you shouldn't have to try so hard."

Krystin's heart rate is still settling. She feels the needles in the corner of her eyes, at the very top of her nose. She doesn't know where Josh is. The only other person she's been able to share this experience with is a thousand miles away, planning her own hometown date. She feels completely and utterly alone.

Krystin reaches around her waist for the mic pack. Penny motions for her to stop, but she switches it off anyway. When she speaks, her voice sounds unsteady even to her own ears. "Why are you trying to ruin this for me?"

The front door opens again, and Josh returns with her parents. Actually, he's walking between them, like—well, like the son they never had. It's all too easy for Krystin to imagine Thanksgivings and Christmukkahs and regular old Sunday mornings with the four of them, passing the coffee and the syrup and the local newspaper with the easy crossword puzzles.

Delia must see the way Krystin looks at the three of them, because she leans over to Krystin, gripping her arm. "Krys, please. You think this is what you want, but it's not. I know you. I *know* you."

But Krystin shakes her off. "You used to."

By the time Josh sits down with Krystin again, her mic is back on and she's smiling up at him. He looks down at her, running a hand through his hair. He looks like he just ran a marathon, cheeks flushed, catching his breath at the finish line. He's warm too, but he's always warm.

On the second couch, Delia moves to make room for Krystin's parents. She's finished her wine, and slides the glass purposefully across the coffee table.

"This was quite the night," Peg says, leaning into her husband. His hand slides easily over her shoulder, his thumb brushing absently across her skin. They've moved as a unit for as long as Krystin can remember. Even when they disagree, they can predict each other's sentences before the words make it out of their mouths.

Delia used to ask how they didn't get sick of it all. She'd throw glances at Krystin when she came over for dinner. *You really buy this?* Krystin did. She never had any reason not to. It should have occurred to Krystin that Delia might extend the same cynicism to her.

"It was an absolute pleasure to meet the folks that made this stunner of a woman," Josh says, planting a kiss on Krystin's cheek. "You know, we all have walls up. Thank you for letting me through your door."

Peg bats a hand. "Oh, you're welcome any time."

Delia is uncharacteristically restrained. Krystin feels like she's already standing at the altar, and the officiator is asking if anyone objects. The seconds drip by slowly as she waits for Delia to jump up and drag her away.

But she doesn't.

They all stand and say their goodbyes. When Delia reaches for Krystin, the embrace is tighter than earlier, and longer. Krystin feels Delia's heart beat into her own. She still smells like green apple shampoo, the same one she's been using for years.

And then the cameras follow them out of the house and down the driveway, where another big, black car is waiting to take Josh away, probably to New Jersey. He kisses her for a long time before climbing inside. Then he tells her he's going to miss her, and she says the same.

The next time she sees him will be at the string-cutting ceremony, after he's charmed everyone else's families and shaken their fathers' hands and told them he'll miss them too. Krystin expects this knowledge to pierce, but she feels nothing. She feels like her arm is asleep and she's poking it with a needle. She's aware of the action, and its consequence, yet numb to the pain.

Stranger is the knowledge that Krystin has spent more hours, multiplied, with Lauren than Josh, and he's going to meet Lauren's parents before she does. Krystin wonders if Lauren's parents will like Josh as much as hers did; then she wonders if they would like Krystin more. Then she goes back inside her home and tries not to think of anything at all.

CHAPTER SIXTEEN

In a perfect universe, Lauren's hometown date would've happened in Manhattan: They'd get dinner at Balthazar, she'd take Josh to a rooftop bar in Chelsea, and somehow finagle a fully financed shopping spree in Soho. In a perfect universe, her hometown date would also involve Damian. But there's no way she could get away with inviting an ex-boyfriend to meet her potential future husband, and production insisted Lauren show Josh where she's really from: not New York, or Newark, but Pinevale, population 6,106, about thirty minutes southwest of Jersey City.

"There's really not much to do," Lauren had tried to tell Penny. "We should just go into the city. I basically live in the West Village, anyway."

"Absolutely not," Penny said. "Come on. Cute local ice cream shops? Diners?"

Lauren paused. "Does Wawa count?"

Penny frowned, typed something into her phone, and shook her head. "Let's think bigger. How far away is the Jersey Shore?" Her eyes widened. "Maybe we can revisit your high school? The site of your first job, or first kiss? Somewhere really formative."

This is why, today, Lauren is back at the Pinevale Deluxe Mall, dressed in a black bodysuit, matching leather boots, and tastefully ripped jeans. She's so focused on the possibility of running into someone from high school that she almost doesn't recognize Josh until he's a few feet away.

"There's my Jersey girl!" His face cracks into a grin, and Lauren gives a little squeal before hugging him.

"I can't believe you're here," Lauren says. "It feels so unreal."

"It's good to be back on the East Coast." Josh takes a deep, satisfied breath, even though the air smells like greasy pizza and an amalgamation of old lady perfumes. "There's really nothing like the tri-state area, huh?"

Lauren can't tell if he's joking, so she just smiles placidly. "I practically lived at this mall," she says. "So, you know, I thought I'd show you around a bit before you meet everyone tonight."

Josh reaches for her hand, then follows her as she leads him up the escalator. "So who am I meeting tonight, anyway?"

"My parents," Lauren says. "Their names are Steven and Trina. And then I told you about my sister, Rachel."

His eyes twinkle. "Anyone I should worry about?"

"They'll all love you," she assures him, but truthfully, Lauren has no idea how this will go. No one in her family has met anyone she's ever dated—probably because her relationships have all been short-lived, kept on the DL, or strictly sexual. They knew Damian, obviously, but sometime around high school, they picked up on the fact that Lauren wasn't his type. They asked her about it once, after he drank a few too many glasses of wine and accidentally made a pretty choice comment about Shawn Mendes in front of Trina. Lauren responded that she was helping out a friend who wasn't ready to come out to his parents, and Trina had just nodded sympathetically. ("That Barbara Thomas is a piece of work," she'd said. "Poor boy. He's lucky to have a friend like you.")

Lauren thinks back to last week, when Krystin asked if she was out to her family. The truth is, her parents wouldn't care about her sexuality. Her town in Jersey isn't necessarily a progressive paradise, but her parents have always believed that science is real, women's rights are human rights, Black lives matter, and love is love. In fact, they have a massive sign on their lawn proudly proclaiming all of these sentiments.

People would like you, Krystin had said, if you did get close to them.

"You good?" Josh gives her hand a squeeze, and Lauren realizes she's stopped in front of a Bath & Body Works.

She blinks. "Yeah. I'm just nervous, I guess. I haven't done this in a while."

"Hey. It's going to be great," Josh says. "I'm so happy I'm here with you."

He looks like he wants to continue, but Lauren abruptly squeezes his arm. "Let me show you some of my favorite places here."

She leads Josh through the mall, brings him to the Francesca's, where she had her first summer job ("It's how I got really into fashion," she explains), and the food court where she went on a very chaste double date with Zach Meyer in eighth grade. As they walk from store to store, it hits Lauren that a lot of her most formative, traumatizing, and thrilling experiences *did* happen here. But it's not like she can tell him about the time she and Rachel had a pretzel-eating race at Auntie Anne's and both ended up throwing up on the floor. It's not like she can tell him that, back in middle school, she used to sneak into Victoria's Secret just for the free lingerie catalogs; that she'd sometimes look at them before falling asleep, thinking, *I just want to* be *them*.

It's not like she can tell him about the time she made out with a girl in the Nordstrom dressing room. As they pass the department store, she remembers trying on prom dresses with Sierra, a bubbly, strawberry blonde from the outskirts of her friend group who joked that Lauren looked *so hot*, that they should just ditch their dates and go to the dance together, and wouldn't that be *iconic*? Lauren didn't respond—there was no way she'd ever ditch Damian, anyway—but then Sierra's zipper got stuck, and Lauren had to help her out of the dress, and it felt weirdly natural as one thing led to another.

Sierra went to NYU, and sometime in college, she came out as bi. Lauren quietly followed her life on Instagram as she publicly dated people of all genders, moved to a charming walk-up in Brooklyn, and posted cute videos every time Pride Month rolled around. Sometimes, Lauren thought about DMing her—maybe they could get a coffee or something, and just laugh about their brief situationship—but she was clearly thriving with a cool, super-queer group of friends. She probably didn't have any interest in reminiscing about her repressed, closeted days with an ex-hookup who was . . . well, still pretty closeted.

Now, Lauren points at a fountain filled with rusty pennies, a few straw wrappers, and aqua-blue water. It used to look majestic, but to her adult eyes it's kind of sad and dumpy. "I kissed Zach right there," she says.

After the mall, they walk around the boardwalk a bit, but it's windy and cold and the cameras can't pick up anything Josh says, so they leave after fifteen minutes. To Penny's dismay, they aren't filming any footage at Lauren's house: Trina put up a fuss about their ongoing kitchen renovations, and argued that they should just go to the local

Olive Garden instead. Lauren's pretty sure her mom is just trying to get out of cooking a TV-worthy dinner—no one in her family can make *anything* besides scrambled eggs, pasta, and frozen meals—but she doesn't exactly want Josh in her childhood home anyway, so it all worked out.

"Mom, Dad, hi!" Her parents both jump up from their seats in the corner booth, and Rachel politely smiles as she puts down a breadstick. "I'd like you to meet Josh Rosen."

"I'm so excited to be here," he says, his voice dripping with sincerity. He looks like he can't decide whether Lauren's dad would be receptive to a hug, so he settles on shaking his hand. Probably a safe bet. "Thank you so much for setting this up."

Everyone at the table knows that Lauren's parents did not set this up: In fact, the network is paying for the entire family-style meal, which explains why Trina's already double-fisting margaritas. If Lauren inherited anything from her mother, besides her silky brown hair, it's her ability to get what she wants.

"Tell me everything," Trina says. "First of all, have you gone on any fun trips?"

Clearly, her parents haven't been watching the season. Lauren takes a seat next to Josh, who places a hot hand on her thigh. "We actually had our first one-on-one date in Argentina," she says. "We learned how to tango."

"Let me tell you, your daughter is a natural." Josh smiles. "She's an amazing dancer, an amazing person—I mean, I'm in awe of her, really."

"That's nice," Steven says, as if he couldn't give even half a shit. He clears his throat. "Where did our server go? I'd love another beer."

"*Dad,*" Rachel hisses. "Don't be rude."

"Who's being rude?" he asks. "I'd like to get our man Joshua a beer, too. Hear a little more about this dating show."

"Journey," Penny interrupts. "Or experience."

"Right." Steven isn't usually one to shirk, but he actually seems startled by the venom in Penny's voice. "Should I repeat that?"

"I'm actually going to slip to the restroom super quickly," Lauren interrupts. "Let you get to know each other."

She almost feels guilty about leaving Josh with her moody sister, buzzed mom, and oblivious father, but then she switches off her mic pack and slips into the all-gender, single-stall bathroom, and in a matter of seconds, Damian is there: hilarious, brutally honest, beautifully familiar Damian, with his dark wash jeans and Calvin Klein button-down. He locks the door behind him and hugs Lauren so tight, she has to pull back to catch her breath.

"God, I missed you," he says. "I know we only have, like, five minutes, but I need to hear everything, especially about Josh. I can't believe I can't sit with you guys and see him up close."

Lauren reaches into her pocket and pulls out a lip gloss. "I'm just glad we pulled this off. I was so scared a producer would catch us DMing."

"Same, girl. But seriously, back to Josh. How tall is he in real life?" Damian's voice lowers. "What does his aftershave smell like?"

Lauren wrinkles her nose. "Shorter than you, and he wears shitty cologne. But Dames, we don't have time to talk about this. I need you to tell me the truth about my edit. How did my hair look in Buenos Aires?"

"Well, some people think you're inaccessible." *There it is.* Lauren's spent so many weeks bullshitting everyone around her, and it's beyond comforting to be real around someone. Well, real around someone who isn't Krystin. Lauren swallows—she can't think about Krystin, because then she'll start thinking about Josh meeting Krystin's family, and Josh moving to Montana and fathering Krystin's wholesome, all-American children, and the whole thing is just a long and arduous mental path she'd rather avoid. "But everyone thinks you're hot, and they like that you aren't a whiner."

"Okay." Lauren nods, processing this. "That's good."

"So you're really doing this," Damian says. "I mean, if you make it past this week, you get an overnight date. Would you ever just . . ."

"Four minutes," Lauren says. "Spit it out."

"Would you ever self-eliminate?"

"No." Lauren frowns. "No, of course not. Why would I do that?"

Damian looks at her like she's an idiot. "Because you don't want to sleep with him? Even though, in my humble opinion, he's the full package. He's, like, the guy you want to bring home to your parents, but *also* hot. And kind of ripped, which surprised me, but you should've seen his hot tub date with Kaydie. Remember that male model I got with junior year?"

"I don't have to sleep with him on our Honeymoon," Lauren says. "They actually encourage you to just spend the night, like, kissing. Talking about vulnerable stuff you wouldn't want to discuss on-camera."

"Right. And there's a lot of vulnerable stuff you need to tell him," Damian says. "For instance, you need to tell him you don't like guys."

"*Shh*," Lauren says, suddenly worried a producer might be waiting outside this bathroom. "Why are you acting like this, anyway? I thought you were rooting for me."

Damian pauses.

"You've got, like, two minutes. Or else they'll think I got food poisoning."

"I can't be your ex-boyfriend forever, Lauren," Damian says.

The bathroom suddenly feels very, very cold. "What do you mean?"

"I want to be gay."

"You *are* gay."

"Okay, well, I want people to *know* I'm gay." He looks away. "If you want to play straight online forever, I can't stop you. But I'm ready to be me."

"'Ready to be me'?" Lauren echoes. "Do you hear yourself?"

"I was always going to come out at some point," Damian continues. "You know that."

"You *are* out," Lauren reminds him. "To the people who matter. To the guys you like. To all of Grindr. Instagram isn't who you really are, Dames. It's just your brand, and—"

"Laur, we've been living this huge lie for over a decade. I'm done," he interrupts. "This is the twenty-first century. I want to go to Fire Island and post about it. I want to post shirtless, oiled-up thirst traps. I *deserve* to post shirtless, oiled-up thirst traps."

"Oh, please." Lauren rolls her eyes. "What, you want to become a gay influencer? You want an endless stream of unsolicited dick pics from married forty-year-olds?"

"Maybe I do," he snaps. "Maybe I want guys propositioning me in my DMs. Maybe I want an actual boyfriend."

Lauren, oddly hurt, wants to scream back that he doesn't need a boyfriend, that he doesn't need anyone. Because he has her, and together they're unstoppable. Instead, she says, "I mean, you never told me any of this. You had *years* to back out. You certainly didn't mind pretending to be metrosexual to get into Lavo."

He gasps. "Girl, tell me you're not implying I couldn't get into Lavo without you."

She ignores him. "I just don't get why you're doing this now. When we found out I was going on the show, you said you'd go along with it," Lauren says. "You promised. You were happy for me."

"Yeah, because I never thought you'd make the top fucking four!" Damian hisses. "Bitch, I've seen you flirt with guys before. Remember when someone made you kiss Jeremy from my frat so he'd buy you guys free drinks? You looked like you'd just tried my mom's spice-free, keto-friendly, vegan enchiladas."

"Check my socials, Damian!" Lauren all but shouts. "I'm a good actress. I'm basically a businesswoman at this point. Has anyone offered *you* over ten K for an Instagram post?"

"Lauren. Watching you put on a show like that week after week after week has started to make me depressed, you know? It was funny at first, don't get me wrong, but . . ." He takes a breath, then looks her in the eye and speaks again. This time, his voice drips with pity. "I love to watch fun, fake, crazy-edited drama on TV. But I don't want that to be, like, my actual life. There are more important things than followers."

Her mind is spinning. He wouldn't actually do this while she was filming, right? She imagines the tabloid headlines, the Reddit posts. The judgment from *Hopelessly Devoted* viewers worldwide; the homophobia. Realistically, it wouldn't impact Lauren's narrative— she could still be his ex, someone he dated before he realized he liked men. She might even get some sympathy points. But the idea of Damian coming out, going to gay bars and pride parties without her—if she's being honest with herself, it almost makes her feel . . . left behind.

As if he can tell exactly what she's thinking, Damian clears his throat and speaks again. "You can come out too, you know. You can leave," he says. "Josh still has other options. You already have your followers. It might even help some people. Like, queer fans of the show, you know?"

Lauren tries to imagine herself on her family's old brown sofa with Damian and Rachel, watching a *Hopelessly Devoted* contestant tell a lead that, oops, she's actually a lesbian. She imagines a guy like Josh—a picture-perfect straight man—listening and under-standing and thanking her for *sharing her truth*. She imagines former contestants showing their support online, denouncing the franchise's most bigoted viewers. Would all that have actually meant something to her?

She doesn't know. Because there's no way in hell that ever would've happened.

It's not like Lauren's never thought about coming out to her parents, to her followers, to the world. In fact, she's been thinking about it a lot more than usual—more than she should—ever since her talk with Krystin. But the idea of exposing her genuine self to anyone, let alone the world? She could get rejected, harassed. People could unfollow her; she could lose sponsorships. People might accuse her of faking her queerness now, or yell at her for faking her heterosexuality before. She's from a blue state; she *knows* there's a huge, vibrant community out there, knows it's not just Damian and Krystin and Sierra Ashbery's utopic little NYU friend group. But would that community even want her?

"Listen, I know it's a big deal, and it's scary. And I know you have this massive platform now, but I think Josh wouldn't care if you left at this point. He has other women," Damian continues. "And your family would be supportive, right?"

Lauren says nothing.

"All I'm saying is, the only person trapping you where you are is yourself." He looks her in the eye. "And that's okay, Lauren. It's your life, and it's totally your choice. But you can't keep trapping me there, too."

"Fine." Lauren's throat feels like it's full of chalk. "I get it. Do what you want, but I'm not self-eliminating."

She's giving Damian everything he wants, but for some reason he starts shaking his head. "I just can't believe you're really doing this," he says. "You're going to hurt him, you know. You're going to hurt her, too. And you're going to hurt yourself the most, and as someone who . . . like, *loves* you, Laur, I can't watch that happen. I just can't."

Lauren can't remember the last time someone said that they loved her. Damian is probably the only person in the world who does, besides her parents, and he's never been the emotional type. She looks away, half afraid that if she doesn't, she might start to cry.

Then she realizes what he said. "Wait, who's *her*?"

Damian snorts. "Again, you're a really shitty actress, babe," he says. "You're eyefucking *Brokeback Mountain* Barbie, like, every time you're both on-screen. You're lucky this show's viewership is too offensively straight to pick up on it."

A series of images flash through Lauren's mind: Krystin at the pool, at the chateau, in Patagonia, on horseback. Underneath her in the ring, covered in mud. Underneath her in bed, naked. Lauren lets out a composed breath. "I need to go back," she says, flipping her perfectly curled hair. "Good luck with your coming out post. I hope you get all the horny comments you want."

She doesn't wait for Damian to respond, just pushes past him and walks back to the table with poise.

"Hey." Josh, ever the gentleman, pulls out Lauren's seat. "Are you okay?"

"Yeah," Lauren says. "Just a really long line."

The table's silent. Eventually, Steven speaks up. "So, Josh. Knicks or the Nets?"

"Oh, let's not talk about that," Trina interrupts. "I want to hear about the sh—*journey* you two have been on. I know you gave Lauren the first impression string."

"I did." Josh beams. "I mean, we had a connection right away. And, um, definitely the Nets, sir."

Steven, satisfied with this answer, nods and finishes his glass of beer in one gulp.

"So how does Lauren compare to the other women?" Rachel asks bluntly. "It seems like you have some pretty strong connections."

Josh looks taken aback. "Well, Lauren is—I mean, look at her. She's so beautiful and strong. And our chemistry is amazing."

Lauren doesn't know which is cringier: the fact that he's talking about their "chemistry" in front of her parents, or the fact that he actually thinks they have it. She feels more when Krystin just walks into a room than she's ever felt during a makeout session with Josh.

"Right," Rachel says. She gives Lauren a quick look, and even though they haven't had a heartfelt conversation in years, she still knows exactly what Rachel's thinking: that he didn't answer her question. "Well, I'm glad you two are happy."

"So happy, really," Lauren emphasizes. She tries to subtly scan the restaurant for Damian, but he must have left right after their conversation.

You're going to hurt yourself the most.

She swallows it down.

After kissing Josh goodbye and watching him exchange another tense handshake with Steven ("Yeah, I'm really not a hugger, but take care," he'd said gruffly)—and after a fifteen-minute, camera-free car ride with her family that was utterly silent, save for Trina's drunken snores from the passenger seat—Lauren finds herself in the bathroom she shared with Rachel growing up. Even more than her bedroom, which she's revamped almost as many times as her Instagram bio, the bathroom feels like a time capsule. There's the tacky P.B. Teen shower curtain that hasn't been replaced in ten years; the dozens of half-empty, flowery lotions no one's bothered to toss out; the faded, cloud-shaped bath mat that's turned a gross, yellowy color.

But as she washes off her face of makeup, Lauren doesn't feel disgusted or depressed by all the bathroom's small, outdated details. It feels like home, somehow, even if it isn't as romantic as the life she wants in New York. Or, for that matter, as charming as she imagines Krystin's Montana hometown to be.

She doesn't know why she keeps thinking of Krystin. It's not like they're, like, dating.

There's a knock at the door, and Rachel slips in. "I need to brush my teeth," she says. "Move over."

It's funny. Rachel's always been different from Lauren—she's someone who coasts through life more naturally and approaches her friends, interests, and probably guys with an unfiltered earnestness. But they have the same dark, shiny hair and the same brusque, unafraid way of entering a room. Lauren says nothing. She just moves a few inches, giving Rachel just enough space to open the cabinet and pull out her toothbrush.

"So. Josh," Rachel says. "He's kind of a nerd. Not like that one Romantic we were all obsessed with. The ex-NBA guy?"

"Victor," Lauren agrees. She definitely wasn't obsessed with him, but his season was good.

"Right. Victor." Rachel brushes her teeth, and then Lauren reaches for her travel toothbrush too, and they both brush in silence for what feels like three minutes. Finally, Rachel spits. "I'm just surprised you're so into this guy."

Thirty seconds later, Lauren spits too. "Why? Not cool enough for you?"

She turns to face Rachel, and for a moment it's like staring into a mirror. Then Rachel softens, and she's just Lauren's little sister, always hyper-excited to spend her Monday nights cuddled up on the couch with Damian, always bursting into her room unannounced and begging her to play a game. "He's fine," Rachel says. "I mean, he's definitely hot. Damian's type, for sure. I bet he's salivating over him."

"Probably," Lauren says. She wonders if she should tell Rachel about their bathroom meet-up, but decides not to. The fewer people who know about it, the better.

"He doesn't seem like yours, though."

"My what?" Lauren puts her brush and toothpaste back into her Kate Spade cosmetic bag.

"Your type."

"And how, exactly, would you know my type?" Lauren snorts. "I don't know yours."

Lauren could swear Rachel looks exactly the way she did at age eight, when she brought up Wedding Garden Special and Lauren shot her down in front of her friends. There's some hurt, and a lot of confusion, and then in an instant, it's all replaced by something like acceptance. "I guess I don't," Rachel says.

"I should go check on Mom," Lauren says. "She had way too many margaritas."

And, just as she did with Damian a few hours ago, she leaves Rachel in the bathroom.

WEEK 7
CONFESSIONALS

Three women remaining.

Delia
23
Krystin's Friend
Bozeman, MT

Uh. [Stares ahead.] Yeah.

Steven
62
Lauren's Dad
Pinevale, NJ

Sure, he seemed like a nice kid. But when you think of the person you want your daughter to end up with, do you think "nice kid"? [Air quotes.] I mean, sure. Josh seemed fine. At least we could talk sports.

Josh
27
Hopeless Romantic
Jericho, NY

I say this every week, but man, these string-cutting ceremonies just get harder and harder. I can't even believe I got to go home with four amazing women and meet their families . . . it's just . . . [Sniffles.] I had to just follow my heart. And my heart's pulling me in three directions right now.

CHAPTER SEVENTEEN

Kaydie is crying when she leaves. Like, really, really crying. She holds Krystin for a long time, and Krystin feels the shoulder of her dress dampen. Josh stands awkwardly on the other side of the room, still holding the golden scissors. He looks down at them, clasped between his thumb and forefinger, then places them gingerly on the gilded platter.

The delicate clatter rouses Kaydie from Krystin's shoulder. She shudders out a breath, then dabs the corner of her eyes so as to not disrupt her makeup, which is already irreparably disrupted.

Kaydie turns to hug Krystin first, then turns to Lauren and McKenzie. She looks at the ground as she walks to Josh, the red string still hanging from her wrist. He asks if he can walk her out, and she nods again, limply.

The cameras, and Jim, follow the two of them outside the chateau. When they're gone, the three women stand in silence.

Lauren is the first to speak. "That was intense."

McKenzie agrees solemnly. She hardly looks at either of them, her fuchsia lips drawn into themselves. Krystin thinks they must be thinking the same thing—that she didn't think Kaydie felt so strongly about Josh. But why wouldn't she? It's eight weeks in, and he just met her parents.

Lauren clears her throat. "Maybe her mom really hated him."

McKenzie scoffs. "As if. How could anyone hate *Josh*?"

"I'm not saying it's *likely*," Lauren replies. "Just that it's possible."

A PA helps them all take their mic packs off. Krystin holds herself still as they peel the tape from her skin.

Holland strides over to them, iPad in hand. "All right, ladies, it seems like Josh is gonna be outside with Kaydie for . . . a while, so I'm just gonna tell you that Honeymoons will be taking place in Costa Rica!" She shakes a half-hearted jazz hand in the air. "Woo!"

The women are silent. McKenzie looks like she wants to melt into the floor. Lauren, on the other hand, cranes her neck around Holland as if she could somehow see through the walls to Josh and Kaydie's conversation.

Holland's hand is still jazzing. Finally, she drops it, along with her smile. "Exciting stuff. Anyway, flight's tomorrow afternoon." Then she rejoins Penny in the corner.

"Wonder what's taking them so long out there," Lauren says, eyes wide to feign innocence, but Krystin knows better.

McKenzie crosses her arms. "Kaydie was a puddle when Josh cut her string. What do you think?"

"We don't know what their relationship is like," Krystin offers, attempting diplomacy.

"Yet." Lauren smooths the front of her dress. Without the mic, the satin lies flat against her body. "We will in, like, two weeks."

McKenzie shakes her head. "I don't wanna think about that right now."

"Why not?"

"What do you mean, 'why not?'" McKenzie's words are razored. Krystin almost expects blood to dribble from the corner of her lips. "He's my boyfriend. I don't want to think about him being anyone else's."

She doesn't wait for a response, just leaves the two of them standing there in the string-cutting room. Even surrounded by production, Krystin feels gooseflesh rise, as if her skin is jumping out of itself to get closer to Lauren. She rubs her hands against her arms vigorously.

Lauren looks at Krystin pointedly. "Cold?"

Krystin drops her arms. "Kinda."

"Well . . ." Lauren steps closer to her, hooking her arm around Krystin's elbow. To anyone watching, it would look like they were simply the best of friends. "Good thing I know what makes you hot."

And all of a sudden she is. She feels blood flush her cheeks, and it feels like a layer of her skin is about to burn off. She lets Lauren lead her out of the room.

McKenzie's door is already shut when they reach the residential wing. Lauren releases Krystin's arm and presses an ear against the door.

"'Teardrops on My Guitar,'" Lauren whispers. "A little basic, but still a classic. She's down bad."

When they turn into their room, Lauren spins around and kisses Krystin so hard she stumbles backward, accidentally slamming the door behind her. Krystin's lips part easily as Lauren slides her hands around Krystin's waist.

The silk of Lauren's dress feels like water under Krystin's hands. Her fingers trace the neckline, slipping effortlessly underneath. She can feel Lauren's heartbeat, the thrum under her sternum. Krystin matches her rhythm. They trade breaths.

Krystin drops kisses along Lauren's jawline.

Lauren sighs. "I . . ."

Krystin hums a response from the crook of Lauren's neck. "Hmm?"

"Missed you," she finishes.

Lauren's never said that before. The confession elicits something like a whimper from Krystin. She tangles her fingers in Lauren's hair, pressing her into herself.

Lauren grips Krystin's hips, sliding a knee between her legs. "Did you, like . . . miss me?"

Lauren tastes good, so good, sweet and bitter and hot. "Yes."

Krystin means it. She can hardly breathe, but she manages; she's at once desperate and utterly calm. And she wants Lauren.

She reaches to her side, gliding the zipper of her dress down until it's a shell that she kicks to the ground. Lauren leaves constellations across Krystin's collar, chest, stomach, mouth. Krystin quivers under her touch, until Lauren slips her fingers inside her, and she feels relief.

Krystin likes a lot of things about sleeping with Lauren. She likes laying her head on Lauren's chest and bobbing up and down with her breath, like when she takes a float out into the middle of the lake and feels the waves bubble underneath her. She likes that Lauren is soft, and smells like sugar. She likes that it feels like the best part of a sleepover, when you're both tired and peaceful and letting half-stitched thoughts unravel as they leave your lips.

Krystin never considered herself a particularly sexual person, mostly because the few times she'd had sex with men, she hadn't enjoyed it. But this . . . she can hardly recognize these feelings. Her body is moving on instinct, her mind trailing behind.

They haven't even taken off their string-cutting ceremony makeup, though now both their dresses are on the floor. Krystin's pretty sure some of her fake lashes have dislodged. Her arms shimmer from Lauren's body glitter.

"So," Krystin says, letting the word take its time in her mouth, "maybe we should talk about Hometowns."

Lauren shifts under her. "Um, okay. Was there something you wanted to, like, know?"

No. Yes. "How did it go?"

"It was . . . fine." Lauren thinks. "Josh talked to my dad about working in sales."

"That sounds nice."

"Does it?"

"I mean, they have something in common."

Lauren laughs. "Sure."

Krystin draws abstract shapes on Lauren's stomach. "What else?"

"We went to the mall. Then my mom got shitfaced at the Olive Garden."

Krystin gasps. "You got to go to an Olive Garden? No fair!"

"We leave for Costa Rica in fourteen hours, and you're jealous of a mid-priced American chain restaurant?"

Krystin pouts. "The closest one to us growing up was forty minutes away. It was only for special occasions. And, like, when you're there . . . you're family."

"Pff. Okay, what about *your* family?" Lauren segues. "I'm sure it was nice to be back in Montana."

"It was," Krystin says, and it's the truth. "We didn't really get to do much. My parents liked Josh a lot. He, like . . . fit in."

Lauren doesn't respond right away. Krystin can hear her heartbeat spike a little. "That's . . . good, right?"

"Yeah. Yeah, definitely." Krystin draws a flower around the freckle below Lauren's left rib cage. "Um, Delia was there."

Maybe she's imagining it, but Krystin thinks she feels Lauren's heartbeat spike a little more.

But Lauren just releases a steady breath. "Oh?"

"Yeah. I didn't know about it beforehand. She was just . . . in my house, sitting with my parents like nothing happened."

"Sounds like you haven't lost your best friend after all."

"That's the thing, though." Krystin props herself up on Lauren's chest. "It didn't feel that way. We just had the same fight we had months ago, again." She pauses. "With cameras."

Lauren sucks air through her teeth. "Yikes."

"And it was so frustrating, like, she just kept drinking wine on my couch, saying the most cryptic shit, like *she knows something I don't*, or—" Krystin can feel herself getting worked up again. She looks down at Lauren, whose expression is entirely blank. "Whatever."

Lauren shifts under Krystin's weight. "I mean. Does she?"

"Does she what?"

"Know something you don't."

"If she did, wouldn't I not know what it is?"

Lauren makes a sound that's supposed to sound like a laugh. "Okay."

Krystin's cheeks feel hot, and not in the way they did about thirty minutes ago. "What, do you, like, agree with her or something?"

"Krystin, I don't even know her. Actually, all I know about her is that she's been a shitty friend to you."

Krystin relaxes a little at the words. They feel like they did in Buenos Aires, like honey melting on her mind. "She said I wasn't ready to get married. I'm just . . ." She rubs her eyes, then remembers her makeup, then remembers she doesn't care. "I'm sick of people telling me what not to do. No one ever tells me what *to* do instead."

A lock of Krystin's hair spills forward onto Lauren's chest. Lauren twirls it between her fingers.

"Well, only you know that," she says. "Right?"

"I don't, though."

Lauren plays with the hair a little longer, then drops her hand. "Krystin," and the way she says it sounds just like Delia. Krystin fights the urge to rip herself away from Lauren.

"What?"

"*Are* you ready?"

"Are *you*?" Krystin feels the conversation rapidly unfolding before her, and she can't catch up to it. "Why are we even talking about this?"

An expression of hurt creases Lauren's face before she has the chance to mask it. "*You* wanted to. You're the one who said we should talk about Hometowns."

"Well, I shouldn't have. This is stupid." Krystin wants to peel herself away, but she feels glued to Lauren's skin. And she can't help but feel that any action would mean something, when she wants it to not mean anything at all.

"Maybe it isn't."

Krystin feels something like tectonic plates shifting under her, and then realizes it's just Lauren pulling herself up. She sits back against the bed frame, arms crossed over her chest.

Krystin pushes herself into a sitting position. She pulls at the sheets, trying to wrap them around her, feeling like a cliché even as she does. Lauren speaks before she can.

"Do you ever wonder what we're doing here?"

"Like, *here* here?"

"You know what kind of *here* I mean."

"Again with the me knowing things." She knows it's dumb even as she says it. Lauren waits for a real answer.

"I don't know what's happening," Krystin says carefully.

Lauren looks at her with a rare tenderness, which, admittedly, is growing less rare as Krystin knows her. "Do you want to?"

Krystin thinks of Josh at her family's home, the way her mother smiled when he kissed Krystin's cheek, the way her father patted Josh's shoulder as they left. She feels an ache in her core for something she hadn't even lost yet.

"I can't . . ." She trails off. Krystin flicks her eyes up to Lauren's, whose features seem to be hardening the longer Krystin waffles. "This just doesn't—it's not—"

"Forget it," Lauren says, and now she's entirely stone. "I don't know what I expected from this."

The ache is shot through with a sharp pain. "What do you mean?"

"Krystin, you don't just fall into bed with someone. I mean, has anything like this ever happened to you before?"

"I . . ." Krystin knows the answer. She's known it the whole time, even though she never thinks about it, or *tries* to never think about it, because it makes everything so much more complicated.

When they were fourteen, Krystin and Delia sat on the floor of Krystin's bedroom. Delia was propped against the wall, face nearly obscured by the fantasy novel she was reading aloud to Krystin, knees pulled up to her chest. Krystin lay on her back, staring at the glow-in-the-dark stars they had plastered to the ceiling a few years earlier. The fan spun lazily in the hot summer air, blowing wisps of hair on and off of Krystin's face.

She'd turned her head to look at Delia. Her eyes were so bright, brighter than the stars in the big Montana sky, darting across the page so energetically she didn't even notice Krystin staring. And then her gaze moved from Delia's eyes to her lips, which moved around the words so effortlessly that Krystin found herself more focused on the shapes they made than the sentences they read.

Krystin thought about kissing her. She thought about springing from the carpeted floor and falling into Delia, about stopping her lips moving with her own, and letting the rest of the story play out between the two of them.

So she did. And Delia didn't stop her. And it felt nice and good, and right. They kept kissing for a little while, until they went to sleep, and in the morning they didn't talk about it. They kept not talking about it until Krystin nearly convinced herself she'd made it all up to begin with, just like she did with Will.

Lauren is quiet while Krystin tells her this, just lets Krystin talk until the end. Krystin searches her for any hint of a reaction, for disgust or disappointment or anger, but Lauren's features aren't twisted or icy. If anything, Lauren looks at her with something like pity.

She nearly stands up to leave before Lauren speaks.

"That makes sense," she says.

Krystin runs her fingers along the ridges in the sheets. "Why?"

"It just . . . does." Lauren rearranges herself in the bed. "With what you told me about Delia, and your relationship, and . . . yeah, it makes sense that you've kissed a girl before."

"But I mean, that's it. That's all we ever did. Just that one time."

"That's okay," Lauren says, soft, and Krystin realizes she's mistaken empathy for pity.

"I don't know what any of this is." Krystin sighs. She feels like crumpling, but she almost doesn't have the energy. "And you—you do. You hooked up with your sorority sisters and God knows who else, and I mean—you *clearly* know what you're doing."

Lauren smirks. "Please, go on."

Krystin blushes. "I kissed one girl *once*, and we never talked about it again, meanwhile you've probably had countless relationships and heartbreaks. Like, enough for a season of television."

"I wouldn't go that far."

Is she playing coy? "Come on, haven't you?"

Lauren runs her fingers through her hair, flipping her part. "Have I broken hearts? Absolutely. But if you're asking me if I've been in a lot of actual relationships, it's a different answer."

"And what is it?"

"None."

"None," Krystin repeats.

"None. I mean, not any long ones. Not serious."

The admission crawls under her skin, burrowing deeper than Krystin expects. She'd thought of Lauren as so sure of herself this entire time, so unfalteringly confident, so—experienced. That Lauren has never been in a relationship feels unfathomable to Krystin. She knows she seems hypocritical but it doesn't feel that way. It's not the same.

Krystin swallows. "I guess I just figured, with all the stories you've told me . . ." She looks at Lauren, waiting for her to finish the sentence, but Lauren just stares forward. "You've been with women. Like, *been* with them. But you've never really dated them?"

Lauren shrugs. "I date and I hook up, but it's never really gone anywhere. I 'experimented' with my high school girlfriends, I've had the occasional one-night stand, but a lot of my relationships, they've just been fun. They're . . ." She pauses, searching for the right word. "Convenient."

Krystin blinks. "Convenient."

She's starting to sound like a parrot, but she doesn't care. She doesn't think she'd be able to string two words together if she tried. The past two months, Krystin has considered Lauren the one who knew what she was doing. Lauren has guided Krystin through everything, and Krystin has wanted all of it. But it's been playacting. Lauren is on a show she doesn't care about, wooing a man she doesn't want. She's wasted two months of her own life for a ring that means nothing to her, because she doesn't want commitment, and apparently never has. Lauren doesn't take anything seriously. Why did Krystin ever think this would be different?

Krystin feels hot and prickly. Her mouth fills with too much spit, and it tastes bitter and coppery. Lauren is looking at her like she wants a response, and the longer Krystin takes, the more it feels like she's the one twisting Lauren's features, as if she was watching her swirl down the sink drain. And the more she looks at her, the less she understands what Lauren wants at all.

"I have to pee," Krystin says suddenly, and scrambles out of the bed, taking the top sheet with her.

Lauren doesn't respond, or doesn't have time to, because Krystin crosses the room in a few large steps and closes the door behind her, almost snagging the sheet in the process. When she reaches the bathroom, she barely has time to turn the lock before gagging into the toilet, eyes watering. She presses a palm to the cold tile, anchoring herself to the floor. Her heart shudders in her chest; her breath stutters between heaves.

When her heart rate begins to stabilize, she unfolds herself onto the floor. The bed sheet tangles around her limply. She steadies her breath. *One, two, three, four, in, one, two, three, four, out.* Her body slouches toward relaxation, her limbs like lead. Lauren is probably wondering where she is, if she hasn't fallen asleep, but Krystin doesn't move from the floor. She just lets herself lie there, blending into the marble.

When Krystin returns to the room, she doesn't slip into Lauren's bunk. Instead, she crawls into the bed across from her and prays she gets enough sleep before their flight to Costa Rica.

She doesn't.

She wakes up a million times, flips her pillow, pulls one leg up near her chest, and rolls onto her stomach. The freaking birds wake her up. By the time she manages to fall (and stay) asleep, she rouses to the sound of Lauren shuffling around the room, zipping and unzipping various travel bags, and folding very loud beaded dresses into her suitcase.

"You're alive," Lauren comments when Krystin groans into consciousness. "I didn't hear you come back last night."

Her voice is steady, nearly void of emotion. Krystin rubs at her eyes, which ache in their sockets. "You must have fallen asleep."

"I didn't."

Krystin forces her eyes open, looking around the room. Lauren's side is nearly impeccable, her bed made, nary a lace bralette hanging from a doorknob. Two suitcases huddle together near the door, her monogrammed travel tote slouched on top. Krystin doesn't think she's seen Lauren's space ever look so . . . tidy.

And then there's Lauren, standing in the middle of it all, holding a compact and applying lip gloss to her perfect lips. She closes the lid with a snap.

Krystin isn't sure what to say. Sorry? But what would she even apologize for? Running off with the top sheet after realizing that Lauren is actually who she always said she was?

Lauren speaks first. "Is everything okay? Like . . ." she trails off, playing with the compact she's still holding. "With us?"

Krystin is suddenly very aware of their differences in dress. She feels ridiculous, still lying horizontal in bed, while Lauren looks ready for a date card. "Uh, yeah," she manages. "Yes, everything is fine." Because it is. It has to be.

Lauren is unconvinced. "You took half my bedding with you when you went to pee."

"McKenzie's still down the hall. Didn't want her to get any ideas."

Lauren lets out half a laugh. She hovers there for a moment, then walks brusquely to Krystin's bed and plants a kiss on her lips. Then she steps back, looks like she might say something, and changes her mind. "See you downstairs," she says, and then pulls her luggage behind her.

Costa Rica is hot and humid. Krystin doesn't know what she was expecting, but it wasn't a blanket of sweat the second she stepped off the plane. It's beautiful, though, even at the airport, because she could see mountains on the skyline, and palm trees literally swaying all around her, and it's everything she imagined a tropical vacation would be.

Except it's not a vacation.

She's not even outside, enjoying the rhythmic waves of the Caribbean, or the squawks of exotic birds. Instead, she stares at the printed wallpaper of their villa's common area, replete with illustrated parrots and brightly colored fruits. The three women are sitting on the couch, while Holland and Penny watch from their perch in the corner. The cameras are filming B-roll as the women wait for this week's first date card, even though they already know what it will be.

Honeymoons.

McKenzie locked herself in her room as soon as they'd gotten there, leaving Krystin and Lauren stranded in the middle of the common area. They hadn't really spoken since that morning, since Krystin was in a rush to get ready, and they weren't seated together on the flight. Lauren had flashed Krystin a couple of smiles, just for her, throughout the day, which Krystin had returned, even though she wasn't sure what they meant anymore.

Krystin told Lauren she was going to hop in the shower before hitting the hay, but then Lauren stepped closer to Krystin, and flicked a finger across her forearm.

And then she asked, "Want me to join you?"

Krystin ignored the shivers Lauren's touch sent down her body—who needs electroshock when the tip of Lauren's forefinger can zap you from the brain to the toes?—squeaked out a frantic "No thanks!" and pulled her suitcase into the bathroom with her. By the time she'd left the bathroom after her hour-long bathing routine, Lauren was in her bedroom. Krystin avoided her the rest of the night.

The next morning, she's sandwiched between Lauren and McKenzie, trying to avoid grazing either pair of knees on the very small teakwood love seat. McKenzie is incessantly running her fingers through the curls she just spent an entire hour perfecting. She wants to tell her what her mother used to say when she was younger, and unused to the feeling of hairsprayed coils: *Don't touch it! The oils in your fingertips will make it all limp.* And then Peg would collapse like a rag doll and Krystin would laugh and forget about her hair completely.

Lauren sits to Krystin's right, examining her nails. She must have gotten them done while she was home in New Jersey; the cherry red Krystin had grown accustomed to has been replaced with an opalescent pink. They're still short, though.

Krystin feels insane, having to talk to herself about this whole situation. She keeps asking herself questions, to which she can only respond *I don't know*, which isn't helpful in the least. She's heard that you're supposed to be your own best friend, but Krystin thinks she needs a best friend who has some different opinions. It isn't the first time she's missed Delia for that reason—but Delia made it very clear exactly what her opinions are.

A knock on the door startles Krystin, even though it's scripted. Lauren stands, like Holland instructed, and saunters to the door.

When she returns, she holds a golden square between her shimmering fingers.

"Krystin," Lauren reads, and Krystin's name sounds like silk in her mouth. "Let's take our love to new heights."

Krystin could swear she heard Lauren's tone falter over the word *love*. Honestly, Krystin tripped over it, too. Had she told Josh she loved him? Had he said it to her? Even in the fog of the past few weeks, there's no way she wouldn't have remembered *that*.

To her left, McKenzie has visibly crumpled. "I'm super happy for you," she says, but her voice is flat.

"New heights," Lauren repeats, flipping the words around on her tongue. "Wonder what that means."

"Maybe we're going hiking," Krystin supplies, figuring it's the least offensive guess.

"Maybe rock climbing," Lauren adds.

"Maybe he's taking you to the highest point in Costa Rica to kiss so you can break some freaking world record about the highest kiss in Costa Rica."

Krystin and Lauren both turn to McKenzie, who's nearly panting after pushing out that entire sentence without a breath. She's red-faced, her lips drawn into a line as if to suck the words back in. For the first time, Krystin notices the half-moons under her eyes.

She watches in silence as the season's rumored front-runner sulks out of the room, a camera following dutifully behind her. Even Holland has an eyebrow raised.

Lauren whistles out a long breath. "I've always thought there was more going on there, but I honestly didn't think I'd see her break," she says to Krystin.

Krystin nods. "I guess I should go get ready," she says, but doesn't move from her seat.

Lauren doesn't move either. She turns the date card around in her hands, then gives it to Krystin. "This is yours."

"Mm." Krystin looks down at the glittering cardstock, runs her fingers over the Sharpied message.

Krystin,

Let's take our love to new heights.

—Josh

It's not Josh's handwriting. Krystin wonders which PA is tasked with inscribing the cards. It feels heavy in her hands, as if she can feel its implications. Krystin doesn't blame McKenzie for leaving the room. She wants to do the same.

Holland approaches the two women, who still haven't moved from their respective positions.

"Krystin," she says, voice bright, "if you don't mind, I'd like to steal you for a few moments before you get ready for the date. It's a big week," she adds, wiggling her eyebrows.

Krystin can't help it—she glances at Lauren. But the other woman is examining her nails again, leaning all her weight on one foot, looking as bored as ever.

"Sure, of course," Krystin replies, and follows Holland out of the room, leaving Lauren alone with Penny and the parrots in the wallpaper.

A few hours later, Krystin stands under the nets and ladders of an adventure course, beginning to understand the meaning of "new heights." (It's very literal.)

Josh stands to her side, staring up at the rope bridges suspended between the soaring trees. He grabs her hand, just like he did before they walked into Krystin's childhood home.

"Ready to do this?" he asks.

"As I'll ever be."

And then they start to climb.

Krystin never considered herself afraid of heights, but she realizes now that's because she's never really been very high up. The first base isn't too bad—about the height of a deer-hunting stand—and she wobbles across the wooden planks of the bridge. Josh follows behind her, stepping confidently onto the next base.

"How're you feeling?" he asks after they climb a few more yards into the sky. The air is heavy with humidity, but they're shaded by the canopy of leaves, sunlight dappling in clusters of yellow.

"Fine," Krystin manages, even though a single glance down makes her knees hurt.

Josh rubs his thumbs into her shoulders, which are already beading with sweat. "Hey," he says, softly, "I've got you."

And the thing is, she believes him—because he's never given her any reason not to. It's enough to make her take a shaky step forward onto a floating stair, clutching the guiding cable above her.

"Keep going," Josh calls from behind her. "You're good."

Krystin nods, mostly to herself, and takes another step, and another, until she reaches the next tree and flings her arms around it.

Josh laughs as he climbs up, reaching his arms around her torso. She stiffens under his touch, and convinces herself it's the nerves.

"You know," Josh says, tugging on the cable. "It's actually kind of nice to see you like this."

Krystin turns around to face him, resting her back against the tree. "What? Scared shitless forty feet in the air?"

Josh chuckles. "No, no, not that. Just . . ." He trails off, looking at the rainforest surrounding them. "You're pretty fearless. All your rodeo stuff, and how you've handled yourself this whole season with the drama. I don't know, you're just—you're human."

Krystin smirks. "You thought I beamed down from Mars?"

"No," he says. "I think you fell from heaven."

Krystin searches for a tinge of irony in his expression, but he's looking at her with a softness that feels earnest. She gestures to the course.

"Should we keep going?"

Josh smiles. "You bet."

The rest of the course passes quickly. Krystin focuses on the vegetation, the feeling of the breeze on her skin. It really is beautiful here, if she doesn't look down. And the zipline to the end of the course fills her with the same buzzing as running with Ringo.

Krystin doesn't regain her land legs until she's showered and changed for dinner. She's wearing one of her favorite dresses she brought, a silky blush gown with iridescent beading that reflects the light. Josh beams when he sees her, pulling her into a kiss.

Krystin pulls away after a few moments. "Lip gloss," she says.

"Right," Josh replies, unbothered. "I always forget!"

He leads her down a stony path lined with palm trees. A small round table is nestled between a few trees wound with fairy lights. Josh pulls out the chair for her, and she sits.

She has to admit, it's romantic. The set designers really outdid themselves here, between the purple orchids and the trios of candles scattered around the space.

"Today was really fun," Josh says, swirling his glass of wine.

"Yeah," Krystin agrees, "if you forget the jelly-leg-inducing death trap part, it was super fun."

"No way! I felt like Indiana Jones up there." Josh mimes using a whip.

"Pretty sure Indie never wore a safety harness."

Josh frowns. "Hey, a man can dream. Besides," he says, reaching his hand across the table to hers, "we bonded pretty hard."

Krystin smiles, but doesn't say anything. Josh takes her silence as a sign to keep going.

"I meant what I said back there," he says, squeezing her hand. "I've got you. Any time, any place, you can trust me. I'll take care of you."

It's everything Krystin has ever wanted to hear.

"I know," she replies.

He takes a sip of wine. "I loved meeting your family last week, they're great. Your friend, though—she was a bit of a hard-ass."

Krystin winces. "I'm sorry about her. She doesn't really like this whole . . ." She waves her hands in the air. "Thing."

"So she didn't like me?"

"It's not that," Krystin insists, though she doesn't know if that's entirely true. "I don't know. This isn't what she saw for me."

"Is it what you saw for yourself?"

Krystin thinks. "I don't know," she admits. "I mean, I know what I see at the end of it: a partner, a family, a home. I didn't necessarily know how I'd get there."

"I see that for myself too," Josh says. "I definitely never thought I'd be the Romantic, but hey." He pauses, looking at Krystin. "It brought me here, to you. Can't complain about that."

Krystin imagines McKenzie back at the villa, streaming more old Taylor, and feels a pit start to open up in her stomach. Or an ulcer.

"And this place," Josh continues, leaning back to admire the trees. "I mean, come on."

"It's stunning," Krystin agrees.

"We'll have to come back some time."

Krystin swallows. Does he talk about his future like this with all of them?

"So, like, after all this," Josh says, swirling his wine around some more, "what are you planning on doing? Since you won't be reigning Rodeo Princess."

Rodeo Queen Montana. Krystin doesn't correct him. It's difficult to conceptualize a life not characterized by early morning drives to the stables, hitching the trailer to her truck, and driving it (and Ringo) to the next county over. And she loves competing, which is why she never stopped too long to think about what came next. Well, that isn't the *only* reason.

Krystin loves competing, but she would be lying if she said she wasn't losing steam. She's tired of constantly being judged (literally), of the hairspray and the nitpicking and the clocks that are always running out of time. But she's known for a long time that if she stops, she'll crash headfirst into the next phase of her life. At the next wedding, she won't be able to use competing as an excuse for why she doesn't have a man in her life, not to mention actually having to *go* on the dates her friends set her up for without a viable reason for flaking. She knows they just want her to be happy, and that should make *her* happy—but instead, she's filled with dread over the prospect of those two things being different.

Krystin watches the candle flame flicker in the breeze. "I'd like to coach," she decides then, half surprising herself even as she says it. "Even if I don't have the title, or am not even competing for it, I want to stay involved. And I would really love to help little girls do what I did," she adds. As she speaks, she realizes how much she actually means it, and it feels good to actually believe the words coming out of her mouth for once.

"Wow," Josh replies. "That's great. So I take it you're not gonna move out to LA with the rest of the Devoted Fam?"

Krystin scoffs, then tries to play it off like a laugh. "Nooo. I don't think that's for me."

Josh looks at his lap, rubs his chin. "You think you'd ever move out of Montana?"

He doesn't say the other part. *For me.* Krystin grips her wine glass, and chooses her words very carefully.

"For the right reason," she says. She doesn't elaborate.

Josh reddens and shakes his head. Krystin lets him draw his own conclusions; it feels like less of a lie.

Over the next hour, they talk about their families. Josh wants to know more about Krystin's parents after meeting them, and Krystin has questions about meeting his next week.

"It's my little brother you have to worry about," Josh warns, eyes widening. "I mean, you watched my season."

Krystin had. Josh's little brother, Jeremiah, had asked Amanda if she'd ever consider going for a younger man, and then attempted to sneak a Bud Light from the fridge. It destabilized the entire night and launched a whole domino effect of trouble—Josh didn't even make it to the string-cutting ceremony. Amanda broke his heart in the same place he took his prom photos.

Josh continues. "I just hope the women I bring to meet them accept them as they are. They're . . . a little wacky."

"Wacky's good," Krystin says. "Not to sound like an after school special, but like, everyone's family is kind of wacky in their own way, right?"

"Wacky might not even be the best word . . ." He trails off, laughing faintly. "They're intense."

There's no arguing with that. Josh's hometown date involved a lot of pointed questions that caught Amanda off guard. Krystin remembers the whisper-shouted argument that occurred between drinks and dinner, even before shit really hit the fan.

"Why didn't you prepare me for this?" Amanda had asked, but it was more of an accusation. Josh didn't have an answer, just gave a pained shrug.

At the time, Krystin had thought Josh was being passive, with his parents talking over each other and his brother making inappropriate jokes. Now, sitting at a small, well-lit table in the middle of the Costa Rican rainforest, Krystin realizes he was embarrassed. It makes her heart fissure in her chest, imagining Josh mortified by the people he loves, all because of someone else's judgment.

"I'm really excited to meet them," Krystin tells him, and Josh visibly relaxes.

They sit for a moment, not speaking. He looks nice here, Krystin thinks, his skin flushed from the warm air, kissed by the sun. And he's looking at her with the open sincerity of a literal puppy, pupils dilated, and she can feel the comfort radiating off of him, just like on the adventure course. He wants her—visibly, seriously, and without a time limit ticking down the seconds.

Lauren might look at her with desire, but she's never once said anything pointing to any kind of future. Josh tells her what he wants: a wife, a family, enough love to fill a dining room table, enough security to never feel unwanted, to never have to go on another stupid TV show ever again.

Lauren has given Krystin murmurs in her ear, breath hot and sweet on her neck. She's made her slick between the legs, dizzy and desperate, and uncertain in ways that have made her life so much harder than she ever wanted it to be. She's given her restless nights and the kind of support Krystin thought could only result after years and years of friendship.

But Josh has never given Krystin any reason to doubt him.

Krystin doesn't want to be confused. She doesn't want messy, unruly feelings that send her into a spiral. She wants to be in control. She wants—fine—the metaphorical fucking reins.

So when a PA approaches them with a platter and another golden card, she's ready. They'll edit this part out in post—when it airs, it will seem like these trinkets appeared magically, another fairy tale flourish in America's Number One Dating Show.

She knows what the card says before Josh reads it: *Will you spend tonight with me?* She doesn't let him finish before she answers: "Yes."

CHAPTER EIGHTEEN

There's a part of Lauren's brain that she can never really silence—the strategic, goal-oriented part that got her this far on *Hopelessly Devoted* in the first place. And right now, as she's making shitty coffee in a kitschy villa in Costa Rica, that part of her brain is screaming and howling like she's back at freshman year rush week or something.

Even though McKenzie and Kaydie wouldn't let up about the optics of going on the first or last hometown date, Lauren knows that the producers of this show are strategic too; she's listened to every teary tell-all on every reality podcast out there, including *When One Door Closes*. From a viewership standpoint, it really doesn't matter if she has the last hometown date or the first overnight date or anything at all, because everything will get edited around in post-production anyway. Lauren's will probably go at the beginning, and the producers will end on McKenzie's, assuming she gives the teariest confession *and* has the steamiest on-screen kiss with Josh.

The disadvantage to going last, though, is that Josh will be all distracted and giddy from his closed-door nights with McKenzie and

Krystin. Her brain snags on the image of Josh and Krystin sleeping side by side last night—even though she imagines them fully clothed, a safe two feet apart, a sharp chill runs down Lauren's back. Krystin's still not back, and Lauren's thoughts are racing. She tightens her fluffy bathrobe, grabs her mug, and walks out to the porch.

She's not going to sleep with Josh. She doesn't *have* to sleep with Josh. In fact, several leads have come forward and shared that they didn't have sex with anyone on overnights, lest they hurt their eventual winner's feelings. Josh doesn't seem like the wait-until-marriage type, but he *definitely* doesn't seem like Hunter from season ten, who infamously fucked all three finalists—and led them all to believe they were the only one.

Lauren doesn't even notice that a car's pulled up to the cottage until the door slams and Krystin steps out. She can't help but falter, just a little bit, at the sight of Krystin, flushed and cozy in her sweatpants and form-fitting tank top. It's too familiar. Lauren's mind unhelpfully, pathetically reminds her that up until now, she was the only person on *Hopelessly Devoted* who got to see Krystin so relaxed and unguarded up close.

It's fine.

When Krystin starts walking up to the porch, though, Lauren can tell that something's off. She does not look relaxed; she does, in fact, look very guarded. There are bags under her eyes, probably from a night spent sharing secrets with Josh. "Hey," Lauren says. "Late night?"

"It was . . ." Krystin turns to look back at Holland and the small team of camera people, ten or so feet away but probably within earshot. "We ended up doing a ropes course. That was the date."

"Mm." Lauren sips her coffee. "So you did reach some new heights, after all." And then, worried the quip might've sounded bitchy, she quickly adds, "I'm glad you had a fun time. Really."

269

But Krystin doesn't look like she had fun. She looks exhausted. "This is for you," she mutters, practically shoving a date card in Lauren's face.

Lauren bites into her lip. She's overcome with the now-familiar urge to ask Krystin if she's okay, to comfort her, give her a hug or something. But then Holland runs up to the women, and fuck. They're swarmed.

"Krystin. Krystin!" Holland taps her on the shoulder. "We need you to give that to her again, in front of McKenzie."

God. Lauren knows she doesn't exactly have the moral high ground here, but making Krystin deliver a date card on her way home from a Honeymoon? And making McKenzie, who's been locked in her room for a day straight, bear witness to the entire thing? Lauren's not exactly sure when this started, but evidently, no one here is having fun anymore.

"Come inside," Holland says gruffly. "We need a redo."

Lauren frowns at the card.

Lauren, it reads. *I can't wait to get even closer. Love, Josh.*

The words sound eerily like a threat.

Holland snatches it back.

The date is tantric yoga on the beach. Of course it is.

"I know it took me a minute to get the hang of dancing," Josh says, reaching for Lauren's hand. "But I have a feeling this will be, um, a really special experience. Even if it's completely weird, we're in it together, right?"

"Well, I've never done this before," Lauren says. "So just don't expect me to lead you through this one."

It's meant to be a cute joke, but the words come out cold. Josh doesn't seem to notice, though. Or if he does, he doesn't care. "Like I said. We're in it together."

Lauren just smiles weakly. He kisses her, softly but abruptly. Are his lips really dry, or her own?

"So you and I are lucky enough to learn the basics from Mary over here," Josh says. "She's an amazing yogi, and she's going to make sure we don't embarrass ourselves too much. At least, I hope she does!"

The yogi doesn't look all that different from the woman who taught Lauren how to tango, but she's wearing noticeably more tie-dye, and her hair is starting to gray. "Tantra might sound scary, but it really isn't," Mary says. "It's just about getting in touch with your own energy, desires, and body. Let's start with a little breathwork. How's that sound?"

Lauren nods. It's windier on this beach than she'd expected—she ties her hair back into a tight ponytail, and tries not to think about the excruciating discomfort of standing across from Josh, just breathing and thinking about her bodily desires. *It's just like meditation*, she tells herself. *Followed by yoga. That's it.*

She's been doing yoga for about a decade. This shouldn't feel more daunting than mud wrestling or even dancing the tango. It's fine, it's fine, it's fine.

"The key here is to breathe in through your diaphragm," Mary says. "Try to feel your breaths in your belly and lower back. And take a step closer! Look into each other's eyes, if you can. It will help ground you."

Josh gives her a small, comforting smile, and as Mary counts to three, they inhale together. It reminds Lauren of the first night she woke up with Krystin in Patagonia, when she was terrified of running into one of the other women and Lauren implored her to *just try to breathe*. When Josh tries to hold her hand again, it reminds Lauren of the first time she and Krystin fell asleep in the same bed, their fingers laced together. When Mary asks them to dig deep and think about what they really, really want, Lauren involuntarily closes her eyes and thinks of gentle, full lips brushing her hip bones. She thinks of the split second between "Did you miss me?" and Krystin's quiet, certain "yes."

She thinks of the pool.

Josh clears his throat, and Lauren's eyes snap open. He's flushed red, and he's staring at her mouth. Lauren wouldn't say she believes in any of this tantric stuff, but yeah—clearly, both of them were able to tap into what they want. She feels borderline sick.

It doesn't get any better when they move to the actual poses. Mary positions them across from each other on a woven blanket. "Now, put your hands on Josh's hips. Josh, wrap yours around her waist. And let's try that breathing again, shall we?"

Josh is in a tee and shorts, but Lauren's in her favorite Outdoor Voices set. She never viewed it as an obscene, sexy outfit before, but with Josh's hands resting on her bare torso, she's starting to really wish she'd worn a tank instead of a sports bra.

The ironic thing is, Lauren's never felt more out of touch with her own body. At some point, Josh sheds his shirt, and Lauren can already hear Penny's questions—*He looked good, right? Did that make you excited for tonight? Give me something.*

But she feels nothing as she and Josh move from pose to pose, closer and closer. She feels nothing as he kisses her goodbye and gives her a dazed, gooey look as she goes back to the villa alone, as she gets in her silky little House of CB dress and paints her lips red. She feels nothing as the same black car that shuttled Krystin back to the cottage shuttles her to the nighttime portion of her date: A table for two is set up on the beach, in the same spot where she and Josh crawled all over each other hours ago. Josh is standing in front of the water, a small bouquet of roses in his arm. He looks like a stock image on the cover of one of Lauren's mom's romance novels. The perfect leading man.

Lauren kicks off her heels before she hits the sand, and then she makes her way to Josh. "Hey."

"Hi, gorgeous." He pulls her into a tight hug, and the flowers brush Lauren's cheek. "You look incredible. Wow."

"Thank you." He looks like he's about to say something else, or maybe kiss her, but Lauren sits down in her seat before he can even pull out her chair.

"So," Josh starts. He sounds nervous. "Our date today was . . . really an experience."

Finally, Lauren feels something. That feeling is dread.

"I guess tantric yoga is a natural next step after tango," Lauren says.

Unless your tango partner is Krystin, her brain supplies. *Then the natural next step is sex.*

Her heart starts pounding, the way her head does after she's had too many glasses of wine. She reaches for the glass of champagne on the table, and takes a strong gulp.

"We're not toasting?" Josh jokes, but there's an undercurrent of worry in his voice.

"Sorry." Lauren puts down her glass. "I had something in my throat, and there's—there's no water."

"Oh, no. Really?" Josh frowns at the table, then moves to stand up. "Let me grab someone."

"No, it's fine." Lauren reaches out and grabs his arm. "Really."

He sits back down, but looks uncertain. Lauren feels a ripple of guilt, a surprisingly strong one, and remembers Damian's words: *You're going to hurt him.*

"Well, I'll make a toast." Josh lifts his flute. "To an amazing night with a one-of-a-kind woman."

"To us," Lauren says, half-heartedly. She feels like she's outside of her own body. *You're going to hurt yourself.*

She thinks of Krystin, home alone at the villa in her Murdoch's tee and boxer shorts. *You're going to hurt her.*

"We've really had quite the journey, haven't we?" Josh asks.

"Yeah. I guess." She thinks, not for the first time, that they've spent more time recapping their own relationship than actually having one. "We've been sent on a lot of sexy dates."

"We have." A smile creeps across Josh's face. "Not that I'm complaining."

"Me neither," Lauren says.

Silence.

"Can I be real with you for a second?" Josh asks. He doesn't wait for her response. "You make me really nervous sometimes. Being with you feels, like . . . unreal. Like I'm the dweeby middle school kid with a crush on the popular girl."

"That doesn't sound like a very good feeling, to be honest," Lauren says, before she can stop herself.

"It feels exciting, actually." Josh stares at her with intensity. "When the hot, popular girl actually gives the dweeby nerd a chance."

It's not like Lauren's really given him a chance to see her as anything beyond fun, flirty, and occasionally a little teary and helpless. And it's not like it's *that* serious. Still, hearing her entire identity distilled down to "hot, popular girl" by a man who allegedly wants to propose to someone next week makes her feel like someone's hollowed her out with a spoon.

"Josh," Lauren says, "I think—"

"I—can I just say something first?" he interrupts. "I know this hasn't been the easiest journey for you. You've had to go outside your comfort zone more times in the past month than you probably have your entire *life*. You almost got seriously injured twice—three times, actually, if we count the time I kept stepping on your toes at the milonga. And the fact that you stuck around because you see a future with me? It's . . ." He shakes his head. "Mind-blowing. It matters. That's what I'm trying to say."

Lauren doesn't know what to say. She only got "injured" during the wrestling date because she was half afraid that if they kept going, she might kiss Krystin into the muddy ground. She was only spared an injury on the horse because Krystin saved her life. And her feet didn't hurt at all after hours of clumsy tangoing, because she was too busy having the best sex of her life to even notice.

She's not still here—in Costa Rica, on the show, in the final three—for Josh. For the right reasons. But maybe she's not still here for followers and fame, either.

She's here because she's falling in love with another contestant.

"I'm falling for you, Lauren," Josh says, clearly interpreting Lauren's silence as a sign to continue. "And trust me. It's a really, really good feeling."

She opens her mouth. Closes it. Takes a baby sip of champagne, just to buy time. And she can't fake it anymore—she just can't. "Thank you for sharing that with me," she says, and then watches Josh's entire face fall.

When a casting director first called Lauren and told her that *you're going to be a Devotee on Season 22 of Hopelessly Devoted!* and to *pack enough cocktail gowns to last you two months!* and to *prepare for the journey of your lifetime!*, she shrieked. She texted Damian. And then she took a train into the city and went shopping.

In the end, she ordered most of her dresses from Revolve, but she did splurge on one from Reformation: an elegant, slinky black number with long sleeves and an even longer slit up the left thigh. It cost more than three times as much as the dresses she wore to the past three string-cutting ceremonies, and it's been shuttled from the chateau to Buenos Aires to Patagonia and back. Every week, she's considered wearing it, and every week, she's decided against it.

Because she bought this dress for a specific purpose: It's the one she'll be wearing when Josh Rosen sends her home. She should have worn it a few weeks ago, really, but then she got carried away with Krystin and just . . . didn't leave.

In any case, tonight's the night. There's no reason Josh *won't* send her home. After she explicitly refused to reciprocate his "falling for you" statement, dinner was tense and awkward, with Josh trying to fill the silences and play off the rejection and Lauren wondering if she could believably fake a stomach bug and leave early. By the time a production assistant passed him a laminated card with a hotel key, it was obvious they would not be spending the night together. Still, he didn't eliminate her on the spot—they shared an awkward, close-mouthed kiss, and Lauren went back to the villa alone. She hasn't seen Krystin at all today; she hasn't seen McKenzie, either, for that matter.

Now she stares at her reflection in the full-length mirror, from her dark red lips to her exposed thigh to her stilettos. She looks even more devastatingly hot than she did in that Manhattan dressing room.

She takes a deep, focused breath and steps into the hallway, but before she can even descend the stairs, Holland steps out of one of the side rooms. "Lauren. Let's chat," she says.

The producers, much like zits and mosquitoes, have a habit of appearing out of thin air, often at inopportune times. Something about this exchange, though, feels particularly confrontational, like Holland's just been waiting to intercept Lauren. There's nothing to do but walk into the room and stare at the camera, the way she's now done dozens of times.

"How do you feel about your chances tonight?"

She knew this one was coming. And she knows exactly how she wants to play it. "I care about Josh so much," Lauren says. "I think . . . I think anyone can see that. But our tantric yoga date was an intense experience for me, and that put us both on edge at dinner. I just hope he knows that, whatever happens, I'm glad we've gone on this journey together."

Holland nods. "It sounds like you think you're going home tonight. Or . . ."

"Or?" Lauren echoes.

"You're sending yourself home."

Lauren's silent. She's positive Josh is cutting her string tonight—she's always wanted him to cut her string, and tonight's circumstances couldn't be more perfect. As an eliminated contestant, Lauren won't come across as some kind of villainous heartbreaker. Josh, on the other hand, will get to maintain a bit of dignity: His ego's probably bruised from last night's rejection, but at least he'll get to reject her right back. It will be a win for both of them, really.

But maybe she should self-eliminate. Maybe she's not on the chopping block, after all. The calculating, always-one-step-ahead part of her brain wonders if Krystin's date with Josh was a disaster too. She *did* look miserable the next morning: Maybe they fell asleep the second they got back to his hotel room. Maybe she told him she didn't know if she liked men at all. Maybe . . .

Maybe this isn't coming from the smart, strategic part of Lauren's mind after all. Maybe it's coming from somewhere smaller, quieter, more hopeful.

"I don't know," she finally says.

The three words just hang there, thick like fog.

Holland leans forward. "It makes sense," she says. "After all, you were the only woman who wasn't intimate with him, right?"

Lauren stills. "What?"

"As a rule, I really shouldn't be speculating with a Devotee," Holland says, in the kind of slick, conspiratorial way that reminds Lauren she's probably broken this "rule" and speculated with Devotees many, many, many times. "But after talking to Josh, it's just . . . evident. You're the only one who wasn't intimate with him. It makes sense that you'd want to leave."

"I don't believe that," Lauren says. "Just because two people spend the night together, doesn't mean they were intimate." Even as she says it, she knows how naïve she probably sounds.

Holland gives her a pitying look. "I can take you to Josh before the ceremony, if you want. It sounds like you two might have some unfinished business to discuss."

Josh isn't the person Lauren needs to see right now. She wants to believe that Holland's just fucking with her head, that Krystin wouldn't turn around and sleep with Josh just *three days* after sleeping with her, after telling her things she'd never told anyone else, after telling her she doesn't even like kissing guys. Lauren wants to believe it so badly, in fact, that she's already concocting all kinds of reasons it logically couldn't have happened.

But then she remembers how *awkward* Krystin was after Hometowns, how she hid in the bathroom and barely kissed Lauren before taking off for her overnight date. How Josh was always the one she wanted, and even her lifelong best friend didn't *fit in* with her perfect, imagined life the way he did. How every single Devotee, even Krystin, has just been a contestant on a game show. They're literally players in a game.

A game that Lauren's been winning for weeks, actually. She just . . . briefly forgot why she was playing it in the first place.

"Lauren," Holland says. "Are you okay?"

"I do want to see Josh," she blurts out. "I need to, actually. Where is he?"

Holland stands up. "Follow me," she says.

They walk down the stairs and into the first-floor lounge. A cameraman is filming some B-roll, probably, of Josh seated on a velvet sofa, looking uncharacteristically stoic and distraught.

Holland coughs from the entrance. "I have someone for you."

"Lauren?" Josh stands up. He looks at Lauren, then Holland. "What's going on?"

"We have to talk," Lauren says. She walks over and guides him to the wall, as far from the camera as possible. "Please."

"Don't we have the ceremony soon?" he asks.

"Not yet." Lauren reaches for his hand and weaves their fingers together. "I just feel like our overnight didn't go the way it should have, and I just couldn't, like, *stand there* and watch you cut my string without talking to you about it first."

"Okay." Josh tilts his body, somewhat shielding her from the camera, which strikes Lauren as sweet. *He's a good guy*, she thinks, which makes her feel even more gross about what she's about to do. But then she thinks about Josh sleeping with Krystin, trading secrets, giggling with her afterward, and she doesn't need to cry, she doesn't need to scream, she just needs some kind of *control*. "What do you want to talk about?"

"What usually happens on overnight dates," Lauren says. "And what . . . *didn't happen* on ours."

Recognition passes Josh's face, and then he looks almost worried—like if he eliminates Lauren now, a bunch of Devoted Fans on Reddit will accuse him of just cutting the one girl who didn't put out.

279

"The thing is . . . there's a reason we didn't take that step," Lauren says carefully, even though her mind is racing. "Even though I wanted to. Even though physical chemistry is important to me—you know it is." She takes a shaky breath. "But, Josh, think of the dates we've had. The dancing. The yoga. I know you're attracted to me, and that's scary, you know? Because sometimes, when I spend . . . intimate time with someone, I feel like the person stops liking me for, like, who I really am. It's suddenly all about my body, or how hot I am, and I just—"

Josh nods. He's listening to her, and *fuck*, he's actually buying this.

"I wanted you to be different." She thinks of Krystin's soft, private smiles, their late night conversations, and it's alarming how quickly her eyes start to water. Damian was wrong. She's an *amazing* actress. "I just wanted you to be different," Lauren repeats, her voice cracking.

"I—okay," he says. It's almost like it's too much for him to compute: His brows are furrowed, and his eyes aren't meeting hers. "But it's not just about sex, Lauren. We could've spent the night together and not been . . . intimate like that. If we're really talking about this right now, it sometimes feels like you're keeping a part of yourself from me. I've felt that for a while now."

"No." Lauren shakes her head. "I mean, you're right, but knowing that I could lose this puts everything into perspective. I don't want to hide myself anymore. I want . . ."

You want to win, she reminds herself, even though she already did. In the past two months, Lauren earned hundreds of thousands of followers, a shiny blue checkmark of verification, and a lifetime supply of ShineGirl essentials.

She never wanted Josh: She wanted him to fall for someone else, send her home, and never think of her again, actually. And now, weeks later, she's here, just one string-cutting ceremony away from a tearful, guilt-free elimination.

But looking at Josh means picturing his hairy, burly body on top of Krystin's, her hands in his hair and her full-throated laugh reverberating throughout the hotel room. And the thought makes Lauren feel like she didn't win at all—like she lost something, actually, something that might've actually been important. And the worst part of all? For once in her fucking life, she was trying to do the honest thing. The thing that wouldn't hurt Krystin, or Josh. She was being *real*, or whatever. Fuck that.

After all, you're the only woman who wasn't intimate with him, right?

"Lauren, I'm sorry." Josh sighs. "Something just feels off. I've been falling for you, I really have, but I don't know what to do. We're flying out to my parents' next week, and—"

"You can't close this door yet, Josh," Lauren interrupts. "You know our story isn't over."

The door cliché, obviously, softens him. His eyes flicker down to her cherry-painted lips, and before either of them can say anything else, he leans forward and kisses her.

It isn't like any of their other kisses. It's rough, forceful, desperate. Lauren doesn't think about Krystin as she yanks his body flush against hers and runs her fingernails down his back. She doesn't think about Krystin as she squeezes his ass, the back of his thigh. He groans and pulls at her with the kind of aggressive enthusiasm that makes her feel like she knows exactly what he's like in bed, but she's not thinking about Josh fucking Krystin as she grinds against his blatant erection, pulls him closer, closer, so close it's hard to breathe, and bites his lip.

"Lauren, I like you. You don't have to do this," he murmurs as she kisses down his neck, but he notably doesn't move away; in fact, he slides a hand under her dress, and even though it's all still very over-the-underwear, she lets out a small whimper.

It's fake, of course. Like everything else that's happened over the past two months.

You're the only woman who wasn't intimate with him, right?

"Give me another chance," Lauren whispers as their kisses turn more languid than frantic. At this point, she's even more unsure about what she wants or why she's doing any of this. She doesn't know what there is left to win. Is she trying to get Krystin sent home, humiliated and heartbroken? Is she trying to prove that, all along, they've been playing the exact same game, that Lauren was actually a step ahead? Is she just trying to forget the way Krystin kissed her first, the way Krystin drunkenly serenaded her at a shitty bar, the way Krystin looked when she—

What Lauren really wants is for this uncensored footage to air on national TV. She wants it to hurt Krystin, damn it. But that won't happen, because Krystin doesn't care.

"You don't need another chance. I like you," Josh repeats, and it's bullshit, it's bullshit, it's bullshit, because he doesn't even know her. Nobody does.

Holland coughs again from the doorway. "Ceremony in five," she says. "Please make yourselves decent."

"I'm really glad you opened up to me," Josh says, as if she actually had; as if she actually did anything, really, besides dry-hump him for five minutes. But he runs a hand through his hair and shoots her a boyish grin, like those five minutes really did change everything for him. "I can't stop smiling."

There's not enough air in this room, this whole damn building. Lauren feels like she might pass out. "I'll see you out there," she manages.

On her way to the ceremony room, Lauren catches a glimpse of herself in the mirror. She manages to smooth her hair, and she uses a tissue to wipe off her lipstick altogether, but her mascara's slightly streaked. It doesn't matter.

She's the last woman there—McKenzie looks solemn but hopeful, and Krystin just looks completely blank-faced. She takes her place between the two of them, and although she feels Krystin's eyes on her body, she refuses to look at her.

Josh makes his entrance, slow and stoic. "McKenzie. Krystin. Lauren," he says, slightly out of breath. "Hey."

No one responds.

"This is the hardest string-cutting ceremony yet." He looks at the scissors like they're an explosive. "I know I say that every week, but this week was . . . wow. I have three incredible women in front of me, and knowing that I have to break someone's heart tonight, it's just—it hurts me too."

Lauren hears McKenzie swallow.

"Krystin, could you come up here?" he asks, and she does. "I'd like . . . I'd really like you to stay another week. Meet my family."

"I'd like that too," she says. Lauren can't identify how Krystin feels, and she doesn't want to. She doesn't even want to look at her.

There's a pause. Lauren doesn't know if their last-ditch makeout session successfully overrode the awkwardness of last night, but at this point, it doesn't matter. If she stays, she wins. If she stays, she proves that she's untouchable, that she doesn't care.

If she stays, she gets another week with Krystin, which feels like a prize until she remembers it's more like a punishment.

"McKenzie," Josh finally says, and Lauren's surprised to realize she's relieved.

She's *done*. She's out. It's all over.

But then, Josh wipes a literal tear from his eye.

"McKenzie," he says again. "I'm going to have to cut your string."

WEEK 8
CONFESSIONALS

Two women remaining.

McKenzie
25
Scaffolding Heiress
Buffalo, NY

[Sobs.] I can't talk right now. I'm sorry, I just can't talk right now.

Josh
27
Hopeless Romantic
Jericho, NY

McKenzie and I had something so special from day one. This was by far the hardest decision I've made on this journey, and I . . . [Looks away.] I don't know. I'm so lost. I have to just trust that this journey will end in true love. That's all I have left.

Krystin
23
Rodeo Queen
Bozeman, MT

I'm . . . honestly, I'm shocked. I think we've all been considering McKenzie a front-runner, from, like, day one. [Pause.] What? Oh, yeah, I'm thrilled. Um, yeah.

Lauren C.
25
Content Creator
Pinevale, NJ

Well, yeah. I think he's really the one, so I'm willing to, like . . . [Pause.] I'm sorry, it's been an emotional night. Do you think we can pick up this interview tomorrow morning?

CHAPTER NINETEEN

Krystin is going to throw up. She can still hear McKenzie's wails from the villa's courtyard, even as she sits on the tall wooden stool in production's Costa Rican confessional room. She tries to uncross her legs, but her stiletto heel gets caught in her layers of gauzy gown and sends her off balance.

Penny sits across from her, waiting for her to be finished. Whatever made her seem approachable to Krystin is gone now, or at least cracked, because Krystin can see past the veneer of Gen Z humor and charming smiles. She's not a friend.

"Do you need me to repeat the question?" Penny asks.

It's not so much that Krystin didn't hear it as she doesn't know what the fuck to say. *How does it feel to be one of Josh's two final Devotees?* Just dandy! Except, when one Devotee likes to tongue-fuck the other, does she still count?

Here's what she's really thinking: If it's come down to Krystin and Lauren, the woman who never cared about Josh in the first place, who fully intends to shoot down any proposal she's offered, to leave

286

before the question's even popped—Krystin is going to win. Lauren wouldn't endure a fake engagement, even for the clout. Which means it's going to be Krystin at the end of this, and Krystin is going to throw up.

"Um," she stutters, squeezing her eyes shut in hopes it will clear her mind. The bright film lights etch eclipses against the back of her eyelids. "I just—I'm sorry, can you hear that?"

She pauses, waiting for McKenzie's cries to echo into the room. Penny just blinks.

"Hear what?"

"McKenzie," Krystin says, twisting around on her stool to look out the window, but there's nothing but swaying trees. "I can hear her, like—I can hear her talking to Josh."

"I don't hear anything," Penny says. "Besides, you're mic-ed, and that's what our sound will pick up. Background noise is what we have sound mixers for."

"Okay." Krystin scratches her forearm absently. "Okay."

"Okay?"

"Yes." *One, two, three, four, in. One, two, three, four, out.* She presses her lips into a smile. "I can't explain in words how it feels to be so close to this journey's end." That part's true. "I didn't know, when I started, the kinds of feelings I'd be experiencing, and—" Lauren's lips hovering above Krystin, her hips arching up to meet them. Josh, his stubble scraping her bare shoulder. "It's crazy to think this all ends with an engagement. I mean, to know. To know it ends with an engagement," she corrects herself, turning to Penny. "Do you want me to say that again?"

"If you want to."

Krystin looks at the camera. "It's crazy to *know* this all ends with an engagement. The past nine weeks have been leading to this moment. I feel really lucky that Josh is confident enough in our connection that he wants to introduce me to his family." That was good, she thinks, that was enough.

It isn't.

"How do you think the other Honeymoons went?"

Krystin thinks they probably went pretty fucking well, if Lauren's meeting Josh's parents and McKenzie, thinking she was going to marry the man taking prop scissors to the red string around her wrist, fell to a heap on the literal floor.

"I think everyone's Honeymoon went differently. People say this every season—this night is for whatever you want, and that means different things to different people. You don't have to be . . . intimate. You can just talk."

"Were you intimate with Josh?"

The memories flash against her vision, as if they're projected onto the walls of her skull, some invasive supercut. Josh's teeth tugging on her ear, covering her body with his, making her feel claustrophobic with his mere presence. Eventually, as she had many times before, she pulled away, feigning coyness when really, she just plainly didn't want to. But it still felt wrong. It still feels wrong—and every time she remembers it, she wants to *Eternal Sunshine* herself, to scrub herself clean again.

The cameras don't know. They were kicked out around eleven, and filmed a blushing Josh closing the door, with Krystin on the other side. But Penny and Holland and Jim and all the other producers don't care what did or didn't happen, because they're going to push the storyline they want anyway.

Krystin doesn't remember when she got this jaded. Maybe it was watching PAs hose down the chateau cobblestones so it always looks like it's just rained, or maybe it was never eating on camera, or pretending to like things she didn't. Maybe she needed to feel something actually real in order to see what was fake.

Krystin clears her throat. "Josh and I used our Honeymoon to continue to learn about each other," she says. Because no matter how she answered, someone would call her a prude or a slut or whatever.

Penny nods. "How did it feel to see Josh send McKenzie home?"

Krystin swallows another wave of nausea. "Seeing McKenzie leave was heartbreaking. It's obvious that she really loved—loves—Josh, and it sucks to see that taken away from her, even though it means I get to stay." It's the most genuine answer Krystin could have given, but it does nothing to alleviate the guilt eating its way to her core.

She closes her eyes again, and when she opens them, she's steady. "This process has been excruciating," she says, staring straight into the lens. "The only thing that has made it worth it is the knowledge that everything I've ever wanted is waiting for me at the end of it."

Lauren isn't in their suite when Krystin returns from her interview. They didn't get a chance to speak before the string-cutting ceremony—Lauren came straight from her Honeymoon. She didn't look at Krystin the entire time; no knowing glances, no winks, no smirks curling up the corner of her mouth. She was utterly unreadable.

Krystin scrubs at her face in the bathroom, rubbing soap in circles all over her face. She keeps splashing water even after the suds are gone. She wishes she could just sink into it.

The front door clicks shut. Krystin hears shoes kicked off, soft thuds leading into Lauren's room. Krystin towels off her face, and for the first time since she was thirteen, doesn't even bother with moisturizer.

"Lauren?" she calls into the suite. It's dark. She hadn't cared to turn on a light, and it seems Lauren hadn't either. Krystin traces her fingers along the wall as she crosses the room, tripping over the corner of the couch. She mouths a silent *fuck*.

She approaches Lauren's room, nudges the already-cracked door open. "Lauren," she says again.

She can see her faint outline, just a vaguely Lauren-shaped darkness. It's silent. Then: "Did you sleep with him?"

The words shatter on the floor. Krystin feels an inverted version of racing Ringo along the fence: the air completely sucked from her lungs, her heart ballooning into her ribs. Except where that makes Krystin feel more alive than anything, now she feels like she's dying. She wants to gasp for air, but she's afraid to make a sound.

"Don't answer," Lauren says, before she can. "I already know."

But she doesn't know, because it didn't happen. "It—I don't know what to say." The words feel stupid even as they come out of her mouth. She doesn't know how to convince Lauren that she and Josh didn't go any further than sloppy over-the-clothes groping, and part of her wonders how that's any better. "I don't—fuck, I don't know."

"You must have some idea."

"Josh—" Krystin swears she sees Lauren twitch when she says his name. "Josh is probably the best man I've ever known. He's . . . everything I've ever wanted."

Lauren laughs, without any humor. "Well, then I'm really happy for you," she says. "Really fucking happy."

And it's this—the way Lauren says the words, her tone entirely even. The way she's knocked down a wall just to brick it back up again; the way that, even in the dark, Krystin can see a hard set to her jaw.

The way Lauren still, even now, won't ever say what she feels.

"This thing we've been doing," Krystin says, "I don't know what it means. I tried to understand it, I tried to understand it with you, but I'm not *like* you, I—"

"Not *like* me?" Lauren hisses. "You mean a lesbian?"

"No!" Krystin reaches for Lauren's shoulder, but it snakes away from her grasp. "I mean that I can't do things without thinking about them, all the time, too much."

"You weren't thinking when you kissed me," Lauren counters. "Which was *your* choice. And it was your choice to kiss me again. I never forced that on you."

"I'm not saying you did!" Krystin is trying desperately to keep her voice even, but she feels the words starting to crack open in her throat. "I'm saying that I have to think very carefully about my decision here. This whole experience here, it *matters* to me. This is my life."

"I *know* that." There's a softness in her eyes at odds with the acid in her voice. "Krystin, I ratted someone out to save *your ass* after the podcast date. I've tried to make sure you were okay, like, every fucking step of the way, weeks before you kissed me in Buenos Aires. I've been on your side with Delia and on your side with Josh, and I—this entire time, all I've done is show you that I understand what this is. That I care about *your* life and *your* future and what *you* want."

"All you've done is make everything harder and more confusing!" Krystin cries. She can already see the end of this, stretching out ahead of her. It's like she's reaching the end of a long tunnel, just to be met with a slab of concrete. She shudders out a breath. "I'm tired of feeling this way. I want everything—I want everything to go back to normal."

"Why?" she asks, and the word is deep and long, brimming with more than it can hold. Krystin's vision has adjusted to the dark enough that she can see Lauren's eyes, fierce and fathomless. "Why him?"

So Krystin answers. "He's always made me feel certain." *Certain that we could be something serious. Certain we could have a family, with Thanksgivings and first days of school, and stability.*

"You know who else he made feel certain? The thirty-two other women he already sent home. Lily. Kaydie. *McKenzie.*" She spits the last name. "Me, if I cared enough for it to mean anything."

"That's exactly it! You don't care about things the way I care about things." Krystin rakes sweaty fingers through her hair. "You care about things like followers, and brand deals, and doing whatever it takes to get what you want. You don't *want* a relationship—not the way I do."

"That's really what you think of me?" Lauren asks quietly.

Krystin is silent. She thinks myriad things about Lauren, most of them good—but that doesn't mean it isn't true.

This time, Lauren doesn't wait for an answer. "Maybe I've done some selfish, bitchy things, like go on a dating show for the wrong reasons and 'lead on' a guy who's dating a few dozen other women. But if you seriously think I just faked everything with you . . ." Her voice catches. "Clearly, I'm not like Josh. At all. And if that's the kind of person you want to be with, we were never going to work out. But just because I'm not like *him* doesn't mean I don't . . ." She turns away, looking out the window. "It doesn't matter. I hope you and Josh buy a beautiful house, and fill it with seventeen babies, and name them all Josh Junior."

Krystin feels a dull ache scrape into her stomach. There's still so much to say; she can see the words flashing behind her vision, but she can't string any of them together. "I'm sorry," she manages, even though she can't pinpoint what exactly she's sorry for.

Lauren steps toward her, then past her, stopping at the door. Krystin stares at her, the way her hair reflects the moonlight. She knows how it smells.

"Look," Lauren says, her voice quieter now, but still sharp to the touch. "I know Holland is capable of manipulating things for the sake of the show, but she wouldn't explicitly lie. I know you accepted

the Honeymoons card, and I know you spent the night in his room."
She takes a breath. "Is that true?"

Krystin hesitates, then nods, because it is, and she can't defend
herself anymore. Let Lauren think what she wants. She's tired of having to explain herself—to Delia, to Lauren, to everyone. It's easier
this way—clean break—and she wants this night to end. "Yes," she
answers, barely a whisper.

Krystin walks slowly toward where Lauren stands, wavering. Lauren shifts her weight, one foot in front of the other. For a
moment, Krystin thinks Lauren might lean into her and remind her
how she smells, and how she tastes. But Lauren just takes another
step, and closes the door.

Josh's house looks different than it did on TV last season. They
changed the landscaping in the front yard: where there had been tat-
tered shrubs, a small tree has been planted, and the walkway is now
lined with daffodils. Krystin wonders idly how they've survived the
early fall, before she remembers the answer—Holland sent someone
to plant them this morning.

"Feels like we just did this, huh?" Josh says, chipper. "Except,
obviously, now you'll be meeting *my* folks. Oh, how the tables, right?"

"Uh-huh." Even though she's been off the plane since it arrived
in New York last night, Krystin feels like the motion sickness didn't
end with the flight.

"Well, no point standing around here. Shall we?" He offers Krystin an arm. She accepts, if mostly to steady herself.

When the door opens—a heavy oak thing, stained a different
brown since its appearance on Amanda's season—Krystin's vision
becomes a flurry of hugs. Josh's mom envelops her first, squeezing her

into her tiny athletic frame. She almost looks too small for her hair, which falls in brassy waves to the middle of her back.

"Sweetheart," she says into Krystin's shoulder. "Let me get a good look at you." She releases Krystin, leaning backward in exaggerated appraisal. Then she turns to Josh. "She's a beaut, Joshy."

"Joshy?" Krystin says.

Josh shrugs, sheepish. "Since I was a kid. Heyyy, little bro!"

And Krystin can hardly believe it, but Josh pulls his little brother into a headlock, and gives him an honest-to-God noogie. Krystin thought she had a pretty good idea of Jeremiah from watching his scene-stealing performance at Josh's Hometown—but the cameras only captured a fraction of Jeremiah's effervescence.

At a generous five eight, Jeremiah Rosen is a blonde, boyish interpretation of his brother, composed of more energy than flesh. He wrestles away from Josh, fluffing out his curls.

"Jerry," Josh says, reaching an arm around Krystin, "I want you to meet Krystin."

"Hi," Krystin says, offering a timid wave. Should she hug him? Do nineteen-year-old boys like being hugged?

Jeremiah matches her greeting, something distinctly mischievous in his grin. "Hey, Special K."

"Jer," Josh warns.

Krystin has already lost the plot. "Like the cereal?"

"Precisely," Jeremiah replies, ignoring Josh's admonition. "Classic, all-American, wheat-based—"

"Wheat-based?"

"A little basic to some, but at the right time, exactly what you need."

"Jer!" Josh is already more exasperated than Krystin has seen him all season.

"Basic?" Krystin wonders aloud.

Josh spins to face Krystin. "You're not basic, babe."

Krystin knows it isn't the point, but she lingers on the word *babe*.

Josh's mother, Wendy, brushes a hand lightly over Krystin's hair. "Come on, sweetheart, let's get you settled."

She leads them through the house and out onto the back deck, the cameras shadowing them obediently. Holland hovers a few feet away.

"So, Krystin," Wendy says as they sink into the outdoor furniture. "Tell us about yourself. Something we haven't seen."

"Um." Krystin reflects, trying to think of something they wouldn't know about her, even after having watched the past eight episodes of *Hopelessly Devoted*, something that doesn't start with an L. "I'm a Cancer?"

Josh's father leans forward in his wicker chair. "Let's just cut right to the chase. How about you tell us why you think you're a good match for our son."

Wendy slaps her husband lightly on his bicep. "David, can we learn a bit about her before launching into it?"

"I think this is the perfect way to learn more about her," David replies. His tone is firm, but he has the same softness in his eyes as Josh, the kind crinkle at the corners that used to make Krystin feel like everything was going to be okay.

"We make a good team," Krystin answers, looking over at Josh, who nods in encouragement. "We bring out the best in each other."

"I think that's true," Wendy says, bringing a hand to her heart. "Seeing you two together the past two months—" She sighs. "It's been a treat. You're an absolute doll."

Krystin smiles, but her heart is still racing. She worries she isn't smiling big enough, so she smiles harder, but then she worries she looks scary, or scared, so she just settles her lips into a gentle curve and hopes for the best.

"Krystin has been right there by my side throughout this entire experience," Josh tells them, reaching an arm around Krystin's waist. She fights the urge to squirm under his grasp, then scolds her own instinct. "She's been my rock."

"Has that been true for you too?" Wendy asks Krystin.

"Oh, definitely," Krystin responds. *You know who else he made feel certain?* "I always knew that he had my back."

She feels Josh flex his fingers into her skin. She wonders if he can feel her pulse.

"Time for an important question," Jeremiah says, brow furrowing. He steeples his fingers on his knee. "The very first time you met Josh, you said you 'know how to ride 'em, cowboy.' Have you—"

"*Jer!*" Josh nearly leaps from his seat. "Jesus Christ, dude!"

But Jeremiah is laughing, having already delivered the essential lines. Krystin shifts in her seat. She breathes through her nose, but it feels like she's sucking air through one of those tiny red cocktail straws.

And then Wendy's at her side, pulling her out of her seat. "Krystin, let's go have a chat, shall we?"

Wendy leads her back through the house and into the kitchen, where she pours them both a substantial glass of iced tea. Krystin inspects it, turning the icy glass around in her hands.

"Don't worry," Wendy whispers. "It's the Long Island way."

Krystin isn't sure alcohol is the best thing for her persistent nausea, but she takes a sip anyway, in an attempt at graciousness. Wendy takes a seat at the kitchen table, then gestures for Krystin to join her.

"You really are just the sweetest thing," Wendy says, watching Krystin as she slips onto the chair. "Your parents really raised you right. I can't wait to meet them," she adds.

"Oh," Krystin says, setting the glass down on the table. "Thank you. But, I mean, we aren't—it's not—"

"I know, I know. David keeps telling me not to get ahead of myself, but I think you know as well as I—well, you know." She winks.

Krystin nods, then slides the tea closer to her. Wendy must take her silence as nerves, because she reassures her:

"Between you and me," she says, voice low, as if Holland and her crew of cameras aren't standing five feet away from them, "I can see it for you. I can see him getting on one knee."

Krystin wonders how strong a Long Island iced tea has to be in order to make your head spin after two sips. "Really?"

"You're going to fit in so well here." Wendy reaches a hand across the table to Krystin's. "You already do. And—" She takes a deep breath, looking up at the ceiling. When her eyes meet Krystin's they're glassy and bright. "After last season, after Amanda, I just—I really hoped that wouldn't break him. It was so hard to watch that." She swallows, clears her throat. "Krystin, let me tell you something. When you have a child, from the moment they're born, they start to leave you. First, they leave your body, and then they leave again for preschool, and then for dates and for college and for work, and they don't stop leaving for the rest of their life."

Krystin must look mildly panicked, because Wendy waves a hand through the air. "Oh, sweetie, I'm not trying to scare you. It's—they leave you, and the most you can hope for is that they find someone else. That the leaving isn't the end—for them, it's the beginning." She dabs at the corners of her eyes. "Anyway, I'm glad he's found you. He deserves it. I'm sure you do, too."

Krystin flicks her eyes over to Holland, who's looking back at her expectantly. "Um, I'm sorry, do you think I could have some water?"

Wendy looks from Krystin to Holland and back again. "Oh! I'm sorry, I didn't even ask." She hops up from the table and fills a glass from the refrigerator door.

Wendy places the glass in front of her, then sits back down. Krystin takes a long time drinking, feeling every gulp stream down her throat.

"Krystin," Holland prompts, when she's finished, "what's your response to Wendy?"

"I think . . ." Krystin begins, looking directly at Wendy, but she doesn't know what she thinks. She just keeps picturing Josh on a white sand beach, or on the top of a skyscraper, or in a fucking helicopter or something, leaning his knee into the ground and pulling out a ring and asking her and asking her and asking her. And then she sees it on her finger, because she knows that if he asked, she wouldn't know how to say no.

And now, at the worst possible time, in the worst possible place, Krystin knows what she wants. Or really, she knows what she *doesn't* want, because even if Lauren wasn't part of all this, Krystin couldn't marry Josh. And the realization makes everything—Wendy's hopeful eyes, Holland's omniscient gaze, the family portraits with everyone dressed in khakis—so much worse.

"I have to talk to Josh," she says, and leaves the room before anyone can stop her.

Krystin finds Josh outside, drinking a Stella in an Adirondack across from David. It feels colder now, the wind's serrated edge skating across her skin.

"Josh," she says once she's close enough. "Can we—" But it isn't a question. Not this time. "I have to talk to you."

"Now?" He looks from his dad to Penny and the cameras. They were clearly in the middle of a father-son heart-to-heart. Penny looks pissed that Krystin interrupted what was about to be very good television. *If they can just wait, I'll give them something better,* she thinks bitterly.

"Yeah, sure," Josh says, once it's clear Krystin isn't moving. "Of course."

He leads her through a footpath along the house's side that opens onto the front yard. The cameras follow shakily behind them; Krystin registers distantly the front door opening, and Holland stepping onto the porch.

"What's up?" Josh asks. "Is everything okay?"

"Um—" Krystin takes a breath, but her lungs quiver. "*Fuck.*"

"Krystin, hey." Josh reaches out for her, leaning into a hug, but Krystin dodges him. He peels back from her, visibly hurt.

"Don't touch me," she says. "You don't—you don't want to touch me."

Josh's brows knit, confusion pooling between them. "What's going on? Why are you so upset?"

"This isn't going to work," Krystin cries. It's the first time she's said it, the first time she's even thought of it as a full sentence. "This isn't going to work," she says again, quieter, for herself.

Josh is incredulous. "What? Is this because of what my brother said? He's a dick, but—"

"No, of course not. I would never—" But she stops herself, because the list of things she would never do is evidently shorter than she ever believed. "Your family is great, truly."

He looks unconvinced. "I know they can be a lot, I mean, I *told* you—"

"It's not them," Krystin says. "I swear."

Josh crosses his arms in front of his chest, realization dawning. "Then it's me."

"It's not you either." Krystin shivers. "Trust me, I wish it was you."

Josh scoffs. "So you're saying 'it's not you, it's me.'"

"I—Yeah, I guess I am."

A breeze rustles through the trees, sending the hairs on her arms on edge. A browning leaf fumbles drowsily through the air, landing at Josh's feet. He bends to pick it up.

"You said 'knew,'" he says after a moment, rolling the leaf stem between his thumb and forefinger.

"What?"

"Back on the deck. You said you *knew* I had your back. Past tense. Like you don't know that anymore."

"Josh." Krystin sighs, her shoulders dropping. "I just meant that was how I felt, in Costa Rica."

"Still," he says, still twirling the leaf. "I don't think you would have said it like that if you saw us at the end of this." He drops the leaf. Krystin watches its clumsy descent.

This is the worst feeling in the world, Krystin thinks. *The worst feeling in the world.* She wraps her arms around herself, clutching at her elbows. The only thing worse would be staying with Josh anyway, without letting him find someone who reciprocates his feelings—without letting herself find the same.

"This isn't the end for you," she says, remembering Wendy's words.

Josh laughs, mirthless. "Isn't it, though?"

"It's not," Krystin insists. The wind sends a piece of her hair flying out in front of her face, and she brushes it back behind her ear. "You have so much ahead of you, Josh, I promise." She almost mentions Lauren, but she knows that pretty soon he won't have her either. It's too much, the gravity of everything, her decisions from the past nine weeks falling like shrapnel all around her.

Krystin hears a whimper, and when she turns toward it, she sees Wendy standing in the open doorway. David comes from behind her, leading her away at Holland's instruction.

She looks at the house then, at its East Coast grandeur, and back at Josh, who became himself inside its walls. And then she realizes, without an ounce of humor, that this is the second time Josh's heart has been broken by a woman in his front yard.

"I don't know, Krystin," Josh says. He rubs the back of his neck. "Whatever you wanna call it, this looks like a clear fuckin' ending to me."

CHAPTER TWENTY

Sharing a Long Island hotel suite with someone you may or may not be in love with—someone who just completely broke your heart, rejected you, and then ran off into the metaphorical sunset with your communal boyfriend—is a special kind of hell.

Luckily, Lauren hasn't had to speak to Krystin once since her generic, emotionless "I'm sorry." There was one time Krystin accidentally walked in on Lauren brushing her teeth, and she just scurried out without another word, but besides that, they had zero contact—and then yesterday morning, she went to meet the Rosens. Lauren stayed behind, watching Bravo and drinking producer-provided mimosas in bed. Krystin never came back. At least, she didn't come back to their conjoined bathroom.

She's halfway through an episode of *Below Deck* when there's a knock at her door.

It's Josh. He looks disheveled, unhappy, and Lauren knows why: She's supposed to meet his parents today. Well, she was supposed to. Josh is three hours early, and there's only one possible explanation.

"Hey," Josh says. "Can we talk?"

The Long Island Marriott is, by far, the least glamorous place Lauren's stayed during her *Hopelessly Devoted* tenure. To his (or, well, the producers') credit, Josh picks a somewhat picturesque area for his breakup with Lauren: a bench near a few large cedar trees, autumn leaves littering the ground that remind her of the rose petals in Buenos Aires. A small camera crew is set up in the corner, and Holland and Penny are there too, with clipboards and venti Starbucks coffees.

"So," Josh says. "Krystin met my family yesterday."

"I'm aware." Lauren shivers. This time, Josh doesn't offer her his jacket.

"And I know you were supposed to meet them today," he continues.

Lauren wants to tell Josh that he doesn't have to do this. The last thing she wants is a speech about how much the Rosens loved Krystin, details about everything he and Krystin have in common, platitudes about how he hopes Lauren stays a lifelong friend.

"The truth is," Josh says, "I don't need you to meet my parents. I know what I want—*who* I want."

Lauren swallows and looks away, focusing on a restless squirrel circling one of the cameramen. "Josh. Hey. It's okay."

"The past week has given me so much clarity. Our conversation after Honeymoons, saying goodbye to McKenzie." He sucks in a breath. "Saying goodbye to Krystin."

"Wait. What?" Lauren turns her whole body to face Josh. "Krystin is . . ."

"She's gone. And because I don't want to start this next part of our journey together with anything but complete honesty, I'm going to be transparent. She . . . eliminated herself." He says the words like he's trying to speak with shards of glass in his mouth.

Krystin eliminated herself.

Lauren must have said it out loud, though, because Josh grabs both of her hands and responds, "She did. But, Lauren . . . it was never Krystin."

"It was never Krystin," Lauren repeats. She's starting to *feel* like Krystin, with the way she's just echoing every word Josh says.

"This entire journey, there's only one woman who's been certain about us, invested in our future. She's beautiful, and she's strong, and I think she could be a kickass podcast co-host."

No. No, no, no.

Josh gets down on one knee. "Lauren, I am hopelessly devoted to—"

"Josh," she interrupts. "Hold on."

He frowns. "Is everything . . ."

"Are you proposing to me?" she blurts out.

Now he grins, but it's unsteady. "Well, I was trying to."

"Why?"

"What do you mean, why?" Josh stands up. He looks embarrassed, guilty, and confused at once—maybe even a little angry. "Lauren. Like I said, I'm not just doing this because Krystin left. What I want is someone who can commit to me. Commit to us."

"Josh. I'm not the one you want," Lauren says softly. Weirdly enough, she isn't thinking about her edit, or the viewers, or even Krystin, who might watch this at home in a few days. She's thinking that this poor, misguided, well-intentioned man actually thinks she could be his soulmate. And he knows absolutely nothing about her. "I mean, what do you like about me? Be honest."

He chuckles. "Lauren. Come on."

"I mean it," she says. "You like that I'm hot, and that I stepped outside my comfort zone on a few group dates, and that I'm here. None of those are reasons to marry someone."

"That's not . . ." Josh looks at the ground, then back up. "Lauren. I really do think you're the one for me. I want to give this a shot."

"You said you want honesty and transparency," Lauren says. "And the honest, transparent truth is, I'm not the one for you. I promise. And no offense, but you're really not the one for me."

"I just don't get it." He glances toward the production team, and Lauren reluctantly looks too. Holland's mouthing a message to Josh, or maybe Lauren. *Keep going.*

"The answer's no. I'm sorry." Lauren's trying to be gentle—and spare Josh some of his dignity—but it's getting harder. "Josh, listen to me. I'm really not the one you want. We're not meant to be together."

"You are." Still, he finally stands up. "Lauren. I know we are."

The words pop out before Lauren can stop them. "Then maybe you're not the one *I* want."

Now he looks thoroughly embarrassed, and maybe a little frustrated. Lauren remembers the way he looked when Amanda eliminated him on her season; the way McKenzie looked when Josh cut her string. *That's* heartbreak, Lauren thinks. This is . . . shame. Rejection. Confusion. And while she still feels guilty for bruising his ego on national TV, his response just affirms what she already knew.

Josh never liked her, let alone *loved* her.

It's a relief, until she remembers *why* he doesn't love her—because she's cold. She's calculating and careless.

Because it's impossible to like someone who's impossible to know.

"I think I should go," Lauren says. "Take care, okay?"

It's a short, easy, but traffic-filled drive from Long Island to Newark. Lauren distracts herself with her phone, but it doesn't even matter that she now has complete, unfiltered access to Instagram, Twitter, Reddit, whatever. She can't bring herself to look up anything related to the show, and even if she emerged with a somewhat positive edit, she knows that's about to be shot to hell when America watches her reject Josh's attempted proposal, proving once and for all she wasn't on this show to find love with the lead.

Her assigned driver heads over the bridge, and Lauren opens a blank text message before turning her phone off altogether. Damian's the only person she could contact, anyway, and they didn't exactly leave things on the best of terms in that Olive Garden bathroom. His account was the first one she checked when she got her phone back; despite their fight, he never did make a coming out post.

But then Lauren realizes there is someone she can text—two people, in fact. Her parents.

"Eighty-eight Oak Street, you said?" the driver asks, once they're stalled in traffic.

"Actually," Lauren finds herself saying, "could you go to seventy-six Thompson Ave? It's on the way."

"Also in Newark?" He punches something into the GPS on his phone.

"In Pinevale," Lauren says. "It's my parents' house."

Her dad, Steven, is the first one to greet Lauren when she shows up, depleted and quiet, with her matching luggage set and a bare ring finger. "Well," he says, clapping his daughter on the back. "I had a feeling he wasn't your perfect match. He had a weak character, if you ask me."

"Actually," Lauren replies, wheeling her suitcases inside, "I think I might've been the problem."

"You?" Steven crosses his arms. "Never."

"Hi, baby." Trina walks in from the kitchen, and her thin, tanned arms squeeze Lauren tight. "How are you doing?"

"I'm fine. Really," Lauren says. "It's just . . . nice to be back here." When her parents just look at each other, she quickly adds, "It *is* okay I came here, right?"

"Oh, honey, of course." Trina rubs her shoulders, and Lauren closes her eyes. For a second, she lets herself feel like a little kid who just got home from a horrible day at school. "We're so glad you're here. Your sister even drove over from school."

"She did?" Lauren softens. She's completely lost track of time. "Isn't it a weekday?"

"A Monday," Steven agrees. "But your mom called her as soon as you texted, and she came over. We thought we could all go to Giovanni's for brunch tomorrow. Whaddaya think?"

"Yeah, I don't know," Lauren says, even though she has literally nothing else to do besides catching up on Instagram and emails. "Maybe."

"Well." Trina gives her one more squeeze, then makes her way back into the kitchen. "Why don't you put your stuff in your room and take a shower? You must be exhausted."

She *is* exhausted. It's hard for Lauren to fully comprehend the fact that, just this morning, she was rejecting a marriage proposal, and tonight she's about to fall asleep in her childhood bed. She feels much older and younger than twenty-five. "I think I will," she says. "And I think . . . I'm down for brunch tomorrow, too. If you're all sure you have nothing to do."

"Nothing at all!" Trina shouts from the kitchen.

Lauren doesn't go to her bedroom—at least, not at first. She leaves her suitcases in the hall and follows the sound of an old Lorde song to Rachel's door. She knocks, but doesn't wait for her to say anything before she walks in.

"Laur!" Rachel jumps up from her desk, and like it's the most natural thing in the world, she engulfs her in a hug. "Oh my God. Are you okay?"

"I am," Lauren says, but she hugs her back. It's a little awkward, but as Rachel's hands dig into her back, she thinks, *This is my sister. My little sister. She drove an hour to make sure I was okay.*

"I mean." Rachel heads back to her desk and pauses her Spotify. "You don't have to tell me anything. But are you sure you're okay?"

"Yeah, Rachel, I'm sure. There's really nothing to tell." But Lauren doesn't leave. Instead, she sits down on her sister's bed, accidentally squashing Ellie, her old favorite stuffed elephant. "It happened. I'm home."

There's a beat. Then Rachel walks over and takes a seat beside Lauren. "I'm sorry," she says. "About what I said at your Hometown."

"Huh? When?" All Lauren really remembers from her conversation with Rachel is her own vague bitchiness.

"When I said Josh didn't seem like your type." Rachel plays with a strand of her hair. "Like, *obviously* he was, I guess. You made it to the very end. Did he choose McKenzie?"

Lauren had almost forgotten that the general public hadn't watched overnights yet. "No," she says. "He chose me. Actually."

Rachel's eyes widen. "Did he propose?"

"Mm-hm." Lauren reaches for Ellie, just to have something to squeeze.

"But you said . . . no," Rachel clarifies.

"I said no." Rachel doesn't have to ask why—the question is implicit. "You were right. He wasn't my type."

"Well." Rachel shrugs. "You were also right. I don't know your type at all."

There's another silence. Then Lauren breaks it.

"It's women," she says. She brushes a stray strand of hair off her white tee. "My type is women."

It isn't scary to admit. If anything, she's only saying it because she can't bring herself to care about anything right now—her self-imposed walls, her brand, her strained relationship with her sister. But then Rachel speaks.

"Alisha Singh," she says quietly.

Lauren feels herself flush, feels her head snap toward Rachel. "Sorry?"

"That girl who used to come over here in middle school. Right?" Rachel sounds nervous, like she's half afraid Lauren might bitch her out. "And Sierra Ashbery. You always used to change your outfit, like, four times before driving to her place."

"Fuck you. I did that before going out with *any* of my friends," Lauren says, but her lips start to curve upward.

"That hostess who worked at the Cheesecake Factory when we were both in high school," Rachel continues. "You *always* offered to go pick up the takeout alone. Like, every time Dad ordered."

Lauren can't help it—she laughs, because Rachel's right. She did voluntarily drive to the Cheesecake Factory every single time, and it definitely wasn't because she cared about doing her parents any favors.

"I'm actually with you on that one," Rachel says. "Her boobs were amazing. And did she have, like, a British accent?"

"Australian," Lauren says automatically, and then they're both laughing. This whole time, Rachel *knew*. Before her stint on *Hopelessly Devoted*, Lauren would have felt furious, humiliated, but now it's just funny. Of *course* she's not slick. Of course she's blatantly, obviously gay. She always has been.

"You're my sister," Rachel says, once their giggles have subsided. "I know we're not, like, friends. But I've known you my whole life. I'm not surprised."

"Then why . . ." Lauren shakes her head. "Why did you nominate me? All those years ago, I mean."

"I mean, honestly?" Now Rachel looks somewhat sheepish. "You and Damian, like, only ever wanted to hang out with me when we all watched that show together. It's the only thing you'd ever text me about—*did you see what she was wearing on* After the Final String, *did you hear who the next lead will be,* all of that. I guess that in, like, a weird way, I thought it would make us closer, or something. Or at least you'd like me more if I got you cast on your favorite show."

Guilt climbs up Lauren's throat. "You're my sister, Rachel. You didn't have to get me cast on *Hopelessly Devoted* in order for us to, like, bond."

As soon as she says it, though, she realizes: She *wouldn't* be right here, having this conversation in Rachel's childhood bedroom, if she hadn't gone on the show. If she hadn't met Krystin. If she hadn't ruined things with Krystin, hadn't humiliated Josh, hadn't destroyed her own reputation. Rachel must realize it too, because she gives her a skeptical look.

"I haven't been the best sister," Lauren admits, more softly. "But I love you. Okay? And I want to change that. I want . . . I want us to be friends."

"I want that too," Rachel says. Her voice is small and hopeful, but becomes more firm as she adds, "And I love you, obviously. No matter what your type is."

Lauren debates telling her sister about Krystin, about Josh, about the entire thing. But then her phone buzzes—it's Damian.

*wtf i had to find out you're home from your mom's instagram????
Girl come downstairs right now*

"Damian's here." Lauren shoots him a quick response. "I should go down there."

Rachel nods. "If you wanna, like, hang out later . . ." She twists another piece of hair. "I'll be around."

"Sure," Lauren says.

She means it.

After a quick jaunt downstairs, Lauren opens her front door to Damian, standing sheepishly with his hands in his denim pockets. "Why didn't you just come inside?" she asks. "My parents are home."

"I thought you were pissed at me." He gives her a look. "You didn't even tell me you were back in town."

"Well, I thought *you* were pissed at *me*." Lauren crosses her arms.

"I kind of am," he responds. "I can't believe you stayed on the fucking show."

Lauren sighs. She doesn't really want to do this inside, so she takes a seat on her front steps. "I fucked up."

"Yeah." Damian sits down next to her. "You did. But you're still, like, my favorite person in the world."

"I don't deserve that." Lauren kicks a rock with her bare, pedicured foot. "I don't think I'm a very good person."

"That's . . . not true," he says carefully. "But I'm not gonna tell you you didn't do something shitty. Because I think you did. How far did you make it, the final two?"

Lauren winces. "He proposed."

Damian lets out a strangled sound. "You're kidding me."

"Dames, she slept with him." Her words are all wobbly, and her vision is blurring in front of her, and if she was trying to hold back tears during her conversation with Rachel—well, now she's crying for real. "We had . . . we had a thing, and she liked me, and for a second I was going to leave. I really was." She can't tell if Damian can even hear her over her sobs, but she can't stop talking. "I found out from a *producer*. And when I tried to talk to her about it, she, like . . . she said Josh was the perfect guy she always wanted and I was a bitch who didn't care about things."

"Wait, slow down." She doesn't know when Damian started hugging her, but his steady, solid body is holding hers. "She called you a bitch? Only I can call you a bitch."

"No." Lauren sniffles. "She wouldn't say that. But she said I, like . . . I only care about followers and being famous and stuff."

"Well." Damian pulls away, just a bit. "That's not true. But it makes sense that she thinks that, right? If that's . . . why you went on the show in the first place. Why you stayed so long."

"I stayed so long for *her*, Dames," she says, her voice still cracking. "I mean, yeah, the influencer stuff—that was part of it. But I knew, like, the second I left . . . I think I just knew I'd never see her again."

He nods. "So Josh . . . eliminated her? And then chose you?"

"She eliminated herself." Lauren wipes her teary, sweaty face with her hands until she's positive her eyeliner is all over her face. "I don't know why."

"You could ask her," Damian points out. "Slide in those DMs."

Lauren laughs, but it's empty. "I don't think so."

Damian shrugs. They're both quiet.

"I do wonder, though," she says. The tears have finally stopped. "Why she left. What she told him."

There's another silence, and then Damian stands up. "One second," he said. "I left something in the car."

She waits, and then he comes back from his Jeep with a Magnolia Bakery box in one hand and a bottle of rosé in the other.

"Damian," Lauren says, standing up. "Are you seriously—"

"You want to know what happened, right?" He shakes the wine bottle like it's a trophy. "It's Monday night. *Hopelessly Devoted*'s on at eight. And if we start watching now, we can catch the end of *Jeopardy!*"

"Yeah, no. I'm shutting this down." Lauren shifts her weight. "They're airing Honeymoons tonight. I'd rather not watch her fuck my ex-boyfriend."

"I mean . . ." Damian gives her a look. "It's not like they show that part."

"Doesn't make it any better."

"Lauren." He puts down the bottle, then the box. He hugs her. Lauren doesn't know if she's ever had so many hugs in one day. "It sucks. But we'll do it together, okay? And maybe as we're watching, you can, like . . . tell me what really happened. If you want."

She sighs.

"Well?" Damian raises an eyebrow. "Is that a yes?"

"One condition," Lauren says, opening her front door to let Damian in. "We should invite Rachel to watch too."

He grins. "Sounds like my perfect night."

Nothing could have prepared Lauren for the discomfort of watching herself on TV. She's pretty sure that witnessing the tantric yoga date is even more excruciating than *doing* it.

"Lauren and I have the physical chemistry down," confessional-Josh says. The show cuts to an image of the two of them breathing heavily and gazing into each other's eyes, and present-day Lauren wants to jump out a window. "But . . . I want to know if our relationship runs deeper than that. Hopefully, we can find out tonight."

"What an asshole," Rachel says, taking a bite of her Magnolia banana pudding. "He's totally keeping you around 'cause he wants to fuck."

313

"I disagree," Damian interjects. "He's actually keeping her around because he's waiting to know her *more*. On a deeper level. Like he said."

"See, this is why you fall for fuckboys," Rachel points out.

Damian sighs. "You can't help who you love."

The worst part, obviously, is watching Krystin's Honeymoon with Josh. But even though there's a lot of kissing and flirting, Lauren finds herself taking stock of the parts that aren't quite right, noticing the way that Krystin always pulls away first. The way Josh's jokes don't really make her laugh, the way her smile doesn't exactly reach her eyes in any of her post-overnight confessionals.

"Just because two people spend the night together doesn't mean they were intimate," confessional-Lauren says. There's a pause. "Right?"

Lauren jumps up. "This is unbearable," she says. "I'm getting more wine."

But she can't pull herself away from the screen. She just stands there in front of the TV, like her father does whenever he insists Trina's soaps are "stupid" and he's "just watching for a second." The camera cuts to Josh's confessional.

"Lauren and I, the dates we've been on . . . they've all been really, um, physical," he says. "Tango, yoga . . . I don't want her to think that's all I want. I hope she doesn't think that."

"See!" Damian points at the screen, vindicated. Then he looks back at Lauren. "Sorry."

"It's okay."

Confessional-Josh's words are kind of . . . comforting. Sure, he never really knew her. He never really liked her—at least, not for *the right reasons*. But he's a good person. He deserves a fighting chance at finding love.

Lauren took that from him. And honestly? Krystin took that from him too.

"Ew," Damian says as TV-Lauren and TV-Josh start making out. "*Now* we can turn this off."

"I'm gonna go try to call someone, actually," Lauren says. "You guys can . . . have fun with this. I'll be back."

Damian gasps. "Are you calling Krystin?"

"Nope."

Lauren leaves before he or Rachel can ask anything else.

For someone with a massive social media platform—and as someone who's probably busy fielding media requests and coping with the trauma of getting dumped twice on camera—Josh is surprisingly easy to contact. All she does is send a quick message asking if he's around to talk. He doesn't follow her on Instagram, but her DM request must have caught his attention. *Perks of finally getting verified*, Lauren thinks as his typing bubble pops up, disappears, and then pops up again.

Don't know if I'm ready to talk but thanks.

Lauren sighs. *please.*

The bubble pops up again, then it disappears again. Then her phone rings—it's Josh, calling her through the Instagram app.

"Lauren," he says. "What's up?"

"Um." She really didn't expect to actually get him on the phone. "Not much. I'm, uh, watching *Hopelessly Devoted*."

"Oh," he says. "It's Honeymoons tonight, right?"

"You're not watching?"

"You couldn't pay me to."

He doesn't sound heartbroken. He sounds . . . a little annoyed, and very defeated, but that's it.

"There's something I should've told you, Josh. Like, a long time before I rejected you on camera." She thinks she hears him let out a small whoosh of a breath, but he just waits for her to continue. Faintly, in the distance, she hears Damian's deep voice and Rachel's cackling laugh. "The thing is, I don't like men. At all."

There's a pause, and then Josh lets out a small, hard laugh. "If you're trying to let me down easy . . ."

"I'm gay, Josh," Lauren says, as softly as she can. "I wasn't straight when my sister first nominated me for the show, and I definitely wasn't straight when we were together, and it's . . . like, it's okay if you don't believe me now, or if you just don't care. I wouldn't give a shit if I were you. I'd probably—I mean, Jesus. I'd hate me."

Josh doesn't say anything.

"If you want to anonymously leak this to Deuxmoi, I won't hold it against you," Lauren tries to joke. Embarrassingly, though, her eyes are starting to well up. "Or bring it to Holland and ask for a redo season, or—I don't know, I could come out on *After the Final String*, explain the real reasons things didn't work out between us."

She pauses, and Josh pauses, too. Maybe he's considering it. The wildest part? Lauren's considering it, too. She imagines the chaos it would unleash in the *Hopelessly Devoted* universe, and in her own life: the Reddit threads and TikToks picking apart every interaction between Lauren and Josh, the harassment and homophobia in Lauren's DMs. The once-terrifying idea of the entire world knowing who Lauren is and what she really wants—who she really wants.

It feels less scary now, though. Or maybe she's still scared, but . . . "I'm so tired of lying all the time," Lauren says. She can hear Josh's breath on the other line. "And I'm tired of hurting people because of it. Good people. And I just wish . . ."

She thinks of Krystin, their fight after the overnights. She thinks of Damian, angry and pleading in an Olive Garden bathroom stall. She thinks of her middle school crush on Alisha and her high school hookups with Sierra and the horrific, humiliating sight of McKenzie bawling as Josh walked her out. She thinks of Krystin, again—in Montana with Delia, maybe, or some guy exactly like Josh, promising her everything she's ever wanted.

"I wish I'd done a lot of things differently," she finally says. "And I'm just really sorry."

"I'm listening," Josh says after a beat. "Just wrapping my head around . . . this. I mean, all those times we kissed . . ." She can practically see his brows furrowing. "You really were just . . . not there to find love, were you? Ever."

"I'm not proud of it." She sinks down to the floor and pulls her thighs to her chest. "But to be honest . . . I mean, I've been watching *Hopelessly Devoted* since middle school, and none of the relationships even last. I really thought none of us were there to find love. I thought it would all be fake."

"You know, Lauren?" He lets out a hollow laugh. "I'm starting to think maybe it is."

"No," Lauren says, and she's surprised by the ferocity in her voice.

"No," he repeats.

"I spent time with those girls, and seriously, they liked you. Not me, obviously," Lauren adds quickly.

"Yeah, yeah, okay. I got that."

She has a feeling Josh is smiling now—something about his inflection is kind, earnest, and it makes her smile too, even as she blinks back a tear. "But people come on this show for all kinds of reasons, and that doesn't mean they won't . . . get caught off guard and fall for someone anyway. Someone who's really special." She thinks of Krystin, and her eyes water even more.

"I see," Josh says slowly.

"Like McKenzie, you know?" Lauren blurts out, suddenly worried he can read her mind. "She wanted to be with you, and for what it's worth—I mean, my word's worth nothing, I guess, but I think you're a fucking catch. You're an amazing listener, and you see the best in people, and you're honest, and . . ." Lauren swallows. "That's really rare. Clearly."

She can hear Josh's breathing on the other line. "Thank you," he says, like he means it. "This is, um, a lot to take in."

"I know."

For a few minutes, they just trade breaths. It's like they're on their cursed yoga date again.

"Well," he says, and then his tone abruptly shifts. "Thank you for sharing that with me."

It takes Lauren a second, but then she realizes—he's making a *joke*. He's parroting the words she said when he told her he was falling for her. "Oh, God," she says. "I'm, um. I'm sorry about that."

"Don't be," he says. "I mean, look. I appreciate that you apologized for the other stuff. It fucking sucks that you led me on."

Lauren nods, even though he can't see her.

"But don't apologize for being honest with me at the beach, or on Long Island," he says. "Or now. I just wish you'd done it sooner."

"I wish I had too." She can't hear the hum of the TV anymore. She wonders if Damian and Rachel nodded off to sleep. "If I can do anything—if you want me to explain myself at *After the Final String*, or . . ." She lets herself trail off.

"It's up to you," Josh says. "But I'm glad you told me."

"Yeah. Of course." There's more she could tell him, of course, but it's not all hers to tell. At the end of the day, it just feels good to have an honest, real conversation with Josh, after exchanging weeks and weeks of on-camera bullshit.

"Take care, Lauren, okay?" He sounds like he has something else he wants to add, or maybe ask, but he doesn't. Before she can say goodbye back, he hangs up.

Maybe he forgives her. Maybe he doesn't. Maybe they'll actually become friends, somehow, once all the dust has settled; or maybe he'll decide he never wants to see her again. Either way, they're contractually obligated to interact at the *After the Final String* special in two weeks, where he'll have the opportunity to call her out, if that's what he wants or needs to do. She's positive that by then she'll be a bona fide *Hopelessly Devoted* villain. Her brand will tank. She'll have to, in her dad's words, *get a real job*.

But Damian was right, as he often is: There are more important things than followers, and she found and lost several of those things in the span of two months. But then she leaves her phone in the kitchen and walks back to her best friend and sister. They're cuddled up on the couch, sipping rosé and dissecting their favorite TV show, and Lauren feels lucky. She feels loved.

"Sorry about that," she says.

"Don't be." Rachel's voice is firm. "Are you okay?"

"I think so. Actually . . ." Lauren plops back down on the sofa, in between the two of them. "How would you feel about watching the rest of Josh's season so far? From the beginning."

Damian looks at Rachel, then back at Lauren. "You're sure you want that?"

"Yeah. I want , , ,"

It feels important, though she can't articulate why. Maybe it's about owning up to what she did, to who she hurt. Maybe it's about watching her and Krystin's story unfold, even if she has to fill in all the blanks herself: their confrontation after mud wrestling, their moments at the chateau, the time Krystin told Lauren she was smart and sounded like she genuinely believed it.

Maybe it's about proving to herself that a part of the show was real, after all. That she *did* fall in love—for the first, for the only time—even if it wasn't with Josh.

"I want to tell you what really happened," Lauren finally says. She reaches for the remote.

WEEK 9
CONFESSIONALS

No women remaining.

Krystin
23
Rodeo Queen
Bozeman, MT

[Interior Range Rover.] I, um. [Turns away from camera.] I feel—[voice cracks]—absolutely devastated. I know that this is my decision, and I think—I know—it's the right one, but—[Sniffles.] The last thing I wanted to do was hurt anyone. Maybe it was always going to happen. [Long pause.] This experience taught me a lot of things, and one of them is to be honest with myself. [Pause. Exhale.] I do have feelings for someone. It just isn't Josh.

Lauren C.
25
Content Creator
Pinevale, NJ

I've learned a lot on this journey, but I think the biggest lesson I've taken away is, like . . . [Looks away.] I don't want to settle. [Pause.] And honestly, I don't want Josh to settle, either. [Pause.] Regrets? I mean, I do have—No, I don't regret rejecting him. We weren't meant to be.

CHAPTER TWENTY-ONE

The stables are empty when Krystin pulls the Corolla into the lot—though, at nearly six in the morning, she's not sure what else she expected. She's still on Eastern time, and besides, she didn't sleep much anyway. She hasn't since she got home nearly two weeks ago.

Krystin treads across the mud, boots flattening the occasional patch of grass. This steadily into autumn, the sun is still at least an hour away from rising; the sky is vast and dark, and so silent. When she was younger, training for her first competitions, she used to get to the stables this early every day. She watched the other girls wipe crust from their eyes, groggy and irritable, their parents and trainers chastising them for complaining about being awake before dawn. And it's not like Krystin wasn't also tired—she was exhausted, and sore, and worried about her calc homework. But Montana is never so silent as in the very early morning, black as a sensory deprivation tank, so incredibly still that Krystin feels as if time is suspended. Sometimes, while making coffee in the kitchen, the only light coming from the microwave, she feels as if she's in deep space. She never feels so calm.

Ringo grunts affectionately when she approaches him. She traces his face, drawing a line from the diamond on his forehead all the way down to his velvet nose. She slips the bridle over his ears, nudges the bit between his teeth. She can see her reflection in his glassy eyes. He bends readily under her instruction, and she leads him to the ring.

The arena gate surrenders under her weight, exhaling a familiar creak. A few red flakes of rust flutter to the ground. Then she places a boot in the stirrup and hoists herself easily into the saddle.

As good as it felt to ride in Patagonia, it didn't feel anything close to Ringo. Their movements are entirely fluid; her hips melt into his; where she ends, he begins. They walk, trailing the fence for a while. She presses her heels into his flank, and he falls into a trot. Again, and they're running.

After a while, Krystin dismounts and drags three barrels into the center of the arena. They bolt from one end of the oval ring; she pulls Ringo in a tight cloverleaf pattern, racing around each barrel and back again. She does it again. And again. And again.

She doesn't think about anything while they run. She doesn't think about Lauren, and her glossy hair and full lips and the swath of skin inside her thighs that feels like silk. She doesn't think about Josh or the way his face crumpled in his front yard, or David pulling Wendy away from the sight of Krystin breaking her son's heart. She doesn't think about Lauren and Josh together, on Long Island, sitting around the same bonfire as Krystin did, holding hands as Lauren lies her way to the life she's always wanted. She doesn't think about how Josh will respond when Lauren finally, inevitably, breaks his heart too. Or maybe she already has—Krystin doesn't even know if they're still filming. All she knows is that Lauren won't marry him either. She never would.

Krystin wipes at the sweat beading on her forehead. Her heart rattles against her ribs. She leads Ringo around the pattern, tighter this time, threading each needle with a lifetime of precision. She imagines judges sitting in the empty first row, sees hundreds of faces filling the barren bleachers. She hears their cheers, their whoops and hollers, and smells cotton candy and buttery popcorn mingled with dirt.

She pulls on the reins, coaxing Ringo to rest. She squints her eyes shut, feeling the blood pump from her heart into every finger and toe. She waits for the room to stop spinning around her, leans forward to wrap her arms around Ringo's neck, brushing his damp coat.

When she opens her eyes, Delia is sitting in the third bleacher row, elbows resting on her knees. Krystin feels her heart jump into her throat. Their eyes meet, and Delia stretches into an upright position.

Krystin clucks and nudges Ringo forward. They walk slowly to the fence; Delia pauses for a moment, then stands, descending the handful of steps and stopping in front of the ring. They meet at the edge, but Krystin doesn't dismount. She just sits there, five and a half feet in the air, afraid that if she stands, her legs won't be able to hold her.

Delia leans against the fence; it whines under her. "Hey."

"Hey."

Ringo takes another step forward under Krystin, and Delia reaches out to pet his nose.

"I think he missed me," she says.

Krystin attempts a laugh, but it comes out more like a sniff.

Delia strokes Ringo's face, brushing hair out of his eyes. When she speaks, she looks only at him. "Was he the only one who missed me?"

Krystin waits for Delia to tilt her head to her, but she doesn't. "No," she says softly. "He wasn't."

Delia's lips break into a faint smile, her eyes still glued to the horse.

Krystin sighs, then kicks her leg out of the stirrup and across Ringo's back, dropping gently onto the loose dirt. "How'd you know where I was?"

When Delia finally looks at her, her gaze is at once leaden and bright. "It's like I said. I know you."

Krystin doesn't say anything. She combs her finger through Ringo's mane, and lets the breathing fill the space. Then she leads him out of the arena and back to the stable, lifts the saddle from his back and onto its rack, hangs the bridle and reins on the tack. It doesn't take too long to brush and comb him, but as the minutes tick by, Krystin wonders if Delia will leave, even as she knows she won't. When she walks back into the arena, Delia is sitting in the bleachers again, reading a well-worn copy of *Mrs. Dalloway*.

Krystin kicks the bleacher softly. "Do you wanna walk?"

Delia nods, tucking the book into her bag. They walk the length of the ring in silence. Outside, the air is crisp and light. The sun, barely broken over the mountains, casts a dull blue over the field.

Delia speaks first. "I didn't expect you to be back so soon," she says, looking at her feet.

Krystin sucks her teeth. "But I thought you knew me so well." It sounds more bitter than she intended. "Sorry," she adds.

"Don't be," Delia responds. "I shouldn't have said that. I mean, even if it's true—" She turns to look at Krystin. "I shouldn't act like I know everything when I clearly don't."

"Yeah," Krystin says. "Thanks." She pauses, bending down to pluck a blade of grass. "You know, I didn't expect to be back either. But I don't really know what I expected." She holds the blade between her nails, then splits it cleanly down the middle.

"I guess that's what I don't understand," Delia says. "What I never understood. What did you . . . want?"

Krystin laughs. "A husband."

"And you don't anymore?"

"I don't know," Krystin starts to say, but then she remembers her efforts to stop lying to herself and others. "No," she amends. "I don't."

Delia nods. "Do you know what you want instead?"

Krystin exhales, a long, steady thing. "I think, my whole life, I've thought that there are paths stretching out in front of me, good ones and bad ones, and if I made the right choices, I'd find the best one. Like, if I trained really hard, and really committed, I could be the best barrel racer in the state. Or if I went on a dating show, and, like, practiced, and tried really, really hard, I'd fall in love."

They'd come to a stop. Krystin tilts her head back to look at the sky, the clouds that feel like they could swallow her whole. Delia's silent, waiting for her to finish.

"When I left the show, I left that path. But I didn't choose another one. I'm just, like"—she waves her hands around, gesturing at the grass—"standing in a field. And I don't know what I'm doing."

Delia sits down in the grass, then reaches up to tug Krystin down with her. She follows suit, pulling her legs near her.

"You don't know what you're doing," Delia says quietly. "But do you know what you want?"

And then Krystin cries, because she does. She feels it so strongly it shudders out of her in heaves, and Delia steadies her with her warmth. When the tears subside, Krystin pulls away, rubbing at her eyes.

"It's funny," she says without laughing. "I think I did fall in love. It just wasn't with the Romantic."

Delia rubs Krystin's back, drawing small circles with her thumb. "Well, no one can blame you for that. He's basically just a golden retriever in a man's body."

"What's wrong with golden retrievers?"

"Absolutely nothing, in dog form."

Krystin laughs, then sniffles. "Did you . . . watch the show?"

Delia pauses, then nods slowly.

"Really? Every episode?"

Delia looks pained. "Yes, Krystin, every episode. I wouldn't have . . . said all that stuff at your parents' house if I hadn't."

"Right."

"Yeah. Did *you* watch it?"

Krystin shakes her head. "I don't want to see it."

Delia tilts her head. "You don't want to know what happened?"

"I know what happened. I was there."

Delia rolls her eyes. "I mean after you left."

The finale aired a few days ago. "I'll have to watch it before *After the Final String*," Krystin explains, even though it doesn't answer the question. The truth is, she hasn't been ready to confront it all yet—the excitement she felt in the early days, the women who shit-talked her, all the times she looked at Josh and lied, to him and to herself. Lauren. "I'm just . . . I'm scared. To go back." Evidently, she's scared of a lot of things.

Delia nods. "I'll watch it with you," she offers. "Whenever you're ready."

Krystin smiles half-heartedly. She picks another blade of grass, rips it in half, ties it in knots. The sun is beginning to spill over the hills.

"So," Delia says, watching Krystin's fingers. "The person you love."

Krystin ties another knot, then flicks away the dismembered green. "It's Lauren," she says, unceremoniously, obviously.

Delia sucks in a breath.

Krystin bites the inside of her lip. It's coming back to her again, and this time she can't ward it off like she usually does, frightening it back with a fiery torch. "Are you surprised?"

Delia considers, leaning backward on her hands. "Do you remember when we were reading in your room? We were, I don't know, fifteen or something."

Krystin waits for Delia to elaborate, but she doesn't. But Krystin doesn't need her to. She remembers it perfectly.

"Yeah," she says. "I remember."

Delia's mouth quirks up at the corner. "I kinda thought you forgot about it. You never said anything."

"Neither did you."

"Mm."

Even after all those years, after years of talking and not talking, of bad dates with boys and new friends and sorority sisters that could never match up to each other—even after all of that in the air around them as they sit in the field, the words scratch in Krystin's throat like pollen. She lets the breeze move through them and settle in her lungs.

"It felt too big to talk about, I guess," she says. Delia nods. "But it was also, like, maybe it wasn't big for you, and then you would have thought I was dumb for bringing it up. Or—"

"Gay?" Delia finishes the sentence for her.

Krystin sighs. "Yeah."

Delia thinks. "Well, I can't say for sure how I would have reacted if you had brought it up, even if I did feel similarly. Obviously, I didn't talk about it either."

"But you thought about it?"

"Of course I thought about it. I mean . . ." Delia splays her fingers in the grass. "Okay, look. While you were busy with all your sorority stuff, I was doing stuff too."

"'Doing stuff,'" Krystin repeats, flatly.

"Don't laugh."

"I'm so beyond laughing."

"Anyway—you remember Sam, right? The girl I met in my photo class sophomore year at MSU?"

Krystin does. As much time as she and Delia spent together, the sorority took up a fair amount of Krystin's time, and she was always relieved when Delia mentioned hanging out with Sam—especially when Krystin had to bail on their plans to get ready for a mixer with the boys from Sigma Nu.

"Long story short, we split a bottle of wine going through our negatives, lines blurred, etcetera etcetera. Sound familiar?"

Krystin grins. "Did you guys take artful nudes of each other wrapped in fur?"

"Relax," Delia says, holding a hand up. "It wasn't deep. I'm just saying, while you were doing all your glitter cult stuff, I had to find other ways to keep myself occupied."

Krystin giggles, then looks up at Delia from across the grass. "Why didn't you tell me?"

"Probably for the same reason you didn't tell me either."

They could talk about it more, but Krystin doesn't have anything else to say. What happened between her and Delia, however big or small it was, was years ago. They'd moved on—maybe not right away, but eventually time felt something like closure. And if time didn't, Lauren did.

Krystin looks at Delia. The sun has started to climb up behind the mountains, and a beam spills over the top, reflecting off of her hair. Krystin is so used to seeing her best friend as a blazing force of impassioned opinions and confidence, she's unprepared to see her at peace.

"How did you . . . know?" Krystin asks.

Delia raises her eyebrows. "How did *you* know?" she challenges.

When a boy liked Krystin, she didn't have to think about it. He handed her a handwritten valentine, or asked her to homecoming, or mentioned something to her friends, who would set them up on a double or triple date that left her pity-laughing at his jokes. When he wanted to kiss her, she let him. When he wanted to do more than that, she let him do that, too.

Krystin hadn't kissed another girl after Delia until she was dancing with Lauren, pressed so close to her that she couldn't stop herself from getting closer, closer, until there wasn't anything between them at all. And Lauren had been right—Krystin kissed *her*, just like she kissed Delia back then. It had been her choice. Because *she* wanted to.

Growing up, Krystin was never near any queer people in a meaningful way. Sure, there were kids that were *different*, "tomboys" who were assumed to grow out of it, even strangers at the gas station and walking through the aisles at Walmart, but sexuality was never explicitly discussed. She didn't see rampant homophobia so much as she never saw a happy gay future represented. And Krystin had always relied on a very clear definition of happiness, characterized by what she knew. She always saw the perfect life as being the one that her parents shared.

But that had never been what she wanted.

Maybe the reason Krystin was so lonely wasn't because she needed a man to share it all with, but because she didn't share . . . anything. She'd been alone for so long, and it was easier that way. But maybe what was easy was that there wasn't anyone questioning her. That she didn't have to question herself.

"You know," Delia says, after a while, "it's kind of ironic. 'Hopelessly Devoted' is a song about heartbreak. I mean, sure, Sandy's devoted to Danny, but she knows the relationship is doomed."

Krystin laughs. "What, the car lifting them both up into the clouds isn't enough romance for you?"

"I'm just saying—it's a little misguided to name a dating show after a ballad about deception and insecurity."

"Funny," Krystin says. "That's exactly what it was."

The kitchen is warm, the air spicy from the onions and peppers sautéing in the pan. Krystin stirs the vegetables with one hand, takes a sip of chilled wine with the other. She can see Delia dancing with Krystin's father in the living room; he grabs her hand and twirls her around, bobbing his head to "Copperhead Road."

"You don't even like country music!" Krystin yells to Delia over the speakers.

Delia just sticks her tongue out.

And Krystin laughs, because she remembers what home feels like. Peg stands behind her, holding her own glass. She looks at her husband, then at Krystin, and Krystin knows what her mother is thinking without her saying it. *I'm glad you're home.*

The song ends, and Krystin hears a knock at the door.

"Who could that be?" Peg wonders aloud, moving to answer.

Krystin stops her. "No, you stay. It's probably another Mormon. I'll get it."

She does, leaving Delia to square dance with her dad. When she opens the door, Josh stands on the porch, one hand in his pocket, the other paused mid-knock.

"Sorry," he says, lowering his hand. "I tried a couple of times. I guess you couldn't hear over the music."

"No," Krystin says, because she doesn't know what else to say. "I didn't."

She steps outside, looking around the porch, the lawn. But there aren't any cameras. Josh is here, in Montana, alone.

"Why . . . are you here?" she asks.

Josh raises an eyebrow. "You mean, why am I here without Holland or Jim?"

331

"I mean . . ." Krystin shrugs, crossing her arms over her chest. "Yeah, I guess."

"Because I think we have some stuff to talk about."

The flush from the wine catches on fire, spreading down from her cheeks to fill her whole body. "Josh . . ." She really does not have the capacity to have this conversation again, or any iteration of it. Watching Lauren reject his proposal had made her feel even worse—it was hard enough to witness his hurt the first time, and even though it was all her fault, she really does not want to relive the pain she caused.

But Josh puts a hand up. "Stop. Before you go there, I'm not here to get you back."

The flush drains. "Oh," she says, mildly embarrassed for assuming he had been, though that explains the missing film crew. There's no way they'd miss something like that. "Really?"

"Really," Josh says, scratching his facial hair, which he's let grow into more than a five o'clock shadow. "Believe it or not, I actually don't want to have to convince someone to marry me. Or even like me."

Now Krystin's hurt. "Josh, of course I like you. I wouldn't have stayed so long if I didn't like you."

"Maybe don't talk about why you stayed so long," Josh says. "Or at least, don't try to make it seem like it was about me."

Krystin leans against the doorframe. "Okay, ouch."

Josh looks different. There's a burning in his eyes, a determination Krystin didn't see at the chateau. Or maybe didn't notice.

"Krystin," he says. "Let's not dance around it anymore." He runs a hand through his curls with a roughness that catches Krystin off guard. "I know about you and Lauren."

"*What?*" Krystin cries. "How?"

"Lauren told me."

"What do you mean she *told* you?"

"She called me," he says. "She came clean, about all of it—not about you, not explicitly, but I put two and two together. And she apologized. Which you also could have done, by the way."

Krystin twitches so hard she nearly knocks her head into the door. Then she almost falls backward, because the door opens.

"Dear God," Delia says from the other side. "Not again."

"Hello to you too," Josh responds.

"Why is he here?" Delia asks, still standing with the door open.

"Yeah," Krystin says, still trying to wrap her head around her secret not being a secret to the one person she never wanted to tell. "Josh, why *are* you here?"

"Listen," he says, and then he's looking at Krystin with a sincerity she associates exclusively with him. "I know I've been giving you a hard time about this." He pauses, sighing. "I'm not over it. It's probably going to take me a little while to get over it. But . . . there was love on the show, even if it wasn't for me. I still want to do what I can to help it happen."

"Ha!" Delia blurts, then turns to Krystin. "As if. *This* guy wants to play knight in shining armor?"

"All right, Delia, I know you don't like me—"

"It's not about whether or not I *like* you. I want to make sure you're not setting up my best friend to be humiliated on the same show she just *dumped* you on."

"Delia!" Krystin shouts. Everything is happening too quickly. "Just—everyone shut up for a second."

They do. Delia draws her lips into themselves, her tic for when she wants to stop herself from saying something she might regret, as if she could hold the words between her teeth. Josh just scratches the back of his neck. Krystin takes a breath.

"Okay," she says. "First of all, Josh, I do think Delia's point stands." She sees Josh's expression flicker into affront. "*Not* because I think you're vindictive. I hope I've made it clear by now that I think you're a really great guy who wants the best for everyone. But I do wonder why you'd want to help the two women who just"—she falters on the words—"broke up with you on television."

"In other words," Delia interrupts, clearly done with her imposed silence, "what's in it for you?"

Josh sighs. "Fine. Yeah, it sucked for two women I was into to reject me." He looks at Krystin. "In front of my parents."

"Three if you count Amanda from last season," Delia mutters.

"I'm really sorry, Josh," Krystin says. "I really am."

"Well, this is one way you can make it up to me," Josh replies. "I need my reputation to be more than the guy no one wants to marry. Just, like . . . let me be the hero here."

Krystin brushes her fingers through her hair. "Josh, I want to do anything I can to help you. But whatever you're thinking, I don't think it's going to work. I fucked things up pretty majorly."

"Krystin," Josh says, fiercely. "I don't think you realize how she feels about you."

She shakes her head. "I gave her a lot of chances to tell me." She looks around her, and realizes she's standing between her childhood crush and her ex-quasi-boyfriend, talking about the girl she's in love with. *This is insane.* She pulls her hair back into a ponytail, then lets it fall back. "I am really sorry, Josh. For everything. I didn't know what was happening to me, and I let you become collateral. It wasn't fair."

"It wasn't," Josh says. "But *I* know you're sorry. Lauren doesn't."

Delia clears her throat. "You said you gave Lauren plenty of chances to tell you how she felt. Maybe *you* have to tell *her*." She places a hand on Krystin's shoulder and squeezes.

Krystin takes a deep breath. "So, what are you proposing I do?"

"Okay," Josh says, and now he looks kind of excited. "You're coming on *After the Final String*, right?"

"Yes," she confirms, though she wishes she weren't. She can't imagine facing Lauren again, let alone McKenzie and Kaydie, and the rest of the Devotees. "It's in my contract."

"Okay," Josh repeats. He's rocking back on his feet, bouncing like a quarterback. "What better way to apologize than in front of a live studio audience?"

"Ha!" Delia laughs. "You're kidding."

Krystin shifts her weight. "Josh, Lauren wouldn't even come out to her family. Do you really think she'd be cool with me proclaiming my feelings on TV? To her hundred thousand Instagram followers?"

"I think she's changed," Josh argues. "I don't know, when we spoke on the phone . . . She said she didn't care who knew anymore. I think her priorities have shifted. Just—trust me."

Krystin's silent, turning it over in her head. "Are you sure Penny isn't hiding behind a tree here? This all sounds pretty *most dramatic season yet*."

"She's not," he promises. "Look, they want drama, but not like this. Besides, if we told them, we'd have to do it their way."

Krystin tucks her hair behind her ear, rolls back on her heels. For the first time since she left the show, she feels the familiar batting in her chest, but this time they feel like they're lifting her up rather than pulling her under. Butterflies. The real kind. "So, what, we're gonna do it our way?"

"No." Josh smiles. "You're gonna do it yours."

Which is how Krystin finds herself pacing the floor of the green room, running over the lines in her head while watching thirty-one women of Josh's season of *Hopelessly Devoted* on the monitor.

"Listen, J," Gabi is saying with a smirk from her seat. "I would have treated you better than eeeeveryone else here." She draws circles around the group with her acrylic-pointed finger.

A chorus of groans rumbles through the women, and the studio audience laughs.

"All right, all right." Josh plays at containing them, but he's blushing. "Let's play nice."

"I *am* playing nice." Gabi splays a hand innocently over her heart. "You could have seen me play really, *really* nice."

Lily rolls her eyes. "Can you keep it in your pants, please?"

"Well," Jen says, "we all know who *didn't*."

Krystin, mid-gulp of her Poland Spring, nearly chokes. Even Josh looks like he's ready to kick Jen to the curb.

"Oh, come on," Jen says over the booing from the audience. "We all watched it!"

"And?" Sara-without-an-H responds, swiveling in her stool to face Jen, who sits a row up and three seats down. "We are *not* here to slut shame."

"We don't know what happened behind closed doors," Sarah-with-an-H says, attempting diplomacy, but Jen rolls her eyes.

"Some things are implied," she insists. "But I'm not surprised you never learned to read between the lines."

"Oh, Christ." Krystin brings the water bottle to her temple, but it's tepid and unhelpful.

On the monitor, Josh waves his hands to dispel the chatter. "Guys, guys. Let's not spend too much time on any one person who isn't here yet."

Only four women are missing from the lineup: Kaydie, McKenzie, Krystin, and Lauren. They'll each be brought on, in the order of their elimination, to talk one-on-one with Josh.

Krystin feels nausea prickling at her. But for the first time, it's not from lying. This time, she's going to tell the truth.

To Lauren. Who doesn't know. Who probably hates her after what she did. Oh, God. She takes another gulp of water, and wishes it was something stronger.

"*Shit,*" Krystin whispers. "Fuck."

Someone knocks on the door, then opens it, popping their head through the crack. It's Penny.

"Everything okay in here?" she asks, eyeing the water bottle in Krystin's grip, then the two empties crumpled on the table.

"Yep," Krystin responds. She gives a thumbs-up to drive it home.

Penny leans forward, opening the door a little more. "You know, I can say it now that we're not filming—you're a really bad liar."

Krystin almost laughs. "You're right."

Penny looks at her for a moment. "Josh is too. Which is how I know you guys are up to something."

Krystin opens her mouth to protest, but Penny stops her.

"I don't care, do whatever you want. This is my last season. I'm going to *Housewives.*" Penny points to the water. "You should lay off, though. You're gonna have to pee while you're up there." Then she closes the door and leaves.

Krystin stands there, mildly stunned. She turns to the monitor, where Kaydie and McKenzie are discussing the sister-like bond they formed behind cameras that Krystin never saw.

"I just think that we both knew each other was serious," Kaydie says, clutching McKenzie's hand, "and we really connected because of that. And that was really what got me through the experience. The sisterhood."

McKenzie nods, even though Krystin never saw her the entire last month, due to McKenzie barricading herself in her room with only Taylor Swift as defense.

But whatever.

Krystin looks away. She paces some more, pees three times, and finally just sits down in the middle of the floor, patting her glittery dress gingerly.

And then she hears Lauren's voice. Krystin swivels to the screen, but she's not there—the voice is coming from outside the door, attached to clip-clopping heels and breaths in huffs. Krystin's stomach drops ten stories. It drops another twenty when it fully sinks in that they're in the same building, separated by just concrete and underpaid production assistants.

The audience is laughing at something Josh said, and Krystin can hardly breathe. She feels like she's at once untethered and impossibly rooted to her body. She can hear her blood in her ears, and she can't feel her hands.

Another knock sounds at the door. This time, Penny opens it wide.

One, two, three, four, in. One, two, three, four, out.

Penny looks at Krystin surrounded by her dress on the floor and says, "You're up."

CHAPTER TWENTY-TWO

"Remember when we talked about building our dream house together and raising a family upstate? Did you already know you were cutting my string?"

Oof, Lauren thinks. She's in her own private green room backstage, nervously snacking on some almonds, watching McKenzie's live reunion with Josh. The producers are, of course, making them both relive her teary elimination. But real-time McKenzie, dressed in a stunning jade green gown, just nods, a bittersweet smile on her face, even as the live studio audience members sniffle and shake their heads. One of the hosts poses a question, and Lauren only catches the answer.

"It's hard to watch back, for sure," McKenzie says. Her voice is shaky, but Lauren's surprised—and oddly proud—that she isn't crying. "But when it comes to Josh, I have no regrets." She turns to face him. "Even if I wasn't the one for him, we *did* build something special. And today, I'm stronger than ever."

The special is hosted by a trio of former Romantics. There's Michael, who hosted the mud wrestling date; Nate from season twenty, fresh off a stint on *Dancing With the Stars*; and Christopher, one of the few OG leads who's still married to his final ribbon recipient. It's Nate who asks the next follow-up. "Josh, how do *you* feel watching this breakup with McKenzie?"

He swallows. "I mean, I feel horrible," he says, and Lauren actually believes him. After all, his season pretty much went south after McKenzie's exit. "Kenzie, you're a really amazing woman. I hate that I put you through this."

Now Michael speaks up. "McKenzie says she has no regrets. Josh, can you say the same?"

He turns red and chuckles. "Well, we all saw how my season ended up. I think it's safe to say that most of us made mistakes. But McKenzie . . . you didn't. You were true to yourself all along. I hope you know how much I appreciate that, especially after watching some of these clips back."

Lauren slinks back into her seat, feeling more than a little put in her place. She hasn't spoken to Josh since that phone call, but hey, at least he followed her back on Instagram. The rest of the women did, too. The nebulous, awkward stretch of time between Josh's proposal and *After the Final String* went the way Lauren once dreamed it would—all the other contestants, even Kaydie and Gabi, left cute, supportive comments on her photos. ShineGirl asked if she'd be interested in an official partnership. Her follower count continued to climb each day, even after Josh's botched proposal aired.

In the end, her edit wasn't bad, really. If anything, commentators online seemed to believe he *really* wanted Krystin, and Lauren was smart enough to realize he was just settling for his second pick. She got a lot of nice DMs. Someone even made a fan account. But none of it meant anything.

The one contestant who notably *doesn't* follow her is Krystin. Damian sent Lauren an eerily thorough Reddit thread, in which a bunch of Devoted Fans theorized they must have been sworn enemies behind the scenes because they were the only two contestants who never liked each other's photos. He also sent her a few comments from someone named ThrowawayAccount2873828, who claimed she'd seen Lauren countless times on lesbian Tinder in New Jersey. The rumor never gained traction, though.

At the end of the day, *Hopelessly Devoted* is a straight show, with a straight audience and straight contestants. Of *course* the viewers thought Krystin and Lauren hated each other, beginning and end of story.

But Lauren can't bring herself to hate Krystin. Even though she doesn't follow her online, she's stalked her social media more than she'll ever admit: her throwback rodeo photos, stunning Montana landscapes. Silly selfies with Delia, who's evidently her friend again— or maybe even something more. It's not like Lauren would know.

She's thought about contacting Krystin herself, of course. She's even gone so far as to draft an unsent DM, something corny and vulnerable and stupid about how it doesn't matter if Krystin slept with Josh in Costa Rica, it doesn't matter if they live on opposite sides of the country, it doesn't matter what Krystin's ready for—or what she isn't. She just wants to be with her again, however she can.

She didn't send it, of course.

"Speaking of meeting the family," Christopher says, and Lauren realizes she zoned out the rest of McKenzie's interview. "Who else is *still* thinking about Krystin brutally leaving Josh heartbroken in his driveway? After the break, Miss Rodeo Queen herself will come out and address this season's wildest breakup—and come face-to-face with Josh for the first time since. Stay tuned!"

Lauren's phone buzzes. It's Damian: *I feel like mckenzie and josh were kinda vibing?*

She shoots back a response: *can't tell, but you have a better view than I do.*

Damian: *damn right I do! I thought josh couldn't get any hotter, and then he grew out that beard . . .*

Lauren shakes her head and turns her phone off. Lauren had received a handful of tickets to the live taping, and she'd obviously given three of them to Rachel and her parents. Things have been good between the four of them: Lauren's been staying at home for a bit, applying to some fashion marketing jobs to supplement her influencer career. She came out to her parents last week, and it went well—much like Rachel, they weren't exactly as surprised as Lauren expected them to be.

But as much as she wanted her family at the ceremony, she needed Damian in the audience too. Although Holland told Lauren she was "giving her a million migraines, seriously," when she asked about inviting her ex-boyfriend to the live taping, she knew she couldn't face Josh and Krystin without her best friend somewhere out there, cheering her on. And Holland *did* seem to calm down when Lauren explained that Damian recently and very publicly came out. ("As long as he doesn't jump on stage and express his love for you when you're chatting with Josh, I'm good," Holland had said. "He literally bleached his hair," Lauren had responded.)

"Krystin's on now," a PA hisses from a few feet away. "You're up next."

Lauren's heart catches as she watches Krystin, clad in a sparkly gold dress and matching earrings, walk on and take her seat next to Josh. She's beautiful, but she always looks beautiful—Lauren's fingers itch to trace her figure on the small monitor.

As the audience claps, a Krystin highlight reel starts to play. There's footage of her first one-on-one with Josh, her performance at karaoke, and finally, her brutal breakup. Krystin, Josh, and the trio of hosts stare solemnly at each clip, and the audience reacts with cheers and gasps.

Christopher is the first to speak when the recap ends. "Let's start off easy," he says. "Krystin, how've you been since the show ended? You've been back in Montana for a little while now."

"I have. I've been . . . good," Krystin says. Lauren's eyes automatically narrow at the vague bullshit, but then Krystin adds, "I won't lie, it's been a difficult few weeks."

"What have you been doing with your time off?" Michael interjects. "Have you gotten back in the saddle?"

Krystin gives a half-hearted laugh. "You guessed it. I have been spending a lot of time in the ring. It's meditative for me."

Lauren's pretty sure the PA is speaking to her again, but she can't bring herself to listen to anything besides Krystin's very sanitized Q&A. She's positive that Krystin's about to continue speaking, but Christopher jumps back in.

"Are you competing again, now that you no longer have a public beau?"

"Not yet. I think it's good for me to take a little time off. And . . ." Krystin looks at Josh, then back at the hosts. "I do still have some things to figure out."

"I'm sure some people are certainly happy you're back home. Let's take another look at your Hometown date, shall we?" The monitor cuts to Josh schmoozing with Krystin's parents, and then Krystin's tense conversation with Delia—the one Lauren heard about in real time, then watched back with Damian, Rachel, and a glass of rosé. It's about a million times more awkward with a live studio audience gasping at every turn. "Delia, your childhood best friend, had some feelings about the show. Josh, how did you feel about that?"

"Pfff, yeah." Josh runs a hand through his curly crop. "I will say that felt like a bad sign. I mean, when you meet someone important to your partner, of course you want them to like you."

"Delia doesn't not like you," Krystin interrupts.

The audience laughs, and Lauren purses her lips.

"Okay, okay," she concedes. "Delia definitely has her criticisms about *Hopelessly Devoted*, but I think she's come around to the process. It does bring people together."

"That's actually a great segue," Michael says. "Because, I mean, let's not beat around the bush, here, Krystin. In your exit interview, you said you had feelings for someone who wasn't Josh."

"I knew this was coming. Yeah. I did." Krystin runs a hand over the skirt of her dress.

Lauren knew this was coming too. When she watched Krystin's emotional limo exit with Damian, he'd put down his glass of wine with such ferocity that it spilled across the glass-top coffee table. "She's literally talking about you," he'd said, but Lauren couldn't entertain the theory. Krystin could've been talking about *anyone*. Someone she'd bothered to follow on Instagram, or text. She could've been talking about Delia.

"You've also said that Josh was the first person you took home. The first person you really dated, even," Christopher continues. "So I think we're all wondering . . . who's the guy?"

Krystin's cheeks flush. "I think the person . . . knows who they are."

Christopher turns to Josh. "Buddy, that must be tough to hear."

"You know, it was hard. But I've had some time to sit with it, and I think it all worked out for the best." Josh pats Krystin's thigh, but it's void of any flirtation or motive. "I actually don't think Krystin and I would have been happy together, for more reasons than one."

Christopher raises an eyebrow. "Is that so?"

Josh nods. "Yes."

He waits for Josh to elaborate. When he doesn't, Christopher switches gears. "Krystin, is there anything you'd like to add before we let you go?"

"I just want to say that I learned a lot about myself during this process. And even though I wish I could change some things, I wouldn't trade that knowledge for the world."

"Lauren." The PA's now given up on whispering. "Come on."

"Yeah." Lauren watches as Krystin and Josh share a hug, then as Krystin waves goodbye and exits stage left. It's surreal to know that she's now somewhere backstage, in another tiny green room with nothing but little bowls of almonds and five bottles of Poland Spring. It's surreal to even know that they're in the same time zone.

And it's surreal to see Josh, too, as she steps on stage and sits where Krystin was seated just two minutes ago. "Hi," Lauren murmurs, just to him. Then she shoots Christopher, Michael, and Nate a sparkling smile. "And hello. Thanks for having me."

"We're so glad you came back," Michael says. As if she had a choice. "Lauren, you and Josh had a heartbreaking journey together. Let's take a look."

The lights all fade. Lauren, along with the rest of the room, watches as select parts of her "love story" with Josh play out on-screen: their first kiss after he gave her the first impression ribbon, their tango date, their Hometown visit. Finally, Lauren watches as TV-Josh tries to propose to her. The montage ends on Josh's "heartbroken" confessional, in which he muses about "so many doors slamming shut at once" in the Long Island Marriott lobby.

"Wow. That was hard to watch," Michael says, echoing Lauren's thoughts perfectly. "Josh, how does it feel to see this lovely lady again?"

He gives her a quick smile. "It feels great. It's nice to see you."

"You too." She glances at the audience. Her family's there, somewhere.

So is his. At least she never had to meet them.

"This is the first time you two are speaking since that tense moment, right?" Michael asks.

"Well," Lauren hedges. "There may have been a phone call. Just one."

Michael wiggles his eyebrows. "Oh, yeah? Is there still hope for you two?"

"Look. I meant what I said—we clearly are not meant to be. And I called Josh to apologize, because I . . . *knew* we weren't meant to be. From early on, actually." Lauren feels calm, measured. It's almost *freeing* to admit.

"In that case, I gotta ask," Michael continues. "Why'd you stick around until the very end, if you knew Josh wasn't the one?"

"I think it's . . . a weird environment. *Hopelessly Devoted*, that is. There's a lot of pressure, and I'm not talking about pressure from the lead, or the producers, or the viewers. I think we put a lot of pressure on ourselves. Pressure to come off well, you know?" She swallows, then looks at Josh. "To keep everyone happy." She thinks of Krystin. "To *be* happy. To have everything figured out."

"What would you say to someone who thought you were just on the show to, say, further your influencer career?" Nate interjects.

Lauren's eyes narrow, and she fights the urge to point out that Nate's been shilling fancy tequilas and multivitamins nonstop since his own season. "I'd say those people don't have to like me. They don't have to follow me, either." She shrugs. "At the end of the day, there's a handful of people out there whose opinions matter to me, and if those people are listening . . . I hope they know that I still care about them. Way, way more than my career as a content creator, or my reputation, or anything like that. And definitely more than any TV show."

She's not sure she's making any sense, and Nate's looking at her like he has no idea where this conversation is headed. "Let's take a step back. Are you talking about Josh?" he asks.

For the first time since she took her seat, Lauren looks at Josh— really looks at him. She can tell he's in a better place than he was during filming; he definitely looks less tired and frustrated than he sounded on the phone. He's watching her, too, and his eyes look friendly and warm.

"Josh is great," she says, honestly. "He's going to make someone really happy. But I'm . . ."

Should she do this? Now that she's actually in the hot seat, she's not sure if a very public sexuality announcement would detract from the general theme of the night, which seems to be Josh's Many Heartbreaks. But then he gives her a slight smile and a tiny, almost unnoticeable nod. And she can't see Damian in the audience, but she knows what he would say: *I've got your back.*

"I like women," she says, and tries to ignore the gasps from the audience. "*Only* women, actually. And there's one who I really like. I don't want to take up the rest of Josh's night with my story, but . . ." She looks over at him, and he's grinning. Is the audience now . . . cheering? Lauren somehow feels outside of her body and rooted in place, all at once. "Maybe I can share more on an episode of *When One Door Opens*. If Josh will have me."

"Wait, Lauren," Nate says. He keeps staring somewhere off-stage—Lauren can only imagine how pissed the producers look. "Are you saying—"

But Josh interrupts him, his voice louder than it's been all night. "Actually, Nate, *I'd* like to say a few words. If you don't mind." He clears his throat. "This might get a little long-winded, but I'm hoping you're all willing to bear with me."

Lauren looks at him, puzzled. Once again, he gives an imperceptible nod of assurance.

"First of all, this isn't new information to me. Like Lauren said, we talked, and I support her. And hey, even if she were straight, it wouldn't have worked out between us—she's way too fashionable for me." There's a low rumble of confused laughs. "But this journey taught me so much. I know I talk a lot about doors, but there's a reason my podcast resonates with so many people."

To Lauren's shock, Josh literally stands up and faces the live audience.

"The truth is, we all have parts of ourselves we keep shut, or even locked. Sometimes, because we want to hide what's inside. We want to pretend it doesn't exist, or we're scared to share it with the world. Maybe you have this beautiful, custom-stained oak door, and you're scared that people might love the door itself . . . more than what's behind it." He pauses for emphasis. "I always thought love would be as simple as meeting that special person and deciding to open our innermost doors to one another—"

Lauren coughs to hide a snort at the innuendo.

"But sometimes, it's a little more complicated than that. Sometimes, a door looks like a push, but it's actually a pull. Sometimes a door gets a little jammed, and you need someone really, really special to open it up just right."

He looks at Lauren, smiles, and then turns to look at someone off-stage. Maybe a producer? Maybe he's trying to bring McKenzie back on and beg for a second chance? Lauren has officially lost track of this metaphor.

"Sometimes, a special person opens your door—no, they help *you* open your *own* door—and then you get a little scared, or a little confused, and you shut the door again," Josh continues. "On that note, I'd like to call someone who's become one of my best friends. She didn't turn out to be the hinge to my jamb, but she's a pretty amazing woman, and she's got an important message to share with someone in this room today—and with our Devoted Fans. Krystin, come back out here."

Out of the corner of one eye, Lauren catches the hosts exchanging panicked, confused looks; out of the corner of the other, she sees Penny in the wing, ripping off her headset and reaching for an open can of Truly spiked seltzer. But then Lauren sees Krystin in her golden dress and perfect curls, walking on stage with rodeo champion confidence and composure, and it's like they're back in the mud wrestling ring—like there's just nowhere else to look. She barely even registers Josh returning to his seat next to her, accidentally grazing his thigh against hers and giving her shoulder a reassuring squeeze.

And then, Krystin looks at *her*, and for a selfish, sappy, scary moment, Lauren thinks that she doesn't regret any of the horrible or misguided things she's ever done, actually, because every single decision she's ever made led her to this evening and this chair and this gorgeous, confusing person smiling at her for the first time in weeks.

"I know you guys might be surprised to see me back out here. But there are a few things I really want—I *need* to say," Krystin says. She laughs, a nervous little half-chuckle, and turns out toward the crowd, just like Josh did a moment ago. "I mentioned earlier that this process taught me a lot about myself. I think the most important thing it taught me was to be honest—with other people, but mostly with myself.

"I've spent my entire life doing what I thought would make me happy, without ever stopping to think about whether it was working. And whenever I felt like it wasn't, I just doubled down and hoped I could make myself happy. That I could make myself want things I thought I was supposed to want." Krystin pauses. For the first time all night, the room is completely silent. "I came on this show because I thought I wanted a husband. I can't apologize for that, because at the time that was true for me. But then I met you."

Now, Krystin isn't just looking at Lauren. She's walking over to her. And, as if they'd actually choreographed this in advance or something, Josh is standing up and moving stage right, giving Krystin the space to sit down next to Lauren on the love seat.

"I did fall in love on this show. It wasn't with Josh, even though I think he's so great, and if I were into men, maybe things would be different. But I'm . . . not." Lauren thinks she hears a lone gasp in the audience, but for all she knows, it came from Nate. Krystin's gazing at her with the kind of intensity that's almost overwhelming—maybe it's that, or maybe it's her golden yellow gown, but looking at her feels like squinting at the sun. "I'm not. I'm into you, Lauren. I'm so, so into you." She shuts her eyes for a second, and takes a measured breath. When she opens them up again, she's resolute—more resolute than Lauren's ever seen her. Which makes the next words feel even more sincere. "Actually, I love you. I love you so much I can't remember what it feels like not to."

Lauren doesn't know what it's like to feel good without caveat—without a lingering, repressed sense of guilt, without the knowledge that everything perfect is temporary or fake or not really hers. It must feel like this. Like this beautiful, fearless, earnest person knows her and loves her anyway, loudly and publicly and fully.

Tears are pooling in her eyes, and she's not sure if they're visible, but Lauren still attempts a smirk. Or maybe it's a smile. "Well," she says. Softly, evenly. "Took you long enough to realize it."

Krystin lets out a small, raspy laugh in response, then blinks a few times in succession, like she's also been trying not to cry. She reaches out two shaky hands and cradles Lauren's head like she's holding something precious and delicate and tangible, tucks a strand behind her right ear. And then she takes a deep breath, and leans in to kiss Lauren on live, national television.

There's clapping and gasping and some cheering that Lauren's pretty sure might be coming from Josh. And there's Krystin, her face warm and damp with tears, kissing her and snaking one hand down to Lauren's waist, then squeezing her hand.

"I love you too," Lauren says, and Krystin lights up like she just won a fifteen-person group date competition. "I love you in a real, certain way, and I know I'm not good at, like, feelings and words, but I think I've been trying to tell you that for a really, really long time now. And I want to keep doing it, Krystin. For as long as you'll let me."

Krystin looks away, then back at Lauren. Her voice is soft and shaky, quiet enough to go unnoticed in the cacophony of cheers and yells from producers. "And I never—" she starts, closing her eyes. "I want you to know that Josh and I never did anything during Honeymoons, nothing that meant anything. And I'm sorry I didn't tell you that sooner."

Lauren shakes her head. "It doesn't matter anymore," she says. "I just want to be with you." It's the kind of cheesy line that a Hopeless Romantic would say, one that would usually make her cringe—the kind of thing she never thought she'd feel, let alone say out loud. But it's true.

Krystin kisses her again, and this time Lauren hears one of the hosts clear his throat. Another waffles, trying to get the show back on track, but Josh's voice is clear in the background, pontificating about how, hey, America wanted a love story.

When they pull away, Lauren lowers her voice, just for Krystin. "I know you can't have a boyfriend if you want to keep your rodeo titles," she says, still a little breathless. "Any rules about girlfriends?"

She tilts her head and gives her a meaningful look. "You know, I'm trying to care a little less about rules these days."

"Okay! Okay," Michael exclaims. "This is really great. And we'll be back with more after the break!" He claps a hand on Lauren's shoulder. As soon as the lights dim, he murmurs, "I'm happy for you two, but you really have to get off stage. We've got, like, a minute and a half left to announce the next season."

"Got it," says Krystin. The girl Lauren loves. The girl who loves *her*.

Lauren hears a few scattered claps from the audience, clearly unsure of the appropriate response to the Hopeless Romantic's extremely public double-friendzone. She locks eyes with Damian, who's crying actual tears. Season twenty-two's thirty-three other Devotees express a range of emotions—Madison's shock, Lily's raised eyebrow, like she knew the whole time, even though she totally didn't. Jen looks like she ate a bad oyster, but Lauren always suspected she was a little homophobic anyway.

Krystin's smiling across the room at Kaydie, who gives her a nod of approval. And then she's smiling at Lauren; and even though the lights have dimmed, and the spotlight has found another focus, Lauren feels like no room could possibly be dark with Krystin in it.

In the corner of her eye, Lauren sees a PA approaching them with the determined gleam she could only attribute to Holland's wrath. But Krystin opens her perfect mouth, and mouths the three words she could never tire of hearing. And then she grabs Lauren's hand and leads her off the stage, out of the studio, and into real life.

INSTAGRAM POST FROM JOSH ROSEN

Liked by itslaurenc *and* 9,250 others

joshrosennn Well . . . it's a wrap! Needless to say, my journey this season didn't play out the way I thought it would, but I have no regrets. I followed my heart, learned how to skydive, and got to know some of the most amazing women I've ever met. I got to be a part of a historic season, in more ways than one. Being the first Jewish Romantic came with a lot of pressure, and I just hope there are some kids who watched my story unfold and thought, "Hey, that could be me." If just one Ashkenazi Jewish kid from Long Island saw themselves in me, it would make everything worth it. Finally, I got to lead the first LGBTQ+ season of *Hopelessly Devoted*. Obviously, this was unexpected, but I believe in opening doors—in this case, closet doors. I am proud to be an ally and #GLAADAllyAwards nominee, and I am proud of my friends @itslaurenc and @krystinwithay for living their truth. Please do not send them ANY HATE. #HopelesslyDevoted is about love conquering all and I could not be happier for these two special ladies. As for me, you know what they say . . . when one door closes, another opens! And be sure to tune in Wednesday to my podcast @onedoorpodcast for a special announcement . . . #hopelesslydevoted #whybemadwhenyoucanbeGLAAD

View all 183 comments

TRANSCRIPT OF *WHEN ONE DOOR CLOSES . . .* SEASON 2 EPISODE 1

Josh: Okay, guys! We're back! [Laughs.] I can't believe it's been months since our last recording. The booth isn't as crowded as it was last time . . . [Pauses.] I'm sure you guys remember *that* one. [Snippet of podcast date. Krystin explains dating experience.] As you know, I've been, well, on the journey of a lifetime trying to find love, and you know what? I found it.

I can't wait for next week's episode, when McKenzie and I will answer all your questions about how we found our way back to each other. But today, we're going to talk a little bit about the most surprising love story that unfolded on my season of *Hopelessly Devoted*. Spoiler alert: It wasn't mine.

We have an exciting episode ahead, because I scored Lauren and Krystin's first full-length, exclusive interview since *After the Final String* aired a few weeks ago—I guess they realized they both owed me one for, you know, brutally dumping me on national television. But hey, no hard feelings! Ladies, how have you been doing?

Krystin: [Laughs.] Hi, Josh. We've been doing . . . well. [Giggles.]

Lauren: I can't lie, it's been really refreshing to be so open—and it's so nice to have some support from the Devoted Fans and everyone else. And dating Krystin is incredible, obviously. I guess I don't have to tell you that.

J: [Laughs.] You sure don't. But let's go back to this idea of being open. You were pretty . . . let's say, *private*, during our time on the show. Do you have any regrets about your decision there?

L: You know, Josh, I've gotten a few nasty comments about how I "wasn't myself" on the show. And what I want to clarify is that, in some ways, I *was* myself. I mean, I've always been that fashion-forward, competitive girl who looks great in a swimsuit or a cocktail dress and isn't afraid to go for what she wants, right? But I *did* deceive people, and I hurt some people I care about, and I'm truly sorry about that. I'm just excited for people to get to know the real Lauren. The Lauren who, you know, is still getting used to putting herself out there. And the Lauren who also really likes kissing girls. Especially one girl.

K: I think what people need to understand is that we've all spoken since the show wrapped. Josh, you and I had a long discussion before *After the Final String*, and I know you and Lauren had a similar phone call around that time. Right? So the live recording wasn't completely out of the blue. I wouldn't have put Josh on the spot like that, and I don't think Lauren would have, either.

J: That's a great point, Krystin, and I'm glad you brought that up. It was actually really important for me to be a driving force in getting you guys back together. I'm not one of those guys who's like, if I can't have you, no one can. I'm pro-women, you know? And I've identified as an ally since I first heard that Macklemore song in high school. So I want the Devoted Fans to know that we're all on good terms.

L: *Great* terms.

K: And Josh, you've had a little post-show romance of your own.

J: [Chuckles.] I have, I have.

K: Tell us about her, stud.

J: [Laughs.] Well, you know McKenzie. She's great, she's the sweetest. I think some people might have some things to say about me going back to the second runner-up, but my and Kenz's connection has always been strong. And she knows that I'm not just with her because I didn't have anyone else. But, if you're listening, you'll be able to ask us all the questions you want ahead of our interview next week! So if you have any burning Qs, or if you really wanna put me in the hot seat, send me an email at onedoorpodcast@gmail.com with the subject line "McJosh."

L: I, for one, am very excited to double-date—I was actually able to form a great friendship with McKenzie once filming ended. I won't lie: During production, I thought she was a little grating and sometimes a tryhard. But now that we're not competing for the same man and she knows I'm completely uninterested in you, we've been able to bond over our shared love for *Reputation*-era Taylor Swift and shopping in Soho.

J: Ha! You know, I've heard a lot about my, quote-unquote, *indecisive nature*, but I clearly have good taste. No wonder it was hard to make a decision!

L: I mean. [Pause.] Okay, I guess I can't really argue with that.

J: Anyway, what's next for you two? When should I expect my Save the Date?

K: Well, we've talked about it, and I think *Hopelessly Devoted* puts you on a timeline, right? For a reason—to get serious quick, to get engaged, whatever—but it's really important to us to just enjoy the journey. We're spending a lot of time together, obviously, but we're not signing any leases yet. We're taking it slow.

L: Well, she is.

K: [Laughs sheepishly.] As slowly as I can with this knockout next to me.

J: Oof! Listeners, you can't see me, but I'm fanning myself because it is getting *hot* in here!

L: Did you miss us, Rosen?

J: You know, I have a feeling I'll be seeing a lot of you two. Speaking of . . . Krystin, have you made it out to the Big Apple, yet?

K: We actually spent an amazing weekend in New York a few weeks ago!

J: Just a weekend?

K: [Laughs.] Just the weekend, for now. Baby steps for this country girl.

L: I don't know, Josh, we'll see. I'll make a city girl out of her yet. [Pauses.] I've already made another kind of girl out of her.

K: Laur!

J: Okay, okay. [Laughs.] I think this is a good time to take our first break. We'll be back soon after a few words from our sponsors.

ACKNOWLEDGMENTS

We'd like to first thank Kristy Hunter and the Knight Agency for loving this book from the moment you read it, for believing in us both as a team and as individuals, and for generally being kind and amazing. You are better than the best.

Thank you to our editor Jess Verdi for much the same—we are so lucky to have your guidance, genuine enthusiasm, and understanding of these characters. Thank you for challenging us to write a better version, and then a better one after that.

Massive thanks to the entire Alcove team: Thai Fantauzzi-Perez, Rebecca Nelson, Dulce Botello, Madeline Rathle, Mikaela Bender, Megan Matti, Stephanie Manova, and everyone else involved in helping books get made. Thank you Stephanie Singleton for creating such a beautiful cover.

Thank you Isabel Martin, Lucy Dauman, and everyone at Headline UK for wanting to print and sell our book in another country.

And thank you Jordan Reynolds, our first reader, and unofficial social media manager. We love you so much.

I've always wanted to write one of these—to thank those who have helped me in all aspects of my life (and to have made something worth thanking them for). Of course, now, like many before me, I'm overwhelmed by the task.

I'll start by thanking Krystin, who does things I would *never* do, but is like me in ways I may not admit. Thank you to Montana (my version of it, anyway) and the people there who more than accept me, but love and embrace me and have knitted me into their lives. I am so lucky to drink copious amounts of wine on porches with you.

Thank you to my classmates at The New School Creative Writing Program, whose work I more than admire, and whose thoughtful and empathetic critiques made me so much better. You saw the earliest versions of these chapters, a significant tonal shift from the Gothic-lesbian-yearning-depression you'd grown accustomed to reading from me, and embraced them. Writing this book felt like eating cotton candy, a welcome reprieve after days spent scraping against the darker recesses of my *sad-girl* brain. I was unfamiliar with this ease. Thank you Mira Jacob, my thesis adviser, for telling me the right path isn't always the harder one.

Thank you to my beautiful friends, who make me laugh and cry, and put up with my neuroticisms, and drive me around, and bitch with me, and take me to Pancake House, and love me. I am so grateful for our friendships (homoerotic and not). And I love you too.

Thank you to my nana for encouraging my imagination at a very young age, and for fronting me the money I needed for graduate school. Thank you to my parents, who are happily divorced, and who never once doubted me. Thank you for defending me to people who said I was getting a useless degree, and for motivating me to learn new things, and to practice them. Your love and support have never wavered, and I am so fortunate to be your spawn (your words).

Thank you to Katy Perry's 2008 classic "Thinking of You," which I played on a loop while writing Krystin and Lauren's fight. As I've said before, this song is actually from the POV of a heartbroken closeted lesbian trying to be straight.

And thank you, at last, Lydia Jane Wang. With you, I've learned the love I want (and deserve). You make everything better, including me. That first night, I asked you if we should make out. Then I asked if we could still write the book. The answer to both of those questions was always yes.

—*Annabel*

First off, I would like to thank my family, which is probably the best family in the world. (I know, I'm biased.) Thank you to my dad, who always cares about the things that I care about—no matter what they are—and gives really amazing advice and pep talks, even though I rarely admit it. And thank you to my mom, who's always been my first reader, who will probably always be my first text message, and who handled it really well when I drunkenly called her from the hallway of an NYU dorm at midnight and asked if she'd still love me if I liked girls.

Thank you to my sister and best friend, Sophie May Wang, who is strong and smart and compassionate. I've never written a single thing that doesn't somehow have her wisdom, her love, and our relationship in it. Inside and out, she's better than I am.

Thank you so much to the rest of the Wang/Michalski family for supporting me (and also reading my sex scenes). A special thank you to Lauren, my beautiful cousin who let me borrow her name and also grew up listening to a lot of my stories that were not as good as this one.

I have too many kind, loving, incredible friends to even name here, which is a statement that would be unfathomable to my teenage self. Thank you to the people who love me, go to bookstores with me, give me their hand-me-down clothes, text me about Taylor Swift and reality TV, send me photos of pugs, and let me sleep on their floor back in college. If you're reading this and wondering if I'm talking about you too, I am. And I love you so much.

Thank you to my amazing, wildly supportive colleagues at *Women's Health* who have pushed me to be a more courageous writer and person. Thank you to the other 2024 debut authors, who have helped me feel so much less alone.

Thank you to Bachelor Reddit, which unironically helped me psychoanalyze the *Bachelor* franchise and come up with funnier jokes.

And finally, obviously, thank you to Annabel Frances Paulsen, my partner in everything. Once upon a time, you told me I really shouldn't read the last page of every book first. I don't know if I'll ever stop doing that—I really like to know if there will be a happily ever after—but you've taught me that there's something better than a happy ending, which is just being happy every day. Loving you is like reading a book where every page is the good part.

—*Lydia*